THE
MUNNARI
WAR

NOVEL THREE

ML BELLANTE

The Munnari War: Novel Three

The Munnari Chronicles Series

ML Bellante

Copyright 2020 ML Bellante

All rights reserved

BookWise Publishing, Riverton, Utah

www.bookwisepublishing.com

Editor, Interior Design, & Producer: K Christoffersen

Cover & Graphics Illustrator: Hugo Solis

Cartographer: Hugo Solis

Library of Congress Control Number: 2020924936

ISBN 978-1-60645-274-5 Trade Paperback $14.99

ISBN 978-1-60645-275-2 eBook $4.99

10 9 8 7 6 5 4 3 2 1

Order online at Amazon.com

MunnariChronicles.com

MLBellanteBooks.com

12/19/2020 version

DEDICATION

*This work is dedicated to the men and women
who serve or have served
in defense of our Great Nation.*

TABLE OF CONTENTS

DEDICATION iii

PROLOGUE 1

CHAPTER 1: A Black-hearted Brigand 5

CHAPTER 2: Gartz Magic 12

CHAPTER 3: An Unfortunate Faux Pas 25

CHAPTER 4: Terror-bumps 37

CHAPTER 5: The Dark One 57

CHAPTER 6: An Unexpected Humbling 74

CHAPTER 7: The Dread of Our Time 93

CHAPTER 8: New Sovereigns 116

CHAPTER 9: A Healthy, Well-Trained Slave 142

CHAPTER 10: The Munnari Blade 148

CHAPTER 11: Reunion 153

CHAPTER 12: Catching Up 168

CHAPTER 13: The Shadows of War 180

CHAPTER 14: The Sutro Seer's Gifts 199

CHAPTER 15: The King's Decree 220

CHAPTER 16: Filling the Ranks 238

CHAPTER 17: Black Flag 245

CHAPTER 18: Helping Friends and Family 256

CHAPTER 19: Okay, We'll Go! 275

CHAPTER 20: The Kings' Champions 291

CHAPTER 21: The Munnari War 306

CHAPTER 22: A United Kingdom 329

CHAPTER 23: A Dreadful Warning 345

PRONUNCIATION GUIDE 373

PREVIOUSLY INTRODUCED CHARACTERS 381

GLOSSARY 387

MAPS 395

PREVIEW OF NOVEL FOUR 399

The Munnari War is Novel Three in *The Munnari Chronicles* series. It is strongly recommended that the series be read in chronological order.

PROLOGUE

Ayascho sat on the ground, his back against his resting tree. It was Master's Day, the day of rest, on the Tondo Estate, and he was enjoying his leisure. One day in ten was set aside for man and beast to rest from their labors. It had taken him a while to become accustomed to how hard he was now expected to work. Back at his Batru village, deep in the Wilderness, he hunted one day in ten. The remaining days, he languished in the village, safe from the gorga's threat, at least until the outlander had arrived. Tondo, the outlander, had changed everything. Amazingly, he had singlehandedly killed the gorga that had plagued his village for so many rains. That was a great blessing, but Tondo had kept secret Ayascho's act of cowardice during the beast's attack on his hunting team, and now he was in Tondo's debt. Only an extraordinary feat could free him from his self-imposed debt of honor. He would follow the visitor until an opportunity arose by which he could redeem himself.

At first, Tondo had been his enemy because the outlander had nearly strangled him, but over their long passage from the village to this strange new land, they had grown to be as close as brothers. They had faced many perils together, and more than once, Tondo had saved his life, as well as the lives of the king's men who had fetched him.

He clutched the gorga fang under his jerkin, and he smiled. He and Tondo had killed a second gorga threatening another Batru village. He had learned that he wasn't a coward after all.

He had been steadied by the outlander's calm in the face of the charging beast and bolstered by Tondo's threat to put an arrow in his backside if he ran again.

Now, here they were, in a land far from the village. It had taken them nearly two-hundred days to make the journey. Just as they had arrived in the kingdom, they had heard the sounds of battle. When he and Tondo arrived at the place where the fighting had just ended, he witnessed Tondo do an extraordinary thing. He had brought a dead man back to life by contending with the gods and breathing life back into him. As it turned out, the young man was the prince of the kingdom. When they were brought before the king, Tondo was rewarded with a title and given an estate with many slaves. For the life of him, Ayascho could not understand why anyone would want to be a slave, but over the intervening days, he had learned slaves had no choice in the matter.

On the estate lived the previous steward's woman and daughter. Tondo had allowed them to remain and reside in the huge lodge that was their home, known as the manor house and often called the Big House by the slaves. He, Tondo, and their new companion and friend, king's counselor Idop, had moved into the guesthouse. It was also a huge lodge, much bigger than the family lodges in his village, but smaller than the manor house by more than half.

His thoughts turned to the village's pretty young women, and especially Nita. He wondered if she had caught the eye of another young hunter. The thought chased away his smile. He thought about the pretty Anterran, Mistress Oetan, Ootyiah. She was the stunningly beautiful daughter of the previous estate master, who had caught Tondo's eye. For many days, Tondo and Ootyiah could be seen strolling together, arm in arm, along the ocean cliffs, sometimes embracing. However, Ootyiah's mother had put an end to their evening meetings, declaring that such an unchaperoned relationship was scandalous. Although his friend didn't say much about it, Ayascho could tell that Tondo was not too disappointed. It appeared to him that Mistress Oetan's views on slavery were distressing to his friend. Any feelings Tondo may have had toward the pretty Ootyiah disappeared when he intervened as she was about to punish the slave girl, Maaryah, by striking her with a whip called a slave-beater. Tondo had blocked the attack with his hand but was badly injured. He now carried a scar across his right palm as a reminder of his act of mercy.

Ayascho could see that Maaryah was developing strong feelings toward her new estate master, but Tondo seemed mysteriously oblivious to that. He showed no interest in any estate woman after his encounter and chastisement by Lady Oetan.

Tondo is certainly an odd one, Ayascho thought. He wasn't Batru, and he wasn't Anterran, although he looked like one, mostly. He even had three names. Most people Ayascho knew had one name, like himself. Some even had two names, like the young estate mistress. But Tondo had three, none of which anyone could pronounce. That was why the Batru chief had named him Tondo, meaning *the visitor.* Ayascho had noticed, too, that the visitor thought differently, and he had great knowledge that would sometimes spring forth like a dam bursting in a stream, often confusing everyone who heard his strange ramblings. After the three temple priests had arrived to train them, Ayascho had seen Tondo contending more than once during their lessons with the master scholar, Varios. Even the priest seemed overwhelmed by Tondo's proclamations. But he did have the inner-power, the power that gave men extraordinary abilities. Tondo had it, the two master priests had it, and even he, Ayascho, had it; awakened somehow by Batru's messenger, Tondo.

It wasn't long after the three priests arrived that Ayascho noticed a wagon approaching carrying two men. One was another priest, a master carpenter, and the other was a man with black skin, even darker than his own. As it turned out, they had been sent by the Sutro Seer to build a large boat, something never successfully accomplished in the history of the kingdom. Everyone said it was impossible because all previous attempts had resulted in failures. The boat either sunk or fell apart; however, Tondo presented the master carpenter with new ideas, unseen before, and a boat model to work from. Estate workers were soon collected, and work began on an entirely new and unique design that held the promise of success.

After the first harvest was secured, Tondo had granted the slaves their freedom and paid them for their labor. Ayascho's heart lifted at the thought, for that was the way things should be. The great god, Batru, had given his children the freedom to choose for themselves to act with goodness or wickedness, and a slave had no ability to choose. Now they could, and most had chosen to remain on the estate and work for the kind man who had freed them.

Ayascho closed his eyes and was about to fall asleep. Suddenly, a worrisome thought literally shook him awake. When the priests arrived, they had warned of a coming era of threat. They said the Sutro Seer had sent them to train Tondo, Idop, and himself in preparation to meet this looming danger. What it was, no one could say, but they, even the priests, could feel the rising menace as they continued their studies and sword training. They all knew they were preparing for a climactic event that would change the course of history.

CHAPTER 1

A BLACK-HEARTED BRIGAND

Neva haptane Soidentee was not pleased with his visitor, Defetane Sassin. Soidentee could see that the man was an uncouth commoner: crude, obnoxious, and stinking of wine. Obviously, the man was glorying in his new rank and assignment, which were given to him by the great and mighty conqueror of the realm, the Sutro Showton. Sassin had been assigned the duty of forming a new and elite formation known as the *Invincibles*. Soidentee didn't like what the brigand was up to one bit. Sassin had called upon the neva haptane to assemble one-hundred of his best warriors. Soidentee was told, these men would be tested, and if they proved worthy, they would become members of Sassin's new elite force.

Though neva haptane Soidentee didn't relish the idea of giving up one-hundred of his best warriors, he had to comply; it was his new master's order. "All right, Sassin, these are the men you asked for. Now, how do you plan to test them?"

"Join me for midday-meal, and I'll show you," Sassin told him with a wry smile.

Soidentee was not at all interested in sharing a meal with the brigand, but he did have a keen interest in the welfare of his men. "All right, Sassin, I'll join you. I want to see what you're up to," the neva haptane told him, a scowl filling his face.

Later that day, Soidentee presented himself at Sassin's camp and was directed to a two-story building nearby. He found Sassin feasting while sitting on the balcony. Below him, two armored warriors with swords and shields battled, the sound of gravetum against gravetum ringing in the air, along with the grunts of the two desperate men as they struggled. Soidentee advanced so he could get a good view of what was happening. He watched as two of his best fighters hacked and slashed at each other. The men were sweating profusely under the hot p´atezas, and each man looked desperate, as though his life were hanging in the balance.

"Soidentee, join me," Sassin offered as he pointed to the empty chair on his right. The neva haptane sat and scowled at the great struggle raging below.

"Why are these men using lethal weapons? I thought this was simply a test," Soidentee carped.

"How better to prove their worth? The master wants only the best in his *Invincibles*, and that I intend to give him," Sassin declared. He grabbed a roasted frizzard leg, tore off a hunk of meat with his teeth, and began noisily chewing. He lifted a zin goblet filled with wine and guzzled it down. He wiped his mouth with the back of his arm and belched. He held the goblet high, and a slave dashed to him and filled it from the pitcher he was holding. "Soidentee, help yourself to the frizzard and wine. It's the best in town."

"You will refer to me as neva haptane Soidentee. Is that understood, defetane?"

"You know, Soidentee, I'm the Showton's right hand; been so for spans. Your rank don't mean noth'n to me. Anyways,

when the *Invincibles* is formed, I'll be the master's most important commander—not you. Your high-brow birth ain't worth
spit. So, ya better just get used to it," Sassin grouched.

Just then, one of the combatants sliced his opponent's
sword arm. The wounded man screamed in pain, and the two
men stopped fighting.

"Why have you stopped?" Sassin yelled.

"The man's wounded; he can't use his sword arm,"
Soidentee pointed out.

"So what?" Sassin grumbled. "If he's gonna be an *Invincible*, he'd better learn to fight with either arm."

The wounded man dropped his shield, retrieved his sword
from the dirt with his left hand, and then the battle resumed.
It was apparent that the wounded man was at a severe disadvantage. He quickly received two more wounds.

"Sassin, enough!" Soidentee shouted. "The man can't go
on. I demand you stop this."

Sassin was smiling, and he guzzled more wine. "I ain't
gonna stop this fight until one of them's dead," he declared,
his words a bit slurred.

"My men aren't death-fighters; they're warriors," Soidentee carped.

"Today, they's death-fighters," Sassin declared. He then
shouted, "You've got him! Now, kill him!" The wounded man
was slashed again, and he dropped to his knees, his sword falling to the ground.

"It's over, Sassin," Soidentee loudly declared as he stood.

"No, it ain't," Sassin roared. "Kill him!" he shouted. The
victor looked up at Sassin, and his countenance became stern.

"You will kill him, or my guards will kill both of you! The *Invincibles* will be merciless. Do it now or die."

"Sassin, stop. I order you to end this," Soidentee demanded.

Sassin pulled a dagger from his belt and held its point against Soidentee's side. Sassin's two guards unsheathed their swords, and each man grabbed Soidentee by an upper arm. "Only the master gives me orders," he grumbled. He re-sheathed his dagger, but the guards still kept Soidentee restrained. The neva haptane was furious, but he said nothing. He worried that the woozy brigand would order *him* to be executed and consider the consequences after he was sober.

The victorious warrior grasped his sword with two hands and plunged it into his suffering opponent, ending his life in one quick stroke. Sassin smiled and shouted, "Well done! You're now an *Invincible*. Your pay is doubled. You'll be given a new uniform. He tossed the man a small pouch of zin coins. The victor retrieved his reward, raised his sword in salute, and left the battleground. "Next!" Sassin shouted. He turned to Soidentee and, in a growl, ordered the guards, "Remove him. And don't let me see your face around here again."

The guards pushed and prodded Soidentee as he retreated from the balcony. He yelled over his shoulder as he was pushed down the stairs, "Sassin, you're a black-hearted brigand!"

"You're right, Soidentee. That's just what the Showton wants!" Sassin answered with a laugh. He guzzled down more wine and then held his goblet high for another refill.

Soidentee was standing in the Outer Hall, awaiting his master's summons. The neva haptane had requested this meeting. He was still fuming from his recent confrontation with the uncouth brigand, Sassin. Door attendant Torbo watched as Soidentee paced. He could see by the army commander's demeanor he was as angry as a wet frizzard. Attendant Neehoer pushed the doors open from the inside and called, "Neva haptane Soidentee, His Eminence will see you now." Soidentee marched through the doors and crossed the long Throne Room. When he was ten radi away from the throne stairs, he stopped and dropped to a knee.

"Soidentee, you may stand. What do you want?" the Showton asked as he waved his scepter.

Soidentee stood, looked up to his master, and began speaking, "Your Eminence, I must protest Sassin's foul use of my best warriors. He's forcing them to slaughter one another for no good reason. He told me he would test them, but he's using them as if they were death-fighters."

"I want Sassin to find the best warriors in the land. They will be my *Invincibles*," the Showton explained.

"Yes, master, I understand, but I was under the impression that those who were not selected would be returned to me, alive. If Sassin has his way, he'll return only dead bodies," Soidentee grouched.

"Neva haptane Soidentee, I've given Sassin free rein to choose those who he feels meet my expectations. I trust him to give me what I want. I don't want anyone interfering."

"He's a black-hearted brigand!" Soidentee growled.

"Yes, he is. That's why I chose him for that assignment. I expect all my *Invincibles* to be black-hearted and merciless. Sassin is the man to lead them."

"He knows nothing of military protocol. He refuses to honor *my* rank and *my* authority. And he threatened me at knife-point."

The Showton chuckled, "He did that, did he? Ha, that's Sassin. I'd wager he threw you out, too."

Soidentee scowled, then he spoke, "Your Eminence, you can't have an army in which a lowly defetane threatens a neva haptane. Discipline will erode, and the ranks will fall apart."

The Showton bowed his head in thought for several long moments. After a long pause, he looked up. "You're absolutely right, Soidentee. I will heed your advice. Neehoer!" the Showton called.

Neehoer scurried to the foot of the platform and kneeled. "Yes, Your Eminence," he groveled.

"See that Sassin is promoted to neva haptane," the Showton ordered.

"As you command, master," Neehoer replied. He stood, turned around, and marched out.

Soidentee was livid, but he kept his thoughts to himself. The Showton could see his demeanor and quietly chuckled. "Soidentee, Sassin has my full confidence, and you are to remember that. I expect you to cooperate with him fully. Is there anything else you wish to present?"

Soidentee was obviously disappointed and angry, but he kept his thoughts to himself. Respectfully, he answered, "Yes, Your Eminence, as you have said."

"You may go," the Showton told him.

Soidentee bowed and exited. The meeting with his master had not gone the way he had expected. That vestang, Sassin, had even gotten a promotion out of it. Soidentee swore to himself, *If that brigand wants any more of my men, all he's going to get are the dregs of the army and nothing more.*

CHAPTER 2

GARTZ MAGIC

Shortly after the first anniversary of Megato Oetan's death, Idop began visiting the manor house on a regular basis. It was obvious, he wished to rekindle an old flame, although Coleman couldn't tell if Lady Oetan was receptive. The prince also found it necessary to visit the estate every forty days or so. He explained to Coleman that the king required his personal report concerning the progress of the unusually designed big boat, as well as the management of the estate; however, he hardly spent any time with the estate's master or at the ship construction site, even though his visits lasted many days. It was clear to anyone with eyes, the prince was smitten by the lovely Mistress Ootyiah. Coleman had asked Idop if there was any chance that the two could bond, considering the disgrace her family name had suffered. Idop told him that her dowry was the key. The larger the dowry, the more likely the bonding would be blessed by the king. Coleman, in his ignorance, considered it a ridiculous custom, but that was the reality of the situation, and there was little he could do to change it.

On one of Coleman's Du-Zet visits to the ship site, as he rode along the lake beach looking for snags and underwater boulders that could become navigation hazards, he found an area of very fine sand. Upon closer inspection, he thought it might be quality silica. He filled a large leather pouch with the sand and took it back with him to the manor. It wasn't until the next Du-Zet before he had time to test his theory concerning the sand. He grabbed the pouch and headed for the blacksmith's shop and its forge. He noticed a couple of four-inch square metal frames hanging on the wall.

"Pendor, I'd like to try an experiment. May I use those frames, your crucible, and the forge?" Coleman asked.

"Certainly, Sire Tondo. What is it you're trying to do?"

"When I was a boy, I made glass in one of my science classes in school. I think this is the right kind of sand," he said, using godspeak terms as he held up the leather pouch. "I'll need the forge made as hot as you can get it."

"What can this sand do? It doesn't look like gravetum ore at all," Pendor wondered.

"This will not make gravetum. It will make something entirely different. If it works out, it will seem like magic," Coleman told him with a smile.

Haro, Pendor's helper, excited to see this magic, volunteered to help, and he pumped the bellows furiously. The crucible, full of silica sand mixed with a crystalline compound and lime, turned a glowing red, then orange, then yellow. It wasn't long before the yellow changed to a near white glow. Coleman took a metal rod and stirred the molten flux. After several minutes, he took tongs and removed the crucible from the flames and carefully poured the glowing liquid into the frames.

"We must let this cool for a bit, and then we will see if it worked," Coleman advised.

It only took the liquid a few minutes to solidify; then, he gave a few taps to the metal frame and lifted it away from the hardening glass. He gently grasped the still hot plate with a leather pad and held it by its corner. "There it is; this is glass," he told Pendor and Haro as he held it in front of his face and looked through the semi-transparent pane.

"What kind of gravetum is that? I can see through it!" Pendor nearly shouted.

"It is magic, Master Tondo. You call it gartz? I think it is clear gravetum," Haro exclaimed in awe.

"It is hard like gravetum, but it shatters very easily." Coleman took a hammer and struck the glass pane a sharp blow, shattering it. He then removed the other pane from its frame and examined it. The quality was poor. The edges were opaque, and the rest of the pane was wavy, and images seen through the glass were distorted, but Coleman was very pleased with this first attempt. He knew the product would improve with practice.

"What will you do with this clear gravetum?" Pendor asked.

"I think the first thing I will do is put glass windows in the guesthouse. The glass will let light in and keep the heat inside the house," he advised.

It didn't take Coleman very long to get a work crew together. He showed the workers how to make glass, and then he made the most promising candidate the boss of the work team. He had them build a small workshop near the lake where the silica was found.

Once the glass panes were made, he had another team build the window frames and install them in the guesthouse. As expected, Idop complained. He didn't like being cut off from the fresh outside air, and he always slept with his bedroom window open no matter how cold it got. Every night, Coleman closed his bedroom window, and every morning, he found it wide open, thanks to Ayascho. However, the students at the school really appreciated the addition because the fireplace gave too little heat, but once the glass windows were installed, the classroom became much more comfortable.

After Lady Oetan saw what Coleman had done with the guesthouse and the school building, she, too, wanted gartz windows in the manor house. After they were installed, Ootyiah commented on how much nicer it was on cold days to be able to let light in and yet keep the house warm and cozy. Before the new windows were installed, if they wanted to warm up the house, they had to close the shutters, blocking out daylight and leaving the house dark and dreary. Maaryah's cottage was adorned with gartz windows, as well. She referred to them as *gartz magic*.

With each new batch of gartz, the quality improved. Coleman realized his new invention could be a big hit in the kingdom after word got around. He came up with a marketing plan that he thought would guarantee success, but only if outside influences developed as he expected. He would have to wait and see.

Coleman didn't have to wait long to initiate his plan. Late one afternoon, a royal courier approached the manor and met with Lady Oetan. After a short meeting, the messenger was on his way again without so much as a night's rest. It wasn't long after the courier left that Lady Oetan came to the guest-house. Coleman, Ayascho, and Idop were nearly prostrate, having had a particularly rough training session with Master Shergus.

"Sire Tondo, I must speak with you." Then, looking around the room, she added, "In private."

"Okay, I will go with you to the manor house. I don't think these two can move," he quipped. Coleman was sweaty and grimy, but he didn't have the energy to clean up before he left. He limped into the manor house with Lady Oetan leading the way. After they entered, he asked, "What is it, Lady Oetan? We saw the courier and wondered what his visit was about."

"Ootyiah has been summoned by the king. She is to bring her dowry. I think the prince is requesting a formal courtship, which could lead to a bonding, *if* the king approves."

"That's wonderful news. What do you need from me?"

"I ask that you stand in as her Advocate since her father has crossed-over," she proposed.

"Yes, I can do that. It would be an honor," Coleman replied as he rubbed a sore bruise on his left shoulder.

"There is another thing I must tell you. This is embarrassing for me to admit, but now I must. Because the king displaced us, Ootyiah's dowry is rightfully yours because its proceeds came from the estate's profits. I was selfish and wanted to protect my daughter's future, so I never mentioned it. I apologize for my deceit."

"I've been aware of her dowry since shortly after my arrival here. You have nothing to fear from me; I would never take it from her," Coleman said in a comforting voice, still rubbing his painful shoulder.

"I fear the king and his counselors will reject the dowry as lacking. When the king bonded with his bondmate, may she rest with calmness, her dowry was thirty-five thousand bhat. Ootyiah's is only twenty-thousand."

"What happened to the king's bondmate?"

"She crossed-over during the Black Scourge, the terrible illness I told you about; the illness that killed many, including all the others of my family." Coleman shuddered at what he heard. He wondered if it was something like the bubonic plague. After his ordeal at Ayascho's village, disease had become his greatest fear. He quickly chased the thought from his mind. Lady Oetan continued, "That was over thirty spans ago. The king has several bound concubines, but he never took a bondmate again."

"Even though there's only twenty-thousand in Ootyiah's dowry, maybe we can offer the king something no one else in the kingdom has ever seen before," Coleman said as he gazed in the direction of the gartz window in the room. He and Lady Oetan both smiled.

"The king will now see the Advocate for Mistress Oetan," came the court herald's call. Lady Oetan, who really wasn't a lady by rank anymore, Mistress Ootyiah, and Coleman entered the Throne Room immediately, followed by two workers carrying a medium-sized chest and four other workers with a large flat wooden container. The king sat on his throne at the top of the royal stairs. The prince was nowhere to be seen. Coleman could see Braydo's huge and dark silhouette standing in the shadows behind the king's stairs. When Coleman reached the foot of the stairway, he stopped. Lady Oetan and the workers kneeled; Coleman and Ootyiah bowed.

"Before the king's face, a daughter in disgrace," the Rhymer intoned in his scratchy, high-pitched voice. Coleman frowned—he had forgotten about this annoying aspect of a meeting with the king.

"The rest of you may stand," the king commanded. "Mistress Oetan, you have drawn the prince's interest, and he wishes to conduct a formal courtship. Now that We gaze upon your loveliness, We can understand why; however, We are of a practical mind, and We cannot allow sentiment or the follies of the heart to intercede in sound judgment. We must warn you, the disgrace of your father does not bode well for this union. Your mother stands before Us as a commoner; she holds no rank. That fact, too, does not help in this matter," the king told the young woman. Tears welled in Ootyiah's eyes. "Yet, Sire Tondo accompanies you. What say you, citizen outlander, and the one who has already caused a stir from one end of Our kingdom to the other?"

"Freed his slaves; the kingdom raves," the Rhymer intoned.

"I stand before the king as her Advocate. I fully support this union and feel it will strengthen the kingdom," Coleman expounded in a loud voice as he looked up at the king.

"Yes, yes, that is all wonderful talk, but it is only talk. What good can come from this union, We ask?" the king questioned.

"It will have my blessing. Mistress Ootyiah is my friend, and I always honor and protect my friends, including the kingdom she will represent," Coleman answered forcefully.

"We do not forget; but will the king regret?" the Rhymer continued.

"Forget? Regret!" Coleman responded with an angry tone. "The king did not *regret* my presence when his son lay dying. He did not *regret* when I returned the prince from the otherside. He did not *regret* that, and I'm sure he didn't *forget* it, either," Coleman was reprimanding the voice in the shadows.

The king grumbled on, "Yes, We have not forgotten the great debt We owe you, nor have We forgotten your powers. And yet, We are unable to see your future. And now, We understand there are masters from the temple teaching you. Have you allied yourself with the priests?"

"The Sutro Seer sent them. I do not have a complete understanding as to why, either. All they have told me is that I need to learn the things they are teaching me in order to defend the kingdom, and I am willing to do that," Coleman was now speaking to the king.

"We have often wondered why the priests summoned you here. Your willingness to defend the kingdom pleases Us, and We will ask no more of you. Let Us now examine the dowry," the king ordered.

Two red-robed counselors stepped forward and opened the chest. It was about two-thirds full of bhat coins interspersed with a smattering of regums. "How many?" one of the counselors asked Coleman.

"Twenty-thousand."

The counselor frowned. "Only twenty-thousand bhat, Your Highness. Very disappointing," he growled in an annoyed tone.

"That's not all," Coleman interjected. "Open the crate," he commanded the workers. After some effort, a four-foot square paned glass window was carefully lifted from the crate. The workers stood it up, one end resting on the floor. Coleman walked over to the window and stood behind it. "Your Highness, this is gartz, and I can fill all the windows in your palace with it, allowing in light and keeping out the cold," Coleman said, sounding like a salesman. The king looked shocked. He quickly stood, trotted down the stairs, and gazed at the window. He tapped several of the gartz panes with a knuckle and passed his hand around to its back, waving it up and down.

"This is incredible; gravetum you can see through. Where did you find this amazing thing?" the king asked in a surprised voice.

"I had my workers make this gartz from sand. Would you like every window in the palace covered with one of these?"

Coleman looked at the shuttered window nearby, walked over to it, and opened it, allowing a reddish beam from the p´atezas to penetrate the gloom, along with a chilling wind that ruffled the king's hair. He then closed the shutter, blocking out both light and cold. "This I offer you as part of the dowry."

The king tapped a gartz pane again with a knuckle and smiled. "From sand, you say?" Coleman nodded. "Fascinating! Who else has this?"

"Only a few buildings at my estate. No other place has it, Your Highness. *Your* palace will be the first in the city to be so adorned. The other kingdoms will envy you," Coleman smiled as he stroked the king's ego. The king's countenance lit, and he returned to his throne.

"We have examined the dowry, including the gartz, and find it all fully acceptable. Our counselors will make the arrangements. Leave the dowry. You are dismissed," the king decreed.

"The king is impressed; the palace soon dressed," the Rhymer continued.

Lady Oetan and the workers kneeled; Ootyiah and Coleman bowed, and then all quickly exited the Throne Room. When the doors closed behind them, Ootyiah gave Coleman a snug.

"Thank you, thank you, thank you," she kept repeating.

Coleman gently pushed her away and held her by the hands. "Now, now, my dear, what would the prince think?" he asked with a smile and a wink.

Coleman soon learned courtships with royals could literally take spans to complete. Lady and Mistress Oetan requested to stay at the city house for a while, and Coleman gave them his blessing to do so; however, he had to get back to the estate and continue his training. Also, the planting season was upon them, but before he departed the city, he made sure word was circulated that he was looking for people willing to work the land for a home and a share of the profits. Before he left, he had his workers measure all the windows in the palace and the Tondo city house. These were easy measurements to take since all window openings were rectangular.

After the palace and his city house had gartz windows installed, he expected many orders for gartz windows would soon follow, and sure enough, within half a span, representatives sent by rezus, tetzus, tetzae, and even a few well-to-do commoners traveled to Tondo's estate to order gartz windows. It was going to be a very successful and profitable enterprise.

He felt it was time to see if Maaryah could stretch her wings a little wider, so he put her in charge of managing gartz production. He had learned during one of their evening discussions that when she was very young, a wicked male slave often stole a portion of her food ration. This had gone on for several detzamars, and she was getting tired of feeling hungry all of the time, so she finally worked up the courage to do something about it. In desperation, she ambushed her abuser near his home and hit him in the face with the broad side of a shovel, breaking his nose and knocking him to the ground. She went into his hovel and took back the stolen food. She then stood over the prone miscreant and warned him that if he ever stole from her again, she would use the edge of the shovel on him the next time. The bully never bothered her again; however, she started carrying a concealed sharpened stick from then on as protection against reprisal.

As she grew into womanhood, the stick was replaced by a small rusty knife—actually a paring knife—she had found in a field. She knew, if she were discovered carrying a weapon, she would be severely punished, but her greatest fear was being accosted—which Coleman had learned meant sexual assault—by a male slave, a foreman, or even the estate master. As time passed, her paring knife was replaced with a small dagger, which she carried even now in the folds of her clothing. She would tolerate beatings, but she would defend her person to the death against sexual assault—it was her great dread, only exceeded by the horror of torment, a form of crucifixion.

The revelation made it clear to Coleman that she had a backbone and was willing to take risks. He wanted her to remain on the estate and continue her studies, so he hired a commoner, one who could read and write, to lead the installation crew. She still had to spend a lot of time at the production site, skipping lessons from time-to-time.

Learning to ride a samaran was a challenge for her at first, but Coleman could see, she was beginning to enjoy her new responsibilities, and she was willingly facing all the new requirements necessary to fulfill her duties. He also noticed that her self-confidence was increasing, as well. Even her posture had changed. She no longer held her head low, with rounded shoulders, but stood erect with her head high and shoulders straight. She was taller than most men, and she found that attribute helped when she had to deal with a particularly stubborn male worker who didn't like taking orders from a woman. Surprisingly, even Idop was beginning to see her as more than just another flaccid woman.

Coleman had made several additional sharecropper agreements with commoners and freed-men not originally from the estate. He estimated that there would be at least a ten percent increase in the area of land planted. Most of the sharecroppers were doing well; however, a few seemed to be struggling, whether through misfortune or self-induced incompetence. He did what he could to advise those in trouble, but he left the responsibility for solving their problems to their own devices. He reminded those who were having problems that if they failed to produce a profit, their contracts would be terminated, and they would have to find employment in a different area, such as estate laborer. He found this warning to be an incentive to those who thought they might take advantage of his kind nature. During some of these discussions, he invited Maaryah to join him. He wanted her to learn how to *play hardball*, as he put it. When he explained the translation, it only confused her, but she understood its intent.

CHAPTER 3

AN UNFORTUNATE FAUX PAS

Late one afternoon, the prince and his contingent arrived at the estate. Lady Oetan and Ootyiah were with him. It had been nearly two detzamars since the meeting with the king. The prince had told him earlier that the king wanted his son to inspect the ship's progress and report back to him regularly. It was fortuitous timing because two wernts before their arrival, Master T'erio had sent word that the ship's hull was nearly complete, and he planned to launch it into the lake soon. After the hull was launched, he estimated, the project would be completed in two or three detzamars.

Lady Oetan's return also brightened Idop's mood. He had grown sullen and depressed as time passed while the lady resided at the city house. Coleman had occasionally teased him about his missing love in the hope of lifting his spirits but to no avail. It was clear, his feelings toward her had grown very strong, and Coleman thought he was going to have to send the counselor on an errand to the city or watch him pine away. The only thing that stopped him from sending the counselor was his concern that Idop might not return. However, her arrival immediately lifted his spirits, and he became less dour and even jovial at times.

The next Master's Day, the day of rest, was chosen as the launch date for the ship. Nearly all of the estate's residents gathered at the ship's construction site to witness the launching, some making wagers on whether the huge boat would float, sink, or fall apart as all previous efforts had. Coleman had no doubt that the master carpenter and Hermanez had done excellent work, but he wondered if the ship was balanced. They could correct a slight list with ballast, but a profound list could cause serious problems. Coleman had discussed this issue with the two builders, but there was no way to determine its balance until the ship was in the water.

Coleman also wanted to know what kind of a ceremony the two felt would be appropriate for the occasion. Neither man had even considered it. The priest was a very practical man and had little notion of ceremony, other than temple rites. Hermanez was a bit of a larker and also offered no suggestions, so Coleman counseled them that since they would have a large audience, including royalty, a *few* appropriate words should be said.

Coleman also proposed christening the vessel, as that was a tradition in his homeland, a tradition that he had to explain to them. He knew the use of champagne was the traditional preference, but all he had was wine, so that would have to do. Both T'erio and Hermanez, mispronouncing the difficult word by calling it *gristening*, thought it a waste of good wine but deferred to the man who had paid for the project.

They also suggested he be the one to say 'the few appropriate words' since he seemed to know more about these matters than they did, even though he, too, had no previous experience. He managed to convince Hermanez to talk a little about his home island across the ocean, and he asked T´erio to spend some time talking about a few of the challenges they faced in creating such a large boat. Both reluctantly agreed, and the time quickly arrived for the ceremony to begin.

A short platform had been constructed for the speakers. Coleman, Master T´erio, and Hermanez were seated on the platform, and when everyone was ready, Coleman stood and welcomed the guests.

"Prince Teg-ar-mos, we are honored by your presence. I also wish to thank Mistress Oetan and her mother for attending. Besides Master T´erio, our guests include Master Varios and Master Shergus, as well as Attendant Pahno. Also, I wish to acknowledge Scholar Pammon and his lovely bondmate, Wandra, as well as our renowned blacksmith Pendor and his helper Haro. I want to thank all who have come to witness this launching, the first of its kind in the history of the kingdom. I have asked Hermanez and Master T´erio to say a few words. Following their remarks, I will offer some final comments before the launch."

Hermanez intrigued the audience when he told them of his origins and his perilous journey across the sea, relating his horror when his small craft was attacked by a terror, and his two companions demise. Master T´erio went into excruciating detail concerning how he strengthened the hull, braced the keel, formed the ribs, doubled the planking, and many minute details that no one could remember nor desired to. Even Coleman felt his eyelids growing heavy by the time of the master carpenter's belated conclusion.

When Master T´erio finally sat, Coleman stood and began to speak again. He thought it best if he kept his final remarks short and to the point. "All should be made aware that the impetus for this project started with the Sutro Seer. He sent Master T´erio and Hermanez to me, knowing that this project would be the result. By his wisdom and the hard work of many, this boat is ready to launch. I wish to take a moment to recognize all those who have been a part of this project. Would everyone who has contributed to this effort please stand."

Besides T´erio and Hermanez, many workers, both men and women, stood, a couple of men waving to the audience from atop the hull. Coleman applauded, and the rest of the gathering followed suit.

When the applause faded, Coleman continued his speech, "As you all know, I am an outlander, too. In my homeland, we have a tradition of launching a ship by christening it as she slips into the water for the first time. I have asked Mistress Oetan to perform the honors. Mistress Oetan, please join me." As Ootyiah proudly stepped to the platform, a worker atop the hull lowered a rope. Coleman tied the handle of a clay pitcher, half-full of wine, to it. He then whispered into her ear, "Do you remember what you're going to say?" he asked.

"Yes," she whispered back.

"Be sure to give it a good heave," he said in a calm voice.

She took the clay pitcher in both arms, pulled it over her right shoulder, and shouted, "I gristen you the *Anterra!*" and then she flung the pitcher as hard as she could at the hull. It hit with a loud thud and shattered, sending shards of clay to the ground as the splattered red wine ran in rivulets down the yellow wooden planks. The audience stood and cheered as workers hammered loose the stays. The ship creaked and swayed, and then it began moving slowly down the slipway, stern first, its velocity increasing as it moved. Everyone could hear the workers atop the hull screaming in terror.

Within seconds, the hull hit the water, sending a huge spray over its stern quarter. The ship rolled left, then right, finally resting with a slight list to starboard—its right side. The spectators stood wide-eyed and silent as the great hull came to rest. The two workers onboard soon stood, raising their arms high, shouting their joy and relief. The spectators quickly followed with cheers of their own. T´erio and Hermanez embraced one another. Coleman was wearing a huge smile and slapping the backs of everyone within reach. His euphoria was quickly tempered as worry crept into his mind concerning the ship's ability to withstand an assault by the monstrous terror of the sea, but keeping his apprehensions to himself, he continued celebrating.

The prince had planned to spend another ten or twenty days at the estate, but once the ship's hull was successfully launched, he decided to hurry back to the palace and report the news of its efficacious launching to the king. He departed for the city that very afternoon.

Before the celebration ended, Coleman asked for volunteers to crew the ship. Hermanez and T´erio believed they would need at least twelve crewmen. Coleman reminded the onlookers of the inherent dangers of sailing a vessel on the open ocean, but everyone already understood that. By the end of the day, fifteen individuals had volunteered: thirteen men and two women. The fact that women stepped forward even surprised Coleman, but after a short discussion with Hermanez and T´erio, it was decided to allow them to try out for a position. Coleman was aware of the old superstition that women onboard a ship was bad luck, but he wasn't going to carry that false notion over to this world. The women were advised that they would have to do the same things the men did, and they would receive no special treatment. The men were advised to treat the women fairly and as equals on the threat of dismissal if they didn't.

By the end of the first detzamar, two men and one woman had quit the training program. When pressed for their reasons, they admitted to either a fear of heights when required to climb a mast to secure the rigging, the hard manual labor, or second thoughts about the dangers associated with the open sea. Nevertheless, the crew's training was going well, even though the ship was not fully completed. Coleman constructed a gumpass and presented it to Hermanez, showing him how to use it and periodically checking to see how comfortable he was with it. The outlander realized its value immediately, and he used it every time the *Anterra* sailed around the lake.

About a detzamar after the boat's launching, Lady Oetan held a special social event in honor of her daughter, Mistress Oetan's fortieth birthday. Tradition called for a tandeban, a coming-out celebration, but since Ootyiah was already being courted by the prince, that was no longer necessary nor desired. The prince made a special visit to the event. Coleman, Ayascho, Idop, Scholar Pammon and his bondmate, the four priests, and even Pendor the blacksmith, were invited; the priests arriving after the other guests had finished eating.

The dinner was delicious, and the conversation captivating, but the most delightful part of the evening was when Ootyiah played the vant and sang. Nearly everyone commented that it was the most enjoyable evening they could recall. When it had completed, the visitors returned to their lodgings. Coleman sat in his chair, weaving a basket, thinking about what Maaryah had told him: she had been born two days after Lady Oetan's daughter. He decided to celebrate her birth with a birthday party fashioned after those of his homeland.

When Maaryah walked into the guesthouse, she was shocked to see not only Coleman and his two companions but also Pammon and Wandra, Shergus, Varios, Pendor, Haro, Doros, Teema, and Tenny—the new guesthouse maid. On the table was a huge birthday cake, with a lit lamp at its center. As instructed by Coleman, everyone shouted, 'Surprise!' which caused Maaryah to take a step backward in shock. Coleman went to her and took her by the hands, leading her to the table.

"Maaryah, my dear friend, today is your fortieth birthday, and I've invited all of your close friends to share this special day with you. This is a celebration like the ones we hold in my homeland. This is called a birthday cake, and the first thing you must do is make a wish and blow out the lamp."

Maaryah was embarrassed by all the attention, but she did as Coleman instructed. "I wish . . . " she began, but Coleman cut her off.

"You must keep your wish secret, or it won't come true," he advised with a smile and a wink.

"Hoy," she said. She closed her eyes, waited a moment, and opened them again, taking a deep breath and blowing out the flame. Coleman clapped his hands, and all the other visitors applauded, as well, and shouted words of encouragement.

"Another tradition we have is the giving of gifts. Here, this is for you. I had it specially made for you with material from the city." He handed her a package wrapped in plain linen and tied with string. Maaryah's hands were trembling as she opened the gift, and when she saw it was a beautiful pale-yellow gown, she covered her mouth with her hands and stifled a cry, a cry not of surprise but of distress. She looked around the room in horror, and then her tortured eyes fell upon Coleman. She began slowly shaking her head from side to side. She covered her face with her hands and dashed from the room sobbing. Coleman was stunned; the priests and Ayascho looked confused; Doros and Teema were staring at the floor, but Idop was looking at him with an unnerving glare.

"I don't understand. What happened? What went wrong?" he asked in a pained voice. No one said a word. "Teema, Doros, can you tell me what just happened?" Neither lifted their gaze.

"I'll tell you what you just did," Idop finally intervened. "You shamed her in front of everyone, that's what you did."

"How did I do that? This is supposed to be a happy time for her. How did I shame her?"

Doros finally managed to work up enough courage to address the estate's steward, "Sire Tondo, in the past, the days before you gave us our freedom, the master of the estate would sometimes favor one of the women slaves. He would show his interest by giving her gifts and special favors. Then, one night, he would visit her," Doros explained.

Teema's eyes searched Tondo's face, and she added, "I cannot imagine a more humiliating experience; in front of everyone like this."

Coleman lowered his head in shame, slowly shaking it. "Let me assure everyone that was not my intent. I would never do such a thing. Maaryah is my friend, and I hold her in the highest regard. I would never purposely shame or humiliate her. My gift is freely given. I expect nothing in return. Please forgive my ignorance."

"It's not our forgiveness you should seek," Pammon told him.

"Yes, of course. Please enjoy the refreshments while I make amends," he said, and then he left the guesthouse in search of Maaryah.

He found her near the cliffs behind the manor house. She was gazing at the horizon as Munnoga's silver glow reflected off the waters. Coleman slowly approached, clearing his throat, not wanting to startle her.

She glanced at him over her shoulder and then scanned the sharp rocks far below. "I almost jumped," she muttered.

"What? You mean you were going to kill yourself because I gave you a gift?"

"No, no, it happened when I first came here as the new guesthouse slave. It was a punishment for not submitting to Foreman Nestor's lust. He expected a house full of men to, to . . . well, accost me," she stopped and took a deep breath, holding back tears. "Remember the first day, the day you scared me, and I spilled wine and water all over the table and floor."

"Yes, I still feel bad about that," Coleman admitted.

"You then made me show everyone my undressed back and the welt from Foreman Nestor's whip. I was so scared I didn't know what to think, but I feared the worst. That night I went to my old home and hid in despair. The next day, I came here. I was going to put an end to my miserable life, but before I could work up the courage to take the step, Teema found me and held my arm. She told me she thought you were different, a kind master who had a special place in his heart for slaves. She told me the cliffs would always be here, and I should wait and see what sort of master you really were. I remembered how you took away the pain from my wound, and I recalled my dreams, so I believed her."

"Dreams; flying free as a bird?" Coleman wondered.

"Dreams of your blue eyes. I never understood what the dreams meant. I didn't know if they were a warning or something else. I'm so glad Teema found me here. You have been kinder to me than anyone I've ever known, but when you gave me a gift, my old fears returned, and I felt like a slave again." She turned her head and looked into his face, searching for the reasoning behind his offering.

"My gift is simply a custom from my homeland. I expect nothing in return other than your happiness. I'm so sorry I made such a dumb mistake. I only want this evening to be happy and fun for you, nothing more. I've made a mess of it. Can you forgive me?" he entreated.

"I know you well enough, Tondo. I believe you. It's just hard to forget the past and put it behind me," she admitted.

"I'm glad you understand I meant no harm. My wish is to honor you. Through my ignorance, I made a regrettable mistake. Please forgive me," he offered.

Maaryah chuckled, "I understand, and I do."

"Can we go back to your party? I've already apologized to everyone for being todo."

"Todo, what's that?"

"Dumb."

She smiled, "What did they say?"

"They realize I wasn't trying to ply you with gifts and favors. I'm the one who should be embarrassed, not you. I understand the cake is good. At least that's what Teema promised."

It was obvious she wasn't ready to return. She hesitated and seemed lost in thought. Coleman said nothing and waited. Finally, she began speaking again, "Teema told me Master Oetan would visit her after he drank too much. She also told me he would hit Lady Oetan when he was drunk. It must have been terrible for both of them."

"That's awful. I can understand why Teema wouldn't say anything about it, but why would Lady Oetan stay silent about his abuse?" he wondered.

She looked at him, a bit surprised by his lack of understanding. "It was too dangerous for either of them to say a word about it. The master was tetzae. Do you think anyone would believe either of them or care?" she reasoned.

"Of course, you're right. That's too bad. They must have lived in fear," Coleman guessed.

"Yes, just as I have most of my life, but I'm getting over it," she confided. "Thank you for giving me a real life, a life where I can make my own choices."

"That's the way it should be for everyone," he said with a smile. She looked into his face and returned one of her own. He saw in her eyes the invitation he had seen before. He paused in thought, weighing the risks of another estate romance. He recalled once again the promise he'd made to himself, and reluctantly, he lowered his gaze.

After a long pause, Maaryah spoke, "Okay, let's go back. I think I'm over my shock," she told him.

"Okay? That's pretty good godspeak," he told her. He took her by the arm, and they walked back to the guesthouse. When they entered, all of the guests applauded and cheered. Maaryah's face lit up, and she smiled. Coleman forced a smile, too, still fully embarrassed by his unfortunate faux pas.

CHAPTER 4

TERROR-BUMPS

The divitz harvest was soon completed, processed into bales, and sold. The sharecroppers earned between seventy-five and one-hundred and fifty bhat each for their efforts. Coleman and Lady Oetan each had a net profit of six-thousand two-hundred and fifty bhat. The king's tax amounted to a little over two-thousand bhat, an amount, Coleman learned, pleased the king greatly, and eased the sovereign's concerns about Coleman's strange estate management. Coleman was very proud of the success his *free estate* was having. It was another good span, with just the right amount of rain and p´atezas warmth. He knew this might not continue, but he didn't let that worry dampen his spirits. He had opened a huge area for cultivation, and he was planning to open more land for the next planting season. All he needed were more people willing to till the soil and work hard. Although he was distressed, having evicted a couple of families who failed in their efforts. He offered them work as laborers, but having been shamed by their failings, they refused his offer and left the estate. However, all-in-all, his first span as the hands-on manager of operations had turned out better than expected.

As the days grew colder, Coleman received word from Master T´erio and Hermanez that the ship was ready for its ocean trials. Coleman had begun referring to Hermanez as boatmaster since he would be the ship's *captain*, a word that no one but the estate holder could pronounce correctly. Since a ship's captain is the master, it was an easy adjustment for everyone to grasp. The *Anterra* looked to be a fine ship, but it was nothing like any wooden vessel Coleman had ever seen or read about. He wasn't well versed in the nautical, but the hull appeared to resemble that of a Chinese junk, while the two masts with fore-and-aft rigging were akin to a schooner, meaning the sails were triangular and rigged in front of and behind the masts, not square-rigged, with square sails hung from spars, nor even like a junk with its batten sails. Fore-and-aft rigging required a smaller crew and also would be easier to handle in coastal waters—something Hermanez had pointed out to him.

Master T´erio had the workers construct a huge wagon in which to haul the ship to the ocean. Coleman hired several teams of thrice to provide the power to pull the ship from the lake and tow it to its new destination, a cove not too far from the manor house. A ramp-like road had been constructed that would allow the wagon and teams to move down to the water, although Coleman was planning on catching a high tide, reducing the distance they had to travel down the road.

A floating dock had also been built and was near the shore, secured by thick ropes. He had hoped that his young thrice would be large enough and trained to perform the labor, but unfortunately, thrice take a lot longer to mature than he expected, probably due to the influence of the Blessing of the City. Numo was doing a fine job with them, but they were too young and not ready for real work yet, especially something as momentous and as potentially hazardous as moving a heavy ship cross-country. They would have to travel nearly one march—around fifteen to twenty miles—and a lot could happen in that distance, but everyone had planned wisely and hoped they had foreseen all potential problems.

When the day came, all went as planned, and the huge boat—huge to everyone's standards but Coleman's—rolled across the harvested divitz fields, leaving deep ruts cut by the wide wooden wheels. Coleman reminded everyone they were to take as long as it was necessary to make the journey, and by midafternoon, he called a halt and let man and beast rest until the next morning. On the following day, travel resumed at midmorning and continued until just before dusk. All rested well, knowing the final day of overland travel would begin in the morning.

The effort began early the next day. By midday, they reached the road leading down into the ocean. The tide was rising, so they waited until late afternoon before attempting to back the wagon down the ramp. By the time darkness fell, the ship was in the water and anchored safely in the cove. The anchors were designed by Hermanez: large, flat, oblong stones with holes chiseled through their tops and secured by ropes. Coleman watched the lights on the ship, wondering how Hermanez and his crew felt now that they were in dangerous waters. He turned and walked to the guesthouse, worried that the ship and his friends could be gone by morning, devoured by a terror.

As dawn was breaking, Coleman rushed to the cove, wondering what he might find and fearing he would find the ship missing. To his relief, the *Anterra* was floating serenely at low tide while several crewmen milled about the deck.

"Ahoy!" Coleman shouted in godspeak, chuckling aloud and waving his arms.

"Good morning!" came a reply. It was Hermanez's voice, and he waved back.

"Bring her to the dock. I want to come aboard!" Coleman yelled. Hermanez waved again and began shouting orders as crewmen scurried around the deck, pulling up the anchor stones and quickly raising a single triangular sail. It took almost a segment for the *Anterra* to maneuver to the dock. By then, a crowd of people had formed around Coleman.

"Don't tell me you're going on that thing?" Idop spouted.

"Tondo, that's not a good idea. The giant water beast will eat you," Ayascho warned.

"The Sutro Seer didn't send us here to train you and then watch a terror take you. You must not get on that boat. I forbid it!" Master Shergus commanded.

"Please, don't do it. Stay here, on land. Let Boatmaster Hermanez and the boaters go by themselves," Maaryah begged.

"It's not in my nature to order men into danger and not lead them. I will not ask anyone to do something I'm not willing to do myself," he was adamant in his obstinance.

Ayascho, Idop, and even Maaryah knew him well enough to know his mind could not be changed. The three master priests, Lady Oetan, and Mistress Ootyiah continued pleading with him, but to no avail.

"The Sutro Seer has called for this vessel, so why would he do that if it was to end in disaster?" Coleman reasoned. This comment silenced the priests' objections.

A short time later, the ship gently bumped into the floating dock as ropes were cast over its side and secured by laborers. Planks were placed from land to the dock and from the dock to the ship. Coleman scrambled aboard, followed by Ayascho and Idop.

"You two don't have to follow me," Coleman advised them, but they would not leave him. Soon, the three temple masters climbed aboard. Coleman smiled but said nothing; however, his mood changed when Maaryah appeared on deck. "This is no place for you," he told her in an annoyed tone.

"Oy, *now* it's too dangerous? Why? I will not watch from the shore; I just can't. I have to be here, with *you*," she pleaded with a hint of desperation in her voice.

"Very well then, but at least find something to hold onto." He turned and faced the others. "By the way, do any of you know how to swim?" he asked. He learned, no one could. "Ha, at this point, if the boat goes down, it won't make a difference anyway. But you all need to learn how to swim."

The ropes were released; the crew adjusted the sail, and they were soon heading into open waters. More sails were raised, and the *Anterra* raced forward at a brisk pace. The sea swells were low, and the wind was strong, pushing the ship forward at a clip that astonished everyone but Hermanez, the boaters, and Coleman. Occasionally, the bow would crash into a swell, sending sea spray over the forequarter. It was an exhilarating ride for everyone onboard.

Coleman and the others knew the area near the cove was a feeding ground for terrors because many large sea creatures congregated there during mating season, but at first, no terror was spotted. After a couple of segments of free running, a woman's voice called from the ship's bow. All eyes turned toward her.

"Terror off the port beam!" she called. All heads turned, each looking toward a different gumpass point, most not knowing which direction she was referring to, but soon, everyone's gaze locked on a huge dorsal fin slicing through the water not far from the ship's left bow.

"This is it; the first test," Coleman mumbled through clenched teeth.

Everyone watched as the huge fin passed them on the left side, circled around the stern, and approached from the right rear of the ship. Master Shergus moved to the ship's stern and raised his right arm.

"What are you doing?" Coleman asked.

"I'll protect the boat. I'll use tzaah to chase the sea beast away," Shergus told him.

Coleman pushed the master's arm down. "Are you planning to go with the ship on every voyage it takes?" Coleman asked. Shergus shook his head. "Then, let it be. The ship must be tested, and it must survive on its own," Coleman counseled.

The fin drew nearer, ever nearer, as beads of sweat formed above Coleman's brow. No one said a word; every breath was stilled, watching the symbol of death drawing closer, ever so closer. The terror's fin quickly sank beneath the surface, and shortly after it disappeared, the ship's passengers felt the *Anterra* rush forward as if pushed by a giant hand.

Everyone held tightly to a nearby fixed object and waited for the worst. The ship's momentum declined, and someone yelled, "Over there!" The fin reappeared off the starboard beam, circled to the right, and came back, aimed directly amidship. Coleman braced himself for the horrible impact he knew was coming. With his free arm, he grabbed Maaryah and held her securely to his side. She grabbed him around the chest and held on tightly. Her eyes closed in fear. The fin raced towards them, and then suddenly, it disappeared below the surface again. Everyone felt the ship roll slightly as the great fish brushed against the hull a second time as if testing its strength. This time, the fin did not reappear. After what seemed an eternity, everyone began to relax.

Coleman released his grip on Maaryah, but she still held him tightly. "It's okay. It's gone. You can relax now," he calmly told her. She remained glued to his side, her grip not relaxing a bit. She finally opened her eyes and looked up into his smiling face, and her expression brightened in relief. "We're safe for now. The *Anterra* passed the first test," Coleman said in a loud voice, evoking a cheer of joy and relief from all the others.

Maaryah reluctantly released her embrace and stepped away. "I'm sorry I was so frightened. I thought we were all going to die," she admitted.

"There was a moment when I thought the same thing, but here we are, safe and sound," Coleman told her.

The *Anterra* sailed back and forth in front of the cliffs near the manor house, daring the terrors to approach. Several times, a huge terror would threaten, but in nearly every case, the monster only made a relatively gentle brush against the hull. Hermanez referred to them as *terror-bumps*, and everyone else started calling them that, as well.

When the p´atezas hung low in the western sky, the *Anterra* returned to the dock and debarked its relieved and exhilarated passengers. Much to the surprise of all, they were met by the prince and his contingent, as well as a large crowd of onlookers, including Lady Oetan and Ootyiah. Coleman thought it was another fortuitous sojourn by the prince. His timing seemed to be impeccable, leading the estate master to wonder if such lucky coincidences were so often possible, for he knew that Counselor Idop's report, indicating the ocean launch was nearing, had yet to be sent to the king. It was becoming obvious, the king, and the prince for that matter, had a set of eyes and ears, other than Idop's, living on the estate.

That evening, Coleman held a meeting in the guesthouse to go over the plans for the *Anterra's* first sea voyage. Hermanez had a strong desire to return to his home island. The prince was interested in commerce, as well as exploration and mapping, wanting to know what the world looked like beyond the horizon. Coleman was mainly interested in receiving a return on his substantial investment. It was decided, Hermanez would sail the ship to his island, engage in trade, and map it by circumnavigating it before returning to Tondo's estate.

Coleman had set aside fifty bales of divitz, five spinning wheels, and three crated gartz-paned windows to be used in trade with those whom the *Anterra* made contact. The prince decided to risk one-hundred and fifty sacks of cereal products collected in taxes, including wheat, barley, and oats. It was going to take more than two wernts for the prince's items to reach the ship, which did not please Coleman nor Hermanez, but there was little they could do about it short of offending the royal, so they had to wait.

When the prince's wagons arrived, they were quickly unloaded, and the sacks of grain were stored in the *Anterra's* hold next to Coleman's items. *It's a very inauspicious beginning*, Coleman thought, as he examined the cargo that filled only a small portion of the space available. Something nagged at his thoughts, but at first, he just couldn't put his finger on it. Finally, it occurred to him that the ship was too light. He feared the ship would bounce over the waves like a cork, so he passed his hunch on to Hermanez. The shipmaster really didn't think that would be a problem since the *Anterra's* own weight seemed enough. Although Coleman had his doubts, he deferred to the man who was going to have to live with the decision.

On the morning of the following day, the priests prayed and blessed the huge boat. The ropes were then cast off, and the *Anterra* was on her way with its master and twelve crew. Hermanez watched the gumpass and set a course due south, hoping to run into his island by dead reckoning. Coleman and the others watched as the ship slowly disappeared into the morning haze.

"May the unnamed god protect them," Master T´erio quietly uttered.

"May he protect the cargo," the prince added.

Coleman didn't say a word. He guessed there were many dangers on the open sea, some even more threatening and dangerous than the terrors. He feared he would never see the ship and its occupants again.

Over a span had passed since Master Varios and Master Shergus had begun training the *Three Amigos*, as Coleman began referring to Idop, Ayascho, and himself. The others just considered the term more godspeak and thought little more of it. Maaryah attended Master Varios's class in the morning, and after mid-day meal, she spent a couple more segments being personally tutored by the master. Master Shergus wouldn't even consider allowing a woman in his class, and Maaryah had no desire to suffer through his punishing lessons.

Shergus had advanced his students to using real swords from time-to-time, but he continued using his two-handed wooden blade, mainly as an instrument of punishment. Several times a wernt, Shergus extended the training sessions into the night. He wanted his students prepared to fight in all conditions, whether it was light or dark. Those classes were especially trying because the *Three Amigos* had no idea when the session and the master's painful retributions would end.

All three students had become quite proficient in their style, but none could approach the master's skill; however, one afternoon, Coleman actually scored a touch on the master's arm; something never achieved before by any of the students. Shergus, a bit taken aback, complimented him on his success, and then the master proceeded to make him suffer for his accomplishment the remainder of the day. By the time his ordeal was over, Coleman clearly understood that the master was prideful. He knew he would be able to use that realization in the future, although he kept his scheme to himself.

Two wernts after the *Anterra* had left the estate's cove, she returned to the cheers of everyone who greeted her. The crew waved enthusiastically, and Hermanez greeted Coleman with a broad smile.

"How did it go?" he asked as soon as the boatmaster reached the shore.

"It took only five days to reach my homeland, and that was against the current and into the prevailing wind. It took only three days to return. When we sailed into the protected bay, no one on land could believe their eyes. When the tide went out, the ship became grounded, making it safe to load the cargo into smaller boats and take to shore. I was able to sell everything for nearly twice the regular price, and I used that money to purchase spices, jewelry, and cloth. I was even summoned to appear before King Em-tom-bono, himself.

"You were right about the weight of the ship; we bounced up and down the whole way to the island. It was a miserable passage; even I got sick. So, after I saw that the cargo hold still had a lot of space, I hired laborers to collect black-rock to fill the empty spaces and give the ship more weight. That made a big difference on the return passage."

"Black-rock, what's that?" Idop asked.

"It's a rock that burns; we use it to heat our homes, but usually it's not necessary because it's always warm on the island, but it's cooler here. Sometimes, we use it to cook, so I thought it a good idea to see if we can sell it here," Hermanez told the gathering.

"Coal? The black-rock is coal? Let me see it." Hermanez yelled for one of the boaters to fetch a chunk of the black-rock. "What about the gartz windows? Was anyone interested; did anyone place orders?" Coleman asked.

"Although everyone was amazed by gartz, there wasn't any interest in putting it in windows. It's too warm on the island, and no one thought gartz-covered windows were useful. I re-crated them and brought them back." Coleman's expression revealed his disappointment.

Soon, the crewman handed Hermanez a hunk of black-rock. He passed it to Coleman, who examined the shiny black stone closely. "This definitely looks like coal. Has anyone ever seen anything like this here?" Coleman asked Idop.

"Not that I know of. What's it good for?" the counselor asked.

"Watch," Coleman said as he dropped the rock to the ground, stepped back, and concentrated. The rock burst into flames and continued burning. "This *is* coal, and it burns just like wood. Does your island have a lot of black-rock?" Coleman asked the boatmaster.

"I really don't know. We just collect it from the western hills on the island and use it whenever we need to."

"We might be able to start a business with this if we can get enough of it. You mentioned spices. What kind?" Coleman asked.

Hermanez rattled off several words no one had ever heard before. "The food here is bland and flavorless. Add some of the island's spices to it, and you'll see a big difference. I'll show you tonight. I'll cook the meal," Hermanez promised.

The ship's cargo was unloaded and stored in the barn. Coleman examined the ship's log and the maps Hermanez had drawn while exploring his island. He also learned, Hermanez had enough cash left over to cover their expenses, but they would have to sell the other items if they were to see a profit. Coleman was confident he would be able to sell the coal during the upcoming cold season, and he hoped the spices would be a big hit, as well.

True to his promise, Hermanez assisted Teema in preparing the last-meal and watched with delight as Lady Oetan's guests ate their fill and asked for more, indicating to Coleman that there would be a great demand for the flavor-enhancing seasoning.

Five days later, just before dusk, the prince and his contingent arrived. Coleman now knew for sure that someone was able to get communications to the palace quickly. Unless tzaah was involved, which the masters told him was unlikely, Coleman felt the only way the prince could get the word of the ship's return so quickly was by means akin to a homing pigeon. Although he had nothing to hide from royalty or anyone else, he had developed a strong hatred for moles within any organization of which he was a part. Such a situation had led to grievous consequences for him in the past and was the primary reason he left the military. He was going to find out who the estate spy was, but he would do so in a surreptitious manner.

When Hermanez and Coleman made a full report to the prince and saw his disappointment at the lack of profit, Coleman offered to buy out the prince's share of the remaining goods. After some thought, the prince decided to wait and see how the sale of the spices and black-rock turned out. If the sale didn't go well, he would accept Coleman's offer. The outlander made it clear to the prince that his offer was only good for the next three days, and if not accepted by then, the prince would be taking the same risk as everyone else. Idop almost gasped at Coleman's blunt offer, but the prince laughed, realizing this was one man he couldn't bully with his rank.

As it turned out, the spices sold out quickly, netting a threefold profit. The black-rock languished until the cold weather arrived in force and then sold out within two wernts, giving the investors a bigger profit than they had hoped for.

Hermanez was granted a ten percent commission since he was instrumental in making the transactions. The boaters shared a five percent cut for their bravery and skill. All in all, it had been an auspicious start to Coleman's new shipping enterprise; however, the prince demanded more.

He desired that the *Anterra's* next voyage be eastward, toward the City of Women and the great salt cache that all three great sister cities were so dependent upon. Caravans plied the trade charging huge sums for bringing the life-sustaining compound to his city. The caravan trails were long and dangerous, a one-way journey requiring more than two detzamars to complete—more than eighty days. Too often, caravans were ambushed and raided by brigands, leading to salt shortages or extremely high prices. The prince contracted with Coleman to deliver a hold full of divitz and cereal grains to the City of Women in exchange for as much salt as Hermanez could barter for.

Coleman also saw it as another opportunity to sell his gartz windows, so he accepted the prince's offer and contracted with him for ten percent of the profits. The prince, realizing seventy-five percent of the income, felt it a good deal and agreed. A rider soon left the estate with orders to return with wagons full of divitz and cereal grains collected from taxes. Two wernts later, the wagons arrived, and their loads were quickly stored in the ship's hold. Hermanez told Coleman and the prince he would travel along the eastern shoreline, mapping as he traveled. When the tide was going out, the ship cast off its lines and made for the open sea, just as a squall blew in from the southwest.

A detzamar later, the *Anterra* returned, looking worn and damaged by her journey. A huge gash scarred her stern, its mainmast had been snapped in half, and its mended pieces held together with rope lashings.

Coleman counted only ten boaters, besides the boatmaster. "What happened?" he asked when Hermanez reached the shore.

"We were attacked by a terror. It bit the stern, snapping the mainmast, breaking the rudder, and then it disappeared. Two men were knocked overboard, and we never saw them again."

"Who was lost?" Coleman asked.

"Ab´as and Ioes."

"When did it happen?"

"The day before yesterday. Everything was going well; then, we were attacked. But the ship held up, and the crew did a fine job saving her and the cargo."

"What about the cargo?" Coleman wondered.

"Full of salt, as much as we can carry. The queen bought everything we had for twice the price we usually sell it for, and I got all the salt at less than half the price the caravan's charge."

"And the gartz windows?"

"The queen ordered forty-two windows for her palace; I've got the dimensions, just as you asked. You will make a fine profit because she was willing to pay a good deal more than you told me to offer," Hermanez said proudly.

Coleman smiled, then turned sullen. "Do Ab´as and Ioes have family?"

"Ab´as was alone; Ioes has a brother. Why?" Hermanez asked.

"I think we should hold a memorial service for them and see to it that Ioes's brother is given all his possessions and his share of the profits. Divide Ab´as's things with the boaters," Coleman advised.

"I'll see that it's done as you say," Hermanez agreed; then he continued, "I hugged the coastline and mapped all the way to the City of Women; they call it Te Femma, by the way. It took almost twenty days to get there. On the return trip, I set a straight course over open water using the gumpass, and it took only six days, even with making repairs after the terror's attack. Now that I know the course, and with your gumpass, I'm sure I can make it in three or four days. Just imagine, a trip that takes the caravans over eighty days, made in only four by water. I think we should build another boat, an even larger one," Hermanez told him.

The memorial service was a grim reminder of the dangers the boaters faced; however, Coleman had no trouble recruiting replacements. The boaters were earning three times as much as a laborer, plus they were returning with exciting stories of faraway places, both especially strong incentives to adventurous young men and a few strong-willed young women.

As the memorial service was concluding, the prince and his contingent arrived, as Coleman expected. He informed the outlander that the royal wagons were on the way.

"Your boat looks like it ran into trouble this time out, but it arrived with a cargo of salt, and that is good enough for me," the prince commented.

Over the next several wernts, the boatmaster had the *Anterra* fully repaired. Hermanez had extra rigging added, which strengthened the masts. Master T´erio increased the protection on the stern quarter, adding arm-long gravetro spikes, a hopeful deterrent to another terror attack. Certainly, not long enough to impale the huge beast, but long enough to inflict a painful wound. When all were sure the ship was as ready as she could be, the *Anterra* set sail again, this time heading west, her hold full of divitz, grains, a gartz window, and even some salt.

Fifty-five days later, the ship returned. The mapping had gone well, but unfortunately, they didn't encounter one living soul during the entire voyage along the western coastline. After such a disappointing exploration, Hermanez told everyone he decided to set a course for his home island to see if he could sell the cargo there. Again, he was welcomed and bartered well, selling everything he had and buying more goods, including spices, black-rock, and a few plants whose fruit seemed to snap some of the boaters out of a lethargic illness. Through his trading skills, he had saved the expedition. He also told Coleman the city officials had built a floating dock, which made it a lot easier and faster to load and unload cargo.

When the *Anterra* was divested of its cargo, Coleman examined the potted fruit trees. "These look to be citrus," he said using the godspeak term.

"We call them the *gods' delight*. Some are very sweet, and some are very sour," Hermanez told him.

"Did you say some of the boaters had become sick?" Coleman asked.

"Yes, they just didn't look right and didn't want to work. A couple of them even got spots on their skin. After we had landed at my island, and they ate the gods' delight, they regained their vigor."

"Scurvy," said Coleman in godspeak. "Your crew was suffering from scurvy. You will need to take a supply of this fruit with you from now on." He went on to explain what little he could recall concerning the disease, which wasn't much.

Coleman found a suitable place to plant the orange, lemon, and lime fruit trees that Hermanez had garnered. Coleman hoped this new fruit would become popular in the kingdom, but he knew it was a must on any future sea expeditions of more than a detzamar.

He had tried raising cereal grains on his estate but with only limited success. The Magheedo Plain was much more conducive to the growing of wheat, barley, and oats, so he realized it would be a losing proposition for him to continue that effort on the estate. It seemed the soil on the peninsula just wasn't rich enough for grains; however, he refused to accept failure.

After some thought, Coleman conducted an experiment and dug down a foot into the ground. There, he found much better soil, which was well below the depth the traditional kingdom plow could reach. He quickly realized, all he needed to do was design a plow that could dig that deep and turn over the soil.

Thus, he gave Pendor a new assignment: the building of a very large gravetum plow. The effort consumed more than half of Coleman's remaining stockpile of blue meteorites. When finished, the plow was so big and heavy, much larger than the ancient traditional plows, it required a thrice or a

team of two draft samarans to pull it, but it seemed to work well. By the time all this was accomplished, the growing season was over, and the early rains made the fields too wet to work, so he would have to wait until the planting season before trying again.

Master T´erio agreed to construct another ship, one nearly half again as large as the *Anterra*. Work began on the day the *Anterra* sailed into the western sea.

CHAPTER 5

THE DARK ONE

The Sutro Showton sat on a chair, his many guards and attendants standing nearby, watching with threatening stares as a groomer began scraping away the master's beard with a sharp sutro gravetum blade. The man, Frotz he called himself, looked worried, and each time he lifted the blade off the Showton's face, everyone could see his hand trembling.

The Showton grabbed the groomer by his wrist, and his Munnevo-red eyes flared. "If you cut me, I'll have one of these guards cut you. Now, stop your shaking!"

The Showton's threat only made Frotz's body quake more. "Master, I'm . . . I'm afraid," poor Frotz stuttered in a quavering voice.

"Here, let me bolster you. Guard, calm this fool. Place your blade against his back," the Showton ordered while pointing to one of his men. The guard stepped forward and drew forth his sword. He stepped behind Frotz and placed its point against the center of the groomer's back. Frotz closed his eyes, inhaled deeply, and attempted to calm himself. He exhaled heavily, opened his eyes, and returned to his task as beads of sweat formed on his forehead and ran down the sides of his face.

Frotz was a groomer, a very good one. Some said he was

the best in the kingdom, and he had served many in the nobility, at least until the king and his followers were deposed and executed. When the new master assumed the throne, he soon learned of Frotz's expertise and decided he needed his hair trimmed and the hair on his face removed. When the groomer was summoned, Frotz assumed he would perform the same service he had for the previous nobles.

When his new master lowered his veil and ordered Frotz to remove the hair on his face, the poor man nearly fainted. He had never seen such a thing, nor had he ever been assigned such a task. Now, here he was, a sword point at his back and a host of stern-looking guards posted throughout the room. The Sutro Showton's wicked red eyes made things all the worse. The groomer ever so carefully resumed his work, wiping sweat from his forehead from time-to-time.

Frotz struggled through his assigned duty, slowly, ever so slowly, scraping away the Showton's facial hair. When he completed that task, he turned to the more familiar and routine job of trimming the hair on his new master's head. When he had finished, he held a polished zin mirror in front of the Showton's face.

The Showton closely examined his reflection. "Hold still!" Frotz was still shaking. The Showton snatched the mirror away from the groomer's hand and examined himself, his free hand rubbing his cheeks and jaw. "Well done, Frotz. You're now my personal groomer." The Showton looked to the guard standing behind the trembling Frotz and commanded, "Move him into the castle. I'll use him from now on." Frotz didn't know whether to cheer or cry. He took back his mirror and simply followed the guard out.

Nevesant entered, his high-quality dark robes flowing as he stepped. He was no longer the boy from Tangundo's early days. He had grown into a young man. He stopped a few steps away from his master and kneeled. "Master, you summoned me?" he asked, his head bowed.

The Sutro Showton answered while still rubbing his naked and smooth jaw and cheeks. "Neva Haptane Soidentee is in need of some good scouts. I want you and your followers to go to him and assist as he deems appropriate."

"Yes, master, as you wish," Nevesant dutifully replied as he looked at his overlord's face. "Master, the hair on your face is gone. Now, you look just like any other man."

The Sutro Showton stopped rubbing his jaw. His red eyes turned angry, and he sprang to his feet. "I am not just like any other man, Nevesant!" he growled. He pulled his veil up, covering his mouth and nose. "Remember that!" he spouted.

"Yes, master. I meant no disrespect," Nevesant whimpered.

"All right, then. Now, take your leave and report to Soidentee," the Showton commanded.

"Master, I and my men can do more than scout. We can sneak into the enemy's camp and kill their commander. I know we can," the young man offered.

"Do you really think you can do that? How do you intend to get into the enemy's camp? How do you plan to get past the guards? The commander's no fool. He's probably a great warrior, too. He'll have your head displayed on a pike in front of his tent. These are serious matters; they aren't games, boy. Now go, do what I've told you," the Showton ordered.

Nevesant was crestfallen. His master had chastised him in front of the guards. He bowed his head, stood, and stomped out. He felt like a fool, and his anger burned. He would prove his worth; he would prove his loyalty; he would prove he was ready to gain more magical abilities.

Neva Haptane Soidentee awoke with a start; he'd felt a presence in his tent. The army commander sat up on his sleeping cot and blinked as sleep fled from his eyes. He quickly realized he wasn't alone. A shadowy figure, sitting on a chair in the center of his tent, quickly snapped him fully awake. He reached for his sword and discovered it was missing.

"Looking for this?" a voice softly uttered as he held up the neva haptane's sword, barely visible in the subdued light.

"Who are you?" Soidentee questioned with only the hint of a quaver in his voice.

"Nevesant," the young man proudly stated. "Not only did I sneak into your tent undetected, I entered the camp unseen, as well; me, T´uft, and Gherd."

"Why in the names of the Five Shadows would you do this? I don't have time for your silly games, boy!" Neva Haptane Soidentee was not a happy man, especially after being awakened from a sound and much-desired nod. He jumped up and attempted to snatch his sword from Nevesant's grip. The young man moved the blade ever so slightly, and Soidentee missed. Nevesant held the sword up, its point aimed at the man's neck.

He smiled as Soidentee's angry glare transformed into worry. A wry smile slowly crept across Nevesant's face. He turned the blade around and handed its grip to the him. Soidentee snatched it out of the air and flung it at Nevesant, its point sinking deep into the ground between the young man's feet.

Nevesant chuckled, "Too late; you're already dead." He pulled the sword out of the ground, wiped its blade on his robe, and handed it back to Soidentee.

"All right, Creeper, what's your point?" he grumbled.

"Don't you dare call me that! Don't ever call me that again! Next time, I'll cut off a piece of your ear," Nevesant threatened.

"Oy, ha, but aren't you the bold one? I should have my guards use the flats of their swords on your backside," Soidentee groused.

"Go ahead, summon your guards," Nevesant challenged.

Soidentee looked at him with a suspicious glare. "Guards!" he called. Two men armed with pikes and drawn swords entered. When they faced the neva haptane, he could see they weren't his guards; they were T'uft and Gherd, his young intruder's companions. The two scouts stood smiling at Soidentee, their pike-points leveled at his gut. The neva haptane shuddered, waiting to see what was going to happen next. Worry began to slither into his thoughts. Had his master sent these three youngsters to assassinate him for some unknown transgression? He waited in silence, his eyes moving from one interloper to another.

Nevesant's smile grew wider as he watched Soidentee squirm. He slowly stood and walked over to the neva haptane. "I've been sent by His Eminence to lop off the head of the army you're facing. I thought a demonstration of our abilities was in order. I want to thank you for being so cooperative."

Soidentee lit a lamp, then turned and faced Nevesant. His angry eyes were boring into the young trespasser. "Get out of my tent! If you ever do anything like this again, I'll use my dagger and take a knuckle from you," he threatened.

Nevesant chuckled and waved his arm, indicating his two comrades should exit. He followed them, but before he passed through the tent doorway, its skins held open by T´uft and Gherd, Nevesant turned, pulled something from his waist belt, and flung it toward Soidentee. The neva haptane looked down and saw his personal dagger stuck in the dirt between his feet. When he looked up, Nevesant was gone.

The three young scouts walked to a clearing not far from Soidentee's command tent. Nevesant stopped and looked up into the night sky. Munnari, the blue moon, could barely be seen as it slowly dropped below the tree line. A gibbous Munnevo, the red moon, hung low, just above the trees. Nevesant raised his left arm in a Showton salute. His two companions followed his lead. "We, the followers of Munnevo, seek your blessing," Nevesant beseeched. The trio lowered their arms.

"Master, where to now?" T´uft wondered.

"We'll ride out of camp tonight and move to a safe place near the enemy's army. We'll rest during the day, and tomorrow night, we will do the same thing, only this time, we'll return with the enemy's commander's head in a poke," Nevesant told his accomplices. His two men looked worried. Had they been caught during their little escapade this evening, they would have simply been punished. If they got caught tomorrow night, they would undoubtedly be killed.

The night had been a harrowing experience for T´uft and Gherd, and yet their master, Nevesant, seemed to relish the danger and threat. They had carried out their secret foray into the enemy's camp and succeeded in their deadly task. The three men moved their mounts to the open area between the two opposing armies, holding their position as the reddish disk of the p´atezas began its daily climb, illuminating the open field between the armies, and revealing the three mounted young men for all to see.

"T´uft, give me your pike," Nevesant ordered. T´uft handed the pike to his master. Nevesant loosed the bloody grain sack tied to his saddle and reached in, pulling out the severed head of the enemy army's commander by the hair, and mounted it on the gravetum point of the pike. He then raised it high for all to see. His heels dug into his mount's sides, and he began his dash across the front of the enemy line, T´uft and Gherd on their mounts closely following, the enemy commander's personal banner dragging behind Gherd's mount and the enemy kingdom's flag dragging behind T´uft's.

The three men's mounts galloped across the front, turned around, and charged back. Just as they completed their sprint, a detachment of mounted enemy warriors charged past their foot soldiers and pursued the three assassins into no-man's-land. Nevesant reined his mount toward his line and stopped in front of his allies, still holding the pike high, daring the enemy to approach. The enemy detachment stopped half-way between the lines, ending their aggressive sortie with angry shouts, threats, and curses. Nevesant laughed. T´uft and Gherd cut the ropes securing the enemy banners to their saddles, and then let their mounts trample their foe's symbols. The three young men slowly entered their army's line, satisfaction, confidence, and hubris etched on their faces. Nevesant tossed the pike with the bloody trophy to a nearby defetane—a low-ranking Showton officer—as he rode to the rear. The defetane stepped forward, and with the help of two of his men, planted the gruesome prize in the ground. All of the Showton warriors began shouting in elation at the assassins' bold success.

Neva Haptane Soidentee was amazed by Nevesant's daring victory and told him so; however, the army commander was reluctant to take advantage of the act, and he refused to order his army forward. The Showton's army was outnumbered, and Soidentee wasn't confident he could prevail, even though the opposing army had been decapitated, literally. Nevesant was furious at the neva haptane's lack of action, so he sent his two subordinates to give a report to their master, the Sutro Showton. A few days later, they returned with a message informing both Nevesant and Neva Haptane Soidentee that His Eminence would arrive soon to survey the situation personally.

King Sen-ro-mun, the ruler of Wenstrif, a large city in the south-land, paced back and forth in his great hall. News from the west became more dire as each messenger arrived. Not that long ago, he learned of King Ben-do-teg's destruction by a gang of murdering outlaws, only to be quickly followed by word of King Gor-bin-den's execution, including his entire house, at the behest of the same heartless brigand ruler. The king had learned the outsider savage had a name: the Sutro Showton. Recently, this monster had turned his rumored red eyes toward the Sen-ro-mun realm. And just today, the king had learned his trusted guard's commander, Vitmon Ronzenb'er, was killed by assassins while he slept. This vile Sutro Showton was despicable and without honor.

King Sen-ro-mun had been counting on his reinforced guards unit to throw back the invaders who now threatened his kingdom. Vitmon Ronzenb'er was the key. He was a strong leader and a smart tactician. The king must now take his place and assume command. That was the only way to bolster his army's flagging morale.

"Muster my personal guards. We ride to assume command of Our army. The evil Showton and his vile warriors must be expunged from the realm," the king ordered.

The Sutro Showton sat atop an elevated platform on his makeshift throne placed in the center of his temporary meeting hall. The edifice was hardly more than a glorified barn, the Great One thought. The rafters were bare, and stringy, dusty webs were evident in many shadowy corners. The floor was simply compacted dirt. If this was the provincial over-seer's seat of leadership, it was certainly a poor province, indeed. The Showton's eyes shifted from the less than regal trappings and focused on the two men on a knee before him, Neva Haptane Soidentee and Nevesant.

"Nevesant, is it possible what I've been told; you slew the enemy commander in his bed?" the Showton wondered, his Munnevo-red eyes open wide above the veil across the lower half of his face.

"Yes, my master, I did. I can be more than a scout," Nevesant blustered proudly.

"So you can, Nevesant, so you can. That is quite a feat. I've underestimated your abilities. Well done!" the Showton praised.

"Thank you, master, but I fear my efforts were for nothing. Our army should have acted a wernt ago. Victory was easily at hand. Yet, here we are, still waiting. Now I've learned, their king has arrived and taken command, bolstering his warriors' will," Nevesant grumbled.

"Neva haptane, with their leader dead, why didn't you strike? It would seem a most opportune time," the Showton wondered. He knew Soidentee to be a competent commander and waited to learn his reasoning for not acting.

"Your Eminence, our young friend here is indeed brave, but he's impetuous and too willingly takes risks. You can afford to lose him and a couple of his men; however, to lose this army is a different matter entirely. King Sen-ro-mun has culled good men and stripling lads from all over his kingdom. He has a core of well-trained guardsmen; many mounted on tanters. He has assembled well more than three-thousand warriors. I barely have two-thousand," Soidentee explained.

"What are tanters?" the Showton asked.

Soidentee gave an arm gesture, and a guard entered, holding a tanter by its bridle. "They are mounts with spiral  horns, strong and rugged. They can easily kill a man or a samaran," Soidentee told him.

"It looks impressive. I want tanters for all my armies. We'll take them from Sen-ro-mun." The Showton turned to Nevesant, "I want you to expand your band. You're no longer simply a scout. Your command will be my manslayers, called upon to perform secretive missions. The Illustrious Showton from my father-land had a powerful supporter called the Dark One. No one knows whether it was a title or a name. Nevesant, you are my Dark One." The young man smiled and bowed. The Show-ton continued, "This is my 1st War Order: Soidentee, I'll summon Sassin and my one-thousand Invincibles. After they arrive, you will command the army, and I will oversee our victory. King Sen-ro-mun, a Worlder, cannot contend with me and my godly powers. His end will be just like all the others of his lowly ilk.

The Sutro Showton sat confidently on his mount, eyeing the formations of warriors arrayed before him. Soidentee's two-thousand men were arrayed in four blocks of five-hundred, each brandishing a long pike. A thin line of slingers, called rockmen, stretched across the Showton army's front. Their duty and purpose was to disrupt the enemy formation as much as possible before the two great hordes made contact. On the Showton's right, Neva Haptane Soidentee watched from his mount. He commanded the main force. He was not pleased. His men were outnumbered significantly. The enemy mass was twice as deep as his own. The Showton's orders were for him to drive his warriors forward and engage the enemy. He feared he lacked the numbers to be successful. It appeared to be a simple battle of attrition, and his force was lacking. Soidentee voiced his concerns to his master, but he was quickly and sternly rebuked. He had learned from past experience, the Sutro Showton's decisions were not to be challenged. Soidentee nervously wondered if he would survive the day.

The recently promoted Neva Haptane Sassin, on the Sutro Showton's left, waited with anticipation. His one-thousand Invincibles had been placed at the rear. This was to be the formation's first trial in battle. Sassin was confident. His men were veterans all, and the best warriors collected from the Showton's expanding domain. Even though the enemy outnumbered the Showton's force, Sassin wasn't worried. His master had overcome the odds before, and Sassin knew he would again. Having a god on your side evened those odds and even tilted them in your favor. He wondered how his master would prevail again, fully expecting a great victory.

King Sen-ro-mun did not want to be here, confronting a brutally cruel sorcerer. *Kings don't conduct battles; their subordinates do,* he grouched silently. Yet, here he was, drawn here because assassins had killed his army's commander. The king's arrival had bolstered his men's dwindling morale, and after he saw his army's superior numbers, his own confidence was lifted, as well; however, something nagging at his center warned him of a great danger approaching. Because his foreboding was unclear, all he could do now was to wait and react to its threat.

"Neva Haptane Soidentee," the Showton called in a loud voice, "it's time! Sound the advance!" Soidentee took a deep and worried breath, gave a hand signal, and a horn sounded. The call was repeated by other horns. Orders were shouted, and the pikemen began a slow, steady, and relentless march toward the enemy line. The rockmen dashed forward, and when close enough to the enemy, unleashed their stones. The enemy was not expecting a shower of missiles, and many warriors were downed by the rockmen's hail. As the Showton expected, the leading ranks of his enemy were thrown into chaos. However, this early success was short-lived as the fallen soldiers were quickly replaced, although presenting a ragged front when the pikemen's advance drove into King Sen-ro-mun's defenders. Men shouted, cursed, screamed in pain, and groaned as two great armies struggled in a death-wrestle.

After a segment, the Sen-ro-mun army's superior numbers were beginning to have an effect. A few of the Showton's pikemen had lost hope and were beginning to pull back.

"Soidentee," the Showton yelled, "get in there and rally your men! Any warrior who runs will answer to me!" Soidentee swallowed hard, dug his heels into his samaran's sides, and galloped off. He knew he was moving toward his doom, but he was a brave man and dedicated to his duty. The Showton turned to Sassin, "Prepare the Invincibles for their advance. They will cut through the enemy like a sharp sword. Now, go!" Sassin returned a smile, gave his master a Showton salute, and quickly moved his mount to the front of his one-thousand black-clad and veiled Invincibles.

The Sutro Showton continued watching the battle unfolding with steely red eyes, waiting for the right moment to act. King Sen-ro-mun had moved closer to the action so he could better determine when and how to administer the deathblow to his faltering enemy.

The Showton felt this was the time to make his move. "Order Sassin to advance the Invincibles!" he called to an aide. The Showton galloped his mount into the center of Soidentee's force. He could see King Sen-ro-mun through the dust, and he raised his right fist and pointed it toward the king. A ball of purple energy blasted forth, hitting the king squarely on the chest, knocking him from his mount. King Sen-ro-mun struggled to his feet, screaming in pain as purple flames engulfed him. After excruciating suffering, the king fell to his face and expired. An instant later, Sassin's Invincibles tore into the king's demoralized men, and they broke. The Invincibles were ruthless, giving no quarter nor accepting any plea for mercy. Every enemy warrior who could not or would not run was put to the sword. For the remainder of the day, the slaughter continued; not one prisoner was taken. It was the Sutro Showton's greatest victory to date.

His Eminence, the Sutro Showton, reclined at his elevated table, watching as his high-ranking officials celebrated their great victory. Sassin, in particular, was reveling in his new-found status. His Invincibles had performed magnificently, and they had carried the day. He was propped on cushions next to a table stacked with an abundance of fine foods and drink. At his side was a buxom temptress wiling her way into his good graces and succeeding. Sassin was full of fine food and wine, but also, mostly full of himself. All that his master had promised in the past had come true.

He stood and raised his cup to his master in salute. "All hail the Conqueror! All hail the Sutro Showton!" he shouted, his words only slightly slurred. The other men in the room stood and raised their cups, giving a shout of victory in honor of their god-like leader.

The Sutro Showton nodded, his Munnevo-red eyes cold and unrevealing of his true feelings. A veil covered the lower half of his face, as usual, and no one could tell if it hid a smile or not. The Showton preferred it that way. He felt it best to keep his underlings guessing; they'd be easier to control if they knew not his mood.

He noticed that Neva Haptane Soidentee wasn't enjoying himself as fully as the other men. He all but ignored the woman assigned to him by his master and drank little. As the celebration continued, the Showton could see Soidentee's mood darken even more.

"Soidentee!" the Showton finally called. The room slowly quieted as all eyes turned toward the two men.

Soidentee stood and presented himself before his master on a knee. "Yes, Your Eminence, how may I serve you?" he offered.

"Neva Haptane, what's your problem? Have I not provided enough for your liking?"

"You have been most generous, my master."

"Then what is it? Why so glum on this joyous occasion? Was this not our greatest victory?" The Showton's red eyes were expressing his displeasure.

"Master, the victory nearly annihilated my army. There is little left for me to command," Soidentee lamented.

"Ha, is that all? Stand up! You think your role has been diminished in our future efforts. Soidentee, put your mind at ease. I have great plans for you, my most skilled commander. Now, listen closely to my 2nd War Order: I want you to rebuild your army. Collect young and strong men from throughout my domain. Train them, push them, prepare them. When they are ready, you are to take them to the coast and advance northward. I understand there are wealthy realms there. Take every city and kingdom you encounter. Send me half of all the booty you take. With the rest, grow your army, garrison the cities, and drive on. I will form other armies, and they will drive south and east, doing the same. In short order, I will own the world, and you will be found at my side."

A smile chased away Soidentee's dispirited countenance. His master was publicly honoring him and promising greater victories to come. "I will serve you with all my might!" Soidentee shouted after he stood. He raised his left arm with a closed fist in salute. The Showton snapped his fingers, and an attendant approached holding a fine wooden box. He opened its lid and held it in front of his master. The Showton retrieved a small leather pouch and tossed it to Soidentee. The neva haptane caught it, and he heard the chink of coins inside.

"Zanth should brighten your mood. Also, I advance you to haptane. Now, return to your table and enjoy the evening. There will be many more victories to come."

CHAPTER 6

AN UNEXPECTED HUMBLING

Training continued for the Three Amigos, and the priests were like taskmasters as they entered the third span of training. Everyone knew of the Sutro Seer's prophecy of dread, commencing sometime during the second or third span, resulting in the training becoming even more intense. Master Shergus had his students engage more often in matches against each other, sometimes one-on-one and sometimes two-on-one. More than once, the master took on all three students himself and soundly trounced them, showing that it was possible to win even when the odds appeared to be so decisively against one.

During a two-on-one encounter, while Coleman was the one, he managed to entangle both Idop and Ayascho in a downed tree branch he pulled into the battle using tzaah. Master Shergus was so impressed, Coleman was given the remainder of the afternoon off, much to the chagrin of the other two. He made sure to rub some salt in their wounded pride during last-meal. Unfortunately for Coleman, Ayascho executed nearly the same trick on him during a one-on-one match the next day, ending with two quick smacks against Coleman's head by Ayascho's wooden blades. Master Shergus laughed when he learned it was vengeance for Coleman's needling of the other two the night before. It took a segment for Coleman's head to clear.

It was during this season, at long-range archery practice on a windy day, that Coleman felt an inner urging. He didn't understand what it was, but he felt the power of tzaah within himself reaching out. He had felt it before, many times during archery practice, but he didn't know what to do about it; however, he guessed it must be something special. On this day, Idop was having a particularly difficult time hitting the target over one-hundred strides away. Coleman intently watched as Idop drew his bow and fired; the target was missed. Ayascho took his turn and also missed. Master Shergus then released his arrow and only managed to hit the lower right corner of his hay bale. Idop readied another arrow, and Coleman felt his inner-power swell again.

"Wait," Coleman ordered. He walked over to Idop and faced him. He then placed his hand on the man's chest and closed his eyes. A force of energy moved from the center of his body, traveled down his arm, and poured into Idop's chest. The counselor's eyes grew wide, and he staggered backward.

"What was that; what just happened?" the counselor stuttered as he regained his balance.

Coleman opened his eyes and took a deep breath. "Now, try again," he simply said. Idop took careful aim and let his arrow loose. It slammed into the center of the target. "Try another," Coleman coaxed. Idop fired another arrow, and it, too, hit the center of the target.

"I can see it, in my mind, I can see the arrow hitting the target even before I let it go," Idop declared breathlessly.

"You have awakened his tzaah. It was an honor to witness it," Master Shergus uttered in a reverent tone. Idop's countenance was radiant. The power he so dearly coveted had finally awakened.

Coleman could see that Idop was nearly beside himself with joy after discovering his new power. However, one evening after spending time with Lady Oetan, he returned to the guesthouse gloomy and morose. "What's the matter? You look like you've lost your best friend," Coleman said in a concerned voice.

"Lady Oetan can't seek an Intervention, and even if she wanted to, she worries about what her daughter would think of it if she did. Also, she has no dowry and feels it would be improper for her to bond again without one," Idop grumbled.

"Maybe there is something I can do. I will talk with her," Coleman offered.

"Please do; I would appreciate it."

Coleman had learned, through his lessons with the master scholar, some of the finer points of the bonding laws of the kingdom. He'd learned that nearly all bondings in the kingdom, at least those of wealthy commoners and all of the higher social ranks, required the woman to provide a dowry. At first, it had seemed a ridiculous requirement to Coleman, but as Master Varios explained its purpose to his questioning student, Coleman learned it had a practical basis and brought stability to the bonding agreement. The dowry was given to the bridegroom as payment for assuming the responsibility for the care and support of the head of household's daughter. If the marriage failed and the husband petitioned an adjudicator for a Writ of Disbonding, the husband was required to return the dowry in full. Since a dowry was generally quite a considerable sum, disbonding was seldom pursued. On the other hand, a woman had no legal right to request a disbonding; however, if her bondmate was shown to be abusive, usually by a public display in front of three or more unmarked citizen witnesses, or found in disgrace by the king, she could seek an Intervention. In such a rare situation, she had the right to ask her father or oldest living male relative to intervene on her behalf. If an adjudicator accepted the Intervention, then he would issue a Writ of Independence, which allowed the woman's bondmate to keep the dowry; the responsibility for the support and care of the woman would then shift to the interventionist. The woman would be allowed to separate herself from her ex-bondmate's home, leaving everything behind, including her children. She was no longer bonded to him, and she was allowed to re-bond, but since she no longer had a dowry, it was unlikely she could do so with respect.

Since Sire Oetan had been disgraced by the king, Lady Oetan was free to seek an Intervention if she chose. Unfortunately, Lady Oetan's father and older brother had died during the Black Scourge, leaving her without an interventionist if she decided to take that course.

An alternative to an intervention for a widow was to become a concubine. Since bondings were not considered to end at death, it was not legal for a bonded woman to bond again upon the death of her bondmate; however, for practical reasons, a woman could become a bound concubine. This was a socially acceptable way for a woman to be supported if her bondmate had crossed-over. The bond of a concubine ended upon the death of either the man or the woman. In this culture, men were allowed multiple bondmates; however, this ancient practice was frowned upon even if a man's bondmate had crossed-over. A man was allowed to have as many concubines as he could support, and there was no social stigma attached to it.

Coleman knew Idop wanted to bond with Lady Oetan, and from what he could surmise, neither wanted to go the concubine route because it placed the woman on a lower social level. Although Coleman didn't think there was much he could do about the legal machinations, but he felt there was something else he could do. It was time to formalize his promise to Lady Oetan—his promise to give her one-sixth of the divitz profits earned by the estate. He took quill to parchment and drew up a document stating such. Master Varios reviewed it and wondered what it was all about since he had never seen anything quite like it before.

Coleman explained, "This document formally requires the Tondo Estate to pay Lady Oetan one-sixth of the estate's divitch profits. She can sell this document, which represents her interest, if she wishes, but I will advise her to hold on to it because the profits she is likely to make over the spans will probably be much more than she could ever sell it for."

"I'm not sure it's legally binding. Women cannot hold property. An adjudicator will have to make a ruling," Varios told him.

"I will go ahead with this and get a ruling later. After all, I'm the steward, not her," Coleman reasoned. He then marched to the manor house and met with Lady Oetan. He handed her the document, waited for her to read it, and then he explained its meaning to her. He could see she was confused, so he began his edification, "As I have done in the past two harvests, I will continue to do, and this document legally requires me to."

"This document is not necessary; you are an honorable man. I trust you," she said.

"I know, but this instrument can take the place of a dowry. Just think of this, for example: over the next ten spans, this document may entitle you to sixty-thousand bhat, probably more, undoubtedly much more. Imagine how much it could earn for you over a hundred spans. It could be called the largest dowry ever assembled." She was stunned by his statement. A tear coursed down her cheek, and, surprisingly, she gave him a gentle snug, then thanked him profusely. "I do this not only for you, Lady Oetan, but also for Counselor Idop," he told her as he wiped the lady's dampness from his cheek. He could see he had embarrassed her. "I also do this for myself."

"How could this generosity benefit you?" she wondered.

"The priests tell us that a time is coming when great danger will threaten the kingdom. It is then I will need Counselor Idop at my side, fully engaged in defeating the unnamed foe, not pining away over a lost love."

An expression of concern covered her face. "Idop has never explained all this to me, even though I've repeatedly asked him why the priests are here. Is that why they're here? What is this threat? Is Idop in danger?"

"He probably didn't want you to worry. I really don't know what the threat is, my lady. The priests have warned us about a threat coming to the kingdom, but only the Sutro Seer knows what it is. All we can do is prepare, and that is why the priests are here and why we're being trained."

Coleman had divided the responsibility for running the estate and given several bosses oversight duties, Maaryah being one. She oversaw the estate manor ground's functions as well as gartz production. She was also made the sutro boss and given the responsibility of making Coleman aware of any problems the other bosses reported. Bosses oversaw the Separation House; the lumber team; divitz planting, growing, and picking; gartz production and window installation.

Divitz profits were still Coleman's largest income, but gartz production and sea trade were quickly catching up. By the time the third harvest was over—Coleman's second full span as the estate's operations overlord—he was able to give Lady Oetan six-thousand-six-hundred-and-fifty bhat as her share of the divitz profit, and he earned the same amount. He also reaped an additional two-thousand-two-hundred bhat profit from gartz window sales and another one-thousand-nine-hundred bhat in profits from sea trade.

He offered to split the ship's profit with Master T'erio, but the priest would not accept it. The Sutro Adept suggested he make an offering to the temple instead. After some thought,

Coleman decided a tenth, what he referred to as a tithe, of current and future sea trade profits would be appropriate, and the priest agreed.

Coleman even started a general store, which earned several hundred bhat profit in its first span. He brought in supplies for the freed-men and commoners to purchase, saving them the long journey to the city. He called it the Company Store, but everyone referred to it as the Master's Shelves. Coleman was especially proud of the fact that his little general store was actually making money. It proved to him, and to others, that paid workers were much better for the economy than unpaid slaves. His store even paid a small royal tax, and he made it clear to the tax collector's representative that the tax payment came mostly from the freed slaves' purchases.

During one of the sword training exercises, Coleman scored another touch on the master. The students could see that Master Shergus was fuming, but he kept his anger under control. He then proceeded to brutalize Ayascho and Idop before inviting Coleman to face him for another punishing bout.

Well, this is it, Coleman thought to himself. *I refuse to allow the master to torture us any longer because of his wounded pride.*

Coleman slowly circled Shergus with his wooden two-handed sword at the ready. He wondered if the master would strike first or simply wait and counter his attack. Neither antagonist took the initiative, at least not in a way that the two other students could see at first; however, initially, an unseen battle raged as the two men's tzaah reached out and lashed at each other. Parries of force and thrusts of energy whipped from each man's center. After several seconds, Ayascho and Idop could see sparks and tongues of flame exploding in the air above the heads of the antagonists. Master Shergus quickly advanced with his two-handed wooden sword, and making a move quicker than the eye could follow, he lunged at Coleman. The student reacted reflexively and quickly parried the physical blow, then countered with a blast of heat that singed the master's eyebrows. Coleman's plan was not to seriously injure or attempt to defeat his master outright. His goal was to tweak and tease him until pride and anger overrode the master's concentration.

The contest continued in this vein for several minutes. Both men were dripping in sweat, but neither said a word nor sought a rest. This had become a duel of wills. Coleman had been preparing for this moment for a very long time, and the master quickly realized his student's resolve. Shergus made another lunge, and Coleman could feel a coil of energy circling around his legs. He parried the master's thrust and countered the master's energy attack by focusing a fire attack on Shergus's wooden sword. The master had to release his energy coils to counter Coleman's fire blast.

The student could feel the master's anger building when he bounced an energy ball off Shergus's head, not powerful enough to stun, but sufficient enough to annoy. Shergus's eyes darkened, and he again lunged at Coleman, spinning, side-stepping his student, swinging his wooden blade at the back of Coleman's neck. Coleman parried the stroke again, instantly dropping the blade under his master's sword and slashing toward the master's ankle. Shergus deftly stepped away just in time. Coleman felt a powerful force of unseen energy slam against the side of his right leg, and it was all he could do to keep his balance.

The master moved in for another attack, but when he did, Coleman quickly brought the pommel of his sword up and hit the master squarely under the chin, momentarily stunning him. He then stepped into Shergus's attack, wrapped his right leg behind the master's trailing leg, and pushed him down, dropping him onto his back with a loud thud. Coleman brought his sword down for a mock killing blow, but it was blocked. He guessed what was coming next: an extreme energy attack that would knock him away, but Coleman was prepared. From his superior position above the master, he bore down with all the energy of his tzaah and shattered the master's energy thrust. He then focused his inner-power on the master's wooden sword. It burst into flame and was quickly consumed, its charred remnants and glowing embers dropping onto Shergus's leather jerkin.

"It's done!" the master grumbled loudly. "I'm defeated." Idop and Ayascho looked at each other in stunned silence as Coleman helped the master to his feet.

"You have learned well, Tondo. It has been a very long time since I have been humbled by one of my students. It gives me much to think about," the master said.

"It was your instruction that allowed me to win this time, and I was lucky," Coleman said, trying to soothe the master's injured pride.

"No need to patronize me! I tried my best to defeat you, but you were the better man, at least on this day. I look forward to our next match."

"I don't," Coleman replied, and then both men laughed.

"You may bring me a sword of your choosing, and I will bless it," Master Shergus told him.

Coleman bowed, and Master Shergus returned it, and then he dismissed the class more than two segments earlier than usual. The master walked to the priests' wagon, but before he entered, he angrily chucked the stub of his wooden sword as far as he could. A couple of frizzards, the tiny barnyard dinosaur-like creatures, scurried to the stub and began squabbling over it, thinking it was a tasty morsel.

After the master swordsman was no longer in view, Ayascho and Idop gathered around Coleman and congratulated him on his remarkable victory. Coleman basked in their praises until they calmed down. "I think all I've done is remind the master not to be complacent. I think our next match will turn out much differently," Coleman advised the others.

"It's still amazing," Idop told him. "I can't recall hearing of anyone ever defeating Master Shergus. You have become quite adept at both sword and tzaah."

"You must tell me all you did with your taah. I could see flames, and sparks, and energy all around the two of you. It was wondrous and horrible at the same time. I thought both of you would die," Ayascho admitted.

"I was holding back. I didn't want to injure Master Shergus seriously. I'm sure he was doing the same. By the way, counselor, what did he mean when he said he would bless a blade of my choosing?"

"Those who have been found worthy are sometimes rewarded with a blessed vessel. The blessing is believed to infuse the item with power from the unnamed god. I've never believed in such things, but I'm beginning to think there may be something to it. A blessed sword from the temple's master swordsman could be a most powerful weapon," Idop told him.

"Hmm, I guess I should get myself a suitable blade then," Coleman said. He then turned and walked into the barn, stopping in front of the few remaining blue meteorites stored there.

He searched the pile with his eyes until he saw one that seemed to beckon to him. He hefted it, examined it closely, and determined it seemed to be a good candidate to forge into a sword. He took it to Pendor's shop at the north end of the barn.

He found Pendor busy at his daily tasks, Haro assisting as usual. "Pendor, I have a job for you. I would like you to turn this into a sword," Coleman held the blue meteorite in front of himself.

"Ha, I'm sure it will do just fine. It's the best sutro gravetum I've ever worked with. It's a difficult task to make a sutro gravetum sword, but I can do it. It will take time, and much effort, sire," Pendor told him as his eyes searched Coleman's face.

"I'm willing to pay handsomely for a quality blade. Tell me, how do you go about turning this stone into a sword?"

"I will melt it and pour it into a mold. It will then be heated, hammered, and shaped until I feel it is done. Then it will be heated and quenched, making it hard and strong. After a good polishing and a first sharpening by Haro, I will give it a final sharpening. It will then be ready for you, sire," Pendor told him with pride.

"Rather than melt the stone, have you ever considered heating it and folding it over on itself several times?" Coleman asked.

An expression of disgust darkened Pendor's mood. "Yes, sire, I did that once. The results were . . . were less than desirable. I swore to the gods; I would never try that again."

"I'm interested in a folded sutro gravetum blade. Do you know of another swordsmith who would be willing to make one?"

"I'm sorry, sire, I don't. Even if you take your request to the city, I doubt anyone will risk doing it?"

"Why's that?" Coleman asked.

"Never has a folded blade been a good one. Most of the time, they shatter, leaving the wielder in a very bad situation. For your own safety, I strongly urge you to stay with the true and trusted blades."

"Thank you, Pendor; I appreciate your advice. I'll have to think about it."

Coleman was hoping to find someone who could make a sword similar to a Japanese katana, but it appeared that the technology of this culture had a long way to go before that could be done. He walked to the guesthouse a bit disheartened, placing the blue meteorite on the center of the main table.

After a good soaking in the bathhouse, Coleman felt much better. He had decided if the only sword he could have made were a typical longsword, that would have to be good enough. When he got back to the guesthouse, he changed into white trousers and a white shirt with sleeves to just below his elbows. He sat at the table, staring at the blue meteorite, pondering and reviewing in his mind his victory over the master swordsman. He wondered what would happen the next time the two of them faced off. He'd left the door to the guesthouse open; he enjoyed watching the frizzards scratching for food, just like chickens had done on his grandfather's farm. He thought, *What an astonishing place this world is—a mixture of the familiar and the bizarre.*

He soon heard footsteps approaching. It was Haro. The young man stood in the doorway and waited for Coleman to acknowledge his presence.

"Yes, Haro, what can I do for you?" Haro looked over his shoulder as if searching to see if someone was watching. Coleman could tell that the young man, relatively speaking, was worried about something. "Come in and join me at the table."

"Thank you, master. I've never been in such a big house before." He stepped into the large room and scanned every wall and corner. Coleman motioned for him to sit across the table from him, and the young man did. He didn't like the fact that Haro had called him master, but the poor blacksmith's assistant looked so nervous, he didn't want to add to his stress by correcting him. Coleman poured Haro and himself cups of water and then waited for his guest to speak. Haro sat, sipping his water, blinking his eyes over and over. Coleman sat patiently while the young man worked up the courage to voice his message.

Finally, Haro gulped, took a deep breath, and began to speak, "Master Pendor has been good to me. I have served him for over twenty spans."

"Yes, go on," Coleman encouraged, wondering where this was going.

"I don't want to dishonor him," Haro continued, "but I would like to make the folded blade, Master Tondo. I've had dreams about a folded blade for many spans. Once, I asked Master Pendor if I could try, but he said no, never again."

"Why is Pendor so against the idea?" Coleman asked.

"More than twenty-five spans ago, he took a contract to make such a sword for a baron—one of the king's cousins. It was a fine-looking sword, I've been told, but it shattered in a duel, and the rezus was wounded, causing him to lose the match and suffer shame. He made awful trouble for Master Pendor; so much so that he had to abandon his shop in the city and come here."

"I see," Coleman interjected, rubbing the stubble on his chin. "I'm willing to let you try, but what will Pendor say?"

"He will not be happy with me, I'm sure. I fear he will not allow me to work for him ever again if I do this."

"You should ask him one more time if you can make the folded blade. Tell him it's for me, and I approve. If he refuses to allow you to do it, then you should quit his service and strike out on your own. You could become a master blacksmith. After twenty spans of learning, you should know a lot about it already."

"I can't do that, Master Tondo, I'm just a helper," he pleaded.

"You're a freed-man now. You can do whatever you wish. If you really want to make a folded blade for me, you may have to do some hard things, risky things. But is it worth the risk? You may fail just like Pendor did," Coleman warned. He wanted to encourage the young man to take his destiny into his own hands, but he didn't want to be overbearing. The fact that he was once the slave master and still the steward of the estate magnified his comments. If Haro were to become his own master, he would have to choose to do so by his own volition.

"I saved most of the money I've earned since you freed us. I think it's enough to have a forge built, and I'll need to hire two helpers. But I don't know where I could build a shop," Haro told him.

"I can see you've given this some thought. Okay, if you find it necessary to leave Pendor, I will let you build your shop at the ship construction site. They've wanted me to move Pendor over there for some time now. The estate can now use two black-smiths. What do you think about that?"

"I'm afraid; I don't want to offend Master Pendor."

"The choice is yours, Haro," Coleman advised.

"Yes, Master Tondo. I must take time to think and pray some more," Haro said as he stared at the blue meteorite sitting between them.

"Go ahead, Haro, pick it up," Coleman encouraged. Haro eagerly lifted the stone and held it in both hands, staring at it reverently for a while. "Let me know when you've decided what you're going to do. I still want a folded blade." The young man set the blue meteorite down, rose to his feet, bowed, and exited the guesthouse.

Idop and Ayascho entered the room. "What's all this talk about a folded blade? What does that mean?" Idop asked.

Ayascho had been listening while sitting under his resting tree. He asked, "How do you fold gravetum?" He pulled his Caver's knife from its scabbard and tried to bend the blade with his fingers.

"In my homeland, there are swordsmiths from a kingdom called Japan who make a sword called the katana. It is famous for its strength, flexibility, and sharpness. I was hoping someone here could make one like it for me."

"What does folded blade mean?" Idop wondered.

Coleman lifted the meteorite. "The hunk of sutro gravetum is heated and pounded. It is then folded over on itself, heated, and pounded some more. The swordsmith keeps doing that until the blade is formed. Each fold creates new layers, just like tree rings. If the gravetum is folded twenty times, there will be more than a million layers; however, I doubt anyone would fold it that many times." They were duly impressed and could hardly believe what he was telling them. Nevertheless, they'd had enough experience with Tondo's outrageous statements to know he spoke the truth, no matter how unbelievable it seemed.

Two days later, Haro returned to the guesthouse and was invited in. The three residents and Maaryah were sharing last-meal together, so Coleman invited the young man to join them. Tenny, the guesthouse maid, brought more food and drink. Idop didn't complain; by now, he'd become accustomed to Coleman's open-mindedness, although he still disapproved.

"So, what is your decision?" Coleman asked.

"I asked the unnamed god, and I'm sure he gave me his blessing. I have decided to become a swordsmith and build my own forge," Haro told the group.

"Good for you. What did Pendor say?" Coleman asked.

"I did as you said, and I asked him one more time if I could make a folded blade using his forge. He said no. He feared, if I failed, you would blame him. So, I told him I would have to leave. I thought he would be angry with me, but he wasn't. He patted me on the head and told me he was my age when he told his master blacksmith he was leaving. He even gave me his blessing. Master Pendor is a very good man," Haro was beaming. "I would like to build my forge and shop at the big boat site, as you said. Is that still all right?"

"Yes, yes," Coleman responded eagerly. "What else do you need to do?"

"I must walk into the city, hire two helpers, rent a wagon, a team to pull it, and buy many supplies. I just hope I have enough coin," was his reply.

"I'll tell you what I'll do to help you get started. I'll let you use an estate wagon and a team of samarans at no cost. That should save you some money. I'll also supply you with the wood to build your shop. How does that sound?" Coleman asked.

"Do you even know your numbers?" Idop wondered.

"Yes, counselor, I learned while watching Master Pendor."

"Hoy," was Idop's surprised response.

"Thank you, Master Tondo. I will try to make the best sword in the kingdom for you. I'm sure I can. It will be my gift to you in thanks for all the things you've done for me; for all of us," the young man was ecstatic.

"Don't get too excited. There's a lot of work ahead of you before you can even start work on the blade," Coleman warned.

"Yes, master, but I won't let you down. I know I can do it. Thank you, thank you."

"Okay, as I understand it, I will help you get started with your new trade, and you will make the sword for me without charge. Is that right?" Coleman clarified.

"Yes, master," Haro replied.

"Please, stop calling me master. Then, it's agreed. Let's seal the contract with a handshake," Coleman said. He stretched forth his hand, and they grasped each other by the forearm. Suddenly, a surge of energy flowed from Coleman into Haro, nearly knocking the young man over. Coleman had to steady him with his other hand, but Haro quickly recovered.

"What was that?" the young man wondered.

"Tzaah!" Idop, Ayascho, and Maaryah said in unison. While Haro recovered, Coleman went to a side table, retrieved the blue meteorite, and handed it to the young blacksmith.

CHAPTER 7

THE DREAD OF OUR TIME

I t had been nearly three spans since the masters had arrived. Coleman wondered when or if the Seer's prophecy would begin. Many others were also aware of the Seer's foreboding message, but no one wanted to talk about it. Each privately hoped that life would continue as it had been, yet they felt the heavy and worrisome pall of dread that hung over them. Training continued under the tutelage of the masters. Master Varios was spending more time during class sessions asking Coleman questions than answering his. Master Shergus continued to push his students hard, but he seemed a bit more reserved than in the past; some might say, a little humbler.

Maaryah kept Coleman apprised of Haro's progress. It took him over two detzamars to get settled, but he was now producing metal fixtures for Master T´erio's new project—a second and larger boat. The master carpenter paid Haro for each fixture upon receipt, earning the young blacksmith enough income to hire another helper; he now had three.

The temple priest made so many requests that Haro hadn't yet started work on the sword he had promised Coleman, but he reassured Maaryah, he would begin as soon as he could. Occasionally, Pendor would inquire as to Haro's progress, earnestly concerned for the young man's welfare. When

Maaryah told him he had hired a third helper, Pendor was surprised. One helper, he could understand, maybe two for a special project, but three helpers seemed too many and a waste of funds.

Finally, after more than three detzamars, Haro began work on Coleman's sword. He finally delayed all other work so he could concentrate solely on that project, much to the chagrin of Master T´erio. The young craftsman focused all his physical, mental, and tzaah energies on preparing the folded blade.

Maaryah related to the others how she watched as Haro heated the blue meteorite until it glowed, and then two of his helpers pounded the lump of metal with heavy hammers as Haro turned the glowing sutro gravetum with tongs. The third helper worked the bellows of the forge, a very tedious and tiring task, she thought. She could see the blade slowly taking form, but she couldn't tarry too long due to her other duties. The news excited Coleman, so he resolved to visit the site on the next Master's Day on Du-Zet.

Haro saw the riders approaching in the distance and instantly knew who they were. This was the moment he'd been dreading for the past two days. Coleman, Idop, Ayascho, Maaryah, and Pendor soon arrived at the young blacksmith's shop.

Coleman was surprised that no one greeted him and his company. "Haro, are you here?" Coleman called out.

The young man's head peeked around the edge of the shop's wide doorway. He then scurried to Coleman, head bowed, and fell to his knees at Coleman's feet. "Forgive me, master, I have failed," the young blacksmith lamented.

Coleman looked into the sky and, in an annoyed tone, said, "Haro, stand up and straighten your back; quit groveling." The young man stood, his head still bowed, refusing to look Coleman in the face.

"What has happened?" Pendor asked.

"I failed, Master Pendor. I thought I could make the folded blade, but I failed. It's ruined. My failure shames me. I'm so sorry, Master Tondo. I don't know what went wrong," Haro bemoaned, almost in tears.

"Tell me what happened," Coleman said in as calm a voice as he could muster. This was disappointing news, but he didn't want to increase the novice swordsmith's distress.

Haro began his explanation while staring at the ground at his feet, "I had finished preparing and shaping the blade. It was time to harden it by quenching. In my dreams, I coated the blade with a special mixture of clay and other things, so when it came time to quench it, that's what I did. The blade was heated, and then, at the right moment, it was dipped into the quenching tank. Something horrible happened. I don't know why."

"What happened?" asked Idop, no longer able to stand the suspense.

"I must show you," the young man told him and dashed into his shop, returning quickly with the blade wrapped in a leather shroud. He slowly uncovered it, exposing a slightly curved, dull-blue tinted blade. Pendor gasped, then chuckled quietly.

"What's the problem?" Coleman wondered.

"Sire Tondo, can't you see?" Pendor asked. "The blade has curved. It's useless."

"A thousand apologies, master, forgive me. It was perfectly straight, I swear, but when I quenched it, it curved. I'm so ashamed," came Haro's heartfelt anguish.

"There's nothing wrong with this blade that I can see. I expected the sword to be curved. If the blade is made properly, it will curve when it's quenched," Coleman didn't know much about sword making, but he had always been intrigued with the Japanese katana and knew a little about how they were made. "Is it strong?" he asked.

"But Sire Tondo, no one has ever seen anything like this bent sword. Everyone knows swords must be straight and sharp on both sides. This one is so thick on its backside, it doesn't look like you could sharpen it properly," Pendor advised.

"No, not all swords need two sharp edges. One sharp, curved edge can be very effective. And the thickness of its spine gives it extra strength. Haro, stop worrying; it looks perfect. When will you finish it?" Coleman asked.

For the first time since Coleman's arrival, Haro looked into his benefactor's face, and a broad smile took the place of his worry. "I must polish it, add the guard, grip, and pommel, then sharpen it. I think another wernt."

Coleman examined the blade more closely. He could see the layering embedded in the metal and the wavy temper line that was like a fingerprint that made each famed masterpiece from his homeworld unique. It also held much of the blue tint from its mother stone. Coleman wondered if the blue meteorite was equal to the honored tamahagane the Japanese used in the making of their famous sword. Only time would tell.

While they were at the lake, Coleman and the other visitors toured the new ship under construction. Master T´erio introduced Coleman to his new assistant builder, Mentas. T´erio told Coleman he would return to the temple after this ship was completed, and Mentas would be his replacement. Coleman thanked both of them for their efforts.

The midday-meal was soon prepared, and they ate together, all except T´erio, who withdrew to his priests' cloister to eat. After a hearty meal, the visitors bid everyone adieu and returned to the estate manor. They arrived just before the p´atezas dipped beneath the horizon. A royal herald awaited their arrival. When they reached him, he unrolled a parchment scroll and began reading it aloud.

"The Great King Teg-ar-mos the Elder has crossed-over. His son, Prince Teg-ar-mos, rules in his place. All citizens are required to mourn the loss of our past monarch until the prince is crowned our new king. All citizens of rank in the kingdom, and all citizens residing in the city of Anterra, are requested and required to attend the great king's entombment procession on the last day of Dzaah. At the conclusion of the mourning period, all citizens will offer their oaths of loyalty to the new king. So it has been declared, and so it must be obeyed." The herald mounted his samaran and rode off.

Coleman then noticed the priests had joined his small group to hear the herald's message. "And so begins the dread of our time," Master Shergus pronounced.

Coleman's estate had gotten the herald's message two wernts before the end of the detzamar of Dzaah, the third detzamar of the *Anterran* calendar. Because he was a person of rank, Coleman was required to attend the late king's services. Mistress Oetan, also a tetzae, was required to attend, as well. No others residing on the estate were under that obligation; however, Counselor Idop told him that anyone in the king's service was also expected to attend—that went without saying. Ayascho would follow Coleman, and Lady Oetan would accompany her daughter, along with Teema. Also, all four priests would be joining them. The temple always attended such official functions as a symbol of the priests' respect for the sovereigns. Doros, Teema, and Tenny dressed the manor house, the guesthouse, and the senior boss's cottage with olive drab mourning trappings.

The day before the party was to leave, Maaryah met with Coleman in the guesthouse. "Please, let me go with you," she pleaded. "I've never been to the big city before."

"It's nearing the planting season, so no, I need you here," he told her. He could tell she was crestfallen. He softened his tone and continued, attempting to uplift her sagging spirits, "Maaryah, you are indispensable to the smooth operation of everything being done here. I rely on you more than anyone else in these matters. I promise you'll be able to go to the city with the gartz team after I get back."

"I don't want to go with the gartz team. I want to go with you!" she nearly shouted. She realized she had revealed something she didn't want others to know. She quickly attempted to recover by clouding her remarks. "I've always wanted to see the palace, and . . . and maybe you could find a way for me to go inside." Her white lie wasn't convincing to Ayascho, who was standing next to Idop. Coleman didn't seem fazed by either statement and placed his hands on her shoulders.

"I promise, I will take you to the palace as soon as I can; after I get back. In the meantime, I need you here. Understood?"

"Yes!" Maaryah huffed. Her grief had instantly transformed into chagrin and anger. She turned on her heels and stomped out of the guesthouse in a snit as tears welled in her eyes. Ayascho's gaze followed her out of the room, and then he looked at Coleman as a broad smile filled his visage.

Idop was the first to speak, "I suppose you're going to let her get away with that insolence. A good slap would change her attitude."

Coleman took a deep breath and shook his head, obviously annoyed by the counselor's remark. "Have you learned nothing? Only a vile and ignorant brute would do that," he shot back at Idop. His angry rebuke gave the counselor pause and made him turn introspective. Coleman sat at the table, unrolled a scroll, and started reading, his thoughts and concentration focusing on the urgent matters he needed to accomplish before leaving for the city.

In a melodic tone, Ayascho said, "I think she loves you."

Idop's head snapped toward Ayascho. "Oy, you jest!" he grouched. It didn't appear that Coleman heard either remark. He was running through a list in his mind of all the things he needed to address before he departed the estate.

"Hoy!" Idop huffed, and then he exited the guesthouse.

Ayascho continued watching Coleman, and after a few moments, he repeated, "I think she loves you."

Coleman didn't respond. He was still deep in thought. Ayascho waited, then shrugged, and finally left the room, heading for the barn. A few minutes later, after making some notations on a scroll, Coleman was sure he had covered all the important issues. He looked around and noticed everyone was gone. He went to his room to change into a robe before heading to the bathhouse.

The journey to the city was slow and without incident. Coleman had the opportunity to ask Master Shergus what he meant by his comment concerning the 'dread of our time.'

The master explained, "The Sutro Seer has warned the struggle with evil would enter a new phase when a significant royal crossed-over, and there was not a more significant royal than the king. His Eminence didn't want that prophecy broadcast to the populace because it might be misconstrued as seditious."

All of the travelers wondered what could have befallen the great king. He was a man of late middle-age, and everyone expected him to remain on the throne for a few hundred spans more. Coleman decided it wasn't worth speculating about; he would have to wait until they reached *Anterra* and receive a full report.

Upon their arrival at the city, the group split and went their separate ways; the priests returned to the temple; Counselor Idop reported to the palace; Coleman, Ayascho, Lady Oetan, Mistress Ootyiah, and Teema went to the city house. As soon as they arrived, they draped the windows and doors with mourning cloth.

Although Coleman had stayed at the large house during his last visit while acting as Advocate for Mistress Ootyiah, this was the first time Ayascho had seen the residence, and it amazed him. It was a very large building; three stories high and built from the ubiquitous sandstone-like blocks that were used in most of the stone structures in the city. The lower level had a foyer for greeting visitors, a grand dining hall that was also used to entertain guests, and a kitchen. The second level had two large rooms; one was the men's meeting room, and the other was the women's. There was also a smaller room that resembled a den or study. Coleman had learned that this room had often been used by Master Oetan for private meetings he held concerning his duties in the Pannera or business dealings concerning the estate. The third level had a master bedchamber with a balcony and four smaller bedrooms; two also with balconies. As they had done during Coleman's first visit, the women insisted, he, the steward of the estate, use the master's suite, and they would use the guest bedrooms. Although Ayascho was offered a room of his own and a private bed, he chose to sleep in the master's suite, reposing on the floor as was his wont.

In the evening on the day following their arrival, Counselor Idop paid a visit to the city house. He informed everyone of what he had learned concerning the king's untimely death. He told them the king had always led a healthy and robust life throughout his five-hundred and twenty-eight spans; however, shortly before his death, he had been complaining of fatigue and dizziness. This malady continued for several days, and toward the end, his vision blurred; then he eventually became blind. He had also complained of a severe head-pounder.

"It sounds like the king suffered from an aneurysm. That's a swelling of a blood vessel, most likely in the king's brain," Coleman explained. He couldn't be sure; it could have been a stroke, but at least it didn't seem to be anything nefarious.

"The prince wants to know if there's anything you can do for his father," Idop stated. The others turned and stared at him.

"Tell the prince it is beyond my ability to heal his father, especially because of the nature of his affliction and at this late date," Coleman responded.

"That's what I told the prince, but I promised him I would ask anyway."

On the day of the king's entombment, a royal caisson carrying his body wended its way through the main avenues of the city from the palace to the main gate, led by the prince riding a magnificent-looking samaran. The caisson was flanked by Pannera guardsmen and followed by fifty or more king's counselors dressed in the traditional red robes of their office; among them marched Idop. Mourners gathered along the sides of the street and on verandas overlooking the procession's route.

King Teg-ar-mos was well-loved by most of the people, and there were many wailings and abundant tears. Coleman, Ayascho, and the women stood on the balcony of the master suite and bowed their heads in respect as the bier passed. The king rested on a polished wooden platform. He was dressed in purple robes, indicating his high status. Coleman thought how interesting it was that even here on this distant world, purple signified exalted station.

Upon reaching the main gate, the procession turned and proceeded down the other main avenue of the city in the direction of the temple and the royal mausoleum. After the cortege had passed, citizens stepped into the street behind the counselors and followed the procession to its destination. Lady Oetan suggested they do the same, publicly expressing their respect. Coleman nodded and followed behind the women with Ayascho at his side.

A place had been prepared near the temple entrance for persons of rank; Coleman and Ootyiah were directed there by one of the Pannera guards. After nearly half a segment passed, an elderly, white-haired man, dressed as a priest in their typical cobalt-blue robes trimmed in zanth, and wearing an ornate breast cover, exited the temple and stood in front of the huge wooden doors at the top of the stairs. The king's bier was carefully removed from the caisson and carried to the foot of the stairway leading to the temple doors. Coleman could only guess, but he thought the elderly priest must be the Sutro Seer. He appeared to be of average height and build, nothing otherwise distinguishing him. As the priest faced the gathering, Coleman could better see the amulet or chest plate. It appeared to have a large blue stone set in its center.

He began speaking in the voice of an aged man: "He served his people in life, and now he returns to the place where all things began. The unnamed god will welcome him and guide him into the presence of his forefathers."

The priest stepped aside, and the platform bearing the king was carried into the temple. People slowly began to disperse and head back to their homes. Coleman was surprised by the brevity of the ceremony; no eulogy, no flowing words of the king's accomplishments, only a simple statement. He had a lot of questions to ask the counselor when he saw him again, not the least of which was the location of the king's final resting place.

Coleman's questions were answered later in the evening when Counselor Idop made another visit. The royal mausoleum could be found in the temple ground's cemetery, which was on the outside of the city wall. The king's body was marched through the temple hall, out a side doorway, and through a private gateway in the wall, which led to the mausoleum. All rezus, king's counselors, and the king's Contingent of the Pannera were gathered there to hear the prince's final words of praise for his father's accomplishments. The king's remains were then placed in a tomb, and the tomb was sealed.

The kingdom would now remain in mourning until the prince was crowned as the new king forty days hence.

All citizens of the city were required to attend the public crowning of the new king. Slaves, freed-men, and commoners would then be required to swear an oath of allegiance to their new sovereign in a public ceremony. All persons of rank were required to do the same in a personal appearance before the new king. Coleman was not fond of the idea of swearing allegiance to a man. As a soldier, he had sworn an oath to uphold the Constitution of the United States of America, and no mortal was above its law, but this oath was much different: an oath to the king—a mortal man—who is the law. He thought the prince to be a fair and honorable person, but men have their weaknesses, and power can subvert the purest heart, for 'Power tends to corrupt, and absolute power corrupts absolutely,' as the Englishman, Lord Acton, had put it. He realized this would be another bitter pill he would have to swallow.

Coleman found little to do while he awaited the prince's coronation. None of the other estate owners invited him to their city homes, and no one responded to his invitations. It didn't take him long to realize he was considered a pariah. He soon learned from Lady Oetan, via Teema's slave contacts, all of the other estate owners were furious with him for what he had done by freeing his slaves. These masters saw it as a serious threat, and many secret meetings had been held for which no information was available. Coleman recalled the prince's words: 'When powerful people in the kingdom see a threat, they usually find a way to eliminate it.' He had been duly warned, and while in the city, he would need to be cautious.

While he waited, he began a project he had wanted to get to for some time but couldn't due to training and estate duties. He had noticed that Master Varios was having difficulty reading text. The master told him his eyesight was declining, and he feared it would become so bad that eventually he would be able to read only large symbols. Coleman knew he needed glasses, but he didn't have the knowledge to make a pair that would help the great scholar. He decided to do the next best thing—make a magnifying glass for him. Before he left the estate, he had two two-inch diameter glass blanks and glass tools poured. He planned to grind and polish the blanks into items that would assist his beloved mentor. It took him a few days to find a city vendor who had the grits and powders that would meet his needs, but eventually, he found them in a craftsman's shop who dealt in wood and stone statues. He started grinding and polishing the glass blanks, and it took several days before both magnifying lenses were completed. One was about two-power, and the other was about four-power. Although each had imperfections—meaning small bubbles in the glass—they were serviceable enough.

Before he presented the gift, he spent another couple of days in the study with paper and quill. No one knew what he was up to, and he wouldn't reveal his purposes to anyone other than to say what he was working on was for the master scholar. When Coleman was finally ready, he stacked his documents one over the other and rolled them into a scroll. He then found Ayascho, and the two headed for the temple.

It was midmorning when they climbed the stairs to the holy edifice and entered through the two huge main doors. Stepping into a foyer, they were greeted by a pair of young priests dressed in cobalt-blue robes. They bowed low, and the two guests returned their bows.

"I am Tondo, and this is my friend, Ayascho," Coleman told them.

"Yes, sire, we know who you are: Tondo the Messenger and Ayascho of the Wilderness. How may we help you?" one of the priests asked.

"I would like to visit with Master Varios. I have a gift for him," Coleman explained.

"Please follow us," the other priest replied.

The foyer had three doorways: one leading to the right, another leading to the left, and a double-door in the center. The priests took the visitors through the left doorway and down a long hall. As soon as they entered the hallway, they could hear singing, which seemed to come from everywhere. As Coleman listened, it reminded him of a Gregorian chant. The sound reverberated off the walls and was difficult to understand, but as they walked, Coleman began to recognize the words:

Hear our plea, O glorious and powerful unnamed god,
We honor thee.
Hear our praise, O glorious and powerful unnamed god,
Guide our path.
To thee, the highest and greatest power in creation,
Protector of all,

Overseer of the weak and the strong,
We lift up our eyes to the blue moon.
Hear our pleas, hear the prayers of your servants.

The priests led the visitors into what appeared to be a library, but instead of rows and rows of shelves stocked with books, they found rows of shelves with cubby holes, the ends of scrolls protruding from their resting places. Several priests studying scrolls were seated at tables scattered around the large room. One of the guides pointed to a table, and the visitors immediately recognized their teacher, even though his back was turned toward them. The two priests bowed low again and exited the room. Coleman and Ayascho walked to the other side of the table where Master Varios was sitting, seated themselves on the bench, and waited to be recognized.

The master took his time, but eventually, he looked up and smiled, pushing aside the scroll he was studying. "It seems I can't get away from you two. How may I help?" he asked.

"I hope we can help you," Coleman said as he pulled two cloth pouches from his belt. He opened a pouch, reached in, and carefully removed a glass disk. He set it gently on its cloth pouch.

Master Varios stared at it for a few moments. "Round gartz? What is it for?" Coleman picked up the disk by its edge, held it in front of his right eye, and blinked. Varios immediately noticed the magnification effect, an expression of awe coming over him. "May I have a closer look?" he asked. Coleman handed him the lens and watched with joy as his mentor experimented with its power on the scroll he'd been reading, grinning and bouncing on his stool with excitement. "I can see the smallest symbols clearly through this eye-gartz disk.

What is it?" the master asked.

"It's called a magnifying glass; however, you may call it an eye-gartz if you wish. It's a gift from your grateful students," Coleman told him.

Varios moved the lens back and forth, examining its effects. While the master was doing that, Coleman set the other lens on the table. Master Varios examined that one, also. His visitors noticed tears welling in his eyes. "Thank you, my friends. These are gifts beyond measure."

"I have something else for you, also," Coleman told him as he unrolled the documents. "These are plans for two types of telescopes; devices that will allow you to see great distances. This one is called a refractor, and this one is called a reflector. After you build these instruments, you will be able to look at the stars and discover things you could never dream are up there."

For the next two segments, Coleman and Master Varios talked, Coleman doing most of the teaching and the master asking most of the questions. Ayascho sat in silence, enthralled by all he was hearing.

On the way back to the city house, Coleman and Ayascho asked a guard if he knew where Sestardus Titus could be found. They were told he was at the royal stables. Titus was talking with one of the disgraced guardsmen from the Prince's Contingent. The poor man was still serving his punishment after all this time.

When Titus noticed his visitors, he dismissed the man and went to them. He bowed to Coleman. "Sire, it is good to see you again, and you, too, Ayascho. What brings you here?"

"We just wanted to see an old friend," Coleman told him as he extended his arm, and they shook. "How are all the men?"

"All are doing well. We are treated like heroes by most of the other guards. We've become legends for having made the trip to the Wilderness and returning alive, thanks to you. How have you been?" Titus asked.

"Very well, thank you. We're still being trained at the estate by Master Varios and Master Shergus," Ayascho told him.

"You're still being trained by Master Shergus? I feel sorry for you, my friends. He has a reputation for being a hard task-master," Titus consoled.

"We can testify, it is a well-deserved reputation, can't we Ayascho?" Coleman told him as Ayascho nodded in agreement. "Were you just talking with one of the guards from the Prince's Contingent, one of those sent to the royal stables as punishment?"

"Yes, sire. They're still here, all eight of them, and I'm afraid they've been forgotten."

"Too bad, I think they deserve better," Coleman told him.

"I, as well," Titus agreed.

"I wanted to invite you and your men to my city house for dinner and entertainment, but I've concluded that it wouldn't be appropriate during the kingdom's mourning period. Maybe after that."

"Yes, that would be best. I and the men thank you for thinking of us," Titus told him. The three men continued in conversation for some time, but Titus had to get back to his duties, so Coleman and Ayascho returned to the city house.

That night, after all of the residents in the city house had gone to sleep, a shadowy figure poked his hooded head above the floor of the master suite's balcony and deftly climbed over the railing. Silently, the dark figure moved through the open doors and into the room. He stopped and stared through the darkness and saw a man sleeping in the master's bed. A smile of satisfaction crossed the shadow's face as he pulled a vicious-looking long knife from his black tunic and softly stepped through the gloom, his bare right foot landing only inches from the sleeping Ayascho's nose. The young man's eyes opened with a start and, realizing a threat, he immediately jumped up and attacked. Coleman rolled to his back and awoke as Ayascho and the shadowy figure wrestled in the darkness. Coleman darted out of bed, grabbed his short sword, and jumped into the fray, clubbing the intruder in the back of the head with the pommel of his sword. The man dropped to the floor in a heap.

"Good job, Ayascho. What happened?" Coleman asked.

"I was asleep, but I felt footsteps passing by me. It didn't seem right, and I woke up just as I saw him raise his long knife to kill you; then, I jumped on him. I don't think he saw me sleeping on the floor."

"I owe you my life; your debt of honor has been paid," Coleman told him as he placed a hand on his friend's shoulder. Ayascho's countenance beamed with joy.

They heard a call at the bedroom door; it was Lady Oetan's voice. "Sire Tondo, are you all right? We heard the sounds of a struggle. Sire Tondo! Sire Tondo . . . ?" Coleman opened the door and found all three women in their nightgowns, standing in the hallway. "What has happened," she asked and then gasped when she saw the sword in his hand.

"We have an intruder. He's unconscious. Teema, fetch the Pannera." She bowed and quickly ran down the stairs.

Coleman searched the interloper, confiscating a short sword and a jagged dagger; Ayascho held the assassin's long knife. He noticed a tattoo on the man's upper right arm: a skull with a dagger protruding from an eye socket. "That doesn't look good," Coleman stated in mock jest.

A short time later, Teema returned with three Pannera guardsmen. Coleman directed them to the unconscious man on the floor. "What does this mean?" he asked the guards as he exposed the man's tattoo.

"That's the mark of the Slayer Cult. This man is a murderer," the senior guardsman told him.

"I can't wait to get some answers out of him," Ayascho said.

"He will never talk; he can't; he has no tongue. That was his sacrifice when he joined the cult," the guard told him.

Another guard found a chamber pot half-full of water and poured it on the assassin. Fortunately for the interloper, it hadn't been used that evening. The man awoke, sputtering and coughing. He sat up and blinked several times as he realized he'd been captured. The guards yanked him to his feet, hit him a couple of times with the flat of their swords, and dragged him down the stairs and out of the house. It was obvious the women were very upset by the intrusion, so Coleman invited them to remain in the master's suite for the remainder of the night. No one slept.

In the morning, Coleman and Ayascho went to the guards' barracks to find out what had happened to the assassin. They learned the man had been taken to an adjudicator before dawn, questioned unsuccessfully, and condemned to death as a member of an outlawed band of criminals. He was told the execution had probably already taken place.

"That was fast," Coleman was surprised by how quickly justice was dispensed in the city. Upon further questioning, he learned that it was unusual for adjudicators to convene their forums at night. He wondered why the adjudicator had acted so quickly. *Was it the result of an attempted cover-up?*

The two returned to the city house to find guardsmen posted out front, two on each side of the entryway. The four guards were standing at parade rest—their right arms holding metrens with the heels of their weapons on the ground, their left hands placed behind their backs, and their heads straight ahead, looking neither to the left nor to the right. The guards' helmet spikes were topped with red streamers, signifying they were from the King's Contingent. The guards' eyes followed Coleman and Ayascho as they approached, and without a command, the four men snapped to attention, moving their metrens in front of themselves, held vertically in salute, startling Ayascho and causing him to jump and reach for his sword. Coleman gave them a crisp US Army salute. He looked up and noticed a red-crested guardsman looking down at him from the master suite's balcony high above. The two men walked into the house and found more guards: guards posted inside the doors; guards at every doorway and window; guards were even posted at the foot of the stairs. The two climbed the stairway as guardsmen snapped to attention and saluted as they passed. There were more guards posted on the second level, and more, yet again, on the third level. Coleman entered the master's suite and found the women still there. The commander of the King's Contingent, signified by a crest of red plumage on his helmet, was standing on the balcony.

The commander turned and walked to Coleman and bowed. "Sire Tondo, I am Megato Ayetoz, commander of the King's Contingent."

"Yes, megato, I appreciate the prince's concern for my welfare, but I think all this is a bit overdone, don't you?" Coleman asked.

Ayetoz replied, "Sire, the prince's orders are quite specific. I've been sent here to protect Mistress Oetan, not you."

At Megato Ayetoz's request, Mistress Oetan moved from her bedroom with a balcony to a bedroom that didn't have one. Nevertheless, guards were posted on all three balconies, as well as in the hallway in front of Ootyiah's room. Lady Oetan and Teema also slept in Ootyiah's bedchamber, making things a bit crowded but giving the women a greater feeling of security. What upset Coleman the most was not the attempt on his life, but the worry and feeling of violation the women now suffered. Coleman slept with a short sword under his pillow, and Ayascho slept with one at his side, moving his usual resting place on the floor at the foot of the bed to a shadowy corner of the master suite.

CHAPTER 8

NEW SOVEREIGNS

Finally, to everyone's relief, the kingdom's mourning period ended. The Zuma, composed of the four zumars—the kingdom lords—quickly gathered in their conclave and officially proclaimed the prince the new king.

The day of the coronation soon arrived. The detachment of the King's Contingent protecting the Tondo city house formed an open double-column in the street and waited for the residents to join them. Megato Ayetoz guided Coleman to a place near the front of the columns; Ayascho took his place at Coleman's left; Lady Oetan and Mistress Ootyiah fell in behind them with Teema bringing up the rear. The commander took the lead and, by his command, the formation moved forward at a brisk pace. Coleman thought it a bit too quick and checked to see if the women in their long garments were having any problems keeping up.

"We're doing just fine, Sire Tondo. Don't you fret," came Lady Oetan's comforting words.

"Mother, do you think anyone else will arrive at the coronation with such an escort? This is so exciting," Mistress Oetan purred.

Megato Ayetoz led the formation down winding avenues, always vigilant, scanning to his left and right and above to the galleries, which lined their route. After they had marched for some time, they approached a hillock that could have once been a quarry for the ubiquitous sand-colored stone, but it was now shaped into an open-air amphitheater. As Coleman got a better view of it, he realized it was huge; it could seat thousands upon thousands.

Coleman's group was escorted through one of the side entrances to a place in the twentieth row. Guards were posted on either side of Coleman's group. The hillock was lined by row after row of sandstone-like benches, extending up its side in a half-circle for fifty or so rows. He could see an empty throne sitting on the stage, a sturdy and ornate table next to it with a crown resting upon it. He was told it was the Crown of Authority, the symbol of the kingdom's ruler.

As Coleman's group entered, escorted by members of the King's Contingent, a hush fell over those who had already been seated. Many fingers pointed toward his group, some obviously toward him and others toward the beautiful Mistress Oetan. It was no secret in the kingdom that she had drawn the prince's attention, and for many, this was their first glimpse of the lovely young woman.

It was also the first time many of the attendees had seen the outlander who had caused such a stir in the realm by free-ing his slaves. He could tell that those in front were of rank; the first several rows were reserved for rezus—members of the royal house. The next row was reserved for the tetzus family members. His row and those nearby were reserved for the tetzae, of which he was one. He learned later that because he was Mistress Oetan's Advocate, Lady Oetan and Teema were allowed to be with him—this also included Ayascho. Although there were many stern faces and angry countenances, no one dared object, considering his party had arrived escorted by members of the King's Contingent.

Coleman couldn't help but notice the angst many of those in the rows to his front felt towards him. After listening to their less than discreet remarks, he wanted to set their hats on fire but thought better of the idea, so he simply nodded and smiled in the direction of the disparaging chatter.

"What's wrong with these people? They hate us," Ayascho said.

"It's me they hate. They see me as a threat to their little fiefdoms," Coleman advised, using the godspeak term.

It took more than a segment for the amphitheater to fill. Coleman estimated more than twenty-thousand people had arrived. "Megato Ayetoz, is there room enough for all the population of the city to be here?" Coleman asked.

"Oy, no; only those of rank and the important commoners, along with their families, are allowed in for the coronation. After that takes place, all those of rank will be dismissed. The commoners who can't be seated now will be allowed in after the gentry are dismissed, along with freed-men and city slaves, and then they will offer their allegiance to the new king. Hopefully, it will take only one seating, but we will see. The king will then go to the palace and receive, in person, the allegiance of all those of rank."

"It looks like it will be a very long day," Coleman said.

"Isn't this marvelous," Mistress Oetan cooed. "Look at all the people."

More guardsmen from the King's Contingent filed in from the sides and stood in front of the stage, facing the gathered throng. King's counselors in their red robes filed onto the stage and formed several ranks behind the throne. When the last counselor had taken his place, drums sounded long and loud, and horns blared. When all of the spectators had seated themselves and turned their attention to the stage, the prince entered from a side alcove, and the onlookers jumped to their feet cheering the prince. They shouted with glee and continued to applaud and roar their loyalty. The noise was overwhelming, and Ayascho covered his ears. He said something to Coleman, but he couldn't be understood over the raucous din. After several minutes, the prince took his seat on the throne, and the people began to quiet themselves and sit.

After all became silent, the Sutro Seer slowly stepped onto the stage from another side alcove and took his place behind the prince. He lifted the Crown of Authority—the crown the prince's father wore on all official functions—and held it above the young man's head.

"May you rule under the watchful eye of the great unnamed god. May you always rule with wisdom. May you strengthen the kingdom and overcome any foe. By the power and authority vested in me as the representative of the unnamed god and guided by his omnipotent hand, I proclaim you King Teg-ar-mos the Younger, ruler of Anterra and all of its provinces."

The crown was slowly lowered onto the newly proclaimed king's head, and the entire amphitheater erupted in cheers and applause once more. The young king stood and nodded to his right, then to his center, and finally to his left; the Sutro Seer discretely backed away and returned to the alcove from where he had entered. The cheers continued for several minutes. It was clear to all that the people loved their new king.

Finally, the young king sat, and the assembly calmed again and took their seats. When the last echo had drifted away into the clear blue sky, a king's counselor step forward and proclaimed in a loud voice, "Citizens of rank are now dismissed, and you may prepare for your appearance before the king beginning shortly after midday."

The first twenty rows stood and began to file out of the amphitheater. It was an orderly process, with the first row leaving first, followed by the second, and so on until Coleman's row; the very last of the ranking families made their way out a side exit.

Coleman's party was met by the King's Contingent and led directly to the front of the palace, and there they waited along with the other gentry until summoned by a king's counselor. It wasn't long before vendors began appearing, having completed their oaths of allegiance. It was a welcome relief for those waiting in the hot p´atezas. Men, women, boys, and girls offered cups of ale, wine, and cool water for a price. Food could be purchased, as well: bread, meats, different types of cheeses, nuts, and fruits. Colorful shade poles were also available for those willing to pay someone to hold them above their perspiring heads.

After more than two segments, people started entering the palace as their names were called. Rezus were referred to as barons; tetzus were referred to as lords; tetzae were referred to as sires. Only male names were called, but when a name was announced, entire families moved into the palace. This went on all afternoon, and during this time, Coleman had to put up with a barrage of snide remarks spoken by many around his group. It was obvious, there was no attempt made to keep their criticisms to themselves.

Mistress Oetan was becoming annoyed as the day progressed, and she quietly mentioned to her mother how she wished the people would stop saying those awful things. Megato Ayetoz assumed her comment was a cue for his intervention, so he took one of the more offensive critics aside and had a long, stern talk with the man. The spiteful comments stopped after that, and Coleman's company was left in peace for the remainder of their wait.

When only Coleman's group remained, Counselor Idop stepped out of the palace and announced, "Sire Tondo, please come with me." Coleman and his party followed the counselor into the palace, the p´atezas having set about two segments before. Lady Oetan had told Coleman that the allegiance to the king was done one family at a time by seniority of rank. It was now clear to all, Coleman was the most junior of all persons of rank in the kingdom.

They were led to the Inner Hall, where they met a throng of people waiting to enter into the presence of the king. It was going to be another long wait. Coleman's group passed the time in whispered comments amongst themselves because no one else would speak to them.

When no others, except guards and king's counselors, remained in the Inner Hall, Coleman's group was ushered into the Throne Room. King Teg-ar-mos the Younger sat upon his elevated throne looking more regal and serious than the young prince ever had. Coleman was escorted to the foot of the king's stairs while his party formed a line behind him. A tired Braydo, the late king's massive bodyguard, glared at him from his post behind the royal stairs. Those not of rank kneeled, while Coleman and Ootyiah bowed. The king nodded, and the others stood. The king's eyes rested upon Mistress Oetan, and she smiled. A grin then crept across the new king's fatigued face.

From the shadows near the stairs came the hoarse raspings of the Rhymer, "Stand forth outlander citizen, guided by his friend in crimson." Obviously, it had been a long day for the Rhyming Baron, too.

Idop ignored his comments and spoke in a loud voice, "Most glorious and powerful King Teg-ar-mos the Younger, Sire Tondo of the Tondo Estate wishes to swear his allegiance to your omnipotent personage."

That's a bit over the top, Coleman thought to himself.

"Yes, counselor, We know well who he is. Please proceed," the king commanded in a tired voice. Coleman could tell the new king was exhausted and just wanted to get this oath of allegiance, the final one, over with.

"Sire Tondo, do you swear to uphold the great chain of being and the law of the land in the person of your monarch, King Teg-ar-mos the Younger?" Idop leaned forward and whispered so only Coleman could hear, "Just say yes."

Coleman hesitated a moment as the word stuck to his tongue, not fully understanding what was meant by 'the great chain of being.' After a short delay and with a little more effort, he pronounced in a loud voice, "Yes!"

Idop smiled in relief and continued with the proclamation, "Most glorious and powerful King Teg-ar-mos the Younger, the house of Sire Tondo is at your command. What do you wish from him?"

"We expect him to serve Us with the same loyalty and fervor as he served my father," came the young king's well-practiced reply. Then the king did something unexpected. Instead of dismissing Coleman as had been done with all the others, he stood and walked down the stairs, stopping directly in front of the outlander and whispered in a low voice, "I will visit you tomorrow at your home."

Coleman thought, *This has a familiar ring.* Then, he remembered Taahso's words shortly before he asked for Atura's hand in marriage; Coleman smiled. The king took one long, last look at Mistress Oetan, and then he exited the room.

"The king is done; now, we can run," the Rhymer rasped, also relieved that the day's tiring ordeal had finally concluded.

"I guess we're dismissed," Coleman said as he turned and walked toward the main doors. He could hear Mistress Oetan's excited whisperings to her mother behind him. He couldn't make out what she was saying; however, he could guess.

After they had exited the Throne Room, Ootyiah stepped in front of Coleman and stopped him in his tracks. "What did he say? What did he say? I've got to know," she pleaded.

"We should prepare for a royal visitor tomorrow," he told her, unable to contain his smile.

His party exited the palace and formed up with the guards. They were escorted to the city house, Ootyiah appearing to float above the ground.

It was midmorning of the following day when Counselor Idop entered the city house and was greeted by Coleman, who'd been waiting all morning for the royal visitor to arrive. "What's going on, counselor? When will the king get here?"

"He's on his way, and he wants me to prepare you for his request," Idop told him.

"Okay, counselor, prepare away. What's this all about? As if I couldn't guess."

"You must greet the king as soon as he arrives. He's a busy man and doesn't want to waste time with pleasantries. He would like to meet with you privately. I suggest using the study. He will then ask to bond with Mistress Oetan. I'm assuming you will grant the bonding and offer your blessing. He will then dismiss himself and return to the palace. A king's counselor, someone other than me, will then work out the bonding arrangements with you. The king does not want any delays."

"I thought royal courtships took many spans before the bonding," Coleman wondered.

"Under normal circumstances, that would be the case; however, with the untimely death of his father, the new king has decided to conclude the courtship much sooner than expected."

"In other words, now that he's king, he makes the rules. Am I right?" asked Coleman.

"Yes, in your usual blunt fashion, that is correct," Idop agreed.

"Now, counselor, it seems I swore an oath yesterday to uphold something I don't fully understand," Coleman said in an annoyed tone.

"Your oath of allegiance to the king?" Idop guessed.

"No, that I fully understand. It's the 'great chain of being' I don't. I've heard you and others mention it, but no one, not even the priests, has ever explained it to me."

"The great chain of being starts with the gods. Power and authority flows down the chain, link-by-link. The king is the closest to the gods and represents their will. The chain's links continue from king, prince, duke, baron, lord, sire, commoner, freed-man, domestic beast, slave, wild beast, fruit and grain, tree and shrub, water and rock, with each link subservient to the higher links," Idop explained.

"How do the priests fit into this chain of being?"

"They neither sustain it nor deny it."

"Counselor, in the future, I expect you to make sure I have a full understanding of anything for which I must take an oath. I don't appreciate such surprises," Coleman scolded.

"Would you have given the king your oath if I had?" Coleman gave Idop a cold stare but said nothing more. He guessed the counselor had protected him from himself.

Coleman didn't need to talk to Ootyiah about bonding with the new king; she had made it clear the night before of her willingness, and he wasn't going to stand in the way. Coleman could sense Lady Oetan's sadness in losing her daughter, but she too favored the union.

A shout was heard coming from the street in front of the city house. "Make way for the king!" Coleman quickly stepped through the doorway and greeted the king with a bow as he dismounted his regally adorned samaran and entered the house, leaving his personal guards in the street for, after all, the house was teeming with guards. He acknowledged Megato Ayetoz, who was standing outside, near the door. Coleman couldn't help but notice the effect the king's arrival had on his neighbors. They gathered in their doorways and balconies to observe the new king as he visited their upscale district.

"This way, Your Highness," Counselor Idop said as he motioned to the stairs. Guardsmen snapped to attention and saluted as the king passed. The three men climbed to the second level, Idop leading the way and stopping in front of the door to the study. Coleman opened it and signaled for the king to enter. The king advanced, followed by his host. Idop closed the door and remained in the hallway.

"I'm sure you know why I am here," the king said. Coleman nodded. "Good," the young king continued, obviously a bit self-conscious now. "I wish to bond with Ootyiah. Do you have any objections?"

"Of course not, Your Highness. The two of you have my blessing."

The king exhaled in relief, then he said, "My counselors will assist you in making the arrangements. Do you understand what this means for you personally?" he asked.

"I'm gaining a son-in-law?" he mirthfully questioned, using the godspeak term.

The king gave him a puzzled look. After a short delay, the king continued, "Your status will increase. As the Advocate of the queen, you will have access to the throne and my ear. Others in the kingdom already see you as a growing threat, and you have recently witnessed what they are willing to do to end your perceived menace. I will protect you and your house under the guise of guarding Mistress Oetan while she resides here, but after she leaves, while you're on the road, and even at your estate, you must always remain vigilant."

"Thank you, Your Highness," was all Coleman could think to say.

"I know you are here for a good reason. My father and I had many discussions about you over the past couple of spans, and we both came to that conclusion. What it is, I don't know, but I have a feeling we shall soon find out," the king admitted.

"The priests have told me that a great dread will come upon us when a significant royal crossed-over. I'm sure that royal was your father."

"Yes, I've heard the prophecy," the king said. Coleman was a bit taken aback. He thought only he and the priests were privy to the Sutro Seer's prophecy. "Don't look surprised, my friend. I'm aware of many secret things, including that prophecy."

It's true, Coleman thought, *the king has eyes and ears all over the kingdom, not the least of which is my estate.* "Yes, Your Highness. One day, I will meet with the Sutro Seer and get some answers," Coleman told him.

"Good luck doing that, my friend. My father met with the Seer three times during his lifetime, and he always came from those meetings more confused and bewildered than when he entered. I have yet to meet with the man," the young king admitted. "Now, I must return to the palace, for I have much to do. I will send a counselor to handle all the necessary arrangements."

Coleman bowed and opened the door for the king. The new king stepped briskly through and hurried down the stairs. Mistress and Lady Oetan were waiting for him in the foyer. The king took Ootyiah by the hands, and they exchanged a few words, and then he was out the door.

Coleman trotted down the stairs and stopped in front of the two women, gave Ootyiah a wink, and said, "The king has asked to bond with you, and I have given him my blessing. We can expect a counselor soon. The king is in a hurry to get hitched, so don't expect any delays." The two women hugged each other, then Coleman, and finally Idop.

Idop told Coleman that the king had informed his counselor of Protocol and Ceremony to be prepared to hold a Royal Bonding, as the wedding was called, in two wernts—twenty days. Idop said the counselor nearly fainted. "Usually, royal bonding plans take a span or more; twenty days is unheard of," Idop told him.

"It seems that with no royal father to fret over the suitability of his son's choice, and no royal mother to fret over bonding details and guest lists, the new king is going to cut to the chase," Coleman said using the godspeak terms.

"I wish you'd stop doing that. I have no idea what any of that means," Idop scolded.

"It means he's not going to let any grass grow under his feet," Coleman said, again using godspeak terms. Idop punched him in the front of his left shoulder. "Ouch! That hurt," Coleman exclaimed.

"You deserved it. I hope that teaches you a lesson," Idop grumbled.

"No way, Jose!" Coleman retorted in godspeak as he rubbed the pain from his shoulder and smiled at Idop's aggravated expression.

It wasn't long before a winded king's counselor trundled into the city house. He quickly bowed to Coleman and was escorted to the study on the second level. The portly man had to stop half-way up the stairs to catch his breath. Coleman, Idop, and the king's counselor stepped into the study to find Lady Oetan and Mistress Ootyiah waiting there.

Breathlessly, the man introduced himself as he bowed to Mistress Oetan, "I am Counselor Stasenar, in charge of protocol and ceremony. The king has made it clear that the bonding is to take place in twenty days, and if that doesn't happen . . . oy, let me put it this way, I will be replaced. I just don't know how it can be done; I'm beside myself; where to start, where to start?" The poor man shook his head in worry and despair.

Coleman wrapped an arm around Counselor Stasenar's shoulders and said, "Calm yourself, counselor; we will make it happen."

The counselor's despair seemed to ease a little, "Do you really think it's possible? It has never been done this way before."

"Haven't you heard, counselor?" Coleman asked, "We are noted for doing the impossible. Now, let's get to work."

Coleman had no idea what he was in for. He had never been involved in planning a wedding on his homeworld, let alone in this sector of time and space. Segment after segment, Counselor Stasenar and the women struggled over the guest list, gown styles, hairstyles, jewelry, menus, entertainers, and such. Coleman even sent a fast courier to Maaryah with orders to have several barrels of the estate's famous wine immediately transported to the city, 'And don't spare the samarans,' he had stated.

By the time they were well into the wedding plans, Coleman had realized, most of the military operations he'd been involved with hadn't required as much planning and preparation. Fortunately, he had the foresight to bring with him a small pouch of gold nuggets, which he was expending like water passing through a sieve. He was really beginning to look forward to the day after the bonding ceremony. *Thank the gods! This culture doesn't engage in bachelor parties,* Coleman thought. That was one thing he didn't have to worry about.

One evening, Idop shared with Coleman's group an incident that had occurred during that day in the palace. One of the king's senior counselors, who was overseeing Counselor Stasenar's efforts, objected to the presence of both Ayascho and

Teema during the bonding ceremony itself. This man, Counselor Mordez, considered the savage to be unwelcome at such a regal affair. He wanted Teema excluded because she was not a house slave anymore and, therefore, not entitled to attend to the needs of the family of the bride. Idop explained, knowing full-well how Coleman would react, argued vehemently for both Ayascho and Teema, almost coming to blows with the influential Counselor Mordez. The dispute grew so bitter that the king himself had to intervene and make a ruling, stating that anyone Sire Tondo deemed to be a family member would suffice. The king ordered the proclamation to be recorded by the scribes. Idop warned Coleman that Counselor Mordez, a man who held much sway with the royal family and other influential gentry members, would make trouble for him in the future.

"So be it then," Coleman said defiantly. "I want all of you to keep in mind that you are now part of my family as decreed by the king," he declared as he looked into Lady Oetan's face." Her eyes widened ever so slightly, but whatever she was thinking, she kept to herself.

The twenty days passed in a flash, and the Day of Royal Bonding, as it was officially titled, was upon them. At midmorning, a royal coach arrived at the city house to take Coleman, Ayascho, Lady Oetan, Teema, and the king's bride to the temple where the ceremony was to take place. The city house neighborhood was atwitter as observers packed the street and balconies. The avenue to the temple was lined by well-wishers tossing flowers in the path of the carriage. Ootyiah smiled her delectable smile and waved to the people as the carriage drove on.

Hundreds of kingdom subjects, possibly over a thousand, had gathered near the temple, hoping to catch a glimpse of the royal bride. Tears streamed down Lady Oetan's face. This was the fulfillment of her greatest hope for her daughter—to bond with a royal—and yet she was losing her most beloved possession to the young king. For her, it was a time of mixed emotions. The carriage stopped near the stairs leading to the temple entrance, but far enough away so the bride could well be seen by all those present. Coleman, dressed in his finest toga robe—sewn some time ago by Maaryah—and Ayascho in his finest, exited the carriage first and helped Teema and Lady Oetan as they stepped out. They were dressed in their best classic gowns; Lady Oetan's was a pale green, and Teema wore the standard white of a house slave, even though she was a freed-man.

Finally, Ootyiah exited to the cheers of the crowd. After her feet had touched the ground, she straightened her gown and smiled. All the well-wishers kneeled in unison, surprising her, as well as the others of her party. She was not yet the queen, but the onlookers honored her anyway.

Her gown was a stunning light blue, her favorite color. Teema had searched the nooks and crannies of every market in the city and found cloth from the City of Women. The cloth was light and sleek, similar to silk, Coleman thought. It caught the p´atezas' rays and reflected them in a rainbow of colors. The cloth had cost Coleman a small fortune, but after he saw Ootyiah in the finished work of art, crafted by Betta, the finest seamstress in the city, he knew it was well worth the price. The gown didn't look anything like her mother's or Teema's classic style. It was a mixing of the old and a style no one had ever seen before, a style influenced by her Advocate, Sire Tondo. She desired to wear something distinctive, a gown to be remembered, but yet, not outrageous.

As she moved, the p´atezas' light reflected in rainbow rays. The gown was a princess-style and hugged her form at the bodice and over the hips to about four inches above the knees. From there, a full skirt flared barely to the ground in front and fell in soft drapes on the sides. Embroidered gold filigrees, looking like a lace appliqué, complimented the round neckline and moved down the front from her shoulders to a 'V' just above her bust. Three gold rosettes followed the neckline across the top of the embroidery. A shiny gold belt accentuated her tiny waist. The gown was complemented and set off by a cape of the same fabric and color of shimmering blue cloth. It was attached to the dress at the shoulders by a gold metallic rosette on each side. The embroidered gold filigree continued under the rosettes and over the shoulders of the cape halfway to her elbows. There were openings in the cape for her arms at the elbows, and these openings were surrounded and hidden by more rosettes and embroidered filigrees. The back of the cape had even more rosettes and filigrees across the top and cascaded in beautiful soft drapes to a train trailing about two feet behind her.

Ootyiah's light-brown hair was braided and gathered on the top of her head in a coil held in place by a gold headband that circled the coils like a crown. A gold rosette at the back of the headband held a narrow, mist-like veil running down her back to her waist, which matched the color of her dress and was streaked with gold thread, appearing like rays of light.

Coleman assisted Ootyiah up the temple stairs, and as he had been counseled, let her enter first and alone. She was met by a pair of young priests and ushered to a private room. The rest of the party followed and were met by several other young priests who guided them to the second level balcony overlooking the temple's Grand Hall.

The huge room, which reminded Coleman of a cathedral, was nearly thirty-feet high, the ceiling supported by large stone columns equally spaced throughout. Geometric designs in varying shades of blue were painted on the walls and columns. In the center of the ceiling was a huge painting of the blue moon, Munnari. The floor was covered in mosaic tiles of varying shades of blue. The ground level of the hall was filled with well-dressed guests of social elites: rezus, tetzus, and tetzae; rezus taking the front ranks, tetzus in the middle, and tetzae in the rear. All were standing, for no benches or pews were anywhere to be seen, having been removed so more guests could be invited to the ceremony, Coleman had been told.

Although a few red-robed king's counselors could be seen scattered amongst the throng on the ground level, many others had taken a place in the balcony. Counselor Stasenar told Coleman's party that the balcony was the place for commoners and non-citizen outlander guests. Coleman was given the choice of standing with the upper classes or taking a place in the balcony with his 'family'; he chose the latter.

The Gregorian-like chant could be heard echoing through the room as the guests conversed in whispered tones.

After a short wait, a herald announced the appearance of the royal bride. Ootyiah entered the Grand Hall, and all eyes turned to her. Gasps escaped the mouths of more than a few guests when they cast their eyes upon her gown. It was definitely different from anything seen before, but it was modest and in good taste, or so Coleman surmised. Ootyiah smiled her demure smile and slowly walked down the center of the Grand Hall. As she did, guests bowed to her. There was no altar to be seen, but there was a large ornate wooden table with a single chalice placed at its center. She continued walking until she was about ten feet from the table, and there she stopped and waited.

The herald then announced the king's arrival. He entered from the rear of the hall, just as Ootyiah had. He slowly walked to the front, receiving the bows of the guests and acknowledged them with a simple nod of his head as he looked to the left and then to the right, repeatedly. When he reached Ootyiah, he stood on her right side, and the couple turned and faced each other.

A gasp of wonder and awe escaped his lips as he gazed upon her loveliness. From a side antechamber stepped a priest, wearing his cobalt-blue robe with a white cord draped over his shoulders. Coleman had assumed the bonding would be done by the Sutro Seer, but that was not to be the case. Although the Seer had the authority to perform bondings, he had stopped performing them some time ago due to his advanced age. Counselor Stasenar had informed Coleman that the senior temple bonder would perform the bonding rite. The bonder stepped forward and stopped in front of the couple. The Grand Hall became very quiet, although the chant could still be faintly heard.

The priest began to speak. "As a representative of the unnamed god, I welcome you to his temple. The institution of the bonding has been given to us as the means to bring joy and stability into our lives. The bonding is meant to last not only through the sojourn of our current struggles in this life, but it continues beyond our mortal trials. The bonding provides security for the couple and for their precious children.

"Mistress Oetan, do you willingly give yourself to this man, King Teg-ar-mos the Younger, to be his bondmate in all that he does? Will you support his righteous endeavors and provide counsel as called upon by him? Will you raise his children following the righteous statutes of his home as he declares them unto you? Will you always honor his name in this life and the life to follow?" The priest paused and nodded.

"All this I promise and more," Mistress Oetan responded.

The priest continued. "King Teg-ar-mos the Younger, will you honor Mistress Ootyiah Oetan as your duly chosen bondmate and always esteem her? Will you care for her and see to her welfare throughout this life and the life to come? Will you seek her counsel in the affairs of the home? Will you teach your children to honor her name in all they do?" The priest paused again and nodded.

"All this I promise," the king replied.

The priest turned and picked up the challis and held it before the couple who turned and faced him. He said, "As with this sharing of the cup, you will share your lives together for now and forever." The priest handed the cup to the king and he drank. The king handed it back to the priest, who passed it to Ootyiah, who also sipped. The priest then returned the challis to the table and faced the couple again. He took the king's left arm by his right hand and Ootyiah's right arm by his left and placed them together. He released his grip and carefully removed the white cord draped over his shoulders and wrapped it around the couple's wrists. "I now declare before the unnamed god and these witnesses that you are now bondmates from this day forth and forever." The king leaned left and gave Ootyiah a snug as the guests began to cheer and applaud.

The priest removed the cord, placed it over his shoulders again, and turned the couple so they faced the audience. The newly-bonded pair stepped together as they passed through the center of the hall, and the guests bowed in homage to their new sovereigns. They exited the temple and stood at the top of the temple stairs. The common citizens cheered upon seeing the royal couple. A majestic carriage waited nearby, and the king helped his new bondmate into it. Then off they drove to the palace.

Coleman and his party made their way to the exit but had to wait until all of the elites had made their way out of the main doorway. Coleman, Ayascho, and Lady Oetan then walked to the palace and the bonding feast, with all its entertainment—which had cost Coleman dearly even after the king's hefty contribution.

The feast went as expected. The guests sat on cushions placed on the floor, and the food was served on low tables—meats, vegetables, fruits, and some exotic foods that recently arrived by caravan. Hermanez's spices could also be found in abundance and continued to be quite popular.

Unfortunately for Coleman's party, none of the other guests would engage them in conversation. When addressed, the other invitees would respond in curt but polite replies, and then they would break off the conversation. It was obvious Coleman and his family were *personae non-gratae*, and they would continue to be socially ostracized even at such a joyous celebration. Lady Oetan was ignored, just like Coleman. She sat on her cushions and enjoyed the meal and entertainment, nodding from time-to-time to an acquaintance she recognized. It was as though being a social outcast had no effect on her.

After three segments, the celebration began to wind down. When all the performers had performed, and everyone had eaten and drank their fill, the newly-bonded couple arose and went to the main doors of the Dining Hall, indicating it was time for all to depart. Guests slowly collected around the doorway and offered their blessings and best wishes to the couple, and then exited.

Coleman and his group were the last to leave. As pleasantries were exchanged, concluding with Lady Oetan giving her daughter a hug and the king a snug, then they departed and made their way back to the city house. Tears were streaming down Lady Oetan's cheeks, an expected reaction to the enforced separation from her daughter she must now endure. Counselor Stasenar had informed Coleman that the newly-bonded couple would seclude themselves for the next forty days, the king responding only to the most urgent matters of the kingdom. After the Period of Seclusion was over, they would go on a grand tour of the kingdom. This grand tour had two purposes: the new king would receive obeisance and the oath of allegiance from the remainder of the kingdom, free and bond alike, and he would introduce the new queen and future mother of the heir to the throne to his subjects outside the city proper. All this was likely to take half a span or so.

Coleman made a mental note to see if there was anything Lady Oetan would be interested in doing to assist with the running of the estate, thinking that might ease her pain and loneliness somewhat.

When the party reached the city house, they noticed the complete absence of guards. After they entered and the door was closed, Lady Oetan let out a cry of anger and frustration Coleman had never heard, nor ever expected, from her before. "I know all of those people; nearly every single one, yet they treated us like the dirt beneath their feet. I have warmly greeted each and every one of them to my social gatherings held right here in this very house. Most I've known for one-hundred spans, a few even longer. How dare they be so rude and act so brazenly arrogant."

"It's not you they're blacklisting; it's me they hate," Coleman told her using the godspeak term. Ayascho stood, blinking his eyes.

"Bahr t´izzing is probably a better term than I would use. I hope it means they're idiots," she shot back.

"Blacklisting," he corrected, and then he continued, "No, not really, but I could teach you a few godspeak words that would better describe them," Coleman replied with a smile.

"That's alright; I'll use my own. Of all the ignorant, ungrateful, snobbish, vestangs . . ." she suddenly stopped, realizing she'd uttered a profanity she really hadn't meant to. It was a word Coleman had heard only from the mouths of soldiers and other gruff men, and he knew it was profane, so he didn't respond but simply grinned. Lady Oetan returned a sheepish smile and began to calm down. "When will we return to the estate?" she finally asked.

"I have no other business here, and my poke is very light anyway. We can leave whenever you're ready."

"Hoy, let's leave first thing in the morning. The sooner I'm away from these . . . these *people*, the better I'll feel."

"Good then. We'll leave in the morning as soon as the wagon is packed," Coleman promised.

There came a rustling at the door, and Counselor Idop entered. He immediately went to Lady Oetan and took her by the hands. "I'm so sorry you had to endure that insolence. It was all I could do to restrain myself. You have incredible self-control," he told her.

"Thank you, counselor. We'll be leaving in the morning, and not a moment too soon, I might add," she informed him.

"That suits me just fine. My duties at the palace are now complete. I'll be spending the night here and leaving with you in the morning." He turned to Coleman and continued. "By the way, my brother would like to speak with you before we depart."

"Your brother, the one who raises samarans?"

"Ha, the very one. I haven't seen him for . . . oy, at least three spans, and suddenly, he shows up at the palace and wants to meet with me."

"Why does he want to see me?" Coleman wondered.

"He's in a bit of a tight spot bhat-wise. He hasn't paid his taxes in two spans, and Ghestor Donatar, the royal tax collector, has run out of patience with him. He asked me for money, and I gave him what I could, but he still needs more. He told me he wants to make a transaction with you concerning his samarans. Would you be interested?"

"Okay, I'll listen to what he has to say as a favor to you. But I won't make any promises. Have him here early tomorrow morning."

"That's fair enough," Idop said as he stepped to the door, opened it, and held a short discussion with a man waiting outside. He reentered and closed the door.

"Who was that standing out there?" Coleman asked.

"That was my brother's slave. I told Endet, my brother, I would send him word tonight if you were willing to meet with him."

"You could have at least let the man in, rather than make him wait in the cool night air like that," Coleman chided the counselor. Idop just shrugged.

After that, they all retired to the study and spent a segment or so in light conversation before turning in for the night.

CHAPTER 9

A HEALTHY, WELL-TRAINED SLAVE

The following morning, everyone was up before it was light. By the time Coleman and Ayascho got to the first level, their arms loaded with bundles of clothes and such, Teema and Idop had already loaded most of the party's personal effects. Within a few minutes, all their gear had been packed up, and everyone went into the kitchen for a bite to eat before they started their long journey back to the estate.

Shortly after they had started eating, they heard a shout at the front door. Everyone knew it had to be Idop's brother. Teema let him in, and she led him to the master's study. Coleman finished his bitter bread, excused himself, then he and Idop headed up the stairs. Ayascho realized it would be best if he remained in the kitchen. He smiled at Lady Oetan but said nothing. She returned his smile but looked uncomfortable.

Coleman and Idop entered the study and found Idop's brother standing in the center of the room. *He looks nervous,* Coleman thought.

"Sire Tondo, this is my older brother Endet."

Coleman reached out with his right hand, grasped Endet by the forearm in greeting, "I'm glad to meet you, Endet. I can tell you two are brothers."

The resemblance was remarkable; they weren't twins, but there was no mistaking they were brothers. Endet awkwardly bowed while Coleman held his forearm, so he quickly released it. "What can I do for you?" Coleman continued.

"I presume my brother has told you about my financial difficulties?"

"Yes, he mentioned something about the ghestor."

"I've had some misfortune lately. An illness struck my herd, and I lost several of my best samarans last span. I was hoping to recover this span, but my best female crossed-over while giving birth. I was counting on selling the chetzy to pay my taxes," Endet explained.

"Chetzy? I've heard that word before, but I'm not familiar with its meaning," Coleman admitted, recalling Master Shergus's oft-repeated slur.

"It's a young samaran," Endet informed him. "It had great promise. Very good breeding; probably would have been as choice as the one I traded to Sire Oetan some thirty spans ago," Endet continued.

"Really? So, you are the one who made the trade. I've seen that one; it's a marvelous animal, the most regal-looking of all the samarans on the estate. So, it came from you?" Coleman asked.

"Yes, I reluctantly traded it for a slave. Master Oetan wanted to give his daughter a gift for her twelfth span, but I didn't want to sell. I was planning to use the female to enhance the herd. I could see that my reluctance to sell was beginning to anger the tetzae, so I quoted him a sale price higher than I expected he'd be willing to pay: three thousand bhat—more than any price ever paid for a samaran. His daughter really favored the beast, and she pleaded with her father to buy it. He didn't have that much money on hand, so he offered me a slave in trade. I had no use for a slave, but he would not let it go. I've learned from past experience it isn't wise to anger a man of rank, let alone an officer of the Pannera; no offense intended, sire. I had to make the trade."

"No offense taken. What happened to the slave?" Coleman asked.

"I've still got him. He turned out to be a good samaran trainer: riding, wagons, pack, he does it all. It worked out in my favor, after all."

"Well, how can I help you? What do you have in mind?" Coleman was in a hurry to leave and wanted to get to the reason for Endet's visit.

"I'm willing to grant you your choice of any one of next span's chetzies if you would pay today. I expect some marvelous young ones will be popping out," Endet told him. Coleman had learned, through the teachings of Master Varios, the Blessing of the City had a dark side. Reproduction of both man and beast was restrained. Offspring came slowly, after many long spans. Coleman wasn't convinced Endet could guarantee any chetzies would be born next span.

"How much?" Coleman asked.

"Only one-thousand bhat, and remember, it's your choice of the best one."

"That seems a little steep."

"T'eeb, sire? I don't understand."

"I don't think I need or want a samaran that costly."

"My tax debt is one-thousand. Because I'm in such a hard situation, I will give you the deal of the span: two samaran chetzies of your choice. Can I say we agree?" Endet offered, the pitch of his voice rising.

Coleman looked at Idop, but the counselor bowed his head, not wanting to say anything. Coleman decided not to put him on the spot. "I'm sorry, Endet, but I really don't have a need for more samarans."

"How about three chetzies for only one thousand? Certainly, you can't refuse an offer that good?"

"I'm afraid I can, and I do. I seriously doubt you can be certain even one chetzy will be born anytime soon, let alone three." Coleman could tell Endet was crestfallen, so he continued, "However, there is something I might be willing to buy."

"Yes, sire, what is it?" Endet was in a near panic.

"Your slave; I will buy your slave. That should give you enough money to pay your taxes and have some left over. What do you think?" Coleman asked. Idop's head snapped back, and his eyebrows furrowed.

"He's a good male, a hard worker, and well-trained. Because I'm in such a prickly situation, I'll do it."

"What is a fair price for this slave?" Coleman asked.

"As you know, sire, slaves are very expensive. A healthy, *untrained* male slave usually sells for three-thousand bhat. A trained one sells for even more. Mine is healthy *and* well-trained," Endet told him.

"How much do you want for this healthy, well-trained slave?" Coleman couldn't believe he was negotiating for a man the way he would for a used vehicle.

"He's still young, strong, well-trained, and has never been seriously injured. He's worth at least five-thousand bhat," Endet declared.

Coleman noticed Idop's eyes flare, and he almost said something. Coleman stopped him with a raise of his hand. "Endet, you wouldn't be trying to take advantage of an outlander, now would you? Because if you were, that outlander might have to cancel negotiations altogether. What do you say to that?" Coleman's expression became stern, his blue eyes turned cold, and he glared at Endet.

"My apologies, sire. I got carried away. I think four-thousand bhat would be a fair price."

Idop relaxed and gave a slight nod. Coleman smiled, "Then it's agreed." He grasped Endet by the right forearm, and they sealed their transaction. "Now I must tell you, I do not have that much money with me. The Royal Bonding has nearly depleted my reserves, but if you bring your slave to my estate on the second Du-Zet from today, that's in twelve days, I'll pay you then. Is that agreeable to you?"

"Yes, sire, I will see you then, and I will bring the slave."

"By the way, what's his name?" Coleman asked.

"Harmon, his name is Harmon, sire."

"Does he have a family, a woman, children?"

"No, sire. I have no other slaves."

"Very well, then. I expect to find this slave in good condition. If he is damaged in any way, the transaction will be canceled. Do you understand?"

"Yes, sire, as you say."

Coleman pulled a pouch from his waist cord, opened it,

and reached in, pulling out four zanth regums. He handed them to Endet. The man looked confused. "This is my guarantee to close the transaction and pay you the rest upon delivery of Harmon. It also means you cannot sell him to anyone else. Do you understand?"

"Yes, sire, I understand. Thank you, Sire Tondo."

"Is there anything else?" Coleman asked. He wanted to get on the road.

"No, sire, you've been most kind."

"Then I will see you at my estate in two Du-Zets."

Coleman and Idop walked Endet to the door, and when he was gone, Idop turned to Coleman and looked at him with an expression of bewilderment. "By the face of the unnamed god, why would you buy a slave? I know what you're going to do; you're going to set it free, aren't you? You are the craftiest man of business I've ever met. You can even turn sand into regums. But this transaction is Munnoga-touched. Are you simply being kind to my brother?"

Coleman only smiled and then yelled into the house, "Let's load 'em up and move 'em out!" His family members were soon happily on their way to the estate.

CHAPTER 10

THE MUNNARI BLADE

It took Coleman and his party, which included the four temple priests, only eight days to return home. It was a relief for all to see the estate buildings as they reached the hillock overlooking the manor grounds, and the ocean's backdrop was a much welcoming sight for all. They arrived at the manor house to the cheers of many residents. It was uplifting for Coleman's party to be greeted with such joy and happiness after the shunning they had endured in the city.

Maaryah wasn't there to greet them; they were told she was at the Separation House dealing with a difficult boss she'd had trouble with in the past. When the shadows grew long, she rode in on her samaran. She hopped down from her mount like an expert, tossed the reins to the waiting Seemo, and dashed into the guesthouse. She found no one there, so she walked outside and waited.

"The men have gone to the bathhouse," Seemo told her.

"Of course, that's where he'd be," she said. Seemo looked at her and smiled. Her visage turned to embarrassment as she realized she had absentmindedly divulged a personal secret to Seemo. She gave him a self-conscious grin and hustled to the kitchen in the rear of the manor house. She knew the men would be hungry after their long journey, and she wanted to make sure Tenny was preparing a feast that would please them.

Later that evening, as Maaryah enjoyed last-meal with the Three Amigos, Ayascho closely watched as her gaze kept drifting towards the handsome outlander. Now that he thought about it, he could recall her doing the same thing many times in the past. He smiled an understanding smile and felt happy for her and his friend, the Messenger.

Early the following day, Haro arrived at the guesthouse with Coleman's sword. It was all the estate master had hoped it would be. It was balanced, light, and it looked beautiful. The grip was wrapped in black leather, and the blade was polished until it gleamed with a blue tint.

"Master Tondo, I must show you something no one had ever seen before, at least not before this sword was finished," Haro said with pride. He held the sword at arm's length with its sharpened edge facing up. With his left hand, he tossed a linen towel into the air and watched as it gently floated down and fell across the sword's blade. As it dropped, the linen was sliced in two by its own weight, its two halves falling gently to the floor at Haro's feet. Everyone was stunned into silence. Haro beamed with pride as Coleman took the sword and gingerly touched its razor-sharp edge. Haro continued, "I have sharpened many swords and daggers for Master Pendor, but never have I seen a blade this sharp. I'm certain it has a magical edge."

"Have you tested it? Is it strong? Will it shatter?" Coleman asked in an excited voice.

"It is strong, and it will not shatter, I'm sure of it. This is stronger than any sword I have ever seen," Haro proclaimed proudly.

"I must take it to Master Shergus. Come with me," Coleman commanded. The Three Amigos, Haro, and Maaryah marched over to the priests' wagon, and Coleman shouted a greeting.

Attendant Pahno opened the door, examined the visitors, and noticed Coleman's sword in hand. "Master Shergus, you have guests," Pahno announced. He stepped aside, and the master swordsman passed through the doorway and stepped to the ground.

"What have you there?" the master asked.

"This is the sword I have brought for you to bless," Coleman told him.

"Let me examine it." The master hefted it, swung it with one hand, then two. He signaled for its scabbard and sheathed it. He then drew it out, dropping the scabbard to the ground, and he took several steps as he parried imaginary blows, the sword moving in flowing arcs through the air. Haro rushed to the scabbard, picked it up, and brushed off the dust. "I have never seen a sword like this," Shergus finally said. "It may have great potential, but I will not bless an untested blade."

"Then, how shall it be tested?" Coleman asked. Master Shergus handed the sword to Coleman and walked to a storage bin on the side of the priests wagon. He removed a gravetum sword and returned to Coleman.

"Hold the sword in front of you." Coleman did as the master said. Shergus swung at Coleman's blade as hard as he could, hitting it with a mighty blow, so hard in fact that sparks flew. The master swordsman examined Coleman's blade and could detect no apparent damage. He then looked at the sword he was holding and noticed a large nick in its blade.

"Very good. Now, you swing," Shergus commanded.

Coleman swung with all his might at Shergus's sword, and the master's blade shattered into several pieces. Haro was beaming.

"Very good, very good indeed," the master said. He returned to the storage bin and removed a sutro gravetum sword. "Now, let's try that again," he waited for Coleman to hold his sword out for another strike. It was quick in coming, and again, the new blade survived the blow, leaving a smaller nick in the master's blade, but a nick nonetheless. "Now, you strike my blade." Coleman's swing arced through the air and sliced in twain the proven blade. "Amazing!" the master shouted as he examined the cut. Haro's smile filled his entire face, and Coleman patted him on the back. Shergus then said, "This young man has crafted a masterpiece. It hardly seems possible. How did you learn your craft, my boy?"

"I have had many dreams of this sword, and Master Tondo helped me," Haro told him.

"I might have guessed you had something to do with this," the master said to Coleman.

"I helped by awakening his tzaah and providing him with some Munnari stone, but he did the work. He is now a master craftsman."

"This is a holy sword, undoubtedly a sword of great power, forged from the sacred stone of the blue moon by one who possesses the Gift. It will be my honor to bless it." Master Shergus dropped the remains and held both of his hands in front of himself with palms up. Coleman gently placed his sword across the master's palms and stepped back. Master Shergus took a deep breath and then stated firmly, "By the power and authority granted to me as Sutro Adept of the Great Temple of the Unnamed God, I pronounce a blessing upon this sword. It will stand as a witness for Good throughout the land, and its righteous wielder will be protected by the power of the unnamed god. It was crafted from the sacred stone of the blue moon; therefore, it shall be called the Munnari Blade." Coleman thought he saw the blade glow for an instant, but maybe it was just a reflection from the p´atezas. Master Shergus returned the sword to Coleman, bowed, turned around, and re-entered the wagon without another word being spoken. Coleman took the scabbard from Haro and sheathed the sword.

"Haro, this is a great sword. Your name will become famous throughout the kingdom as a sutro swordsmith," Coleman prophesied.

"I want you to make a sword for me," Idop told him.

"I want two swords," Ayascho quickly interjected.

"And I want you to make another one for me; actually, for Master Shergus. I'll present it to him as a gift for all his hard work in training us," Coleman told him.

"I don't know how I will find time to make all these swords. Master T´erio is beginning to lose patience with me. He has a lot of things he wants me to make for the big boat," Haro admitted.

"You should spend your time making swords. I'll have Pendor assigned to Master T´erio's projects," Coleman decided.

CHAPTER 11

REUNION

The day of rest soon arrived on the Tondo Estate, and Coleman stayed near the guesthouse in excited anticipation of Endet's arrival. It had been agreed that on the day of rest, Coleman, Ayascho, Idop, and Maaryah rotated the duty of preparing meals, and in that order. This particular day, it was Idop's assignment. Idop always complained when it was his turn, telling the others it was women's work, and Maaryah should do it; however, his complaints fell on deaf ears. Teema and Tenny would prepare the food the night before, and basically, all the others had to do was collect it from storage and deliver it to the guesthouse. Idop had already gone to the manor house to gather the food and drink for the morning meal. Ayascho was off somewhere, Coleman didn't know where for sure, probably watching the ocean waves from atop the cliffs and the terrors feeding; Maaryah was in the bathhouse. She had worked out an arrangement with the men to stoke the fire early on every Du-Zet if she could use the bathhouse first thing in the morning. It was an agreement the men were willing to make since Doros, the one who usually kept the water heated, had the day off.

Coleman sat poring over estate documents, never able to escape the daily drudgery of managing the estate's affairs. He was going to have to make some difficult decisions soon. He had not anticipated paying the expenses for a royal bonding nor spending four-thousand bhat for a slave, so he would have to curtail or eliminate many of the projects he was planning this span, primarily indoor plumbing. Nevertheless, he felt very happy to make the sacrifice. At the very least, he would grant a man his freedom, and freedom was something that was beyond price.

Ayascho soon entered and sat at the table across from Coleman. "I see you are buried in documents again. Why don't you rest like everyone else does? After all, you expect everybody to relax on this day."

"Thank you for your concern, my friend, but it seems I'm always falling behind, even with Maaryah's and the other bosses' help. There's still more to do than there's time in the day."

"Maybe you should spend less time in training," Ayascho suggested.

"No, it's important for me, and the rest of us, to gain the skills the masters are teaching. The estate's affairs come after that."

"And what about your affairs? You should find a pretty young woman," Ayascho said with a coltish grin.

"I have no time for that."

"All you do is train and work. I never see you rest or take time for yourself," Ayascho observed.

"Ha, it was much easier when Nestor was here, but I don't miss him," Coleman admitted.

"Neither do I," Maaryah said as she entered the guesthouse. "He is an evil and wicked man, and he enjoyed inflicting pain and suffering on others."

"Yes, I'm glad he's gone, too, but now I'm afflicted with all this pain and suffering," Coleman told her as he pointed to the scrolls gathered on the table.

"Maaryah, you look very pretty today," Ayascho told her with a big smile. She blushed and dipped her head. She was always self-conscious and had a hard time accepting compliments; it was as though she couldn't believe what she was hearing. But Ayascho was right, and she was almost radiant. She wore the pale-yellow gown Coleman had given her as a birthday present, and it highlighted the jet-black braid that draped over her right shoulder. Her golden-amber eyes sparkled in the early morning light. The gown was drawn tight around her waist by a white sash, and it accentuated her hourglass figure. The men had become accustomed to her wearing the formless, white utilitarian gown, with under-trousers for riding, and they considered her just another one of the boys; however, on this particular morning, Coleman and Ayascho leaned back and drank in her loveliness.

Finally, after a long look, Coleman spoke, "Oy! You look wonderful. Is that the gown I gave you?"

"Yes, it is. I wanted to wait until you returned from the city before I wore it. Do you like it?" she asked.

"I sure do; and even more, I like how you look in it," he continued. Her embarrassed grin turned into a full-grown smile, exposing her gleaming white teeth.

Just then, Idop stumbled into the room, his arms holding a large charger of food. He mumbled something under his breath as he tried to straighten a sandal strap that had slipped off his heal. He held the charger over the table and waited for Coleman to push the scrolls out of the way. He set the food down and then turned to Maaryah as air rushed past his teeth.

"You can't be the same simple and plain Maaryah that has been attending Master Varios's classes, can you?" His eyes reached out and searched her from head to foot. "This Maaryah is . . . is fascinating. Nice gown."

"Thank you, counselor, and you too, Ayascho and Tondo. You're all embarrassing me," she said, a bit flustered by all the male attention.

"I don't know about you, counselor, but I've never considered Maaryah simple or plain. She has become a beautiful swan," Coleman extolled. "Come here and sit next to me. I want to make these two cads jealous," Coleman said, using godspeak terms. Maaryah's smile grew even larger as she sat next to him.

"Ayascho, I think the outlander just insulted us. Shall we beat some respect into this brigand?" Idop countered in jest.

"Yes! I agree, but let's wait until after we eat. I'm hungry."

"Agreed; however, I've got to go back to the manor house and get the wine and water," Idop told them, and then he exited.

Maaryah scooted close to Coleman and gave him a glowing smile. Ayascho lifted a loaf of bread above the table, closed his eyes, and silently offered a prayer. The other two waited in respectful silence, and when he finished, they all began to eat. Idop soon returned with two pitchers and sat next to Ayascho across from Coleman and Maaryah.

Through bites of food, Idop began the conversation, "Don't forget, my brother is supposed to arrive today."

"Yes, counselor, I'm ready to receive him," Coleman replied.

"What's this all about?" Maaryah asked.

"It seems the estate master hasn't freed enough slaves yet, so he bought one from my brother while we were in the city. He's supposed to deliver him today and collect the rest of his money."

"You bought a slave? But slaves are so expensive," Maaryah said in surprise, and then she turned and looked into Coleman's face, searching his eyes for a clue to his reasoning. "What are you going to do with this slave?" she asked.

"You know as well as I do what he's going to do. This is the slave master who has no slaves," Idop said in a sarcastic voice.

"I was once a slave," Maaryah reminded him. Idop raised his cup, giving her a sarcastic salute.

"What is freedom worth?" Ayascho wondered. "I would give every slave their freedom if I could. It is the right of every person to choose for themselves."

"In this case, freedom is worth exactly four-thousand bhat," Idop told them, causing Maaryah to gasp.

"Every slave should be given their freedom," Ayascho continued.

"Well said, my friend. Even a man from the Wilderness, where all are freeborn, understands that basic principle. Look, here sits Maaryah, once a poor slave girl. Now, look at her! Not only is she beautiful, but she is also able to run the estate in my absence. How different is she from you or me, counselor?" Coleman asked as he stared at Idop. Maaryah's gaze fell upon Coleman, and her smile grew even larger.

Idop stopped munching his bread and pondered Coleman's question for a moment before he replied, "But it has always been this way; it's the great chain of being. It's how order is maintained," came his rationalized defense.

"There is no great chain of being. That's simply a means for the powerful to retain their status, and it has always been wrong!" came Coleman's stern retort. He wanted to continue the debate with Idop, but the poor counselor was outnumbered three-to-one. If his friend were to change his opinion of slavery, it must come over time and on Idop's own terms. Too much pressure today would only cause him to entrench deeper in his traditional and misguided view. Coleman decided to change the subject. "Tell me, Maaryah, what's happening at the Separation House?"

"Boss Fidus doesn't want me as his manager because I'm a woman, and he tries to cause as much trouble as he can. He won't do what I ask him to do. As a matter of fact, he often does the opposite simply to spite me." Fidus was a commoner Coleman had hired from the city. He was passably literate and seemed to be a good person to make a boss. Unfortunately, the man had his prejudices, and he didn't like taking orders from a woman, especially one carrying a mark.

"Do I need to get involved?" Coleman asked.

"I don't think so. I prade hard-bahr with him before your return. I told him to do as I say or I will terminate his contract. He said, 'Only Sire Tondo can do that.' Then I told him, 'Sire Tondo has given me full authority during his absence.' You should have seen the look of surprise on his face. I almost laughed."

"Good for you. You have my full support. By the way, say it like this: *played hardball*," Coleman coached.

"T'ade harn-b'ahr," she repeated, causing Coleman to wince.

"Ayascho, *you* try," he coaxed.

"Pra har-bor," Ayascho mumbled.

"Counselor?" Coleman asked.

"All of you sound like you've got rocks in your mouths. Hoy, alright, paze har-bworh."

"Well, my lady and cavaliers, that was awful. Now, let's try something even more hopeless. Everyone say Lulubelle," Coleman ducked as Idop and Ayascho threw biscuits at him, and Maaryah nearly pushed him off the bench. They all laughed and continued their meal, exchanging humorous jabs and retorts.

Coleman appreciated the camaraderie his friends were developing. Idop had already accepted the savage Ayascho as his equal. That occurred after a couple of quick chops to the head by Ayascho's wooden swords during training. Idop was slowly getting used to Maaryah, no longer referring to her as 'that slave girl,' but she still had a long way to go in his eyes because she was a lowly woman trying to act with authority in a man's world.

Ayascho, surprisingly, had adjusted to this new culture quite easily. He still practiced his beliefs, but he accepted everyone he met as his equal and ignored bigoted remarks cast at him by racists. Maaryah was gaining the self-confidence she so woefully lacked when she first met Coleman. He had seen her face-off against more than one obstinate male bigot. It was clear, she had a tough hide and a real backbone, probably developed over the many spans as an orphan surviving on her own. Yet, he felt it was more than that, maybe an inborn trait.

The group bantered humorously for more than a segment before going their separate ways. Idop returned the charger and pitchers to the manor house kitchen and then spent the rest of the morning with Lady Oetan. Coleman and Maaryah watched as the counselor and lady walked arm-in-arm through the courtyard entrance and towards the cliffs overlooking the ocean, Teema following at a respectful distance. Ayascho went to the barn and brushed his favorite samaran while Coleman and Maaryah remained at the table, pouring over records and updating documents.

Before they knew it, Idop was back with another plate of food. He placed it on the table and went for the pitchers. Ayascho returned, as well, smelling of samaran. He washed his hands, arms, and face at the wash table before he sat down. Idop returned with two pitchers, placing them on the table, but he didn't sit.

"I'll be taking midday-meal with Lady Oetan," Idop told them.

"How is she doing now that her daughter is gone?" Coleman asked.

"She's very lonely. She broke into tears several times during our walk."

"You can always invite her to join us for our meals. That might help," Ayascho offered.

"I will remember to invite her. I think she would enjoy that. She says the manor house feels larger now than it ever has."

Idop soon left, and the others ate their meal while sharing light conversation. About the time they finished, they heard the sound of samarans approaching; it was Endet and his slave.

Both men looked tired, and so did their sweaty mounts. Obviously, they had been riding hard for several days. If Coleman hadn't met Endet before, he would not have been able to determine who was the master and who was the slave. Both men wore the same type of outfit: a simple tan jersey with sleeves to just below the elbows, leather trousers, and brown sandals. Both wore hats that looked like Stetsons. Cowboys, was Coleman's first impression of the duo.

The two men hopped off their mounts, and the slave took both sets of reins and waited. He was a tall man, around six feet in height, and he towered over his master by half a head. Endet brushed the dirt from his body with his hat, sending clouds of dust into the air. Coleman went to greet him just as Idop joined them.

"Welcome to the estate," Coleman said in greeting while holding out his arm. Endet grasped his forearm, quickly released it, and bowed.

"As you required, sire, I have brought my slave on Du-Zet."

Coleman examined the man from a distance. "He looks well. Is there anything in particular I should learn about him?"

"As you required, he's in good health and uninjured," Endet told him. "Hello again, my brother," he reached out his arm, and he and Idop shook in greeting and embraced. Seemo approached and waited for instructions.

"I can have Seemo, here, feed and water your animals. They look tired. Seemo, do you mind?" The samaran caretaker shook his head.

"Yes, that would be good. I have to get back to the city in four days, or the ghestor will send the Pannera after me," Endet told him.

"You might kill your samarans if you drive them that hard, especially after little rest. I'm sure you realize that," Coleman said.

"I'm in a hard place; I have no other choice. The tax collector gave me his final notice just before we left the city. I presented him with the four regums you gave me. He granted me only a wernt to pay the remaining tax. He threatened to turn me over to the slave traders if I didn't pay in full," Endet told him in a concerned voice.

"Seemo, bring two fresh samarans for Endet. I can loan you two, and you can return them for yours later," Coleman offered.

"That would be very helpful. Thank you, sire." Seemo headed to the barn, and Endet's slave took the two spent samarans to a water trough and let them drink.

Coleman invited Endet into the guesthouse, and Idop followed. "We've just finished eating, but there's plenty left over. Help yourself," Coleman suggested.

"Don't mind if I do. We've been eating in the saddle and only resting when it got too dark to travel. Wouldn't want a samaran breaking its leg in some varmint's hole," Endet told him. It was then he noticed Maaryah sitting at the table, reading a document. "Hello, my lady. Sire, is this your bondmate?" Maaryah looked up, and Endet noticed the mark on her forehead. "Oy, excuse me, sire, I meant no offense."

Coleman gave him a cold stare, not for an offense to his person, but for Endet's bigoted inference about Maaryah. In a stern voice, the estate master grouched, "This is Maaryah. She helps me run the estate, and she manages everything in my absence."

"Really? And very lovely, too. I am sorry, my lady, if I offended you," Endet said with deference, seeing he had angered the estate master and now desiring to get back on his good side, worrying that his ungracious comment may have affected the desperately needed transaction. He took a slice of cheese and bit into it, all the time, nervously waiting for Coleman's reaction. Maaryah smiled a broad smile, nodded, and returned to her reading.

Coleman relaxed. "Sit and eat. Help yourself to the wine," he offered.

"If you don't mind, sire, I'd rather stand. I've been in the saddle for so long, my backsides hurt."

"Very well. Where did you get that hat? It reminds me of a style from my homeland," Coleman asked.

"There's a hatman in the city which makes them. They work real good for us samaran herders."

"I'll have to find him the next time I'm in the city," Coleman said as Endet continued eating and sipping wine. Coleman let the man eat without interruption.

When Endet had finished, he turned to Coleman and said, "If you don't mind, sire, I would like to conclude our transaction. As I said, the ghestor will be sending out the Pannera to fetch me if I don't make my tax payment within days."

"Of course," Coleman said as he walked into his bedroom and returned with a pouch of coins. He poured them onto the table and stacked the regums in three stacks of ten, with six loose coins.

"There you are, three-thousand six-hundred added to the four-hundred I've already given you. That comes to four-thousand, the agreed price," Coleman declared. Endet's eyes widened as he stared at the fortune in front of him. "It's all yours," Coleman told him as he handed him the empty pouch.

Endet collected the coins and dumped them into the leather poke. "Thank you, sire. You have saved my skin. I'm in your debt. It's good to see you again, brother, but I must now leave. Lady Maaryah, it was a pleasure to meet you," Endet said as he prepared to exit the guesthouse. Maaryah looked up and smiled again, beaming with delight. It was then that Coleman realized, Endet must be the first person ever to refer to her as a lady formally. He smiled, too.

Seemo and the slave, Harmon, had moved the saddles to the fresh mounts, and they were waiting for the men to exit the guesthouse. Endet walked to his former slave and placed his hand on the man's shoulder. "Harmon, you've been a hard worker and a good friend. I hated selling you, but business is business. Just work as hard for your new master as you have for me, and you won't have any problems." With that, he mounted, took the reins from Harmon and the rope lead for the other samaran from Seemo, and ambled off. Coleman scrutinized Harmon closely as he watched his ex-master ride into the distance. Harmon then turned and looked into his new master's face. Coleman saw anger and hurt, but Harmon quickly lowered his gaze.

"I know this has to be terribly degrading for you, and I'm sorry for all this, but it's for a good purpose, and it's ultimately for your benefit," Coleman informed him. "Please, come with me." He returned to the guesthouse with Harmon following, who stopped in the doorway, hesitating to enter. "Please, come in and sit at the table," Coleman encouraged.

Harmon reluctantly stepped forward and gawked at the interior of the house. It was obvious he had never been in such a fine dwelling before. He removed his hat, holding it in his hands, and sat on the bench at a corner of the table. Maaryah looked up and smiled, then returned to her reading. Idop also entered, soon followed by Ayascho, who had been sitting under his resting tree.

Coleman took a seat across from Harmon and rubbed his chin in thought for a few moments. "Harmon, do you understand what just happened?" Coleman began.

"Yes, master; Master Endet just sold me to you. He said he was going to, and now he has," Harmon told him, his tone expressing his timidity.

"I'm glad you understand, and again, I want to apologize for having to do it."

"Master, I don't understand."

"First, let me tell you that there are no masters of men on this estate, and there are no slaves here, either. Everyone who works for me does so of their own free will and choice. They can come and go as they please. If they wish to work for me, the holder of this free-estate, we work out an agreement. The worker promises to perform a task for me, and I promise to pay them for what they do. Do you understand?"

"Yes, master, I think so," Harmon looked confused.

"Let me put it this way: I grant you your freedom. As soon as we can have an adjudicator draw up the papers, pay the royal tax, and a markerman changes your mark to freed-man, you will no longer be a slave. Do you understand?"

Harmon's eyes grew wide, and a broad, toothy smile filled his face. "Why would you do that? Master Endet said you paid four-thousand bhat. I know that's a lot of money," Harmon said, not able to comprehend the gift he'd just been given.

"I think slavery is an evil institution, and I will do everything within the law to end it," Coleman told him with emphasis.

Maaryah looked up and smiled, placing aside the scroll she'd been reading. "I was once a slave, too, but Tondo freed me and all the others on the estate; all two-hundred and fifty," she told Harmon.

"I can't believe this. Just like that, I'm free. I can't believe it. Am I dreaming?" Harmon was nearly beside himself by the sudden turn of events, and he was having trouble grasping this new reality.

"I know it's a shock, but it's a happy one. You'll quickly get used to it," Coleman told him with a wide smile.

"Tondo, you haven't introduced us," Maaryah reminded him.

"I'm sorry. Maaryah, this is Harmon. Harmon, this is Maaryah; she helps me manage the estate," Coleman said with a mischievous smile. Harmon bowed his head, and then Coleman could see a memory slowly come forth from the recesses of Harmon's mind. Harmon leaned forward as he stared at Maaryah. Coleman could see she was becoming uncomfortable under his long gaze. "What is it, Harmon? Tell us what you're thinking," Coleman encouraged, his smile becoming a toothy, lighthearted, and larkish beam.

"Many spans ago, I was one of Master Oetan's slaves on this very estate, and I had a woman and a daughter. My daughter's name was Maaryah," he told them.

Maaryah's head snapped up, and she searched Harmon's face more closely. "Papa? Papa, is that you?" she cried. They both jumped up and met with an embrace as tears streamed down Maaryah's face. Ayascho's eyes filled with tears, and Idop's were wide in surprise. Coleman had to swallow the lump in his throat.

"My baby girl, I thought I'd lost you forever. Let me look at you." He held her at arm's length. "My goodness, child. You were so boney before but look at you now. You're beautiful! You remind me so much of your mama. Is . . . is she with you?" he asked.

"No, Papa, she crossed-over many spans ago," Maaryah sadly told him. She could see pain in his eyes, but it quickly passed.

"My wonderful little girl. I thought I would never see you again. I can't believe I'm holding you," he said as he pulled her into his embrace. They clutched each other, and after what seemed a long time, they separated, and he held her at arm's length again. "Do you still have the birthmark on your . . . "

Maaryah cut him off, "Papa, not in front of the men."

Coleman smiled, "I think the rest of us need to give Harmon and Maaryah some privacy and some time to enjoy their reunion. The two of you take all the time you need. The rest of us will leave you alone, won't we?" he said to Idop and Ayascho. The other two quickly took account of themselves and rushed out with Coleman on their heels.

"Tondo, did you know he was Maaryah's father?" Ayascho asked.

"Of course he did, but how, that's the real question?" Idop wondered.

Coleman just smiled and walked into the barn and began feeding the animals. Even though it was the day of rest, the animals still had to be cared for, and today was his turn.

CHAPTER 12

CATCHING UP

"**M**aaryah, you're so beautiful, just like your mother, and the gown you're wearing, it's wonderful," Harmon said.

"It was a gift from Sire Tondo. He gave it to me on my fortieth span. He says it's a tradition in his homeland to give someone gifts on their day of birth."

Harmon gazed upon his lovely daughter with a worried expression. "Has the master plied you with gifts and favors?" he asked with deep concern in his voice.

"Oy, no, Papa. Tondo has never done anything like that. He has been kind to me, and he helps me learn things I thought I could never do."

"Who lives in this house?" he asked.

"Sire Tondo, Ayascho, and Counselor Idop," she told him.

"Who lives in the Big House?"

"Lady Oetan lives there alone, now that Master Oetan has crossed-over and her daughter has bonded with the new king."

"Why does the master live here? Shouldn't he be living in the Big House?"

"It's a long story, Papa. I'll tell you all about it later," she promised.

"Where do you live, my daughter?" he asked, more than a little worried by these strange arrangements.

"Follow me, and I will show you." Maaryah noticed her father eyeing the remaining food on the table, so she grabbed the tray and a pitcher. She walked out of the guesthouse and headed for her cottage nearby. "This is where I live, Papa," she told him, beaming with pride. "I designed it myself and managed its construction." They entered, and she set the food and drink on the table. "Please, Papa, have some food." Harmon took a small loaf of bread and began eating as his eyes scanned the cottage's interior. "Sire Tondo wanted me to have my own place after it got too crowded in Teema's room in the manor house. He told me it would be a second guesthouse, but I knew he said that to try and trick me. He's so smart, but sometimes he's so silly."

"Quiet, child, someone might hear you," Harmon warned in a whisper.

"Don't worry, Papa, he's not like that. He's not like any master you've ever seen or heard about before. He treats everyone with respect. He says all men are created equal, and he means women, too." She smiled and looked through the open window, gazing toward the horizon.

Harmon studied her countenance for a moment. "You love this Master Tondo, don't you? Are you allowed to love him?" Harmon asked. Her faraway look quickly changed, and she lowered her head and turned it until her chin was nearly on her right shoulder. She didn't respond. "I know you are hiding something from me, my daughter. I remember how you would turn your head like that when you were a little girl."

She smiled and looked at her father. "Yes, Papa, I love him."

"Does he love you?" he asked.

"He treats me like a friend, that's all. He's so busy doing all the things he must do before the evil time begins. He has no time for anything else. Sometimes, I just want to shout my feelings, but I'm afraid he'd tell me he doesn't have the same feelings for me. I would just die if that happened."

"Evil time? What are you talking about?" he asked.

Maaryah then explained all that had been going on at the estate for as far back as she could remember, telling him everything from before Tondo's arrival to the present day. She told him about the masters from the temple and the training the three men were engaged in. She also told him about her own training. All the time she was doing this, her father ate portions of the food before him and sipped a cup of water from time-to-time. He said very little, mostly listening as worry began to overtake his countenance.

When Maaryah finished, he took her in his arms and cradled her with her back to his chest, as he had done when she was a young girl. "I wish I could have been here for you, especially after Mama crossed-over. You have suffered a lot, but you have become very strong through all those hardships. I can see, the master relies on you very much," he told her.

"Tell me about yourself, Papa. What happened after they took you from us?"

"I worked for Master Endet, helping him with his samarans. He's a good master, and he treated me well, but I always thought about Mama and you. I wanted to run away and come back here, but I knew I would be caught and punished. Once, I tried to leave in the night, but Master Endet saw me and told me not to do it. He said he would have to inform the Pannera—it was the law. So, I stayed."

"Did he punish you?"

"No, I think he understood. He really didn't want a slave, but he had to take me because Master Oetan wanted the samaran for his daughter. He was always good to me and called me his friend."

"Master Endet called me 'lady' today, three times," she told him, beaming with pride.

"And so you are, my sweet Maaryah. If it weren't for your mark, no one would think you were ever a slave. This Master Tondo seems to change people. Do you think he can change me, too?" Harmon asked.

"He already has, Papa. You're now a freed-man—that is, as soon as he can make all the legal arrangements and pay the tax."

"Why would he do this? What will he want from me? What did he want from the others he freed? What did he want from you?"

"It's his nature, Papa. He never wanted anything from those of us he freed. He doesn't want anything from you, either. He just wants to help others, even more than himself. One day, when I was still a slave, Mistress Oetan was going to scourge me with a slave-beater, and he blocked her attack. It hit him in the palm of his right hand and cut him badly. He still carries a scar from the wound, a scar that was meant for me," she told him. Harmon looked at her in disbelief, but she continued, "Since the day he arrived, no one was ever beaten again; not one of us. And now, we all have our freedom. It's marvelous."

"He must be sent by the gods," Harmon concluded.

They heard a rustling near the doorway; it was Coleman, and he stepped in carrying a rolled-up blanket. "Harmon, is this yours?" he asked. "I found it near the guesthouse."

Harmon jumped to his feet and bowed his head, "Yes, master, it has all my things in it."

"Maaryah, you've been talking with your father all afternoon, and you haven't told him what the first rule of the estate is?" he asked.

In a practiced tone, she said, "Papa, the first rule of the estate is, 'No one calls Tondo master.'"

For the first time, Harmon looked into Coleman's blue eyes and searched them. Coleman held out his right arm to shake Harmon's, but when he did, Harmon took Coleman's hand and looked at his palm, scrutinizing the healed wound. Harmon then grasped Coleman by the forearm, and they shook.

"Mistress Oetan was wrong, and I stopped her. I only wish I had arrived on the estate sooner so I could have stopped Foreman Nestor from doing what he did," Coleman told him.

"What did he do?" Harmon asked. Coleman looked at Maaryah and waited to see if she was willing to show her father the welt on her back. She turned and exposed the back of her left shoulder, showing them the nasty-looking scar she carried. "He's no longer employed here. He left as soon as the first harvest was over." Maaryah covered her shoulder, turned around, and straightened her gown. "I think it would be a good idea if you stayed here, with your daughter, for the time being. Is that okay with you, Maaryah?" he asked.

"Okay," she replied, which made Coleman smile.

"Harmon, why don't you take the next couple of days to get used to your new surroundings? When you're ready, we can negotiate a work contract; that is if you want to stay here," he told him. Harmon simply nodded his agreement. "Endet said you know samarans very well. Maybe we can come to an agreement concerning that."

"Yes, master, that would be good," Harmon told him. Maaryah smiled, for she knew what Coleman was going to say next.

"Don't call me master. You are your own master from now on." He turned and addressed Maaryah, "Oh, by the way, Counselor Idop has invited Lady Oetan to join us for last-meal. Be sure to bring your father. I would like to introduce him to her."

"Are you sure that's a good idea? She can barely tolerate me," Maaryah told him.

"She's going to have to get used to the idea sooner or later. She's just as dependent on you as she is on me for her income, and the sooner she accepts that, the better."

"And Papa, too?"

"Why not? He's part of the estate family now," he told her as he left her cottage and headed toward the cliffs.

Dinner in the guesthouse that evening began at dusk. Coleman had placed a shiny new brass-colored fork at each place setting, forks that Pendor had made some time ago. Coleman had many laughs as he watched the others fumble with the new utensil. Most resorted to the tried and true finger method, but Maaryah worked hard at conquering the unfamiliar device; Harmon followed his daughter's lead and stuck with it, as well.

Lady Oetan, examining the collection of Tondo's guests, minded her social graces, as she always did, but it was clear she was uncomfortable with the mix: slave, freed-man, savage, commoner, and tetzae outlander. She admitted she had never seen such an odd collection of people attending a meal at the same time. However, she did enjoy herself, especially when Coleman and Ayascho once again related their stay with the Caver people and the odd foods they had been served there.

Poor Harmon looked miserable. He sat with his head bowed, and he wouldn't look anyone in the eyes. Coleman knew the man had dignity; now, all he needed was to gain the self-confidence that had been denied him all his long life. Maaryah was encouraged to share her experiences while running the estate during Coleman's group's stay in the city. She had managed to keep things smoothly running even though she had to deal with many unexpected problems. Coleman closely watched Lady Oetan as Maaryah continued her review. As she explained how she handled each situation, he noticed Lady Oetan's expression change from social politeness to real surprise and then esteem. Although she wasn't boasting, Maaryah was telling everyone how she, a marked woman, had taken on the role of a foreman and found solutions to each problem the same way the lady's late bondmate or Nestor had, but without resorting to violence. Coleman could see the Lady's respect for the young woman increasing.

When the dinner party was over, everyone went their separate ways. Lady Oetan returned to the manor house escorted by Counselor Idop; Ayascho went to his bed on the floor of the bedroom; Maaryah and her father went to her cottage; Coleman sat in his chair, weaving a basket. He looked at the empty bench, the one Maaryah usually sat on as she did her sewing. He heard Idop return, go into his bedroom, and he said 'goodnight.' Coleman stopped his weaving and stared at the empty bench again and sighed. He soon placed his unfinished basket on the floor and turned in for the night himself.

Soon, everyone settled back into their normal routines. The temple masters continued training the Three Amigos, although the masters seemed to quicken the pace. Harmon agreed to work as a samaran trainer. Seemo took good care of the creatures, but he had little knowledge about training or breeding them. Harmon told Coleman he thought he could help in getting some of them to breed, which had been a problem on the estate in the past.

After several wernts, Haro completed the swords Ayascho, Idop, and Coleman had commissioned him to make. Coleman presented a blue folded blade to Master Shergus, who received it with appreciation. Coleman had also designed a tomahawk he wanted Haro to make. He had carried one on nearly every Ranger operation he'd been involved with and found it to be a most useful weapon and tool. Maaryah continued her lessons with Master Varios, but only in the afternoons. Her other responsibilities required her to spend the mornings seeing to those duties. She would spend the evenings with her father in her cottage, and only occasionally did she eat meals with the men as she had done in the past.

The *Anterra* continued exploring the ocean and coasts. Hermanez had determined that the Ancient City was located at the northern end of a great gulf. Several other coastal cities, besides the City of Women, were discovered and engaged in trade. Officials from the southernmost city so far discovered, Bondaros by name, welcomed the mariner with open arms. Hermanez estimated that Bondaros was at least two-hundred and fifty marches by land from Anterra. That would make it well over three-thousand miles away, Coleman guessed; however, by sea, it would take only twenty to thirty days to make the voyage, which was direct and avoided the convoluted route required by land.

Hermanez also told him he had traded for several sacks of grain, called mayzie, he had never seen before. The grain came from a city located on the coast north of Bondaros, by the name of Panemento. He reached into a pouch at his waist and pulled out a handful of the grain.

Coleman examined the yellow kernels. "This looks like corn. I'll make arrangements to plant it and see what happens," he told Hermanez.

All-in-all, it had been another successful expedition. Hermanez and the boaters planned to rest several days before heading out again. He told Coleman, his next exploration would start at Bondaros and go south where he had been told mountains of ice drifted in the sea. Coleman warned him that the mountains of ice could be very dangerous and to give them a wide berth. He went on to explain the hazards of icebergs.

A welcome back dinner was held in Hermanez's honor that night in the manor house. The attendees included Counselor Idop, Lady Oetan, Scholar Pammon and his bondmate Wandra, Ayascho, Coleman, and Maaryah. Although Harmon had been invited, he chose to exercise his newly attained freedom and not attend. The thought of last-meal in the Big House with the bondmate of an ex-master was more than he was willing to endure, especially after such an uncomfortable experience he'd had during the guesthouse gathering.

Hermanez was asked to share his adventures from the last expedition, which he happily did. There were several terror-bumps; a violent storm that was likely a gale, Coleman guessed; and many exotic sights in the cities where they stopped. He also mentioned that he'd been told about a rising power in the southland, but no one could give him any details.

After everyone had finished eating, Coleman coaxed Maaryah into sharing her pleasing singing voice with the group. Her song was a lullaby, something she said her mother had sung to her when she was a child. Her voice was clear and vibrant, not nearly as well-trained as Ootyiah's, but very pleasant, nevertheless. When she finished, everyone applauded, and there were many requests for an encore. After some prodding, she relented and offered another child's song, which relaxed the listeners to a point where their eyelids grew heavy.

Counselor Idop then shared some palace chatter he had learned while he was in the city. It pertained to several of the elites in the kingdom, but no one Coleman knew personally. It all sounded like idle gossip to him, not worth thinking about, but Lady Oetan was enthralled.

Scholar Pammon shared how well the school was doing. He had changed the school sessions from all day to only the morning segments. Parents had complained that they needed their children home earlier in the day so they could do the many chores their families needed to be done. He said most of the adults had dropped out because they had too much work to do during the day, so he started holding classes at night for a segment or two. Several of the adults had returned, and he was hopeful more would soon join. It was another enjoyable evening for all the guests. Even Maaryah was becoming comfortable with these social events.

When the gathering concluded, Coleman strolled to the cliffs to watch the waves crash against the rocks far below. The tide was out, and a sliver of the beach could be faintly seen stretching into the darkness. He looked into the heavens and watched in wonder as Munnevo began to eclipse Munnari, causing a shiver to race down his spine. He heard footsteps approaching from behind, and when he turned, he saw Maaryah coming towards him.

"Hello again, stranger," he said in greeting.

"What do you mean?" she asked.

"I hardly see you anymore, ever since your father arrived."

"I've been helping Papa adjust to his new life. He still can't believe he's free. It might help if we get him to an adjudicator and a markerman."

"Yes. I must apologize for not getting that done by now. I'll have to take him into the city, and that's a place I prefer to avoid, especially after my last experience there," he admitted.

"I understand. Papa's not in a hurry, but sometimes he asks me if he's really free."

"I'll move it up on my list of priorities," Coleman promised as he looked into the heavens again. Maaryah did the same.

"Look at that!" she exclaimed as she noticed the eclipse in progress.

"Ayascho's people believe that when the red moon passes in front of the blue moon, something bad will happen," he said with noticeable apprehension.

"Do you believe in such things?" she asked.

"If you had asked me that before I came to this world, I would have said no, but now I'm not so sure."

"What does that mean?" she was looking at him a bit bewildered.

"I mean, since I left my homeland. I think Ayascho's beliefs are beginning to affect me," he admitted, annoyed with himself for his absent-minded revelation. He slipped his arm in hers as they stood side by side. He noticed she drew closer to him, and their sides touched. "I miss our end of day talks. My evenings are just not the same, now, without you there," he intimated.

"Really? I didn't think you missed me at all. You hardly ever said a word. Most of the time, you simply weaved your basket and thought in silence."

"Yes, I do miss you. I sit in my chair and look at an empty bench, and I feel lonely. At first, I thought I'd get over it, but I haven't. I really do miss you," he admitted.

She smiled and faced him. "I've missed you, too," she confessed as she looked into his blue eyes. He searched hers and saw an invitation. He recalled seeing it before. *Dare he violate his promise to never again become emotionally involved with a woman from the estate? Dare he, the estate master, allow an estate woman into his heart once more? Dare he risk friendship for something greater?* Maaryah's smile and golden-amber eyes were so inviting. He pushed his concerns aside and pulled her closer, waiting for her reaction. She pressed her body against his as her arms embraced him around the neck. Just as he bent to kiss her, he heard footsteps rushing toward them. He quickly stepped back and watched as Ayascho dashed out of the darkness.

"Tondo, the evil moon eats the good moon. It is a bad omen! Something awful will happen," he warned.

"It just did," Coleman grumbled in a disappointed tone, and then he smiled and gave Maaryah a wink. The three talked for a while. Then Coleman escorted Maaryah back to her cottage with Ayascho following along like an unwanted stray puppy.

CHAPTER 13

THE SHADOWS OF WAR

At midafternoon of the day following Munnevo's eclipsing of Munnari, while under the tutelage of Master Shergus, Ayascho was the first to notice a lone rider approaching at a fast pace. The four stood in silence and watched as the rider ambled closer, then Idop finally spoke. "It looks like a royal courier. The king has a message for you."

"What's the difference between a courier and a herald?" Coleman asked.

"The news a herald announces is important, but not urgent. A courier always carries an urgent message from the king. Prepare yourself for some important news," Idop warned.

When the courier arrived, Coleman stepped forward. "I am Sire Tondo, the steward of this estate," he told the young man.

"Sire Tondo, I bring a message from the king," he dismounted and handed Coleman a leather tube. Coleman uncapped it and removed a parchment scroll, broke the wax seal, and began reading to himself.

"Tondo, what is it? What does it say?" Ayascho asked worriedly.

"It says, the kings of Terratia and Otterina have allied, and they demand the king surrender kingdom land on the Magheedo Plain. He has refused, and he expects the two kings to declare war on the kingdom. The king orders all citizens of the Tondo Estate to answer his call and defend the realm. Cavaliers, I believe we've just been drafted," Coleman told the onlookers using the godspeak term.

"If that means we're going to war, then I agree," Idop told him.

Coleman's mind was racing. Nearly all of the men who now worked on the estate were citizens and subject to the king's call. The only exceptions were Ayascho and Harmon, and of course, the women. Unlike other estates where a master could drop everything and march off to war, leaving his work to trusted slaves, Coleman didn't have that option—at least this is what he initially thought. He realized he'd been put in a very bad situation.

The king's order required him and nearly every other male to leave, and who knew how long they would be gone? It could be wernts, detzamars, maybe a span, or even more. He finally turned to Idop and asked, "You've dealt with military affairs like this before, haven't you? What can we expect from this threat?"

"Never have two cities allied against one, at least not in my lifetime. Our kingdom will be outnumbered two-to-one. Our only hope for victory is to man the Teg-ar-mos Wall, if there's time before the enemy approaches," Idop told him.

"How effective are the other armies? Will they attack the Wall?" Coleman asked.

"Perhaps, but I doubt it. The cost in lives would be too great. My guess is, they will cut us off from our food supply, stop all food from coming from the Magheedo Plain, and simply wait us out; let the city starve until the king is forced to surrender," Idop warned.

"And what happens if the king surrenders?" Coleman wondered.

"We would lose land on the Plain and probably have to pay tribute. For us, it would mean high taxes to pay the tribute, maybe even food shortages. The king could become a vassal of the other kings, subject to their rules and whims. They might even displace the kingdom stewards and pass their holdings to those of their families and their trusted lackeys. They could even have the king executed and replaced by a subordinate of their choosing."

"Didn't you once tell me, the Blessing of the City is tied to the House of Teg-ar-mos?" Coleman watched as Idop lowered his eyes. The estate master scanned the fields and then the faces of those present. "Okay," he began, "courier, what's your name?"

"Iroesadeen, sire."

"All right, Iroesadeen, you rest, and I'll have someone take care of your samaran. I want you to return a message to the king after we've organized, probably tomorrow morning."

"Yes, sire. The king is expecting your reply."

"Good. Counselor, I want you to ride north and east; tell the men we will meet here in the morning, at first light. Tell them, their king summons, and we are going to war. Ayascho, you ride to the south and west and do the same. Tell them, the estate master expects every able-bodied man to be here in the morning. Master Shergus, what part do the priests play in all this?"

"We will defend the temple with our lives. The Sutro Seer will decide how that is to be done. I will send Attendant Pahno to fetch Master T'erio and the others," Shergus told him.

"Very well. I must find Maaryah. Her life is about to get much more complicated," he declared.

Coleman found her in the Separation House and told her what was happening. He ushered her back to the guesthouse where they spent the rest of the day and well into the evening pouring over documents and making plans to save the harvest now that nearly all of the men were leaving for no one knew how long.

"What about Papa?" she asked.

"Technically, your father is still a slave, and it's against the law for him to carry a weapon. He will stay here and help you."

Idop and Ayascho returned at nearly the same time, but by then, it was the midnight segment. Coleman had a burning question that had bothered him ever since he had sent Idop on his way. "What happens to the other estates when war comes? What becomes of their slaves? Do they remain and continue their labors?"

"Absolutely not! The slaves will be sent to the city and watched within the city walls by members of the Pannera. That's so they can't run away. The estates will be abandoned until the war is over," Idop explained.

"Oy! I will not abandon this estate. There is much that can be done to support the war effort right here," Coleman promised.

"Who will manage the estate? Who will work the fields?" Idop asked.

"The women will do the work, and Maaryah will manage the estate in my absence."

"That's not possible. The men may be gone for a season or more," Idop warned.

"So be it, but I will not allow the estate to be abandoned. The women can do what needs to be done; with their labor, they may very well save the kingdom." Idop looked skeptical but said nothing more.

Coleman had delayed the meal until his two friends returned, and then everyone ate. After that, they turned in for a few segments of rest before the gathering in the morning. Before he went to bed, Coleman walked Maaryah to her cottage, and they were met by her father. As she said goodnight, Coleman could see worry and despair on her face. He took her by the shoulders and looked into her golden-amber eyes.

"We've known this trouble was coming; it's what we've been preparing for. I'm sure everything will work out okay. When I think of the estate, I will know it's in your capable hands, and I will not worry. I wish there was more time for us." He gave her a snug on the cheek and a kiss on the forehead, then he turned and was gone.

She watched him disappear into the darkness, covered her face with her hands, and began to quietly weep. Harmon put an arm around his daughter and directed her into the cottage, closing the door behind them.

The men of the guesthouse were up and about long before dawn. Harmon, Seemo, and Numo were rousted out to harness samaran teams for three wagons. It was going to be a long journey, and the wagons were to carry needed food and supplies.

Coleman took an inventory of the weapons available. He found twenty gravetum swords and twenty gravetum daggers. Master Shergus joined him and offered fifteen swords, ten gravetum, and five sutro gravetum. He also presented Coleman with ten metrens. It was a good start, but Coleman knew he needed many more weapons if he were to arm all the men he was expecting to take with him.

After the wagon teams were harnessed, several families arrived for the meeting, and Coleman put the men to work loading tents and sacks of grain into the wagons. By the time the p´atezas broke the horizon, nearly all of the men had arrived, and although they were not required to bring their families, their loved ones also joined them; many bondmates and children were weeping. Maaryah had made arrangements for food and water to be available for the host of men she expected, but she was surprised by the number of women and children, having made arrangements for only the men. She quickly adjusted and put some of the arriving women to work assisting with food preparation.

After everyone had arrived, Coleman counted noses, wrote his response to the king, and handed it to the courier, Iroesadeen. The courier quickly mounted his samaran and galloped away.

"What did you tell the king?" Idop asked.

"I told him one-hundred and fifteen men will arrive in the city in ten days."

"That's good. I'm sure he will order us to the Wall, so expect another message before we get to the city," Idop advised.

Coleman organized his men into squads of ten men each; the squads were led by estate bosses. The elderly and those too young were told to remain behind and help work the estate. Plans had been drawn up the night before to plant more corn and as much grain seed as remained from Coleman's previous failed ventures. He instructed Maaryah to use the new plow for the cultivation, digging deep to overturn the dark, rich soil below.

He also decided to have work on the new ship continue, and he asked Master T´erio if he was willing to do that. After consulting with deity, the master agreed. Coleman took the responsibility upon himself and ordered the shipbuilding crew to stay and continue their work on the ship.

"We may need the new boat to help supply the city," Coleman reasoned.

Just before midday, all was in order, and the company moved out. One-hundred and fifteen men, three wagons were drawn by draft samarans, with Coleman, Ayascho, and Idop riding mounts; those not driving the wagons were on foot. Many women volunteered to accompany their bondmates and act as cooks and/or laundry women, but Coleman told them they were needed on the estate. He estimated how much he would need in funds, took that sum for himself, and left the remainder for Maaryah to use in managing the estate's affairs; it was a significant cache. She now realized just how much he trusted her, and her feelings for him grew even stronger. Also, he left her what was remaining of the gold nuggets he had brought from the Wilderness, which was only a small pouch full. He explained to Maaryah that it was to be used to finish the new boat.

There was much weeping and sadness as the men departed. Women and children hugged their bondmates and fathers in one final embrace before they headed off to war. It tore at Coleman's heart, but it wasn't the first time he'd witnessed such a scene. He had deployed many times before on a distant planet, but never like this. Never had he felt so responsible for the welfare of those under his command. He hoped upon hope for a peaceful solution to this dispute, although that prospect seemed remote. The wagons took the lead, and the men spread out on both sides. The priests' huge wagon brought up the rear, carrying Master Shergus, Master Varios, and Attendant Pahno. As the party crested the hillock overlooking the manor, the men waved their final farewells, gave a hearty shout, and then they were gone.

Coleman pushed the party hard, wanting to get at least half a march in before nightfall on the first day of travel. After five days, Iroesadeen, the courier, returned with another message from the king. Coleman was instructed to lead his men to the far eastern end of the Teg-ar-mos Wall. He was promised he'd be provided additional weapons upon his company's arrival. Coleman set a course that would bypass the city and cut at least a day's march off their journey, and he said farewell to the priests, who continued on their way to the temple. His group was making good time, traveling more than half a march per day.

As often as time and daylight permitted at the end of each day, Coleman saw to the men's combat training, primarily with wooden swords provided by Master Shergus. He quickly became very disappointed with their skill and their progress. Idop advised him not to expect too much. The counselor also told him that the armies they would be facing were no better trained. The bulk of all three armies were made up of untrained conscripts, pulled away from their daily lives as farmers, merchants, laborers—any grown able-bodied male—and required to serve as militia until released by their kings. Nevertheless, Coleman would see that his men were as prepared as he could make them, not only for the sake of the kingdom but for their own well-being.

It took Coleman's group only fifteen days to reach the Wall. A small contingent of ten militia led by a Pannera sestardi was all that was to be seen. Coleman quickly got his men into the defensive positions on the Wall and prayed that the enemy would not approach until more forces and weapons arrived.

Fortunately, after another ten days, the entire Wall had been manned, and still, the enemy had not been seen. During that time, a wagon load of weapons was delivered. In addition to the weapons, one-hundred farmers and merchants arrived, sent by the king, and placed under the tetzae outlander's command.

Coleman settled his men into a daily routine of guard duty on the Wall, training, doing construction to strengthen the stone bulwark, and occasionally getting some rest and relaxation. When his group consumed a wagon load of food, he would send a wagon along with a couple of drivers, selected by lot, to the estate to restock their supplies. This also gave the two men some time with their families before heading back.

This routine continued for two detzamars, yet no enemy had been spotted anywhere along the Wall, although rumors persisted that an attack was only days away. After more than three detzamars—one hundred and thirty-five days to be exact—enemy scouts were finally spotted near the main gate at the center of the Wall. Over the next several days, the enemy host massed. It was a great mob of tens of thousands of armed men. They could be called the brethren of the Anterrans, but their motives were anything but brotherly.

Hundreds approached the Wall, remaining just out of the range of a thrown metren or rock, and taunted the men atop it. "You cowards on the Wall, prepare to watch it fall!" they shouted over and over. Young King Teg-ar-mos stood above the massive gates and watched the horde of jeering and profane antagonists before him.

After a segment of their verbal abuse, the enemy force silenced themselves as four regally adorned men stepped from the mass. King Teg-ar-mos immediately knew who they were: the kings of Anterra's sister cities, King Pen-dow-mon of Otterina and King Men-dre-dor of Terratia. The two kings stopped well out of range of any known deadly missile, standing proud and commanding. A few steps behind them were their sons and heirs, Prince Men-dre-dor and Prince Pen-dow-mon.

King Men-dre-dor, a stocky man of average height, was the first to speak. "Young King Teg-ar-mos, it would be beneficial for your people if you submit to our demands. You can avoid much suffering and many deaths by doing so," the king shouted.

"Turn your forces around and go home," the young king shouted back, "and peace will return to the land."

"Do our armies frighten you, my little chetzy?" King Pen-dow-mon blustered disparagingly. He was a tall and lanky man.

"Does my formidable wall discourage you, King Pen-dow-mon?" the young king retorted.

"It only separates you from the grain fields. We will simply wait for you to come forth and kneel before us, begging for food," King Men-dre-dor yelled back, and then he chuckled.

"You will waste yourself upon these stones, or your men will tire of a never-ending wait," King Teg-ar-mos promised.

"We will see, my young chetzy," King Pen-dow-mon shouted back, and then the kings and princes withdrew. Within moments, a huge wagon full of dry wood doused in oil was pushed by several men toward the gates. As it neared the wall, a man tossed a burning torch into its load, and its contents burst into flame. The wagon bounced along, picking up speed due to the gentle slope, and crashed against the massive wooden gates, its load of oil-drenched wood burning furiously. This was a contingency for which the defenders were prepared, having stored several barrels of water above the gates. The barrels were poured, and the fire was soon extinguished. King Teg-ar-mos drew his sword and raised it high above his head to the cheers of the men on the wall.

It took but a short time for Coleman's men to receive the report of what had just happened. Since they were at the far eastern end of the Wall, about a march away, they did not witness the events. Coleman and his men continued to guard their section of the defenses and train. He knew idle hands would lead to problems, so he kept his men busy, unlike the defenders on the rest of the Wall. Drunkenness and fights seemed to be a common problem elsewhere; however, Coleman's group had none of these issues.

He also made sure that US Army sanitation standards were upheld, at least as closely as could be followed with this primitive technology, and it negated many camp ailments, such as dysentery, which were afflicting other groups on the Wall. If any of Coleman's warriors violated the rules, they were given extra duty for a period of time pursuant to the severity of their violation.

Coleman also made arrangements for the men to write letters to their families. A handful of his men could read and write to varying degrees, and Coleman encouraged the literate ones to assist or write letters for those who couldn't do it for themselves. In his regular communications with Maaryah, he requested that she make the same arrangements on her end. Fewer women were literate, but those who were, happily assisted the others; however, the demand outweighed the resources, considering all the other tasks the women were performing, so Maaryah found it necessary to call upon Lady Oetan for help. She resisted at first, but when Maaryah persisted, explaining that Tondo needed her help, she reluctantly tendered her services.

As Lady Oetan read the letters from the men to their bond-mates and children, and wrote letters for the women, her feelings for these freed-men—these ex-slaves—grew as she came to understand their worries, their loves, their sadnesses, were no different than what she, herself, had experienced many times in the past.

After Scholar Pammon had returned from the estate with a wagon load of supplies—his R and R, as Coleman referred to it, meaning rest and relaxation—he shared with Coleman what he had seen and learned concerning how the women were fairing. Pammon's wife, Wandra, had told him of a humorous encounter the women had with the thrice, Lulubelle. After the fields had become workable, Maaryah had instructed some of the women to hitch the thrice to the new plow and begin plowing a field near the estate manor grounds. None of the women had ever dealt with a thrice before, and most were terrified at the prospect of dealing with the huge beast. A couple worked up enough courage to attempt to lead Lulubelle to the plow, but she refused to budge. Coleman knew from experience the thrice could be stubborn if she chose to be, and when she was in one of those moods, it was nearly impossible to get her to do anything.

Lady Oetan had been observing their struggles from a distance and decided to join the effort. She stepped in front of the beast, wagged her finger at the thrice, giving Lulubelle a severe scolding. The thrice still refused to budge, so she took Lulubelle by one of its horns and attempted to pull the beast forward. Lulubelle huffed, and with a flick of her head, sent Lady Oetan flying, flinging her into a nearby mud puddle. Lady Oetan was covered from head to toe in mud, and the other women couldn't contain themselves and began quietly snickering.

Just then, Maaryah arrived riding her samaran, jumped off, and helped Lady Oetan to her feet. She then whispered something to her. Lady Oetan, totally humiliated but unbowed, stomped over to the thrice, grabbed the beast by the ear, and led her to the plow, verbally chastising the thrice all the way. The other women quickly harnessed Lulubelle to the plow.

Lady Oetan then stepped in front of the three-horned beast again and scolded her for being so unruly. The thrice gave her a mournful bellow, which many took as an apology. Having made her point, the lady turned on her sandaled heels and marched to the manor house with as much dignity as she could muster through the dripping mud covering her.

Pammon also told Coleman, Harmon was an indispensable help to the women. The only problem being, there was only one of him, and he couldn't be everywhere he was needed. The poor man was working from before the p´atezas rose to well after dark, just as his daughter was. He had confided to one of the elderly male freed-men remaining behind due to age that he had to make sure Maaryah succeeded in her duties as estate manager, and he would do all he could to see that she did.

As the defenders neared their fifth detzamar on the Wall, Coleman was summoned by the king. He left Idop in command and headed toward the king's tent, Ayascho at his side. They made the journey in less than half a day, pushing their sama-rans hard. When they arrived, Coleman could see he was not the only one summoned. A dozen or more regal mounts waited nearby, being cared for by slaves. He learned many tetzae, tetzus, and important barons had also been called to the meeting. Coleman was allowed into the king's tent, but Ayascho was denied, so he remained with the mounts. Coleman found about a score of elites and a few king's counselors discussing the progress of the war.

Coleman heard one of the counselors say, "Your Highness, the city is running low on food. The residents will need to go on half-rations in two or three detzamars so we can continue feeding the men on the Wall."

"If we do that, they will rebel," another warned.

"Only the women, children, and aged men are left. It wouldn't be much of a rebellion," another huffed.

"Don't forget about the slaves. If they rebel, the Pannera wouldn't be able to handle it. We would have to pull a substantial number of men off of the Wall to put them down," one of the tetzae cautioned.

"How many slaves are in the city and the provinces surrounding it?" the king asked.

"Twelve to fifteen thousand, Your Highness; maybe more."

"About half are strong males," another advised.

"If we hope to continue resisting, we must purge the slaves. It's the only way to hold out longer," a counselor warned.

Coleman didn't like what he had just heard and decided to enter the discussion. "Counselor, what do you mean by 'purge the slaves?'"

"Collect them and kill them, or force them into the enemy's camp," came the counselor's cruel and heartless answer.

"You can't summarily kill slaves; it's against Slave Law. It's also not feasible," Coleman warned.

"The king is the law, outlander, and your sympathy for the slaves will find no allies here," a counselor fumed.

"Counselor Mordez, let me hear what Tondo has to say. Why isn't it feasible?" the king asked.

Coleman gave Mordez a cold stare as an inner feeling warned him to be wary of this man. He turned and addressed the king, "Your Highness, as soon as the slaves learn of the threat, they will scatter, or worse yet, they will fight. You need to keep the Wall manned, and you cannot afford to pull men off it to chase down every slave in the kingdom, who will likely threaten our rear with raids against supply points. If the slaves are forced into the enemy's camp, they will be turned against us in one form or another."

"Oy, outlander, what is your solution?" Mordez countered.

"I have ordered my estate manager to have the boat, *Anterra*, bring as much food from the far eastern cities as possible, and it is being stored at my estate. I've also planted grains, which are being harvested as we speak. I know it's not enough to feed everyone very long, but it will help us hold out longer. Provide me with more wagons and teams, and I can have it delivered to the city. I've asked Master T´erio to finish the new boat as quickly as possible. Also, workers on my estate have planted several fields of corn, and it will be harvested soon. That will help a little, as well. We should also consider reducing rations for everyone, those on the Wall as well as those in the city, by a smaller portion, not by half. I think by small adjustments like this, we can hold out longer."

Many attendees were surprised by Coleman's preparations and ideas. A quiet murmur began as individuals whispered their awe at his foresight; however, Counselor Mordez was not impressed.

"Why isn't your estate manager on the Wall, and who are these harvesters? They should also be on the Wall," Mordez angrily stated.

"My manager is a woman, and so are the harvesters," Coleman told him.

"Women? That's ridiculous! What's gorn?" Mordez asked.

"It's a grain. People in my homeland eat it."

"I doubt these small adjustments will be enough. Even if what you say can help, we will still be out of food in a span. Then what?" Mordez questioned.

"This can't be easy for the enemy, either. Who will plant their crops? Who will harvest their fields?" Coleman wondered. A whispered buzz began again as others discussed Coleman's comments. Mordez looked around and saw he was losing the debate. Coleman noticed him nod to one of his counselor allies.

"The enemy can easily let half their force return to the fields while the rest keep us trapped here, unable to do anything but watch and wait. I tell you, we are in a hopeless position. We must consider accepting their terms," the supporter of Mordez offered.

The king scowled, and then he said in a loud and determined voice, "We shall fight on the Wall. We shall fight on the peninsula. We shall fight in the city. We shall never surrender!" His angry eyes scanned the gathering, and then he continued, "I expect all of you to offer constructive ideas to defeat this threat. The thought of killing or banishing slaves is not palatable, but I will consider it as a last resort." Coleman noticed Mordez's snide smile. "In the meantime, we will pursue Sire Tondo's suggestions. We must plant and harvest what we can and reduce rations by a tenth." It was now Coleman's turn to smile.

"Everyone knows the peninsula doesn't grow grain well. We can't eat divitz," Mordez warned.

"I've been experimenting with a new plow for cultivating the land. The reports I'm getting say it's working. I just need to prepare more land, and I need more harvesters," Coleman told the gathering.

Just then, another arrival entered the king's tent; it was Master Shergus. "Ha, the temple's master swordsman. Is the Sutro Seer prepared to support our efforts?" the king asked.

Master Shergus kneeled before the king. "The Sutro Seer desires to converse with Sire Tondo, Your Highness," Shergus told the king while kneeling.

"Typical of the priests; they'll speak with this outlander, but they have no time for their king," Mordez said sarcastically.

Shergus stood and confronted the counselor, his hand on the hilt of his partially drawn sword, and he growled, "It's a good thing when the unnamed god gave you a fool's tongue, he also gave you a fool's face; otherwise, I would soil my sword with your fool's blood." Mordez blanched at the threat from the temple's master swordsman.

"Did the Sutro Seer tell you anything more?" the king asked.

Shergus pushed his sword fully into its scabbard with a loud snap while glaring menacingly at Mordez. He turned and faced the king, "Yes, Your Highness. He said, this meeting is for the benefit of the kingdom, and he urges you to allow the Tondo leave."

"Then, so be it," the king replied. He walked over to Coleman and held out his arm. Coleman grasped it, and they shook in friendship. "You may be the key to our salvation. I will send wagons and slave harvesters to your estate and instruct them to stay there and help. Have your manager return the wagons full of food. What is your manager's name?"

"Her name is Maaryah. You met her when you visited my estate."

"Ha, the guesthouse slave. How is it possible she can now run the estate in your absence?" the king wondered.

"She manages the estate better than any foreman I have ever seen," Master Shergus interjected.

"So be it then. At this point, I will accept anyone's help, man, or even woman, who strives to save the kingdom. Now, go with my blessing," the king told Coleman.

Sire Tondo bowed and turned, Counselor Mordez partially blocked his path, so Coleman threw his shoulder into the man, knocking him out of the way. Shergus grinned and followed Coleman out of the tent. They mounted their samarans, and Coleman told Ayascho what had just transpired. Ayascho was instructed to return to Idop with the news. Then the men rode off, Ayascho heading east; Coleman and Shergus ambling south.

CHAPTER 14

THE SUTRO SEER'S GIFTS

It was about a seven-day march from the Teg-ar-mos Wall to the city. Coleman and Shergus made the trip in less than three. It was dusk when they arrived in Anterra and passed through its guarded gates. They immediately rode to the temple and dismounted. A couple of attendant priests took charge of their tired and sweaty mounts. Shergus led Coleman through the temple doors and down the right hallway, the temple chant caressing their ears. When they reached the end of the hallway at the opposite end of the building, the hallway turned left and continued until it came to a spiral stairway made of stone and wide enough for two men to ascend side-by-side. Shergus led Coleman up the stairs, and they continued until they reached the third level. They moved down another hallway, which Coleman felt was heading toward the front of the temple until they came to an ornately carved set of double doors made of wood and reinforced with shiny brass-like metal bars. They stopped in front of the doors and waited. Shergus placed all of his weapons on a side table and waited for Coleman to do the same.

The priest then took a deep breath, "We will now enter the Hall of the Guardians. When you are asked your name, respond with 'Tondo, the Messenger.' If you value your life, say no more nor any less. The Guardians brook no fools, and they can kill you before I can stop them," Shergus said, looking nervous, the first time Coleman had ever seen him in such a state.

"Who are these Guardians? What are they?" Coleman asked.

"They are powerful beings sent by the unnamed god to protect his holy temple. They are ever watchful, always standing guard, protecting the sacred chambers. You are the first outlander to pass through these doors."

"Should I bow or offer my respects in any way?" Coleman asked.

"Only do as I have told you; nothing more, nothing less," Shergus answered. Coleman took a deep breath, and Shergus pushed the doors open.

The hall was lit by torches in sconces on the right and left walls, equally spaced along the long and wide hallway. Coleman saw the flames jump as the doors opened, making the shadows dance. The ceiling was at least twenty feet above

him, and the walls, floor, and ceiling were constructed of bare sandstone-like blocks. In rows, down both sides of the hall, stood tall and fierce-looking creatures. They had the appearance of men, but if they were men, they were giants. Each one stood at least eight feet tall, and each was standing on a pedestal that was two feet high, giving the titans the illusion of being even taller. At first, Coleman thought they were men in plate armor, and they may well have been, but it was an armor he had never seen before in this world nor his homeworld; it shimmered in the torchlight. The creatures were covered from head to foot—not one bit of flesh was visible. Their heads were helms of zanth-colored metal, highlighted with cobalt-blue, two delicate wing decorations adorned them, and a visor slit that revealed nothing but darkness. Pauldrons of blue highlighted by zanth covered their shoulders and included a large ridge that protected their necks. A decorative, large, round disk was attached to each side with blue streamers that draped over their shoulders, front and back. Their arms from their shoulders down were covered in cobalt-blue metal. Gauntlets of zanth-colored metal covered their hands and forearms. Their breastplates were also cobalt-blue. They wore a skirt of blue chainmail that protected them from waist to foot. Beneath the skirt, Coleman could see feet shod in blue metal highlighted with zanth. Each creature held a huge greatsword, its point resting on the pedestal, its grip held by both hands. The swords' pommels were gems resembling blue sapphires. The greatswords were the same color as Coleman's Munnari Blade, only highlighted with zanth inlays.

Shergus delayed for a moment, and then he stepped into the room. The giant on the left turned its head, a blue light of a laser-like beam streamed from its visor slit and scanned him from head to foot. "Who wishes to pass?" a metallic voice asked.

"Master Shergus of the Temple of the Unnamed God," came his answer.

"You may pass."

Coleman stepped into the hallway, and the colossus on the right turned and scanned him. "Who wishes to pass," it asked in its metallic voice.

"Tondo, the Messenger," was Coleman's simple reply.

"You may pass."

The two men quickly marched down the hall; Shergus kept his eyes fixed on the double doors at the far end of the hallway, and Coleman looked as if his head were on a swivel. When they reached the opposite end, Shergus opened the doors and stepped through with Coleman on his heels.

Shergus shut the doors and took a deep breath. "That always unnerves me," he admitted.

"I take it you've passed this way before," Coleman commented.

"More times than I can recall, but it always has the same effect on me."

"I can see why," Coleman declared. "Are those warriors men?"

"They are man-like, but I wouldn't call them men. Their race is much more than the race of mortal man will ever be," Shergus told him as he wiped a trickle of sweat from his brow.

"What is this place?" Coleman asked.

"This is the Outer Sanctum."

"Now, what do we do?" Coleman wondered.

"We wait for the Sutro Seer."

Coleman looked around the chamber. It was twenty feet from front to back, side to side, and floor to ceiling. In each of the four corners was placed tall, zanth-colored, standing oil lamps, which reminded Coleman of menorahs. Each lamp had ten arms with ten cups, and each cup was lit, bathing the room with a soft glow. The walls, floor, and ceiling were covered in intricate geometric designs of inlaid zanth, which reflected the light from the lamp cups as the flames jumped and quietly sputtered. In the center of the room was a small altar or pedestal, about two feet square, and on its top was a lit brazier of zanth-colored metal. Smoke drifted from the small fire, filling the room with an aromatic odor. Coleman could see vents in the ceiling that let the smoke and heat escape. The opposite wall of the room was covered by a white curtain with a large blue circle in its center, at least five feet in diameter.

"Where is the Sutro Seer?" Coleman asked.

"He's in the Inner Sanctum," Shergus replied and pointed to a small bench against the left wall near the curtain. A pair of sandals rested beneath it.

The two men waited patiently, and Coleman marveled at the craftsmanship of everything in sight. Occasionally, he thought he heard a sound on the other side of the curtain, and he looked to Shergus for direction. The master stood quietly, and with little movement, his eyes closed, and his lips were moving in silent prayer. Coleman felt awkward, not knowing what to do, so he just stood where he was and waited.

After what seemed an interminable period, probably no more than ten minutes though, a rustling sound came from the opposite side of the curtain, then an aged hand appeared on its left side and gently pushed it open just enough for a man to squeeze through. After he exited, he quickly closed the curtain, and carefully sat himself on the bench, slowly putting on his sandals, his hands trembling with age. He was dressed in the blue robes of a priest; however, his vestments were trimmed in zanth. He wore a breastplate that appeared to be zanth and secured by its four corners, a single blue sapphire at its center, which was at least four inches long by more than two inches wide, and protruded more than an inch above its mounting. As the Seer moved, a star with six lines danced across the gem's surface. Coleman could tell that the Seer was very old, much older than anyone he had seen so far on this world.

When the Seer finished tying his sandals, he looked up and smiled at Shergus and Coleman. His face seemed to shine with radiant light. Shergus opened his eyes but said nothing. Coleman continued to wait, not wanting to do anything that might profane this holy place. The Seer continued to smile, and his eye's rested upon Coleman. He stood and walked to them, all the time, his gaze fixed on the visitor. Finally, his eyes moved to Shergus.

"Master Shergus, it is good to see you again, and thank you for bringing the Tondo to me," he began as he reached out to the master with both hands and took him by the forearms.

"Your Eminence, thank you for assigning me as his mentor. Not only has he learned well, but he has also taught his teachers many new things. He fully embraces the good seeds. He is all you told us to hope for," Master Shergus confided.

"Yes, my son, your report pleases me, but I must determine for myself whether he truly is the one I'm expecting." The Seer then turned his gaze to Coleman, "Come here, my son. Sit on this bench, and let me look at you." Coleman did as he was instructed and sat. The Seer remained standing and looked down into Coleman's face. "You have the eyes of our revered blue moon. That is good. It is said that the eyes are the windows to the soul. Do you mind if I peer into your soul?" Coleman didn't object and silently nodded his permission. The Seer's dark-brown eyes seemed to bore into Coleman, touching his inner persona. The visitor did not move under the Sutro Seer's burning scrutiny; he tried to relax, although he could feel the tension in his neck and arms. After what seemed an eternity, the Seer stepped back and closed his eyes; his lips moved in a silent 'thank you,' but not to Coleman—he was addressing deity.

After several seconds, the Seer took a deep breath, opened his eyes, and spoke. "We all possess both the seeds of good and evil within ourselves. You have nurtured the good seeds. You are indeed the one we have been promised, and you are the only one who can struggle with the coming evil on equal terms; however, you can be defeated, so take nothing for granted," the Seer warned.

"Who or what is this evil I will face? Is it the war that is now being waged against the kingdom?" Coleman asked

"That is a part of it. Evil powers, goaded on by the Tempter and its masters, are reaching out in all directions, seeking to drive men to embrace evil seeds in the pursuit of power and a desire to enslave their brothers and sisters. You are the hope of the world."

"Did you bring me here to fight this battle?" Coleman wondered.

The Seer chuckled, and a broad smile filled his countenance, "No, child, I have no such power. The great unnamed god seeks to bring balance to all things. That is why you are here."

"Will I ever return to my own world?" Coleman asked. He noticed Shergus's expression of surprise.

"This is your home now. You must embrace it and embrace who you have become. I urge you to continue nurturing the good seed of compassion and not let the evil seed of cruelty grow during your tribulations," the Seer advised.

Tondo felt a strange, tingling sensation pass through his body. He paused for a moment then asked, "What am I to do?"

"I cannot tell you. What you must do will come from within, from here," the Seer said as he placed his palm on Tondo's chest, over his heart.

"Do you mean tzaah will lead me?"

"Tzaah will help you, but the power comes from your soul. The Whisperer speaks directly to it and can guide you if you but listen. Do you know of the Whisperer?"

"Yes, Master Varios and my friend Ayascho's people have told me about it."

"The people of the Wilderness have knowledge of such things? I'm astonished," the Seer admitted.

"When I was with them, I had a dream or a vision. Can you help me understand it?" Tondo wondered.

"Tell me about your vision, and I will try." Tondo spent the next several minutes relating what he had seen in his vision so long ago. When he finished, the Seer said, "Yes, yes, of course. You have seen the shadows of war unleashed and approaching. It is a warning and a call to prepare," the Seer told him.

"And the little girl, what does she represent?" Tondo asked.

"You will meet her in time. Your fate and hers are intertwined," the Seer replied.

Tondo wanted more clarity, but he could tell the Seer was becoming fatigued. "Please, sit and rest for a while," Tondo offered as he began to rise.

The Seer raised his hand and stopped him. "There is one more thing I must do before you leave. I must bolster your inner-power." The Sutro Seer reached out to Tondo with both hands, and they grasped each other by the forearms. Both men were quickly enveloped in radiant golden light, and Tondo could feel energy flowing into his center; their eyes closed. Shergus was amazed by what he saw. Tondo couldn't help himself and stood, but the Seer held his forearms tightly and did not let go. After nearly a minute, the aura faded away. The Seer relaxed his grip and began to collapse. Tondo held him tightly, turned him, and sat him on the bench. The Seer leaned against the wall, totally spent by what had just happened.

"Your Eminence!" Master Shergus shouted in worry.

"Shush," the Seer commanded, "you are in a holy place. Let me rest now. I will be all right."

"Please, let us help you," Shergus begged.

"No, no, my son. I must return to the Inner Sanctum and restore my strength, but there is more I must offer before the Tondo leaves."

"Your Eminence," Tondo began, "you have done too much already. Please rest." Tondo could feel the goodness emanating from this man.

"I will have plenty of time to rest after you leave, but now I must do all I can to see that you are prepared. The city is running low on food," the Seer stopped and took a few deep breaths.

"Yes, and some of the king's counselors are suggesting he purge the slaves—kill them or drive them out of the kingdom and into the arms of the enemy. That would be horrible," Tondo told him.

"Yes, child, but you can solve the king's dilemma. The great unnamed god, in his wisdom, has counseled us to prepare for this time. The temple has enough food in storage to feed ten thousand, maybe more, for two spans. I've been counseled to give it to you so you can build an army and defend the temple. How you do it is left to your discretion," the Seer stopped talking and took several more deep breaths.

"Master Shergus, tell the Tondo about the sacred stones we have gathered," the Seer ordered.

"Yes, Your Eminence," Shergus responded and then faced Tondo. "When you told me about the blue stones you had collected while in the northern wasteland, I reported it to the temple. His Eminence sent a large caravan to retrieve as many of the sacred stones as could be found. The collection is being kept in temple storehouses."

The Seer then stood and grabbed Tondo by the upper arms, helping to support his weight. "You have access to all we have, and it is your duty to use it wisely." With his right hand, he reached into his blue robe and pulled out two six-inch diameter zanth-colored disks and handed them to Tondo. Each had a large blue sapphire in its center. "Master Shergus will instruct you in their use. I must now return to my ruminations and regain my strength. Please, Master Shergus, help me with my sandals." Shergus kneeled and removed the sandals from the Seer's feet. Tondo held him steady, and then the Sutro Seer slowly walked toward the left side of the curtain with Tondo's help. When they reached the curtain, just as the Seer was about to pull the curtain aside, he warned, "Avert your eyes, my child; the glory of this holy place may blind you." Tondo did as he was told, and the Seer quickly passed to the other side.

Tondo looked at Shergus and then down at the two disks he held in his right hand, "What are these?" he asked.

"Quiet, I will not discuss it here. Let me have them." Tondo handed Shergus the disks. "We must leave," the master priest told him. The two men quickly and quietly left the Outer Sanctum and marched down the Hall of the Guardians. When they reached the opposite end, Shergus pulled the sapphire from one of the disks and held it in front of the Guardian on his right. The Guardian scanned it with its blue beam and nodded. Shergus did the same using the other stone with the Guardian on his left. He stepped through the doors with Tondo following closely behind, and then the master closed the doors. Shergus took a deep breath and relaxed.

"What was that all about?" Tondo asked.

Shergus handed him the two sapphires. "Keep them safe. I will hold on to these until you need them," he said as he slipped the two disks into his jerkin.

"What are they?" Tondo asked again.

"They are summoners. When you place the stone in the center of the disk, the Guardian assigned to that stone will instantly appear. For the first time in this age, the Sutro Seer has authorized the use of the Guardians outside these hallowed walls. Remember, they can only be used to defend the temple and its lands. His Eminence trusts you with their tremendous power, so use it wisely, but be forewarned, if you act unrigh-teously, they'll turn on you, and you'll be slain."

"Can they be used to break the siege?" Tondo asked.

"I don't see how. As I said, they can only be used to defend the temple's domain and the innocent. As long as the enemy doesn't attack, the Guardians will do nothing. It will be up to you to break the siege before we all starve." Shergus counseled.

They picked up their weapons, and Shergus led Tondo to a storehouse full of blue meteorites. The large room had blue stones from one end to the other: large stones, small stones, and all sizes in between. There had to be literally tons of them. He was told this was only one of several storehouses containing the sacred blue stones gathered from the wasteland.

Tondo began to form a plan as he examined the cache. When he had seen enough, he and Shergus left the temple and started their trek back to the Wall. As they rode down the streets of the city, they passed slave after slave, some doing odd jobs, but most seemed to be idle.

"This cannot be good. These men and women need to be put to work," he told Shergus. The Master nodded in agreement.

By the time they reached the Wall, Tondo had worked out the first draft of a plan in his mind. Shergus wondered what he was thinking, but except for a question here and there along the way, Tondo said little to him during their entire journey. They arrived at the Wall in the early afternoon of their fourth day of travel and found the king standing above the huge gates. The two men quickly climbed the stairs of one of the flanking towers, and when they reached the top and peered over the embrasures, they were stunned by the sight before them. Hundreds upon hundreds of the enemy host had gathered, several teams holding long ladders. Obviously, they were preparing to make an assault.

Tondo approached the king and bowed. "Your Highness, what's happening?"

"I've just had another meeting with King Men-dre-dor and King Pen-dow-mon. They expected me to surrender, but I refused. They have threatened to attack the Wall, and by the looks of it, they will."

Tondo appraised the enemy host before them, and he realized it was either a show of force or a probe to determine the resolve of the defenders, for it was too small to be an all-out assault. He turned to Shergus, "Place the summoners," he commanded. Shergus pulled the two disks from his jerkin and set them on the wall walk about six feet apart. Tondo took out the two blue sapphires and placed one in the center of each disk, and then he stepped back. The stones began to glow with blue light, and then a small whirlwind of light spun skyward from each one. In less than five seconds, an image appeared and began to take form. As the image solidified, it became recognizable as a Guardian. In less than ten seconds, the transformation was complete, and two giant Guardians stood above the gates, scanning the enemy from left to right and back again. The king and his entourage retreated several steps when the giant warriors were fully formed. All were astounded and fearful of what they had just witnessed.

Tondo stood between the Guardians and faced them, his back to the enemy host. "If they attack the Wall, you must stop them. Don't use lethal force unless you must." Both Guardians nodded in acknowledgment of their orders and waited.

Suddenly, the shout of hundreds of voices reached the defenders' ears as the enemy mob surged toward the wall. Both Guardians stepped forward like a well-drilled team and leaped up and over the merlons, dropping nearly thirty feet to the ground and landing with a thud, unaffected by their plunge. They hastily marched forward and loosed their huge greatswords from their backs, increasing the distance between each other as they advanced. After a march of fifty feet or so, they stopped. The Guardian on the left held its greatsword in its right hand and lifted it on its right side until it was parallel to the ground. The other Guardian did the same, its sword was in its left hand, and the tips of the two swords were separated by no more than a foot. The men in the front ranks of the charging horde saw what had just happened and froze in place. The men behind them pushed the front rank forward as the leading men screamed and wailed in terror.

The Guardians waited for the front of the bulge of humanity to reach them, and when it did, they began their work. They tore into the mass of men with sweeping strikes, like harvesters mowing down wheat with their scythes; however, they used only the flats of their blades, yet they knocked men hither and yon. Most were bloodied, many had broken bones, and others lay unconscious. As Tondo and the others watched from atop the Wall, they could see the enemy host surround the two Guardians, but soon, the mob refused to advance. The Guardians stood in the center of two cleared, overlapping circles of downed and groaning men, waiting for someone to come within reach of their weapons. No one else dared.

When it was obvious the assault on the Wall was broken, the Guardians marched back to the bulwark, the terrified enemy opening pathways for them. When they reached the Wall, they jumped in unison and landed with a loud clank atop the wall walk. They turned and faced the dispirited enemy horde and stood frozen in place. The men on the Wall gave a mighty cheer, and King Teg-ar-mos pulled his sword from its scabbard, raising it high above his head, as though he, personally, had been the one to defeat the enemy.

Tondo crossed his arms over his chest and stood, shaking his head from side to side. He leaned over and whispered in the king's ear, "When you are finished celebrating your great victory, we need to talk." The king nodded, then began strutting back and forth in front of the Guardians as the defeated host below marveled at what they had just witnessed and suffered.

After several minutes, the king sheathed his sword, walked to the tower on his right, and went down the stairs, Tondo and Shergus following after him. They headed for the king's huge tent and entered. Several gentry and counselors also entered and gathered around the king, waiting for him to direct their next actions. Tondo stood with his arms crossed, looking annoyed.

The king noticed his stance and said, "I must do that to bolster the morale of the defenders. This waiting has unnerved them, but today's victory will strengthen their resolve. Tell me, Tondo, will those creatures continue to fight for us? Are they temple Guardians?"

"Yes, they are Guardians, but their purview is to defend the temple and the land around it. They will not break the siege," Tondo responded.

Counselor Mordez chose to make his sour thoughts known, "What good will that do us? As our food supply dwindles, will they simply watch us starve?"

"The counselor has a point. We can't remain on the Wall forever. What did you learn at the temple?" the king asked.

"Many things, but this for sure: the Guardians will not break the siege. It is up to us to solve that problem."

"Then, we're no better off than before." Counselor Mordez continued, "Our fate is already sealed."

"Nonsense!" Tondo roared. "How much food is left?"

"We estimate we have enough food to feed fifty thousand for half a span. That includes citizens and slaves," one of the counselors told him.

"We're getting reports of petty theft in the city, as well. The Pannera has caught several slaves in the act, and we're told it's getting worse detz-by-detz," Megato Ayetoz told the gathering.

"As I said before, we must get rid of the slaves. The sooner, the better," Counselor Mordez grumbled as he glared at Tondo.

"Idle hands are the devil's workshop," Tondo declared using the godspeak term.

"What's that supposed to mean?" Mordez asked in an annoyed voice.

"It means we need to put the slaves to work, and it wouldn't hurt to do the same with the men on the Wall. I hear that drunkenness and fighting are common problems everywhere," Tondo noted.

"Everywhere but in your duty area. Why is that?" the king wondered.

"My men are kept busy, either on guard duty, repairing the Wall, or training for battle. I keep them too busy to drink and too tired to brawl with each other. I suggest all the commanders do the same."

"Yes, that seems wise," the king said. "Megato Ayetoz, see that all of my commanders receive instructions to do the same."

"As you say, Your Highness," Ayetoz replied.

"We still have a slave problem. They are depleting our food stores, and they're becoming unruly," Mordez declared.

"I may be able to solve both problems," Tondo offered.

"What do you have in mind?" asked the king.

"The law stipulates that masters are required to feed their slaves, right?" Tondo commented.

"It's a time of war. All that rubbish is held in abeyance," Mordez replied.

"Your Highness, is that true? Have you suspended established kingdom laws?" Tondo asked in surprise.

"These are extraordinary times, but I do not yet see the need to set aside the old laws," the king replied. Tondo glared at Mordez, and the counselor glared back. Tondo could tell they were in a battle of wills, and he knew that should he fail, the kingdom's slaves would suffer a horrendous fate.

"I can relieve both problems we're having with the slaves. If you put them in my charge, I will see that they are fed and kept busy," he told the king.

"How do you propose to feed that many slaves? You've already promised the food from your estate and what food your boat can carry to the king. Are you going back on your word now, outlander?" Mordez's comment was laced with disdain.

"I will continue to give all the food my estate produces and all the boat can carry to the king, as promised. I will feed the slaves with food from the temple stores. The Sutro Seer has been preparing for this day, and he has given me permission to use the temple's reserves," Tondo explained.

"If we purge the slaves, we can use the temple stores to feed the citizens and hold out longer," Mordez proposed.

"The temple will not give it to you. Will you try to take it from the Guardians? You've seen what two can do. There are many more," was Tondo's sharp retort. Mordez said nothing and continued glaring at the outlander. Tondo responded with a cold smile in return. He then faced the king. "Besides, the counselor's idea would only delay the inevitable. We need another plan of action," Tondo declared.

"I think you already have one. Let me hear it," the king declared.

"Give me charge of the slaves. I will turn them into an army, and with them, I will break the siege," Tondo announced. A murmur erupted in the gathering, and Mordez laughed.

"Arm the slaves? You're out of your slave-loving mind," Mordez said with utter contempt.

The king gave Tondo a look of scorn, then said, "For the sake of argument, let us follow your reasoning to its logical conclusion. Let's say I approve your plan, and we arm the slaves; then what?"

"I will train them into an army never before seen by anyone in the three kingdoms. An army of such great power, they will be able to break the siege and win this war," Tondo promised.

"Your slave army will only be a fraction of the size of the enemy's. How can you possibly believe a rabble of dung creepers could defeat fifty thousand freeborns?" Mordez knew he had the upper hand.

"The enemy's fifty thousand is only an untrained mob. A much smaller force of well-trained, well-equipped, and well-motivated men will defeat them. In my homeland, similar situations have ended with the smaller force winning many times in the past," Tondo countered.

"I find that hard to believe. They are just slaves, after all, only suitable for emptying chamber pots and shoveling frizzard stink. They'll be slaughtered," Mordez chuckled.

Tondo smiled, "Oy, counselor, you say you want the slaves purged. If I'm wrong, then they'll be purged; however, if I'm right, they will save the kingdom. Your Highness, what do you have to lose?"

The king stood in thought for a few moments. "I see your point. But can they be trained to fight? Will they fight, or will they run when they first lay eyes on the enemy?"

"Your Highness, you can't seriously consider this outlander's muddle-headed plan. I can hear the other kings mocking you now," Mordez lectured.

The king's eyebrows furrowed, "I don't like that prospect."

Tondo took a deep breath and began to expound, "Have I not proven myself in the past? People laughed when I freed my slaves, and now my estate produces more than it ever did, providing an ever-increasing sum for the kingdom's tax collector. People scoffed at the idea of building a boat to sail the domain of the terrors, but I succeeded. I am now growing food crops on the peninsula when everyone, including the counselor here, said it was impossible. Let me build this slave army, and you will be the victor. King Men-dre-dor and King Pen-dow-mon will kneel before you."

"Empty promises!" Mordez shouted.

"Counselor, what plan do *you* offer?" the king asked. Mordez was silent. "Ha, I will consider what Tondo has offered."

"Your Highness, there is one more thing I must mention," Tondo said.

"Yes, what is it?" the king wondered.

"Men must have a reason to fight, and slaves are no different. Give them a powerful incentive, and they will walk through fire for you."

"What are you suggesting," the king asked.

"I only suggest you keep that in mind as you consider my plan," Tondo told him, knowing full well what he was implying.

The king was about to say something, but he stopped and looked deeply into Tondo's face. Finally, he said, "Everyone is dismissed. I wish to be alone. We will reassemble in the morning." The king began rubbing his forehead. "Summon my physician," he ordered.

Tondo and Shergus waited until all the others, except Mordez, had left. The king's senior counselor stood scowling at the two but said nothing. Then he, too, exited. Tondo and Shergus bowed to the king and also left just as the king's physician approached with his satchel of apothecary supplies. They walked to a tent that had been erected by temple priests, which acted as a place of worship—a tabernacle—for the men on the Wall. They entered and found it empty.

"You are a sly one, you are," Shergus said with a chuckle. "You planted the seed of freedom, and now you expect the king to nurture it."

"We will learn in the morning if the seed sprouts and bears fruit," Tondo pronounced.

Shergus invited Tondo to stay with the priests that night, and they dined on a meal of ventana and vegetables, a priest staple. It was the first time Tondo had eaten ventana, and it reminded him of couscous. After they had eaten, they talked about Tondo's plan, and then each man found a secluded corner in the tabernacle and went to sleep.

CHAPTER 15

THE KING'S DECREE

The next morning, Tondo and Shergus arose just as dawn was breaking and ate a breakfast of leftover ventana. When he finished eating, Tondo left the tabernacle tent and looked to the area above the gates, expecting to see the Guardians in their silent vigil. To his dismay, they were not there. He dashed up the stairs and found only the two summoning disks, but the blue stones were gone. Soon, Shergus arrived.

"Where are the Guardians?" Tondo asked, almost in a panic.

"They must have returned to the temple sometime during the night. That is where they renew their strength."

"Will they come back?"

"No, not unless the Seer sends us the summoning stones."

"Did you know this would happen?"

"Did I know? In all truthfulness, I didn't. I only suspected they might return to the temple, but I wasn't sure. I've never seen the Guardians outside the temple before, and I could only guess what they would do," the priest answered.

"Okay, it appears we are on our own again."

"The Sutro Seer is very wise and receives counsel from the unnamed god. Worry not, you are his messenger, and he watches over you."

"Does he also watch over the kingdom?" Tondo wondered. "Only if it's worthy."

Several tetzae, the four kingdom tetzus, and a few important barons gathered near the king's tent and waited for his call. Megato Ayetoz had already reminded them of the king's decree to use Tondo's methods to train and busy their men. Several of the gentry asked Tondo how he went about training his troops. He held a short lecture on what he'd been doing over the past several detzamars. He quickly terminated his instruction when a counselor exited the king's tent, held the doorway covering aside, and declared, "The king will see you now."

The men slowly filed through the entryway, by rank and seniority, Tondo being the very last one to enter. Master Shergus entered with him, and no one dared to object. He kneeled to the king, and after the king nodded, he stood. The king waited until all had assembled. He sat upon an elevated throne, about four feet off the tent floor. He looked serious and stern; Tondo thought he was wearing his 'game face,' ready to do battle with someone.

"Barons, lords, and sires," the king began, "I have spent the entire night contemplating Sire Tondo's words, and I have reached a decision." He paused and waited a moment as all eyes fell upon him. "The slaves present a serious problem for the kingdom. They deplete our food supplies, and now, there are reports of petty theft in the city, and it is getting worse over time. Although they are only slaves, the prospect of slaughtering them is too distasteful to contemplate. Who here would wish to lead such a venture?" The king looked at the many faces gathered, but no one spoke up. After several moments of silence, the king continued, "And neither would I. Also, if we send them into the enemy's camp, undoubtedly, they will be used against us as Sire Tondo has warned. He offers a solution that I cannot ignore. Therefore, sire, I desire that you build your slave army. I have also considered what you said about incentive. I agree, even slaves must have a reason to fight, and I doubt they would if all they had to look forward to was continuing their lives in slavery. Therefore, I will free any slave who serves in your army— after your victory, that is." A murmur began between members of the assembled gentry. "Men of honor and rank, I hear grumbling; you may freely voice your concerns," the king ordered.

"That could be half the slaves in all the kingdom, Your Highness," one tetzae lamented, "How will we run our estates without slaves?"

Another member of the gentry spoke up, "We will be ruined without slaves. My land will lay fallow!"

"If we lose this war, we may lose our holdings altogether," Tondo warned. "You'll find that men who have a stake in success will strive more diligently for it. All you must do is harness that energy. I have, and my estate increases in productivity every span," Tondo declared. He continued, "Your Highness, I'm sure some of the men who will volunteer for this army have women and children. What about them?" The king frowned and rubbed his forehead.

"That's too much," Lord Agganor, a tetzus, fumed. "Your Highness, we maintain some leverage over these slaves if we keep their women and children. If we don't, they will have no reason to work the estates. Tondo's foolish compassion for the slaves will destroy the kingdom."

"The kingdom is on the path to destruction in more ways than one already, my lord," Tondo told the gathering. "I can guarantee victory if the army is motivated. If it isn't, we will fail, and the kingdom will fall."

"Traitor!" Lord Riazon, another powerful tetzus, bellowed. The tent erupted in shouts and angry words, all aimed at the outlander. Master Shergus placed his hand on the grip of his sword, preparing to unsheathe it.

Tondo's hand quickly covered the master's. "Do not draw your blade," Tondo quietly warned. "Emotions are running high because everyone is frustrated. Let me handle this." The priest relaxed. "Let's run through this logically," Tondo said in a loud voice, "For the sake of argument, let us assume that the slave army is defeated, and nearly all are killed, including their outlander commander. What will the rest of you do next?" No one answered, so he walked over to Lord Riazon and faced him. "My lord, will you lead an army of starving defenders in a desperate battle of last resort? Or will you remain on the Wall until all the storehouses are emptied, waiting for starvation and disease to lay waste the kingdom's defenders? Either prospect doesn't bode well for you or the king. Of course, the king can surrender, kneel to Men-dre-dor and Pen-dow-mon, pay the tribute, relinquish a good portion of the Magheedo Plain, and then face the anger of a starving populace. All here could lose their holdings, as well. What say you, my lord?" Lord Riazon was fuming but said nothing. Tondo put his hand on Riazon's shoulder, "I am not your enemy, and I am not a traitor. I am trying to save the kingdom. I've learned, this is an unprecedented situation, and we must make some difficult decisions if we are to prevail. Unfortunately, that is the nature of War." He removed his hand and walked amongst the gathered men. "The enemy has no idea what we're planning, at least not yet. And when they realize all they have to do is defeat a lowly slave army, they will be lulled into overconfidence, not preparing, and waiting for our attack. When it comes, they will be devastated, and the war will be won."

"Has your optimism no bounds? Either you are the most extraordinary man I've ever met, or you're a fool," Lord Agganor asserted.

"If we win, I'm extraordinary. If we lose, I'll be dead, and the slaves purged," Tondo proclaimed in a loud voice. This declaration set the men back on their heels. This outlander was willing to face death for the kingdom in a hopeless battle, surrounded by worthless slaves. Yes, he was extraordinary, or he was a fool.

"Your Highness," Lord Riazon called, "let this outlander have his way. If he's right, I will be the first to honor him. If he's wrong, at least we will be rid of him and the slaves." His statement made Tondo chuckle.

The king looked around and saw most of the men nodding in agreement. "Very well then, by king's decree, any slave who serves in Tondo's army will be granted his freedom, including those deemed to be of his family, predicated upon victory. Let the scribes record it. Let the heralds proclaim it. Send for my physician!" the king ordered as he rubbed his forehead. "This affair has given me another head-pounder."

Tondo and Shergus bowed to the king; he nodded in recognition while rubbing his brow, and they exited the tent. It wasn't long before a scribe also exited, rushed over to the heralds, and handed each a leather tube containing an official parchment scroll. They quickly mounted their samarans, one dashing off to the east, one to the west, and the third went south, in the direction of the city.

"We have much to do. Let us return to Idop and Ayascho and begin putting my plan into action," Tondo told Shergus. They, too, mounted and dashed off toward the east.

Tondo spent the next three days strategizing and organizing with the others, planning the recruitment, structure, and training for his slave army. Many of his freed-men on the eastern section of the Wall wanted to volunteer, but he convinced them that their service was best utilized by remaining on the Wall with the other citizens.

After he had felt his plan was ready to be implemented, he ordered several of his men to take a wagon and locate three hundred bricks, bringing them back to camp. He had another group of men clear a large flat area, removing all the brush, and cutting the grass low using scythes and swing blades. After the bricks had arrived, he arranged them in a formation in the cleared area and placed several guards around it.

When all was ready, Tondo, Idop, and Shergus went to fetch the king for an important meeting. Ayascho was left in command of the defenders after receiving a few final instructions from Tondo. Building an army from scratch would be a major undertaking, and he would need many resources that could only be made available by order of the king. When they arrived at the Wall's huge gates, they found the king on his perch above them. It was obvious something was afoot. The men climbed the stairs and found King Men-dre-dor and King Pen-dow-mon making new threats against the young king.

"What's going on?" Tondo quietly asked Megato Ayetoz.

"The other kings are threatening to make examples of those poor priests; they plan to execute them. The enemy kings are angry because the Sutro Seer has allied with King Teg-ar-mos."

Tondo turned and examined the ground in front of the Wall. The two kings were standing about seventy-five feet away. Behind them was a row of ten priests, recognizable by their blue robes, kneeling, their hands and feet bound. Behind them stood two large men brandishing huge, heavy swords.

"Tell the Sutro Seer, another intervention by him on your behalf will result in the execution of every priest in our two kingdoms. Let him know that this is an example of our will," King Pen-dow-mon shouted.

"Leave the priests in peace. They have done nothing to you," King Teg-ar-mos shouted back.

"Why would they do this?" Tondo asked.

"They must demonstrate their power," Ayetoz told him.

"Do they really think this vile act can change our resolve?" Tondo wondered.

"It's not our resolve that concerns them. It's their own men's steadfastness they're worried about. If the Seer does nothing, they will regain what they lost to the Guardians," Ayetoz counseled. The two kings turned and stepped behind the executioners, each raising an arm, and then they dropped them simultaneously. The two swordsmen advanced and began their grisly task. After four priests had been slaughtered, one of the executioners hesitated and turned, looking toward the kings. King Pen-dow-mon drew his sword and shouted something, resulting in the executioner returning to his appalling duty. In only a few moments, all ten priests had been decapitated; their bleeding and twitching corpses lay sprawled on the blood-soaked grass.

Master Shergus went into a rage and shouted oaths and epithets at the wicked kings. He rushed down the stairs with Tondo on his heels.

"Open the gates!" Shergus shouted.

Tondo caught up to him, grabbed him by the shoulder, and spun him around. "Stop! It will do no good for you to do this!" he yelled at the priest.

"I will kill them!" Shergus shouted as he glared at Tondo. It was such a fierce and angry stare that it unnerved the outlander, and he released the priest's shoulder.

"What good will it do? You will never reach the kings. You'll kill many of their men, but their guards will eventually kill you, and those kings will still have their way. They have shown everyone their wickedness. With this barbaric act, they have sealed their own fates. When our army is ready, I swear, they will not survive the battle," Tondo told him.

Shergus looked deeply into Tondo's raging blue eyes and slowly began to calm himself. "I know every one of those priests by name. I will see that you keep your oath, Messenger," Shergus declared. Tondo nodded in response.

The king rushed down the stairs and joined the two men. "That was the most despicable act I have ever witnessed! Surely, the Sutro Seer will act. Will he send more Guardians to mete out justice?" the king asked.

"The Sutro Seer will do what the great unnamed god directs, nothing more," Shergus told him.

"Maybe the unnamed god will have mercy on those murdering kings, but I won't," Tondo declared as his anger stirred and radiated from his bosom. The others took a step back and watched as a red glow emanated from him. It soon subsided, and his appearance returned to normal. "We must meet with you, Your Highness," he said. "Our army will need many resources that only you can provide."

"Ha, let us retire to my tent, and we will discuss it," the king told him.

"Your Highness, I have prepared an exhibit I want you to see. It is at my camp on the east end of the Wall," Tondo explained.

"Yes, I will go and see this thing you have prepared." The men mounted, and the King's Contingent joined them. Several king's counselors also joined the group, including Counselor Mordez and a few of his allies.

"Your Highness, bring only your guards; leave your counselors behind," Tondo ordered. All who heard the command looked at Tondo as if he were Munnoga-touched.

"What's this?" the king growled.

"It's for a good reason, Your Highness. I will explain after we leave," Tondo promised.

"Very well, then. Counselors are to remain here," the king ordered. The counselors reined up their mounts, and Mordez scowled at Tondo but did not advance. After the king's party had traveled a short distance, the king asked, "Why didn't you want my counselors along?"

"I don't trust all of them, especially Counselor Mordez," Tondo told him.

"I know you two don't agree on things, but Mordez is my senior advisor, and I rely on his judgment."

"He and his allies are not to be trusted, Your Highness," Tondo warned.

"Why?" the king asked.

"I have a feeling that he places his interests before those of the kingdom, Your Highness," Tondo warned.

"Do you have evidence of this? Show me your proof," the king demanded.

"I cannot. It's only a feeling from here," Tondo told him as he thumped his chest.

"I certainly can't disgrace a man based on a feeling. Counselor Mordez was my father's most trusted adviser with many spans of service to the kingdom, and I rely on his wisdom and experience."

"I'm not asking you to disgrace him. Nevertheless, if I were you, I would keep an eye on him. I don't trust his motives."

Shergus entered the discussion, "Your Highness, Tondo has the Gift of Discernment, and it would be wise to listen to the Messenger."

"Oy, what do you suggest I do with him?" the king asked Tondo.

"We have a saying in my homeland: 'Keep your friends close and your enemies closer,'" Tondo instructed.

"What does that mean?" the king wondered.

"It means keep him nearby and watch him closely."

"I don't consider Counselor Mordez an enemy, but I will give what you say some thought, my friend, although I have seen nothing to warrant your concern," the king told him.

Shergus then cautioned, "Your Highness, one seldom sees the viper before it strikes." The king did not respond, and his thoughts turned inward.

By midafternoon, the party arrived at Tondo's camp. As they approached, Ayascho ordered the men to form up, and they gave the king three cheers, as Tondo had instructed before he left. He could see, the king was pleased by his men's display of loyalty. Realizing there would not be enough time to return to the king's headquarters at the center of the Wall before nightfall, Megato Ayetoz had his men set up the king's temporary lodging a discrete distance from the Wall defenders' tents.

A table had been placed near Tondo's cleared area, and sitting on it were several bricks; each brick was twelve inches by eight inches and four inches thick. They were of the ubiquitous sand-color and reminded Tondo of paving stones from his homeland. Two of the bricks had been marked with grid lines across part of their faces: six rows by six columns. A couple of other boxes were also drawn on the bricks. Tondo invited the king to the table, and he picked up a brick and began explaining the markings.

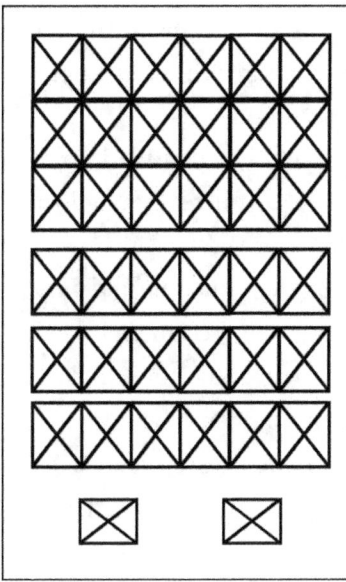

"Your Highness, this brick represents the basic unit of the army I will build. Each box represents a man, and there are six ranks of six men. Each rank is commanded by a neva sestardi. The entire formation is commanded by a neva megato officer and a sestardi non-officer, who stand at the rear of the formation and direct it. In my homeland, this is called a platoon, but because of the difficulty others have pronouncing its name, Counselor Idop suggested we simply call them bricks."

"Yes, I can see why," the king interjected.

Tondo continued, "You can add bricks together to form larger units. My plan is to put four bricks side-by-side to form a foot troop. The troop will be commanded by a megato and a sestardus, and these leaders will position themselves to the rear and middle of the formation. Behind them will be another brick, divided into three paired ranks. This brick will act as support and a rear guard. These men will be held in reserve and committed at a critical moment, or they can be used piecemeal as replacements for the wounded. Each troop will also include twenty-two non-combatants: twelve water carriers and ten medics or, as Counselor Idop suggested, med-men—men who care for the wounded."

"How many men in this army?" the king asked.

"I don't know yet; as many as we can raise from the slaves willing to join. I'm hoping for seven to eight thousand fighters and an equal number in support," Tondo guessed.

"An equal number in support? When it's all added up, that could be every slave in the kingdom. Do you really need them all?" the king was flabbergasted.

"The men will not have time to do anything but train and prepare for battle. I will need washerwomen to sew and clean their clothes, cooks for their food, fletchers to make arrows for the bows, and a host of others to perform duties I haven't even considered yet."

"I see," the king responded, and then he noticed a brick with different markings sitting on the table. "This brick is marked differently. Why?"

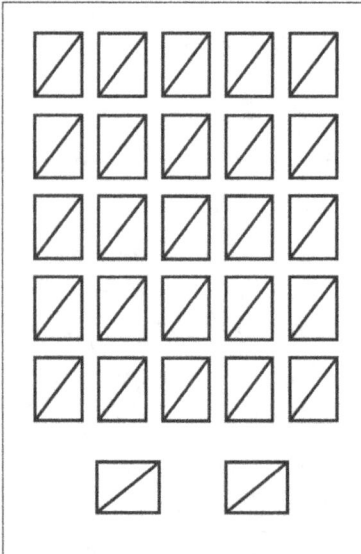

"This is a samaran brick, and it represents the cavalry—the samaran soldiers—men with bows, long metrens, and curved swords riding armored samarans. This will be the shock force of the army," Tondo told him.

"Shock force? Samaran soldiers? Armored samarans? I don't understand." The king was confused, for never before had such terms been used to describe elements of an army.

Tondo nodded to Idop, and the counselor took a deep breath, bowed to the king, quickly mounted a samaran with barding, and rode away. When he was some distance from

ML BELLANTE

them, he drew his bow and nocked an arrow. He dug his heels into the samaran's sides, and the mount took off in a flash. While standing in the stirrups, Idop quickly fired three arrows into a hay bale near the table. He continued his charge, heading directly for the king and Tondo. He replaced his bow with a long curved sword, holding it leveled in the king's and Tondo's direction. When it was obvious he wasn't going to stop, the king quickly retreated a few steps, and two king's guards placed themselves between the king and the rapidly advancing Idop. Tondo didn't flinch and remained in his place. At the last instant, Idop altered course and passed by at full gallop. He then turned his mount around, trotted back to the others, and dismounted. The king appeared to be as mad as a wet frizzard.

"Don't be angry with the counselor, Your Highness," Tondo began, "he was following my orders. I wanted you to experience the terror our enemy will face when the battle begins. This was only one rider. Imagine the horror of facing hundreds like counselor Idop bent on killing you."

"I see your point. An excellent demonstration," the king was obviously relieved, and so was Idop.

"The samaran brick has twenty-five mounts and riders plus a sestardi and neva megato to lead them. Four samaran bricks make a samaran troop, commanded by a megato and a sestardus. If you step this way, Your Highness, I have a display of the army formation laid out for you to examine." Tondo led the king to the cleared area, where he had positioned bricks representing the army's organization. "You'll notice, the samaran troops are on the flanks, and the foot troops are in the middle," Tondo told the king.

"What do those blocks of wood in the center represent?" the king asked, pointing to five square wooden posts about a foot long, standing on end.

"Those are archer towers—archers are men with bows and arrows. Each tower is the height of five men and has four levels. The lowest level holds foot warriors who protect the archers. Each upper level will have twenty archers, and they will shoot their arrows over the heads of our soldiers and into the enemy formations. The towers will be on giant wooden wheels, and they'll be pushed by teams of thrice. They will serve as the main defense for the army's center," Tondo explained. "I expect the enemy to charge our center, but the shock and surprise of the arrows, something they've never seen before, should take the fight out of them in a hurry," he explained.

The king paced back and forth, examining the display before him. He rubbed his chin, turned around, and headed in the opposite direction, all the time staring at Tondo's little army of bricks and wood. After several minutes had passed, he returned to Tondo and the others. "I see the power in this. No one has ever seen anything to compare with it. Is this the way battles are fought by your outlander cities?" he finally asked.

Tondo laughed and said, "Yes, about two to three thousand spans ago." Everyone looked at him in bewilderment. He simply smiled in return.

"Ha, you may proceed with your plan," the king decreed. "What else do you need?"

"I will need at least three thousand samarans, arms, and armor for all the fighters, thrice to push the towers, and probably many other things I'll think of later. Also, since there is no longer a prince, I'd like to borrow Sestardus Titus and the Prince's Contingent, as well as the men still serving their punishment in the royal stables. They will act as my initial trainers."

"Who are these men serving in the stables? Are they more slaves?" the king wondered.

"They were once members of the Prince's Contingent. Have you forgotten?"

The king lowered his head in thought for a moment, then said, "Ha." He then lamented, "All these things you're asking for may drain the kingdom's coffers."

"Your Highness, unfortunately, the cost of victory is high."

"Hoy, I will have one of my counselors assigned here to relay your needs to me," the king said.

"I would prefer one of the officers from the Pannera, Your Highness. As I said earlier, my trust in some of your counselors is weak."

"As you wish. Megato Ayetoz!" the king called.

The commander rushed to the king's side and bowed. "Yes, Your Highness."

"I want you to assign one of your officers to work with Sire Tondo. He will report directly to me."

"Yes, Your Highness, by your command."

"Also, Sestardus Titus and his men have been reassigned to Tondo, along with the men serving their punishment in the royal stables. See that they are notified. Have them report to Sire Tondo, along with all their equipment," the king ordered.

"Yes, Your Highness. Is there anything else?" The king looked at Tondo, and the outlander shook his head.

"That will be all." Ayetoz quickly left and started talking to several members of his staff. The king turned to Tondo again, "Since you are the commander of this army, you will need a Pannera rank. I bestow upon you the rank of megatus, and I transfer Counselor Idop to your command. Also, I grant you the authority to promote and demote who you wish for this army of yours up to the rank of neva megatus."

"Thank you, Your Highness, but this is your army. They will be fighting for your kingdom," Tondo reminded him.

"And for their freedom," Ayascho added.

Tondo invited the king and his men to join him for last-meal. There was no banquet, no special preparations, nothing that royalty would normally expect. Instead, the king was invited to partake of the same food the men ate.

"I'd have expected a kingdom sire's meals to be a bit . . . how shall I say it . . . a bit more robust, even in these unfortunate times," the king commented.

"I eat like this every day, with the men. If a commander is going to determine how well his men are fed and what their morale level is, he must see firsthand. It is one of the ways I gauge the effectiveness of my soldiers, Your Highness," Tondo informed him.

"I think we can learn something from this, megato," the king told Ayetoz.

"Yes, Your Highness, especially now that food is becoming scarce," Ayetoz surmised.

"Your Highness, I have another suggestion I'd like to offer," Tondo continued.

"Ha, what is it?"

"You should have a floating dock built closer to the city. That way, it would require fewer resources to move food from the ship to the city."

"I agree. I will issue an order to that effect first thing in the morning."

CHAPTER 16

FILLING THE RANKS

Tondo estimated that the city and its defenders were consuming four hundred and fifty to five hundred of his outlander tons of food each detzamar. He guessed the *Anterra* could carry fifty to one hundred tons of cargo, but she could make one to three deliveries during a forty-day period, depending on how far she had to travel, affected by the wind and the weather. Tondo's estate was producing about two thousand five hundred tons of gorn in a harvest. In short, there was a significant deficit, and time would soon catch up to them. The temple storage was going to help, but it, too, was limited, and in less than two spans, the kingdom would be on the verge of starvation. Completion of the new ship would help alleviate the shortage, but that was still several detzamars in the future. In his regular communications to Maaryah, Tondo asked if it were possible to have two harvests of gorn per span. Her reply indicated that it was already being done, but she desperately needed additional harvesters. This request was passed on to the king, who sent several more wagon loads of slaves and Pannera guardsmen to the estate. It was late in the season by the time the additional help arrived, so no one was sure if the second planting could be harvested before the rains began.

Tondo promoted both Idop and Ayascho to the rank of neva megatus, a rank roughly equivalent to a field grade officer—major, lieutenant colonel, or colonel. His rank of megatus, he assumed, was equivalent to that of general grade—most likely one or two stars—although it was difficult to make a direct comparison to the ranks of his homeland's military.

He assigned Idop the duty of locating and preparing a training area for the expected thousands of slaves who would soon join the slave army. While he was doing that, Tondo and Ayascho went into the city to start collecting recruits. When they arrived, they were greeted as heroes by the slaves, having heard the king's declaration from the heralds. By this time, every slave in the kingdom knew the outlander had already freed the slaves at his estate, so they were certain the king's proclamation wasn't an evil trick.

Nearly every slave they met wanted to join the army and gain their freedom: the strong and healthy, the lame and halt, those too young and those too old; women beseeched them, as well. The press of flesh became so great that Pannera guards had to threaten the slaves with drawn swords and metren points to back off or suffer the consequences.

The two men quartered their mounts in the Pannera stables and continued on foot to Tondo's city house. This became his headquarters and recruitment center, much to the chagrin of the upper-class women residents as they watched a steady flow of what they considered riffraff invading their stately district. Many complaints were registered with the Pannera, but by royal decree, nothing and no one were to interfere with the outlander's mission.

Tondo was looking for one hundred men who he and the other freeborns would train, and they, in turn, would train others. The first one hundred had to be exceptional individuals, capable of accepting and giving orders. Tondo knew nearly every slave was capable of taking orders, that's all they'd done throughout their lives, but he was looking for men who could also think for themselves and lead others. That would be more challenging, considering how the slaves had been treated from birth.

He began interviewing men that very day. It took ten very long days to identify five hundred potential candidates. He then ran them through tough physical tests, ending with a long-distance run. About half failed to pass these tests and were dropped, but they were encouraged to try again when recruitment continued after the first batch was trained.

The final tests were mental challenges to see if the candidates could solve various puzzles Tondo developed; such as, 'Three men are standing in a room, two fathers and two sons. How is this possible? Answer: one man is a son, the second man is the son's father, and the third man is the father's father (grandfather).'

At the conclusion of the mental tests, there were one-hundred-twelve men remaining. Tondo decided to increase the initial number to include all of those who had made it to this point because it gave him a reserve in case of injury, illness, or failure to progress. Each recruit was required to place his mark on an enlistment document and declare his willingness to serve in the army for a term of no less than twenty spans. Tondo recalled what a problem short enlistment periods had caused during the history of his homeland, and he didn't want that repeated here. It would be much easier to release the men from this long-term agreement than it would be to extend one of shorter duration or seek their re-enlistment. Each man made his mark; none refused, considering that twenty spans were really not that much time while under the influence of the Blessing of the City. Tondo and Ayascho also chose fifteen women who had volunteered to serve as washerwomen, cooks, and fletchers. They were also required to place their marks on contracts that stipulated they would serve for a term of no less than five spans. He then made it clear to all the others—the ones who had not been selected—that he or his subordinates would return soon and select another batch of trainees. This would continue until the army was fully manned. He warned, a candidate would be summarily rejected for army service, and consequently freedom, if they had been found guilty of a punishable offense, such as thievery. Tondo later learned that the petty theft problem the city was experiencing ended that very day.

Coleman and Ayascho gathered up their recruits, the supporting women, and marched out of the city toward the eastern section of the Wall. Tondo had secured four wagons from the temple full of food and supplies. The commander of the city guard offered to send some of his men along to keep the slaves under control, but Tondo would not allow it. To his thinking, these men were now soldiers, not slaves, and he wanted them to begin thinking of themselves in that way. Before they left, he and Ayascho selected leaders of tens and a leader of the one hundred. These men—these slave leaders— were to take responsibility for seeing that their commanders' orders, those being Megatus Tondo and Neva Megatus

Ayascho, were carried out. Training of both leaders and men began that very instant.

After a day of traveling, Tondo's contingent was met by one of the estate's freed-men with word that Idop had found a suitable training area about two marches from the city. He led the group to that location. They were met by Neva Megatus Idop and Sestardus Titus, including all the men of the Prince's Contingent, as well as the eight men finally dismissed from their punishment in the royal stables, now fully equipped and ready to resume their duties.

The One Hundred, as Tondo referred to the initial one-hundred-twelve recruits, were ordered to erect their tents, ten men to a tent, as had been done during their journey. The men were allowed to rest, and the cooks prepared last-meal. Tondo told them, training in earnest would begin at first light.

As dawn began to break, Tondo had Titus's men roust the recruits from their tents as a horn blasted Reveille—well, it really wasn't the actual tune, just something the hornman came up with under Tondo's direction. A quick first-meal was offered, and then training began. Tondo modeled it after Basic Training he had received in the United States Army many spans ago. There was much physical conditioning, military protocol, including how to address officers—the megato and megatus ranks—as well as the non-officers—sestardi and sestardus ranks.

Training included drills in marching in the morning, the afternoon, and the early evening. These drills took on a much more important emphasis for Tondo than his own marching drills had. He realized his warriors would be using many of these maneuvers in actual combat.

Even though the One-Hundred were hand-picked by Ayascho and himself, more than half didn't know their right from their left. Tondo finally resorted to having every man tie a red strip of cloth to his right sandal and a green strip to his left. Every day began with an inspection to make sure each man had his colored strips tied to the correct foot. Tondo made sure everyone wore the strips, including his officers, non-officers, and trainers—up to and including his two sub-commanders and himself. It took many days for all the recruits to get used to the concept of right and left, but they eventually got the hang of it. The colored strips remained a part of every man's uniform because the leaders knew the problem of determining right from left would be repeated by other groups of recruits.

About this time, Tondo got word that the new ship had been launched in the lake. Master T´erio had not bothered with a gristening ceremony because everyone was busy with their vital daily chores on the estate. The ship was given the name *Zerio*, the name of the prevailing southwesterly wind. A crew of twenty had been selected from volunteers on Tondo's section of the Wall and included a handful of experienced boaters from the *Anterra*. Boatmaster Hermanez wanted to be the commander of the new, larger ship, but Tondo didn't want him pulled away from his important responsibility of securing food stocks for the city. Hermanez was an excellent negotiator, and he had struck many personal relationships with the officials of the various cities the *Anterra* visited. Tondo didn't want to pull him away from the vitally important responsibility of securing food for the city simply to train another crew, so the *Anterra's* first mate was chosen to captain the *Zerio*.

About two detzamars later, the new ship was hauled overland and launched into the ocean. A few days later, she set sail for Hermanez's island. Sometime after that, Hermanez learned that because there were no extra food stocks remaining, having been depleted by the *Anterra's* frequent visits, the *Zerio's* master set sail for the southeastern cities along the eastern coastline of the great gulf. That was the last anyone ever saw or heard of the ship. It just seemed to have disappeared, whether by storm or terror or some other hazard, no one knew. It was a devastating blow to Tondo when he learned of the ship's loss with all hands. The loss of life was terrible, but it had also depleted his Wilderness gold in its construction. Now, he had nothing to show for his substantial investment, and he lacked the funds to begin anew. Reluctantly, he ordered the boat construction crew to join the men on the east end of the Wall.

CHAPTER 17

BLACK FLAG

Haptane Soidentee waited nervously to be summoned before his master, the Sutro Showton. He had been ordered to report in person to his illustrious leader to explain something he failed to grasp. As Soidentee paced back and forth in front of the huge doors of the Throne Room, he wiped away a trickle of sweat that had run down the side of his face. The Northern Army, which he commanded, had been moving swiftly for nearly two spans, but it had recently been checked by the improved defenses of the opposing kingdom. Soidentee knew that his master did not tolerate failure or even the appearance of failure. He had learned over the past spans that his new master was merciless when it came to disciplining those who fell short of expectations. Soidentee was a competent army commander, and he had sent scores of wagons loaded with booty back to his master. He hoped that would favorably influence the upcoming meeting; however, when it came to a meeting before the Showton, no one felt secure.

The heavy doors swung open, revealing a stern-looking Showton adviser glaring at the nervous haptane. "The Sutro Showton will see you now," the advisor grumbled in a threatening tone.

Soidentee's unease was confirmed by the adviser's sullen visage and bitter tone; he was in serious trouble. He took a deep breath, straightened his back, and stepped forward at a military gait. The echo of his footsteps reverberated through the Throne Room as officials, dignitaries, and guards silently watched him approach his master's elevated throne. When he was about twenty-five radi from the platform stairs, the Showton raised his scepter, indicating he had advanced close enough. Soidentee dropped to a knee and bowed. Silently, he thought, *If the Showton allows me to stand, I'll be all right.* He waited and waited, but his master didn't say a word. *What does he want me to say, if anything?* His mind was reeling as he plotted a defense should he be accused of some great offense.

After an intolerable delay, the Showton finally spoke, "Haptane Soidentee, why have you forced me to summon you?"

Soidentee squirmed under his master's grumbled words. The Showton hadn't allowed him to stand, and his worst fears were now fully realized. His very life may be under threat. He absentmindedly cleared his throat and began speaking, his voice constricted and at a higher pitch than usual, belaying his fear. "Your Eminence, I came as quickly as I could, without delay." He knew it wasn't an answer to the question, but he felt it a safe enough response to possibly gain an insight into his master's thinking and the purpose for this summons.

"Haptane, I didn't ask you about your travel. I want you to explain to me why it was necessary to summon you here in person to explain yourself." The Showton's voice was growing louder, and it echoed off the stone walls, ceiling, and floor.

Soidentee shifted nervously on his knee. He didn't want to rattle off a list of supposed transgressions he may have committed. Self-incrimination could be suicide. *May as well plead igno-*

rance, he thought to himself. *If I'm to be condemned, it will come from the Showton's mouth, not mine.*

"Oy, I'm waiting, haptane, and you know very well, I'm not a patient man."

"I'm sorry, Eminence, I don't know," Soidentee responded from a knee, his head still lowered in a submissive bow.

"Haptane, must I spell it out for you? Alright, I will. The Northern Army has stopped advancing. Why? Neither the Southern Army nor the Eastern Army have slowed. Why, then, the Northern?"

"Your Eminence, King Deg-an-tus has fortified all the towns and villages in his kingdom. The rulers of these places feel safe atop their walls. None are willing to surrender. Each one must be placed under siege. It is a time-consuming process."

The Showton's threatening red eyes softened a bit, and he adjusted the veil covering the lower half of his face. He leaned back on the throne and pronounced, "Soidentee, you may stand." A relieved haptane stood and looked up to his master. "Soidentee, you're my best army commander, but you still have much to learn. The kind of war I am waging is ruthless. Therefore, you must be ruthless in your approach to war. I don't know why you and the others called your little skirmishes in the past war. They were little more than mob scuffles or shouting matches. I'm bringing a much more deadly game, one you must embrace or be passed over. What's it to be, haptane? Do you still wish to conquer, or would you rather go home and sip the gant your warriors love so much?"

Haptane Soidentee answered without delay, "I wish to conquer, Eminence!"

"That's good, Soidentee, that's good. I was prepared to place Grebsanto in command of the Northern Army, but the firmness of your answer convinces me to grant you a second chance; however, if you fail in your duties, I'll replace you and take your head. Do you understand?"

"Yes, Your Eminence, but the walled cities are hard to crack. No one has ever faced such defenses before; not my army, and not the Southern or Eastern armies," Soidentee demurred.

"It's not your army, haptane, it's mine! Is that clear?" The cowed commander nodded in submission. "Be ruthless, Soidentee; be ruthless." The haptane stood, staring up at his master with a blank expression. The Showton exhaled in exasperation. "Soidentee, give them the black flag."

"Eminence, I don't understand. What does that mean?"

"The black flag is a warning. It means you will take no prisoners. If a city doesn't surrender, you are to slaughter every man, woman, and child within its walls."

"Everyone, Your Eminence?"

"Yes, everyone. When the word gets around, no city will risk that fate. Most will surrender without a fight; you'll see. If any won't submit, make them a bloody example of your will."

"I will do as you say," Soidentee meekly replied while looking at his sandals. He had done some awful things while under the Showton's command, not the least being the murder of King Gor-bin-den by his own hand. Now, this. *Slaughtering the innocent was abhorrent,* he thought, but what was he to do? He had freely chosen to follow the Showton, and now he painfully realized the cost that must be paid to remain in his master's good graces.

The Showton stared down at his submissive haptane, wondering if he was up to the task. Soidentee was a good army commander and a hard one to replace. His idle threat to install Grebsanto was just that, an idle threat. Grebsanto didn't have the skill nor the self-confidence to lead an army. *No, I'll have to stick with Soidentee and push him when necessary,* the Showton thought. "Haptane, you're dismissed. And remember, be ruthless. That's what the black flag means. Don't let me ever hear a report that a city's residents still live after you've hoisted the black flag."

Soidentee lifted his head and gave the Showton a salute by raising his left arm and closing his fist. He turned and marched out of the Throne Room.

It took Haptane Soidentee over two wernts to return to the Northern Army. He hadn't received any messages from Neva Haptane Grebsanto since he'd left his command; therefore, he felt little had changed since his departure. That depressed him even as much as his appearance before his liege, the Sutro Showton. If the leaders of the city his army had under siege wouldn't surrender, he was going to have to do something he would regret. But it was his master's wish and his command. Soidentee inhaled deeply and straightened his back. 'Be ruthless' was the Showton's order, and so he must be.

The army commander rode to his headquarters, a stately home he had commandeered after placing the city under siege.

The three warriors who had journeyed with him took and cared for the tanter mounts. When he entered his office, he found Grebsanto sitting at his desk, reviewing a scroll. The neva haptane looked up, recognized his commander, and jumped to his feet.

"What's the status? Any change while I was gone?" Soidentee grumbled.

"No, haptane, nothing has changed. The men on the wall are still as stubborn and insulting as when you left. By the way they toss insults, you'd think our presence gives them great sport," Grebsanto observed. Soidentee frowned.

A warrior entered and placed a saddlebag on Soidentee's desk. "One of your traveling companions said you wanted this."

Soidentee didn't respond at first. He untied a flap on the saddlebag and pulled out a large black banner. He tossed it to the warrior. "I want you to find a place high enough and clear enough for those fools on the wall to see it if I choose to display it. Make sure it's ready in one segment. I plan to parley with the city leaders shortly. If they don't surrender, I'll raise my right fist. When you see my signal, display the black flag."

"As you command!" the warrior replied. He turned and marched out.

"What does the black flag mean?" Grebsanto wondered.

"Slaughter!" Soidentee grouched.

Soidentee took the time to refresh himself and consume some food before he and Grebsanto marched out of army headquarters.

The army commander led the way as they headed for the city's main gates. They stopped a stone's throw away and waited. It wasn't long before four city dignitaries appeared above the gates. Both parties stood staring at the other, neither voicing a word.

Finally, a city official spoke, his tone hostile. "What's ya want? We don't got all day."

It was the same boorish peasant Soidentee had dealt with in the past. *If he's the best they have, they don't have much,* the haptane thought to himself as he scanned left then right, examining the wall. Obviously, it had been constructed in a hurry. It was simply rough-hewn stones stacked atop one another. A person could climb the twenty radi if he chose, but it couldn't be done easily when under attack by the men above. He knew he'd lose a lot of men in an assault, and that was why he had delayed. He truly wanted to avoid a battle, so he crafted his words carefully. "You and your men have proven worthy adversaries. Your resolve honors you." He waited for a response, hoping for a positive reply.

The four city leaders held a short conference before a reply was formulated. Their spokesman turned and glared down at the two Showton army commanders standing below him. "Ya think ya can soften us up with your pretty words, does ya? We ain't hear'n none a that. Go away! Just go away. Youse wasting our time."

Soidentee chafed at the man's ignorant and defiant reply. The fools on the wall were slowing his advance, and his master was prodding him forward from behind. He felt trapped. He lowered his head, and Grebsanto watched in surprise as his commander's shoulders slumped. And then he straightened his back and looked up. "This is your final warning. Surrender or die! If I must take this city by force, I will see that every one of you—man, woman, and child—are killed. No one will be left alive. What's it to be?"

There was another short discussion atop the wall, and then the spokesman returned to his position above the gates. "We's don't believe ya. Yer empty threats don't scare us none. Go away and leave us alone. Tell that Showton of yern, we ain't ever gonna be ruled by him; no, none of us."

Soidentee clenched his teeth. Under his breath, he uttered a frustrated, "Fools!" He raised his right fist. From the top of a two-story building, the black banner was displayed. Soidentee looked at the banner and then to the men on the wall. "You're all dead men! And so is everyone else we find within these walls." He spit on the ground, turned, and marched back to his headquarters with Grebsanto following.

After Soidentee and Grebsanto returned to army head-quarters, the haptane ordered, "Prepare the men for an assault. Prepare ladders and ramps. We will attack in the morning."

Grebsanto gave his commander a worried look, and then he spoke, "Haptane, our losses will be high. I'm sure they can't hold out much longer. We should wait."

"His Eminence is tired of waiting. We must attack. Tell the men that once inside the city, they are to kill everyone—

man, woman, and child. Leave no one alive," Soidentee ordered. Grebsanto didn't move and stood silently, looking at his commander. "You have a question?" the haptane finally grouched.

"No! I will do as you say," Grebsanto said with a Showton salute. He turned and exited. Soidentee sat, grumbled a curse under his breath, and proceeded to review the scrolls on his desk.

A brilliant blood-red p´atezas rose that morning. It foretold what the day would bring. Grebsanto had made sure the men had been rousted out of their beds long before daylight. All had enjoyed a good first-meal and were now formed up in ranks on three sides of the walled city. Its back was against the great sea. Soidentee stood on a second-story balcony, listening to the black flag fluttering in the gentle morning breeze. *It's a beautiful day,* he thought. He cleared his throat and ordered the man standing beside him, "All right, sound your horn." The man placed the horn to his lips and blew the prearranged signal. From below, a hundred more horns, scattered throughout the army, sounded. The explosive roar of thousands of voices shattered the still of the morning air. The warriors lurched forward in a frenzied assault, some teams carrying long ladders, other teams carrying ramps, but mostly individuals scrambling to the wall and up the stacked stones.

At first, the defenders did well, picking off scores of assailants with rocks and thrown weapons. But once the first wave of attackers crested the wall's top, the farmer and laborer conscripts broke and ran for their lives. It wasn't long before the main gates were swung open, and a tide of Showton warriors poured into the city. Then the killing began. The warriors' bloodlust was burning hot, and they cut down anyone they saw. Soidentee watched the slaughter proceed from his balcony perch. To him, it was an awful display, and he hated what it was doing to his men and his army. It was indeed ruthless, undoubtedly as ruthless as his master had commanded.

The p´atezas was now high overhead, but the bloodbath had not abated. Haptane Soidentee was still overseeing the butchery from his perch when a defetane scrambled up the stairs and dashed over to him.

Soidentee looked the man over and saw that he was splattered in blood from helm to sandals. It was an appalling sight. "Yes, defetane, what is it?"

"Haptane, we have found something incredible. You have to come see it," the winded warrior pronounced.

"What is it?" Soidentee wondered as he turned his gaze back to the burning city.

"I can't explain it. I've never seen nothing like it. I can show it to you."

"All right, defetane. I need to go into the city anyway."

Soidentee and his retinue tramped down the stairs and to their tanter mounts. The defetane led them into the city. Small fires burned everywhere; screams were heard everywhere; dead lay everywhere. To his left, Soidentee watched as a detachment of his warriors chased down a small band of city residents. They became trapped against the side of a building, and his men began slashing and hacking them to pieces as they laughed. From Soidentee's right, he watched a young woman dash from an ally, pursued by a sword-wielding warrior. The woman, hardly more than twenty spans and carrying an infant clutched to her chest, dashed up to him. He could see the terror in her eyes. She lifted the child up so he could see the infant's face. The warrior chasing her stopped and waited.

"Please, master, please spare my son and me," she begged.

He looked at the warrior and then to the detachment that had just finished their gruesome task, an awful work that he had ordered. Everyone was staring at him, waiting to see what he would do. The infant's squalling howl annoyed him. He lifted his right leg, placed it on the young woman's abdomen, and shoved her away, hard. She fell to the ground, clutching her child to her chest, cushioning her infant son from the fall. Her head slammed into the hard ground, stunning her. The warrior who had chased her looked to his commander and waited. Soidentee nodded, and in two quick and lethal hacks of the warrior's blade, the woman and infant were butchered.

CHAPTER 18

HELPING FRIENDS AND FAMILY

After two detzamars—eighty days—the first batch of Tondo's slave recruits had completed their basic training. All one-hundred-twelve men were successfully graduated and promoted to the rank of neva sestardi, equivalent to corporal. Each man received a blue horizontal stripe as an emblem of his rank, worn on the center of their chest cover. Their duty now would be to assist in the training of the next batch of recruits, which would comprise one thousand men. Before the first round of training had ended, Tondo sent Ayascho, Idop, and Titus to the city to select the next group of recruits. Their job was to find one thousand men and two hundred women. He wanted the new group to arrive about the time the first group finished their training. Several of the neva sestardies were promoted to sestardi, gaining a second blue stripe, and Tondo, Ayascho, and Idop began selecting officers. By the time the second batch of recruits were half-way through their training cycle, the senior officers had identified ten men to be promoted to neva megato—a rank equivalent to a lieutenant, indicated by a single vertical zanth-colored bar, also worn on the center of the chest.

The king approved all of Tondo's requests, and soon, many blacksmiths had been transferred to the training area, including Pendor and Haro, and all began making swords, shields, and other implements of war. The temple was sending daily loads of the blue meteorites the priests had collected near the crater beyond the Mountains of Magheedo. The blacksmiths then fashioned the stone into two-edged short swords similar to the Roman gladius, a design Tondo had recommended. The warriors also carried two javelins that were called metrena and weighed about three depuza—roughly three pounds. The metrenas' wooden shafts were socketed, allowing them to be separated in half for easy transport. The weapons' deadly tips were made of Munnari gravetum.

Other crafts-men and women were making linen armor for the average foot soldier. This armor was made by stacking several layers of divitz and leather together. It reminded Tondo of some of the body armor he'd used while he was with the Rangers made from Kevlar III; at the time, the latest and greatest body protection material. The divitz/leather mix couldn't stop a bullet, but it didn't have to. It resisted sword slashes and cushioned the body from the trauma of heavy blows, as well. Stiff linen helms for the men were also constructed. Cheek guards protected the men's faces. Each helm was topped by a pair of inward curved linen horns.

These faux horns were intended to give the warrior a fierce appearance and added to his height, which was expected to intimidate an unseasoned enemy. Tondo's foot soldiers were to be equipped with a large shield that protected his warriors from chin to below the knees. The men were also protected by layered divitz and leather greaves covering their lower legs.

Little combat training had yet been given to the recruits. The focus was on basic and simple commands and marching drills. *The soldiers seemed to pick all this up quickly enough,* Tondo thought, *but the real test would soon begin. Could they be made into fighters with a warrior's heart and zeal?*

The third and final group of recruits were gathered by Tondo, Idop, and several neva sestardies, sestarduses, and neva megatoes. The slaves could see that men they knew were now holding positions of authority. This excited them even more, and the final recruitment topped out at more than six thousand men and an additional six hundred women. Several hundred young boys were accepted as drummers, others who were fleet of foot were chosen as messenger boys, and others were to become water boys. Several hundred more women were selected to become nurses and fletchers. All these concepts were foreign to everyone but Tondo.

By the time the army was fully organized, it had nearly seven thousand five hundred combatants and an equal number of noncombatants and support personnel. The warriors equaled the number Tondo had originally told the king. He had over-stacked the number of support personnel to make sure every slave in the city had the opportunity to gain his or her freedom. The king was no fool and fully understood the outlander's scheme, but every mouth Tondo accepted into the slave army was a mouth that was filled by the temple's stores and not by the king's dwindling supplies. Although the food shortage problem had abated somewhat and the fear of starvation had been relaxed, everyone knew the city was still going to run out of food eventually.

Titus and his men soon volunteered to join the army as more than just trainers. At first, they had been skeptical of the whole idea of a slave army, but as time went on and they saw how the slaves responded to their training, these freeborn men, citizens all, wanted to become part of Tondo's surprisingly dedicated army. Tondo petitioned the king on their behalf, and the king granted them permission to join the army.

Over time, every member of the Prince's Contingent received one or more promotions. Titus himself regained officer rank and was eventually advanced to sutro megato and made commander of the center wing, consisting of several troops of foot soldiers responsible for holding the center of the line and protecting the archer towers; undoubtedly, the most important of all the wings, Tondo told him.

The most difficult portion of the training was with the archers. None of the soldiers had ever seen a bow before, and at first they were awkward in its use. Tondo knew from the histories he had read long ago it took years to train good archers. He didn't have years nor spans, only detzamars. He made sure the basics were taught and received. He knew they would be firing into a closely packed mob, so he didn't think the archers needed to be particularly accurate. He hoped the surprise would be enough to stop the enemy in their tracks. If he were wrong, the day of battle would be a very long day, indeed.

The king continued to grant all of Tondo's requests. It wasn't long before Tondo realized that if he were going to command the progress of a battle, he needed an elevated and mobile platform from which to observe his men as well as the enemy's dispositions. It was then he asked for and received a lead raster—one willing and capable of more than just following the raster in front of it. Tondo knew that standing atop such a colossal beast would give him a wide panoramic view of the entire battlefield.

When the raster arrived at the training camp, it was led by none other than Myron, the merchant whom he had met in Ayascho's village many spans before. Tondo could see that Myron was not pleased with the king's order.

"Sire Tondo, please, please take good care of my raster. It is the only leader I have, and I would be ruined if I didn't get it back. Please make sure it is well cared for," Myron begged.

"It's good to see you, Myron. Where is Zoseemo?" Tondo asked.

"He is here, somewhere in your army. The king's declaration enticed him to join while I was on the Wall. Sire, if this war goes on much longer, I will be utterly ruined," the forlorn merchant lamented.

"I really don't know of anyone who can handle rasters other than Zoseemo. I'll have him care for your raster," Tondo promised.

"That boy may think he's the raster master, but he spoils them too much. If he were to care for this one, it would soon lose its ability to lead. You need a real raster master," Myron told him.

"Someone like you, maybe? Yes, that would solve both our problems. What do you say to that?" Tondo asked.

"Me, a warrior in an army of slaves? Please, sire, don't make me do it. What have I done to you to deserve such cruel treatment?"

"Now, now, don't you fret, Myron. I'm not ordering you to do anything, but if you want your raster cared for properly, I suggest you stay with it. Take a couple of days and observe what is being done here. After that, we'll talk, and you can tell me if you're willing to join us," Tondo offered.

"I will take the time and watch, sire, but I don't think a bunch of lowly slaves can change my mind." Five days later, Myron joined the slave army; his assignment to care for and lead Tondo's command raster.

During a commanders' meeting, which also included two sutro sestarduses, the highest non-officer rank equivalent to master sergeant—with three blue horizontal stripes under three blue chevrons—Titus suggested the army be given a banner. He produced an ensign he said was crafted by Sestardi Pontus. It was a blue circle surrounded by a white background. When he displayed the flag for all to see, Tondo noticed Master Shergus cringe, and the priest looked at him with concerned eyes. The banner looked much like the curtain that separated the Outer Sanctum from the Inner Sanctum in the temple.

Tondo took the banner from Titus and examined it. "In my homeland, a white flag represents surrender," he told the gathered men. He then held the flag by one of its corners and let it hang loose. Nearly all of the blue disappeared in its folds. "This will never do," he declared. "I like the idea of having a banner, and I like the blue circle representing the blue moon; however, we need to change the background color to something other than white. Does anyone have a suggestion?"

The commanders stood in silence for a few moments, then Ayascho spoke, "Zerr, may I suggest a pale-yellow. You know, the same color as the gown you gave Maaryah." His statement raised many eyebrows on the marked men. Realizing their concern and noticing Tondo's scowl, he clarified, "It was a gift to his friend. He expected nothing in return from her. Isn't that right, zerr?" Tondo nodded.

It had been a topic of some discussion early in the organization of the army as to what protocol should be used in addressing officers. Tondo thought calling each officer by his rank was redundant and unnecessary. He suggested that all officers be referred to as 'sire', a title easily understood by the soldiers. Idop objected, fearing the gentry, especially those of the tetzae rank, would vehemently object to such use by slaves for slaves of the appellation applied to themselves, the men of the tetzae gentry. Tondo then suggested 'sir' be used: a godspeak word that no one could object to. After some discussion with the other leaders, it was accepted as the appropriate appellation given to officers; however, the soldiers rendered the word into 'zerr', and that pronunciation stuck.

Tondo waited a bit longer, but there were no other suggestions concerning changes to the flag's appearance, so he looked at Shergus, and the priest nodded his approval.

"Very well, then. Titus, see that it's done."

"Yes, zerr," he replied.

"Zerr, I have another suggestion," one of the commanders announced.

"Megato Bryone, what is it?" Tondo asked.

"We should put the same symbol on our shields."

"Good idea. I like it. Are there any objections?" Tondo scanned the room and saw all his foot commanders nodding in agreement—the samaran soldiers didn't carry shields. "Okay, make it so. There is one other thing that needs to be addressed, as well," Tondo added. "People are referring to this army as 'Tondo's slave army.' I really don't like that." He didn't share this with the men, but he had gotten reports that several of the king's counselors, goaded on by Mordez, had been warning the king that Tondo was building an army to depose his liege and make a separate peace to end the war. He had done all he could to allay such concerns, but he could tell the king was still worried. "I want to call this army the Teg-ar-mos Brigade. Are there any objections?" No one responded. "Okay then, so it shall be, and let it be reported to the king."

After Tondo had examined the first finished brigade flag, he thought it a bit too drab for his liking. He sent it back to the seamstress and had her add black crossed short swords over the face of the blue circle. This gave the banner a more potent look, and many of his men commented on how the blue moon with crossed swords reminded them of their marks.

After learning this, the image pleased Tondo even more, and he accepted this new flag as the final version. The men of the brigade cheered when they first saw it. He ordered the foot soldiers to add the image of crossed swords to their shields, also.

One day, the relief wagon meant for Tondo's freed-men on the east end of the Wall came into the army's camp. Harmon, Maaryah's father, jumped off, collected his gear, and waved the wagoners farewell. He then searched for Megatus Tondo and found him sitting on a samaran observing a brick of men going through their marching drills.

"Sire, I am Harmon, and I'm reporting for training," he told Tondo.

Tondo turned upon hearing a familiar voice. A look of surprise and then annoyance crossed his face. "What are you doing here? You are a freed-man, and this army is only for slaves."

"I'm still a slave, sire. You never took me to an adjudicator."

"That's because circumstances didn't allow it. But I still consider you a freed-man. Now, hurry; you can catch the supply wagon and eventually make your way back to the estate," Tondo told him as he pointed to the wagon slowly moving across the open plain in the distance.

"I have decided to fight, sire, and I know I can be of help to you. I'm sure you can use a good samaran trainer in your army," Harmon told him.

Tondo certainly knew that was true. His men had been having problems training the samarans the king had provided to the army, and it was delaying the drills for his samaran soldiers. His feelings were divided, he wanted to keep Maaryah's father from harm, yet he could use Harmon's help with the mounts.

"Maaryah needs you at the estate. I've been receiving great reports about how helpful you've been."

"Sire, now that the king has sent others to help her, I'm not needed the way I was when this all started. I want to help save the kingdom."

"What's the incentive for you? You already have your freedom, and we are going into a battle in which we will be heavily outnumbered. You could be killed or maimed. The kingdom has forced you to be a slave all your life, so why would you want to risk all to save it now?" Tondo wondered.

"I want to do all I can to protect my daughter's freedom. I feel I can do that here, with you, not back at the estate."

"What does Maaryah think of all this?" Tondo asked.

"In all honesty, sire, she doesn't like it, but she doesn't like you being here, either. It is a hard time for all, and hard decisions must be made. If I am truly a freed-man, then let me choose for myself what I'm to do."

Tondo thought for a moment. There was little he could say to counter Harmon's logic, other than to summarily dismiss the man. He wouldn't do that. He dismounted and took Harmon by the forearm, "Ha, so be it. You are now a member of the Teg-ar-mos Brigade. I will see that you are assigned to a brick, and you'll begin your training immediately."

"Thank you, sire. I will be your best warrior," Harmon promised.

"I have no doubt you will be," Tondo told him with a smile.

After six detzamars, the army was fully formed, and all the recruits had gone through their basic training. It was now time to begin combat training and large unit drills. The soldiers understood and had practiced close-order drills in small units from single ranks of six men to bricks of thirty-six. It was now time to form the bricks into troops and see how things progressed.

True to his word, Harmon proved to be a good soldier. He quickly advanced from basic warrior to neva sestardi and then to sestardi. He was identified by several of the neva mega-toes as someone who really knew how to handle samarans and could be of great value in preparing and training the animals for combat. It wasn't long before the first brick of samaran soldiers had been selected and, of course, Harmon was chosen as the brick's sestardi.

Tondo had remained distant from any discussions concerning Harmon. He didn't want to show favoritism in any way, so he would only advise the leaders to choose wisely. He and Harmon had become friends at the estate, but contact with each other now was limited due to the demands on Tondo's counsel and Harmon's training schedule; however, there was one encounter they had that sealed their relationship. It occurred after Harmon had been promoted to the rank of sestardi. He was eating his midday-meal in the shade of a tree. Tondo rode by and noticed him there, so he went to the mezz, as it was called by the soldiers, and got some food. He then made his way to Harmon's tree, and when Harmon noticed him coming, he stood and saluted. Tondo returned his salute, told him to continue with his meal, and then sat with his back against the same tree trunk.

"It's good to see you again, Sestardi Harmon. Congratulations on your recent promotion," Tondo said as he began the conversation.

"Thank you, zerr, and thank you for recommending me for promotion."

"Sestardi, I had nothing to do with your advancement other than signing off on the promotion. You earned it by your performance and hard work. Your diligence to duty was noted by your commander. Keep up the good work."

"Thank you, zerr. Have you received any messages from Maaryah lately?" Harmon asked.

"I receive correspondence from her once a wernt. She is very diligent in that regard. Now, I know how she came by that trait," Tondo told him with a smile.

"How is she? Does she ever say how she's feeling? When I left, she was exhausted, and I worry about her health," Harmon admitted.

"She has never said anything about her health. She only refers to her duties as the manager of the estate. And a very good one, I might add. She is helping to save the kingdom," Tondo told the proud father. "You should send a message to her and let her know how you're doing. It might lift her spirits to hear from her father."

"I'm reluctant to do that, megatus. I can't read or write, and I'm afraid I would break down and cry in front of the scribe. I miss her so much."

"After the day is done, come to my tent, and I will write the message for you. I have a towel you can use," Tondo offered with a smile.

"You are too busy to waste time to scribe for a heartsick papa," Harmon protested.

"I'm never too busy to help a friend. Besides, I wouldn't want my best sestardi morose and inattentive to his duties." Harmon smiled and turned inward, perhaps crafting a message to his daughter in his mind, Tondo thought. After a few moments, Tondo spoke again, "Tell me about Maaryah's mother."

"She was a beautiful woman, much like her daughter. She came from the City of Women," Harmon began. "She told me, the women there are the rulers of their families and leaders of city affairs. Her mother was a merchant and traded goods with the caravan masters who passed through the city. Somehow, she got into money problems, and a debt was called. She was unable to cover it, and the whole family was sent to Debtor's Camp: her mother, her father, older sister, and brother. No one came forth to pay the debt, so the family was taken to the slave traders and sold into slavery to pay the shortfall. Maaryah's mother, Maariah, was eventually sold to a caravan master. She was only nine spans—those were outlander spans. He took the caravan to the Ancient City, and she was sold again to Master Oetan's foreman, who put her to work in the Separation House as a runner. Eventually, she was sent to the fields, and that's where we met. Maaryah reminds me so much of her: she was also tall, even taller than her daughter, and had the same black hair and the same good heart." Harmon stopped and lost himself in a memory for a bit. Then he continued, "Maaryah is very fond of you. She tells me you're the kindest man she's ever met."

"Your daughter is a wonderful person. I'm so glad I was able to free her and the others. Look at what she's become. She's an example to everyone that slaves are just as capable as freeborns," Tondo told him.

"Yes, sire, but do you have feelings for her? Is there room in your heart for a woman with a mark?" Harmon boldly asked. Tondo was taken aback by Harmon's direct question. He turned inward and pondered. The sestardi waited patiently for his commander's answer.

It took a long time coming. Just as he was about to speak, a neva sestardi rushed up to them and saluted Tondo. Both he and Harmon stood, and Tondo returned the man's salute.

"Megatus Tondo, my commander needs your advice. He has a recruit who is failing to perform, and something needs to be done about it."

Tondo had become accustomed to urgent calls like this. The problem with promoting so many men so quickly was they didn't have time to develop their own leadership skills and confidence, and coupled with the fact that they were all recently slaves themselves, didn't help. "Tell your commander I will be there shortly. Where is your brick located?"

"Over there, by those bushes, zerr. We're in combat training."

"Very well, you're dismissed." The neva sestardi saluted and dashed back to his unit. "Oy, a commander's duties are never done. You have given me something to think about," he told Harmon. "Don't forget, I'm willing to write messages for you." Harmon nodded, then saluted. Tondo returned to his samaran, mounted, and trotted off to his summons.

When he arrived, he was saluted by the neva megato in command of the brick. Tondo returned his salute. "Neva Megato Pemmet, right?" he asked.

"Yes, zerr!" the brick commander responded, proud that his megatus remembered his name.

"Okay, what's the problem?" Tondo asked.

"That man isn't applying himself to his training. He has been taught what he must do, but he is either too lazy or too stupid to do what he's been taught. I think he needs to be scourged," Pemmet suggested pointing to one of his soldiers.

"Megato, that's what is done to slaves, is it not?" Tondo declared.

"Yes, zerr!" the neva megato eagerly responded.

"If you can remember anything, remember this: you and your men are no longer slaves. You are warriors and are to be treated like warriors. Let this man stand in place of a training dummy and have the brickmen take turns practicing on him. He'll either learn quickly or regret it."

"Yes, zerr, I'll see that it's done." Tondo waited while the recalcitrant soldier was informed of the megatus' decision. The man grinned slyly, guessing he'd just escaped a good scourging. Tondo returned a knowing smile and waited. After three severe encounters with members from the brick, the now bruised and humbled malcontent began to apply what he'd been taught in his own defense. By the time the entire brick had a go at him, he'd become very bruised, exhausted, and quite proficient. Megatus Tondo then nodded to Pemmet, and the man was allowed to rest. When he fell back into his rank, he followed his commander's orders precisely and with vigor.

Later that evening, after all the training had ended for the day, and Tondo had finished making his rounds through the camp, he returned to his tent where he found a wooden tray full of food under a cloth covering waiting for him. As he began to eat, he heard footsteps approaching.

"Megatus, may I enter?" It was Harmon's voice.

"Yes, sestardi, please come in." Harmon lifted the tent flap and entered. "I'm just starting my last-meal. Are you hungry?" Tondo asked.

"No, sire, I've come to ask if you'll write the message to my daughter we talked about earlier."

"As soon as I finish eating, I'll be happy to do it." That was the beginning of regular meetings Harmon and Tondo would have. Harmon began visiting his megatus and estate master every Du-Zet, the day of rest, something Tondo had instituted from the very beginning of training.

After the first samaran troop was mustered, Harmon was promoted to sestardus, and by the time all samaran troops had been formed, he'd been promoted to the rank of sutro sestardus—equivalent to master sergeant, the highest non-officer rank so far authorized. He was the senior non-officer for the entire left flank, which was under the command of Neva Megatus Ayascho.

One evening, after Tondo had made his evening inspection of the camp and was preparing to go to bed, Idop entered his tent and sat at the small commander's table and waited to be acknowledged. "What can I do for you, neva megatus?" Tondo asked.

"Lady Oetan has written to me and declared her interest in seeking an Intervention. She is wondering if you would be willing to be her interventionist?"

"I thought she was worried her daughter wouldn't want her to seek an Intervention," Tondo wondered.

"She has received Queen Ootyiah's blessing in the matter, so she has decided the time has come to act."

"Certainly, I would be honored to be her interventionist. Does this mean she will soon bond with someone?" Tondo asked with a wink.

"Not until after the victory is won. There is no time for personal matters, megatus. I will not take leave from the army while training continues. She already understands this, and she fully supports my decision. After the war is won, we will bond."

"Congratulations, my friend. You are indeed a lucky man."

Nearly a detzamar later, Lady Oetan sent word to Idop that she had arrived at the Tondo city house and was ready to proceed with the Intervention. Tondo and Idop rode into the city shortly after that, and the Intervention was conducted before the only adjudicator remaining in the city, an elderly man, too old and frail to defend the Wall.

"Sire Tondo, is it your wish to act as the interventionist for this woman?" the adjudicator asked in his aged voice.

"Yes, it is. I will assume responsibility for her care and support."

"What is her relationship to you?" the adjudicator asked.

Tondo looked at Lady Oetan and then to Idop. He didn't know how to answer, and from their expressions, neither did they. He took a deep breath and then responded, "Write down that she is my sister."

"Oy, I don't see the resemblance, and there seems to be a significant age difference, but I am an old man, and my eyesight is failing me. How shall I record her name?"

Again, Tondo was stumped. He'd always known her as Lady Oetan, and never once was her common name ever mentioned. Again, he looked to Lady Oetan and Idop.

"I am Sevootyiah," she declared.

"I see," said the adjudicator suspiciously, his eyebrows furrowing. "A brother and sister who don't seem related, and a brother who doesn't even know his sister's name. This entire matter is very dubious," the adjudicator warned.

"This lady has been declared a member of my family by royal decree from the king himself. You may refer to palace records if you wish," Tondo advised. "Please proceed." The forcefulness of his statement resolved the issue.

"Sire Tondo, I will take your word on that." He then recorded something on his official record scroll, signed another parchment, placed his seal on it, and handed it to Tondo. "Sire, the former bond is officially broken, and you are now responsible for your . . . your sister's welfare. I hope you are satisfied. These proceedings are concluded," the adjudicator declared.

The three quickly left the adjudicator's forum and returned

to the city house. After they arrived, Sevootyiah gave Tondo a snug and thanked him. "Please stay the night and enjoy the comforts of your house," she offered.

"I'm afraid I have been gone from my men too long, my lady. I must leave soon."

"At least you can stay for a good meal. Teema has prepared the last of the meat," she pleaded.

Tondo licked his lips. "I certainly can't pass up one of Teema's famous creations. I will join you for last-meal, but I must leave at first light; however, Neva Megatus Idop, you have my permission to remain for another day."

Idop took a long look at Sevootyiah and watched as she nodded. "Zerr, I will return with you. I also have duties that must be attended to."

The three enjoyed the finest meal any had enjoyed in over a span. Sevootyiah invited Teema to join them, which made Tondo smile because it wasn't that long ago it wouldn't have even been considered. All enjoyed each other's company and the respite from their worries. Shortly before the midnight segment, everyone turned in for a few segments' sleep before the men's departure. The next morning, while it was still dark, everyone was up and about. The men's samarans were saddled and readied. Teema gave each man a linen-wrapped bundle of food for the trail. Idop and Sevootyiah embraced and exchanged snugs, then the men mounted, and rode out of the city, heading northeast, their samarans ambling onward at a good clip.

CHAPTER 19

OKAY, WE'LL GO!

Several days later, on a wet and windy day of training, Tondo and his two senior lieutenants were together observing a couple of bricks facing off against each other. It reminded Tondo of two football or rugby teams from his homeland lined up for a scrimmage or a scrum. He noticed the men slipping and sliding while pushing one another in opposing line formations. A couple of the men fell and quickly scrambled to their feet while the others laughed. Tondo was not amused.

"This is not good. When we engage the enemy, there will be much pushing and shoving. The ground will be slick, either by mud or blood. I must do something to improve our men's footing."

Later that day, Tondo retired to his commander's tent, sat at his camp table, and started drawing in the dim light of an oil lamp. When he was done, he had designed what he called a battle sandal. It looked like an open-sided boot with the toe and heel covered by stiff hide. He also designed a hobnail—a small cleat-like spike that could be screwed into the underside of the thicker than usual sole. Every foot soldier was to be outfitted with two pairs of sandals: a normal sandal for regular daily use and for marching, and a battle sandal that would be worn in combat training and during actual combat. When put into practice, the battle sandal solved the slipping problem.

The season changed, and the training continued no matter what the weather was: hot and bright, cold and damp, windy or calm. Nearly one span and five detzamars had passed since the start of training. The king was beginning to lose patience with Tondo's deliberate and methodical approach to the army's drills. He demanded action, and he wanted a resolution to the siege. Food supplies were growing short, and it was now very clear the *Anterra's* efforts, as well as those of the Tondo Estate, were not enough to cover the deficit. Tondo had also been informed that the temple's food stores were nearly exhausted, also. He had less than two detzamars to do something about it.

One afternoon, after reviewing all the dire reports of the approaching food shortage, Megatus Tondo called his senior commanders to a council of war. It was time to poll the army's leadership and gain their input concerning the readiness of their warriors. The senior leadership consisted of the three top leaders, Tondo, Ayascho, and Idop; plus seven others chosen for their military prowess, intelligence, and tenacity. The seven held the rank of sutro megato and commanded a wing of five to seven troops. Fayeetez, Gheedan—not the sharp-eyed soldier from the long trek out of the Wilderness but another by the same name—Biatys, and Savas led the samaran wings. Pydeez, Nestess, and Titus led the three wings of foot soldiers. Titus also commanded the five archer towers.

When asked if their commands were ready for battle, to the man, they said their units were prepared and willing. They added, their warriors wanted to fight; the sooner, the better; their training having become redundant and boring. The commanders felt the army was as ready as it would ever be to break the siege.

Just as a date was about to be discussed, Master Shergus joined the meeting. "Megatus Tondo, I have word from the Sutro Seer," he immediately announced.

"What is it? Is he warning me again that the food supplies are running out?" Tondo asked.

"No, sire, he has received counsel from the great unnamed god, and he suggests the day for your attack."

"Don't stop there, Master Shergus, tell us what it is," Neva Megatus Ayascho urged. Tondo nodded his agreement.

"Five days hence is the day the battle must be fought," the master informed him. "His Eminence earnestly recommends you follow this counsel. The fate of the kingdom rests upon your decision."

Tondo looked around the room and saw the determination in the eyes of his subordinates. Neva Megatus Idop was the first to speak. "Megatus, we are ready. Just say the word, and we'll prepare the army for its march to the gates."

Tondo lowered his head in thought for a moment as he felt the heavy weight of the decision he must now make. He soon lifted his head and firmly issued his order. "Okay, we'll go! Ready your men! You will begin your march to the Wall in the morning. Each troop will form up, and the order of march will be as we have discussed previously. Neva Megatus Idop and Neva Megatus Ayascho will ride with me to inform the king of my decision. Sutro Megato Titus will be in command of the army during the march to the Wall. Are there any questions?" None were forthcoming, so Megatus Tondo dismissed his commanders. Master Shergus went to the nearby tabernacle to pray.

There really wasn't much for Tondo to do after he dismissed his senior leadership. One of his messengers started a fire in front of his command tent. Tondo found a camp chair and sat near the warming flames, his hands extended, soaking in the heat. He contemplated his army's training and hoped he had done all that was needed to prepare his men for the great struggle ahead.

Well after darkness had fully engulfed the camp, Ayascho and Idop approached. "Tondo, do you mind if we join you? There is nothing left for us to do. Our subordinates have everything well in hand," Ayascho told him.

"Please, find a chair or a log to sit on and warm yourselves by the fire. It's a little cool tonight," he said. The two quickly joined him. "After I dismissed the commanders, I realized there was nothing left for me to do, as well. I have been reviewing all of our preparations in my mind, trying to think of anything we've overlooked, but I believe we are as prepared as we can be," Tondo told his two senior subordinates.

"Do you really think we have a chance against such a large army as the two wicked kings have?" Ayascho asked.

"Our men are well armed and armored. Our mounted soldiers are also well-armed and armored, and their samarans wear barding. The training has readied them for this battle. I sometimes feel sorry for the enemy host. They won't know what hit them," he told his two senior lieutenants with all the confidence he could muster; however, Ayascho knew him too well.

"I can see there is something you are not telling us, Tondo. What is it?" Ayascho wondered.

"My only concern is the depth of our line. If the enemy penetrates it, we may be hard-pressed to close the gap," he warned.

"I doubt they will. I have never seen such a powerful army, and neither has our enemy. Their numbers no longer worry me," Idop admitted.

"Yes, I agree, but I always have nagging concerns. I'm sure the men will perform brilliantly," Tondo confirmed. "How is Sevootyiah doing? Is she still staying at the city house?"

"Yes, she is. We are both grateful for your generosity in allowing her to remain there," Idop told him.

"I've seen her and Teema around camp from time-to-time, especially on Du-Zet. What's she doing?" Ayascho wondered.

"She visits with me, and then she helps the men write messages to their families. It's something she started doing at the estate after Maaryah's promptings, and now she volunteers to do it for our men," Idop told them.

"It sounds like her heart has softened toward the slaves," Tondo observed.

"It has, now that she has learned they have the same loves and worries as everyone else. I must admit, I have grown fond of these men—these slave warriors. They're the best soldiers I have ever commanded. You were right, as usual, Tondo. They are no different than freeborns," Idop acquiesced.

Tondo smiled and said, "Well, it only took a war and a slave army to change your mind, but may the gods bless you for your willingness to alter your thinking. If you don't mind me asking, what are yours and Sevootyiah's plans after the battle?"

"We have already agreed to bond, that is if I survive."

"I have a feeling we will all survive, my friends," Tondo told them.

"It's comforting to hear the Messenger say we will," Ayascho stated in a relieved voice.

"Tell me, Ayascho, is there someone special waiting for you in your village in the Wilderness—a woman, I mean?" Idop wondered.

Ayascho gave a sigh, "Yes, there is if she hasn't bonded by now. Her name is Nita." He turned and faced Tondo. "I never thanked you for saving her life. I thought I hated you back then, but you saved her from being sent into the trees to die. I am grateful for what you told us. You were right, and her life was spared. If I ever return to my village, I will bond with her, if she'll still have me."

"I only did what I thought was the right thing to do. The Tempter beguiled her, and she succumbed in a moment of weakness. She is a good girl and very beautiful, too," Tondo told him with a smile.

"What about you, Tondo? Is there anyone special in your homeland?" Idop asked.

"There was, but she left me before I came here. She said the voyage was too dangerous, and she didn't want me to take it. But I wouldn't listen to her, so she became angry and left me," he told them.

"There were many women in the village who wanted to be your mate, but after you grew hair all over your face, they lost interest," Ayascho chuckled.

"I did that because I didn't want them chasing me all around the village. I was more afraid of them than a charging gorga," he laughed.

"What kind of woman are you looking for?" Idop wondered.

"Well, let me think," Tondo began. "She would have to be intelligent."

"You mean like Maaryah?" Ayascho added.

"And she'd be beautiful."

"Just like Maaryah," Ayascho added again.

"And she'd have a kind heart."

"Yes, just like Maaryah," Ayascho stated.

"Are you trying to play Cupid?" Tondo asked.

"What's that?" Idop wondered.

"It's a god from my homeland who helps people fall in love. What's your point, Ayascho?"

"Haven't you noticed how she looks at you? She has loved you for many spans. Probably from almost the day she met you. I can tell," Ayascho told him with a smile. Tondo went silent and thought for a while.

Idop watched him and then shared his thoughts, "I can see you and Maaryah together. I'm surprised I never noticed it before. It's the perfect match."

"You've given me a lot to think about. Both of you are right. I feel like such a fool for not realizing this before. There was a time when we almost kissed, but we were interrupted. That was the night the red moon passed in front of the blue moon."

Ayascho took on a sheepish look. "Sorry," he mumbled. Idop punched him in the shoulder, and they all laughed.

They continued to chat for some time, then Ayascho and Idop departed to get some rest. After the two left, Tondo returned to his tent, wrote a message for Maaryah by the dim light of a single oil lamp, folded it, sealed it with wax in three places, and wrote her name on its face. He then sought Master Shergus and found him in the tabernacle the priests had erected in the camp.

"Master, I have a favor to ask of you."

"Yes, what is it?"

Tondo handed him the sealed message. "If I don't survive the coming battle, please give this to Maaryah."

A knowing smile crossed the master's face as he accepted the message. He then quoted from the Temple's Tome of Life, "The heights of joy, the depths of sorrow." Tondo took a seat on one of the benches and meditated for a while; one may have thought he was praying.

The three senior army commanders arose well before light. They took the time to get into their armor since they didn't plan to return. Haro was one of the blacksmiths who the king had assigned to Tondo's army, and after all the weapons and armor had been crafted for the soldiers, Haro spent many long wernts creating a set of special armor for his benefactor, Tondo. It was a form of scale mail, constructed of small, thin but sturdy scales of Munnari meteorite, and it carried the signature blue color of the sacred stone. The armor was light and flexible and melded with several thin layers of cloth and leather cushioning to absorb the impact of both sword and mace.

By the time the three commanders had geared-up, their war-samarans had been readied by aides. Tondo checked to make sure all of his weapons and Taahso's wrap had been packed in his bedroll. He gave some final instructions to Titus, and then they were off to meet with the king. It wasn't long after the three senior commanders left, the lead brick of the brigade also departed, leading the army on its northward march to the Wall.

Tondo and his companions' mounts were healthy and strong, so they arrived at the Wall in only one day of hard riding. It would take the army three days to cover the same distance. They arrived after dark and presented themselves at the king's tent, waiting for him to summon them. It wasn't long before Counselor Mordez exited, and he gave Tondo an angry, cold stare as he passed.

"You may enter; the king is awaiting your report," a king's counselor told them in an annoyed tone. They entered and found the king standing, his elevated throne having been pushed to a corner of the huge tent. Tondo bowed, Idop and Ayascho kneeled, and when the king nodded, they stood.

"Ha, the commanders of my slave army. What news do you bring?" the king asked with a hint of frustration in his voice.

"Your Highness, we are here to tell you, the army is ready to go into battle and is on the march. I expect it to arrive at the gates in three days. The battle to break the siege will be fought on the following day. The Sutro Seer has told us, the blessing of the unnamed god will fall upon us on that day," Tondo told him.

"Really? I was just informed by Counselor Mordez, the army will never be ready or willing to fight, and I've been wasting the kingdom's dwindling resources. The treasury is nearly empty, and so far, there's little to show for it," the king grouched.

"I've warned you about that man, Your Highness. He has no real knowledge of how prepared we are. The men are ready and willing to fight for you. The siege will be broken, and you will be the victor in four days," the army commander declared.

"Sire Tondo, your confidence always amazes me. I have been receiving reports for wernts about how things are falling apart all over the kingdom. It has become so bad that most of my counselors have lost hope. And now, you arrive and make such a declaration. It's like a breath of fresh air in a stale tent. You have raised my spirits and given me new hope," the king admitted. "Do you really think you can defeat the combined forces of those vile kings?"

Idop chose to answer the king's question, "Your Highness, I have never seen an army like this one. Tondo has crafted it into something that can defeat any enemy. The slaves are the most proficient and deadly warriors I have ever seen. You will have your victory."

"It gives me great comfort to hear those words coming from the man who once commanded the Pannera. It just seems too unbelievable," the king said.

"Don't listen to those doubters, Your Highness," Ayascho warned. "They don't know what they're talking about. In four days, you will see. Tondo and Idop are right."

"Why you—a savage from the Wilderness—why would you join this fight. What is my kingdom to you, anyway?"

"I have learned to trust Tondo. When I do what he says, things turn out for the best. I know he is the Messenger, and he has been sent to us to do a great thing. That is what I fight for," Ayascho declared.

For the next segment or so, the men talked about strategies and tactics. The king had many questions, and the three commanders took turns answering each and every concern he raised. By the time they were done, the king looked like he'd been rejuvenated. His confidence had returned, and his worry lessened. When he dismissed the three, they moved to a large tree some distance from the king's camp, cared for their samarans, ate some gornbread— the new staple in the kingdom given to them by a king's aide— rolled out their blankets, and went to sleep.

The three awoke as the p´atezas cleared the horizon and shined on their little camp. Ayascho managed to find some wood, and Tondo started a fire using his tzaah. Idop mixed some water into a pouch of wheat flour from the temple stores and wrapped the thickened dough around a stick. He slowly cooked it over the flames until it was done, then the three shared it for first-meal.

"We should return and meet the brigade," Ayascho suggested.

"Titus is a good man. I'm sure he has everything under control," Idop told him.

"We should make a final examination of the ground where the battle will be fought," Tondo told the other two.

They went to the great gates of the Wall, climbed the tower stairs, and headed east, all the time looking at the terrain in front of the Wall. After they had walked for half a segment, they turned around and headed in the opposite direction. After they passed the gates, they walked for another half-segment, examining the terrain in that direction.

"Well, this is good ground for samarans; few trees and only low bushes. I expect we'll have no trouble with the archer towers, either; as long as it doesn't rain," Tondo concluded.

"Yes, I agree. What do you think, Ayascho?" Idop asked.

"The ground couldn't be better. We have everything on our side. But I agree with Tondo about rain. I will pray to the great god to give us good weather," Ayascho promised.

"While you're at it, say a word for me too," Idop appealed.

"Say a word for us all," Tondo added. He thought for a second and then continued, "There are no atheists in foxholes," he said using the godspeak terms. The other two looked at him, waiting for a translation. "It means all warriors believe in the gods when they go into battle."

They discussed the placement of the various units of the army, how they would move, and where best to attack and defend. As they had determined earlier, Idop would command the right flank, Ayascho the left flank, and Tondo would command the center, where he expected the brunt of the enemy's attack to be concentrated. Tondo warned his subordinates not to let the right and left samaran wings open too large a gap between the foot soldiers in the center of the line. If necessary, they were to close any gap with warriors from their Headquarters troops and accompanying Brothers troops. The Tondo, Idop, and Ayascho Headquarters and Brothers units were composed of handpicked men who not only served as guards for the senior leaders but also as an elite reserve force. Tondo didn't want the flanks of his foot soldiers to be turned. He wanted to keep the enemy off balance and not allow them to gain any successes. His goal was to demoralize them before they could mount a significant threat, for he knew morale and resolve would be the most important elements in the coming showdown.

They continued discussing the deployment of the army as they walked back toward the gates. As they approached the western gate tower, they noticed some activity coming from the enemy camp far in the distance. A large number of soldiers could be seen advancing towards the Wall, led by royal banners.

"I think the kings want to parley with King Teg-ar-mos. I wonder what they're up to?" said Idop. They waited and watched as the horde of enemy soldiers stopped, and the two kings proceeded alone, stopping just out of range of a thrown stone. King Teg-ar-mos scrambled up the tower stairs and stood above the massive gates.

"Young king, we wish to negotiate. We've decided to end this confrontation in a . . . shall I say . . . a civilized manner," King Men-dre-dor shouted.

"What's the matter, are your men tiring of their long wait?" King Teg-ar-mos shouted back.

It was now the audacious King Pen-dow-mon's turn to speak. "Don't think we have lost our resolve in any way. We would rather end this now and allow our men to return to their homes and prepare for the planting season, but we can continue to hold you captive until your people begin eating one another. I can only imagine the suffering they must be going through by now. Even a young king needs to eat. Here, let us present you with a gift." Three men carrying sacks of grain advanced and dropped their loads in front of the two kings. "This is for you, my little chetzy. Eat well tonight, but you should take note of the hungry eyes of your guards as they watch their king fill his belly while their's rumbles with hunger," King Pen-dow-mon yelled for all to hear.

King Teg-ar-mos bristled at Pen-dow-mon's oft-repeated slur, comparing him to a young, docile samaran. "You overestimate the effect of your siege," the young king shouted back. "We have plenty to fill our stomachs and enough to spare. Keep your tainted grains!" The king shouted, but his words seemed hollow and unconvincing.

"Enough of this bluster!" King Men-dre-dor bellowed. "King Pen-dow-mon and I have decided to make an offer you'd be a fool to refuse: a Battle of Champions. Bring forth your strongest and most skilled warrior, and we will do the same. Let them decide the fate of this war. Why force your people to suffer any longer?"

The young king thought for a moment, then responded, "I think not!" he yelled. "I see no advantage in that. My wall is strong, and my men are fully capable of defending it. I even have an army preparing to break your siege soon. Swagger and huff all you wish, but your offer bores me."

"We've heard of this slave army of yours, led by a savage beast-man from the Wilderness," King Pen-dow-mon shouted at the young king, almost spitting his words. "How far you have fallen, my little chetzy. How foolish it is to allow yourself to be embarrassed by such a pathetic scheme."

"He's the Messenger, a representative of deity!" the king yelled back, defending his friend and the man who'd saved his life.

"So, he is the supposed Messenger and slave-lover. Is he that beast-man? Since you hold such faith in this outlander, call him forth to act as your champion, then. If he wins, he will save the lives of many poor, witless slaves whom he loves so much," King Men-dre-dor roared.

King Teg-ar-mos looked over to Tondo. "What say you, megatus? Many lives could be spared if you win."

"Don't trust those wicked kings, Your Highness," Idop warned. "They are treacherous and conniving."

"If I were to do this, what about the warriors you promised to free? Your Highness, they will not go back to being slaves. I doubt even I could convince them to return to that dismal life."

"If you win, I'll consider it the army's victory. I will honor my word, and the slaves will be freed just as if they had won the battle themselves," the king promised, although his words were not convincing to Tondo, and he felt a warning of deception rising at his center.

"This is not a good idea, Tondo. I have a terrible feeling about this. I know they are trying to trick us," Ayascho now warned as he slapped his chest, the center of his tzaah.

"I understand, but it's an offer I can't refuse. Isn't it better for only one to die, rather than thousands?" Tondo stated, concerned not only for his own men but also for the poor conscripts of the enemy's armies.

"Don't do it, Tondo," Idop warned again.

"My mind is made up; I must accept the challenge. Your Highness, I will be your champion, and I expect you to honor your word."

"Are you sure? They are wicked men. You saw what they did to those unfortunate priests. They may not honor their word," the king cautioned.

"Then, it will be abundantly clear to their men, they fight for wicked and dishonorable kings, weakening their resolve even more. Idop, if I fall, you are to take command of the army," Tondo ordered. "I go now to prepare."

"Use my tent, and my aides will provide anything you need," the king said. Tondo nodded and trotted down the stairs, gathered his equipment, and disappeared into the king's tent.

"Oy, my little chetzy, we are waiting for your answer, or can you find no champion to defend your honor?" King Pen-dow-mon shouted with a cruel laugh.

"You will have your Battle of Champions!" King Teg-ar-mos shouted back. The two kings smiled, turned, and walked back through their line, disappearing into a sea of humanity.

CHAPTER 20

THE KINGS' CHAMPIONS

After Tondo had been in the king's tent for a while, Master Shergus rode into camp, made a few inquiries, then went to the king's tent, and dismounted. Just as he was about to enter, Tondo came out; at least that's what Shergus and the others guessed, but if it was him, he looked entirely different. The man wore Tondo's specially crafted blue armor, but his hair was different, and his face was painted. Several of the king's guards actually stepped back in shock of his fearsome appearance.

"What have you done to yourself?" Ayascho asked in amazement.

"They think I'm a beast-man, so I'll look like one," he growled. His hair was cropped and shaved into a Mohawk, and he had a four-inch-wide band of red war paint across his eyes, from ear to ear. He looked wild and threatening. He had changed into his leather battle tunic, with thick pteruges—heavy leather strips that hung below his waist, protecting his groin and upper legs; his torso was protected by his specially crafted blue scale mail. The Munnari Blade was tucked into his belt, extending along his left side; a tomahawk at his right hip and the pommel of a blue gladius-like sword peaked above his right shoulder; a quiver of arrows showed above his left; he carried his bow in his left hand.

Master Shergus examined him from head to foot, then smiled and began speaking, "Is this what a warrior from your homeland looks like? Very impressive; however, you must leave your bow and arrows behind. Only hand-held and thrown weapons are allowed in such a contest, so they would be deemed dishonorable in a battle of champions."

Tondo's look of surprise and anger made Shergus winch. "What the hell!" Tondo cursed in godspeak. He was expecting an easy victory and only wished to disable his opponent. He did not like this unexpected turn.

"This is a battle of honor. You must obey the traditional rules, or it won't be acceptable," Shergus sternly explained.

Tondo handed Ayascho his bow and quiver. "Ridiculous rule!" he spouted.

Shergus put both of his hands on Tondo's shoulders. "By the power vested in me, I give you the blessing of the unnamed god. He will guide and protect you," Shergus proclaimed. "Now beware," Shergus warned, "I'm sure their champion has the inner-power, too."

The men walked to the Wall and stopped before the closed and barred gates. "Open them!" Tondo commanded in a loud voice. Several guards sprang into action, and in short order, the huge gates swung open, revealing the remains of the charred wagon pushed there so long ago.

"Clear that rubble!" Master Shergus shouted to the guards.

It took only moments for the wreckage to be cleared away. Tondo strode through the opening and marched forward, stopping about a stone's throw from the Wall. He heard the gates close, leaving him with an isolated feeling. There he waited as his excitement and nervousness increased, his heart pounding in his ears.

It wasn't long before a burly man of average height cleared the enemy mass and advanced with deliberate purpose towards him, stopping about fifty feet away. He was wide of shoulder and had a barrel chest. He appeared to be wearing a gravetum breastplate that covered his chest and back, buckled at the shoulders. He carried a shield on his left arm, and he brandished a longsword in his right hand. A mace was hanging at his right side. Unexpectedly, another man cleared the enemy host and advanced to the other champion's side. This one was much taller, nearly as tall as Tondo himself. He was muscular and wore leather or hide armor. Two short swords hung at his sides, and he carried two metrens, one in each hand; two antagonists were not what Tondo was expecting.

"This is outrageous!" he heard King Teg-ar-mos shout from atop the Wall.

"Two kings, two champions!" shouted King Pen-dow-mon, and then he laughed.

Tondo's resolve only strengthened. He expected treachery, and this was it. Nevertheless, he was ready for a fight, and his confidence did not flag.

His two foes began to advance, expanding the distance between themselves as they began to flank Tondo on either side. He could feel their tzaah reaching out to him. He detected two powers, one stronger than the other, but which tzaah belonged to which champion? He couldn't tell. Tondo expended much energy as he sparred with them, slapping away their probing thrusts of inner-power as he watched them prepare to flank him on either side, now only thirty feet away. He felt the weaker power push with considerable might, and he blocked it just as the tall man threw the metren in his right hand at him. Tondo quickly stepped aside, drew his Munnari blade in a flash, and sliced through the metren's wooden shank as it passed harmlessly by. The second metren was already on its way before the first one reached him. Tondo took another quick step and sliced it in two, as well, rendering both useless. The stout man rushed him as he struck down the second metren, and Tondo fleetly stepped aside as the man's first swing found only empty space. The tall man unsheathed his two short swords and began waving them in the air in a cascade of death and defiance.

Tondo unleashed his tzaah, and the wooden shank of one of the grounded metrens flew through the air and struck the tall man squarely on his armored shins, causing him to stumble, but he didn't go down. The tall man regained his footing and continued to advance as his two blades sliced through the air in a rhythmic torrent of threat. At the same time, the shorter champion turned and slammed his shield's edge into the back of Tondo's armored left side, and then his longsword slashed at Tondo's neck. Tondo's Munnari cuirass cushioned the shield's effect, and his parry caused the burly champion's sword to miss. He deftly stepped behind his attacker, avoiding the slashing blades of the taller man.

Suddenly, the shorter man's shield burst into flame, and he had to quickly discard it. Tondo could feel the burly champion's anger as his tzaah lashed at him like a whip of hot energy. Now, Tondo knew this was the man with the weaker inner-power. Again, he slapped it aside and advanced toward the shorter man with lightning speed as he swung his two-handed sword. His foe attempted to parry the blow, but Tondo's Munnari Blade cleaved through the man's longsword and bit into his foe's left shoulder, slicing through his gravetum armor and biting into flesh, but not as deeply as Tondo had hoped. The man howled in agony and fell to the ground, spritely rolling away as his ally quickly advanced toward Tondo again, both of his blades swirling in an avalanche of death. Tondo swung his blade up, and it shattered the sword in the man's right hand. In an instant, he felt a jarring pain as his hands were hit by something solid, knocking the Munnari Blade from his grip and sending it flying out of reach, landing in the dirt several yards away. He didn't look to find out what had caused it, but in one quick motion, he stepped into and behind the tall man as he unsheathed his blue short sword. Tondo rammed the sword's point into the tall man's back with such force that its bloody tip protruded from the front of the man's body on the right side. The big man arched his back and reflexively twisted, wrenching the sword from Tondo's injured grip.

Now, Tondo could see that the shorter man had regained his feet and was holding a mace in his left hand while his right applied pressure to the wound in his left shoulder. At the same instant, the tall man swung wildly at Tondo, and his blade slashed across Tondo's abdomen, but the sword ricocheted off his armor, missing the pteruges, and rending his naked right thigh, cutting deeply into flesh and muscle, causing his leg to buckle, and he fell to the ground. The tall man then collapsed and crawled away on hands and knees, howling in agony, the pommel and grip of Tondo's blade protruding from his back and its point from the side of his abdomen.

Tondo attempted to regain his feet, but his injured leg wouldn't respond. He lashed out at the other champion with his tzaah, but the burly champion simply lowered his head and advanced like a man charging into a gale, using his own tzaah as a defensive shield. Tondo quickly grabbed his tomahawk and threw it, guiding it with his inner-power. The blade slammed into the man's head, just below the hairline, and he dropped like a stone, twitching in the throes of death.

Tondo's one remaining and wounded adversary had regained his feet and advanced towards him, the bloody blue short sword still through his body. The enemy champion's remaining sword was leveled, ready to finish off the stricken and unarmed Tondo with blade and slashing bolts of energy. Tondo deflected the energy assault, causing multi-colored sparks to shower both antagonists. He prepared to receive his foe's attack. Tondo had no physical weapon left to fight with. His foe crept closer, looking for an opening in which to strike the killing blow. Tondo prepared a fire attack, and a ball of flame burst from nowhere and engulfed his attacker. In a flash, the flames exploded and scattered in all directions, the tall man having dispersed Tondo's assault with his inner-power.

The tall champion continued to advance; his pace was halting, and he stumbled forward, Tondo's short sword tip still protruding from the front of the man's body. Tondo saw his Munnari Blade lying nearby but out of reach. As his assailant lunged, Tondo's right hand swept through the air, and his Munnari Blade flew toward his assailant, slicing into the tall man's neck, sundering head from body. His torso dropped like a stone, convulsing in spasms of death.

Tondo crawled to his sword and used it as a crutch to regain his feet. He stood on his left leg, held his bloody blue sword high above his head, and gave a roar of victory and relief. The men on the Wall cheered and began shouting, "Tondo! Tondo! Tondo!" The fierce-looking outlander basked in their adoration as blood gushed from the wound in his right thigh.

After several moments, the king raised his arms, and the shout subsided. "King Men-dre-dor, King Pen-dow-mon, my champion has prevailed. You have lost, now you must submit!"

The two kings stepped forward in unison, and King Pen-dow-mon began to speak in a loud and angry voice. "We will not! This man is an evil sorcerer, for only one learned in wicked arts and dark magic could have defeated our two champions. I declare this contest a fraud, and you deserve to be executed for your deceit. Kill the child king's sorcerer!"

A large group of men charged toward the exhausted and wounded Tondo. He crafted a small fireball in the air in front of himself and blasted it into several of the charging men, immolating three attackers in an instant, but the others continued their advance, undeterred. He loosed another fireball, and two more of the charging horde died a flaming death, yet the remaining gang continued their charge. He launched a third attack, but it lost power as it advanced and dissipated before it reached the onrushing host. Tondo felt weak, but he held his sword high and balanced on his left leg, preparing to receive the enemy's assault.

From the periphery of his vision, he saw two flashes streak past him on either side; they were Ayascho on his left and Shergus on his right. Ayascho swept his arm in an arc across his front, and at least two-score of the charging host flew backward, falling to the ground in a heap of groaning bodies. Shergus nodded his head, and another two-score fell on their faces, as if tripped by an unseen rope, others stumbling to the ground over their comrades' prone bodies. Tondo's two defenders continued to advance, Ayascho with swords in both hands, and Shergus gripping his blue blade. Idop galloped up to Tondo on a samaran, jumped off, and threw the stricken king's champion onto his mount from the right side. Tondo grabbed the samaran's neck and swung his left leg over the saddle. Idop slapped the mount's haunches, and the beast charged back through the gates. Idop then went to the dead champions and retrieved Tondo's remaining weapons.

The three men made a guarded withdrawal through the gates, which were quickly slammed shut and barred. Tondo was helped off the samaran and carried to the king's tent, where his wound was treated by the king's personal physician. Idop instructed the physician on how to suture a wound properly, having observed how Tondo had done it while treating the prince. Before the physician completed his work, Tondo passed out from either the pain, loss of blood, or exhaustion—most likely a combination of all three.

Tondo awoke when it was night, and he could tell that dawn was still a long way off. Taahso's wrap lay over his body. He lifted his head. "Water, give me water," he weakly called. In an instant, Ayascho was there with a waterskin. Idop and Shergus quickly joined him as they wiped the sleep from their eyes.

"You've looked better," Idop jokingly told him.

"I've felt a lot better, too. How long have I been out?"

"Only a few segments. You've lost a lot of blood, though," Shergus informed him.

"My thanks to all of you for saving my life. I had nothing left after the battle. What's happened since then? What have the kings done?"

"Our king challenged the other kings' treachery, and he threatened them with the army, but they only laughed at him," Idop said.

"Yes, and then they made sport of him, the army, and you," Ayascho added.

"Good. Their overconfidence will be their undoing," Tondo told them. "Has anyone informed the army of this fight?" The three looked at each other, then shook their heads.

"I saw one of Mordez's allies heading south. I don't know why. Maybe he was sent to announce your victory to the city," Idop guessed.

"I suspect that messenger was sent to make mischief. I want you two to leave right now and meet the army. Tell them the challenge was won and I'm alive. Hurry now," he ordered. The two sub-commanders saluted and dashed out of the tent.

Master Shergus scowled and said, "We need to talk."

"About what?" Tondo wondered.

"I thought I trained you better. Look at you; you're a mess."

"Give me some credit, master; I'm the one who walked away . . . in a manner of speaking, that is."

"You neglected your training while building the army, and look what your dalliance has come to. After this is all over, I'm going to take you to task for allowing yourself to be touched."

Tondo frowned, "Unfortunately, twenty-two segments in a day are not enough to do all that was needed to be done. I've been in more battles than I wish to recall, and never once did I get the slightest wound. Now, I've earned a Purple Heart, but who's going to present it to me?" he lamented using the godspeak term. Shergus cocked his head and wondered what the Messenger was rambling on about. "Never mind," Tondo mumbled with a tired smile. He lifted both of his hands and noticed they were bandaged and swollen. He flexed his fingers and felt their stiffness, and the movement caused him pain. He removed the wrap from his legs and saw another bandage lying loosely over his injured right thigh. He lifted it and saw a huge gash, more than four inches long, sutured together, but already healing.

"Yes, that's an ugly wound, my friend, and it will leave an impressive scar, something you can boast to your children about," the master told him. "I've never seen anyone heal so quickly, though. The unnamed god looks favorably upon you." Tondo smiled and adjusted his wrap.

"Get me a damp towel; I want to get this war paint off my face." Shergus looked confused and then did as he was asked. Tondo scrubbed his face until it was clean. He leaned back, closed his eyes, and quickly fell asleep.

He slept all morning and into the afternoon. Master Shergus stayed at his side the entire time. When he awoke, an aide fetched some food for him—a block of gornbread—and some water. The king paid him a visit, and they talked for a short time. Tondo wanted to get out of bed, but Shergus and the king's physician wouldn't allow it, so he napped off and on for the remainder of the day.

A short time after last-meal, a messenger from the army arrived, sent by Ayascho and Idop. "What news do you bring?" Tondo asked the young man.

"Here, zerr," he said as he handed his commander a short leather tube. Tondo opened it and read the note. Shergus waited for him to say something.

"I knew it. Someone started a rumor that I'd been killed in the fight, and the commanders saw a drop in the men's morale. Ayascho and Idop have things under control now, but they suggest I meet the army so the men can see for themselves that I'm alive. First thing in the morning, I will ride out and meet the army as it arrives." Shergus was about to voice an objection, but Tondo cut him off, "No matter what anyone says about it. What's your name, son?" Tondo asked the messenger.

"I am Tretrio, zerr; second man, third rank, first brick, Ayascho Headquarters Troop. And a messenger," he replied in a strong and proud voice.

Tondo smiled. "Now, that's the response I would expect from a real warrior. What do you think, Master Shergus?"

"He seems to be a credit to your army. Tell me, young warrior, what do you think of this coming battle?" the master asked.

"We will prevail, zerr!" Tretrio shouted, but a sad look crossed his countenance.

"What is it, my boy? You look worried," Tondo said.

"Zerr, I know we will win, but I don't think I'll be around to see the end of the battle," the young messenger replied.

"Why is that?" Tondo asked.

"I have this feeling, zerr, a feeling that I will not survive the battle. I've felt this way for a long time now. I think I'm a coward," he admitted.

"Death is always a warrior's companion, so straighten your back, boy!" Master Shergus grouched.

"Master Shergus, he has. Otherwise, he wouldn't have earned a place in Ayascho's Headquarters Troop." Shergus nodded in recognition. "Tretrio, find a chair or a bench and sit beside me," Tondo told the young man, and the messenger complied. "Let me tell you about another young man who thought he was going to die in his first battle. He was no older than you . . . come to think of it, he was a lot younger. Well, this young man had a premonition that he would die in his very first battle. He had trained hard as you have; he prepared the best he could as you have; he listened to his leaders, just as you have, but he always had a nagging feeling in the pit of his stomach that he was going to die."

"Yes, zerr, that's how I feel," Tretrio admitted.

"The day of his first battle arrived, and this young man rode into the very thick of the fighting. Men on his right and on his left were wounded and carried from the fighting by the med-men. The battle lasted all afternoon, and by the time it was over, many warriors on both sides had lost their lives." Tondo stopped and gazed at the tent ceiling, seemingly lost in a memory.

"Megatus, what happened to the young man? Was he killed?" Tretrio asked.

"He survived; you're talking to him," Tondo admitted. Master Shergus smiled at the revelation, and Tretrio's expression turned to wonder.

"But megatus, you couldn't have been afraid. You are the bravest man in the world. Many say you can't be killed because you're the Messenger, the one sent by the great god."

Tondo lifted his bandaged hands and then uncovered his legs, revealing his stitched up thigh. "If I can be wounded, I can be killed. That's how the great god keeps me humble," he told the young man.

"Were you afraid when you faced the two champions?" Tretrio asked.

"Yes, I was. A man who goes into battle and says he's not afraid is either a liar or a fool. I'm neither, and you aren't either. It's how a man handles his fear that makes him courageous or a coward. If you let fear take hold of your heart, then you'll be a coward; however, if you take control of your fear and turn it against your foes, you will be brave and powerful. Let me look into your eyes," Tondo ordered. Tretrio leaned forward, and Tondo gazed into the boy's dark-brown eyes for several seconds. "Yes, I see a brave man. You'll do just fine. Your leaders will be proud of the way you handle yourself."

"Zerr, will I live?" the young man asked.

"Only the great god knows that. All I can tell you is, you'll be brave in the coming battle."

"Thank you, zerr. I won't let you down."

"I know you won't. Now, go and get something to eat. The aide over there will help you."

"Yes, zerr, and thank you, zerr." Tondo smiled as the boy stood, saluted, and exited the tent.

"Did you really see bravery in that boy's eyes?" Shergus asked after Tretrio had left.

"What I saw was a young man who needed to hear he'd be a brave warrior in the coming battle."

First thing in the morning, even before dawn began to break, Tondo struggled out of bed, wrapped his right thigh tightly, and hopped out of the tent, Master Shergus supporting him and protesting all the way. Shergus helped him onto a samaran, then mounted one himself, and off they ambled, heading south. By midmorning, they could see dust clouds in the distance, so they rode another segment and stopped. It wasn't long before the lead unit of the army appeared, led by Idop and Ayascho riding atop the howdah of Myron's raster.

When the lead brick saw their commander, they broke into cheers and began shouting, "Tondo! Tondo! Tondo!" with each step they took as they marched by. Myron was ordered to move the raster to the side of the road, and then a rope ladder was lowered. Idop, Ayascho, and Shergus helped Tondo climb the ladder to the howdah. When he reached the top, he stood, supported on his left leg, his injured right hand tightly gripping the flag pole that held the army's blue and yellow banner. There he stood in full view of every passing unit, fully geared-up in his blue Munnari scale mail, and with Taahso's wrap draped over his shoulders.

As each brick passed, the men took up the chant, "Tondo! Tondo! Tondo!" There was no longer any doubt that their revered leader lived, and the army's morale climbed to new heights. There he remained all day, and when his grip on the flag pole weakened due to his injured hands, Idop, Ayascho, and Shergus took turns supporting him. By the time the last combat unit had passed by, he was exhausted, and his wounded thigh was bleeding again; however, he wanted to remain for the benefit of all the support personnel, too, which were strung out behind the main body of the brigade. His lieutenants and Shergus argued otherwise, so he wearily agreed and had Myron guide the raster into the direction of the army's march, and they headed north with the bricks.

The army stopped a short distance from the Wall and made camp. Tondo called one last commanders' meeting that evening and issued his final orders for the upcoming battle, telling them it would take place on the following day. The king was impressed by the orderliness and discipline of the soldiers. He invited Tondo to his tent for last-meal, but Tondo was too exhausted from standing in the hot p´atezas all day, so he declined, expressing great regret.

CHAPTER 21

THE MUNNARI WAR

By morning, Tondo's wounds were much better, but he still couldn't put his full weight on his right leg. His hands were healing quickly, also, and the flexibility of his fingers had improved, but his hands were still swollen. He would have preferred to wear his wrap throughout the coming day, but it had become such a prize to him, he didn't want to risk losing it in battle, so he left it behind. He allowed his men to take the time to eat a good first-meal, and then he assembled the army near the massive gates of the Teg-ar-mos Wall.

He hobbled up the gate tower stairs and was standing above the gates, nearly fifty feet above the army, leaning on a metren for support, the king at his side. He scanned the army below and mumbled to himself in godspeak, "The die is cast." Speaking loudly to his warriors, he shouted, "Men of the Teg-ar-mos Brigade, today we go into battle. This is the moment you have been preparing for these many days. You are ready for this fight, and you will prevail!" he shouted. "You joined this army to gain your freedom and freedom for your families. You trained and prepared for your king!"

The chant of "Teg-ar-mos! Teg-ar-mos! Teg-ar-mos!" began and continued until Tondo raised his free arm for it to stop.

When the din silenced, he continued, "Look to the man on your right!" He paused. "Now, look to the man on your left! These are your brothers! Today, you fight for them!" The men cheered, and the foot soldiers began banging their swords against their shields, causing such a racket that birds nesting in the Wall took flight and scattered in all directions.

This went on for some time, then Tondo raised his arm again, and the cheer slowly subsided and stopped. He stepped down the tower stairs, trying not to limp, using the metren as a crutch until he got to his raster, which was positioned next to the stairs. He stepped onto its howdah, assisted by the commander's hornman. Tondo stood, gripping the flag pole.

"Open the gates! Hornmen, sound Advance! Drummers: March Beat!" he ordered. Half a dozen men with horns began sounding, including the young hornman riding with him on the howdah. The massive Wall gates swung open. As soon as the horns stopped, the drummers, who were standing in two parallel lines at the gates, took up March Beat as Tondo's raster proceeded through the opening. He continued forward, and several columns of the Tondo Headquarters warriors mounted on samarans funneled through the gates and then quickly fanned out in line formation between Tondo and the enemy. These mounted men would act as a screen in case the enemy chose to attack before Tondo's army had fully deployed.

For the next couple of segments, brick after brick passed through the gates and between the lines of drummers, taking up their assigned positions. From his perch atop the raster, Tondo could see everything unfolding just as planned. The enemy was also marshaling. He could see groups of men rushing from the east and the west to join the steadily increasing horde before him. Excitement filled his bosom, but he sensed a darkening feeling beginning to overtake him. He worried that it might have something to do with his weakened state or loss of blood, and he shook his head in an effort to clear his mind. As his men continued their deployment and the enemy mustered, Tondo felt as though he was going to faint. The darkness seemed to be invading his vision, and he clutched the flag pole tighter.

Finally, the last brick in his army assumed its position; the drummers finished their beat with a drumroll and then went silent. The foot soldiers had assembled their metrenas and waited. Tondo still labored under the feeling he was beginning to lose consciousness, and he tried again to shake the darkness from his head, but his vision continued to darken even more, and he felt chilled. His worry increased.

The young hornman standing next to him asked in a concerned voice, "Megatus Tondo, why is it getting darker? It can't be the end of day yet."

So, the hornman sees darkness, too, Tondo thought to himself in relief. He grabbed a corner of the flag, held it in front of his face, and looked into the sky.

"It's an eclipse!" he shouted in godspeak. "One of the moons is passing in front of the p´atezas!" he yelled in surprise using world-speak. He squinted his eyes, but all he could see was the black disk of a moon. He couldn't tell which moon was causing the eclipse. His entire army, the defenders on the Wall, and the enemy host to his front were all looking skyward; everyone was transfixed on the startling event. Tondo began hearing words of fear, of bad omens, and of an evil day from the men nearest him. He wondered how he could steel his men's resolve, for he knew morale and resolve were to be the most important elements in the coming battle.

As the final sliver of the p´atezas disappeared behind the black disk of the moon, the star's corona lit up and turned a cobalt-blue. Tondo noticed his blue Munnari armor glowing, and he unsheathed the Munnari Blade and held it high above his head. It, too, was glowing blue. His men began to cheer, and each lifted his Munnari weapon—sword, bow, metrena—high into the air as the entire army glowed under a halo of blue light. Tondo heard an audible groan of despair coming from the enemy host as they spied the phenomenon, and the entire enemy mass literally took a step backward in fear of what they were beholding. Tondo kept his sword raised high above his head, only lowering it when the eclipse's totality ended, and the corona disappeared. The foot soldiers began banging their assembled metrenas against the sides of their shields, and the noise echoed across the field of battle, further seeding doubt and dismay in their enemies' hearts.

Tondo waited and let the pounding beat work more fear and doubt into the thoughts and hearts of the enemy. As darkness was chased away by the returning light of day, he looked over his formations, noting each unit's unique ensign. He could tell, all was in readiness; it was time to launch the attack.

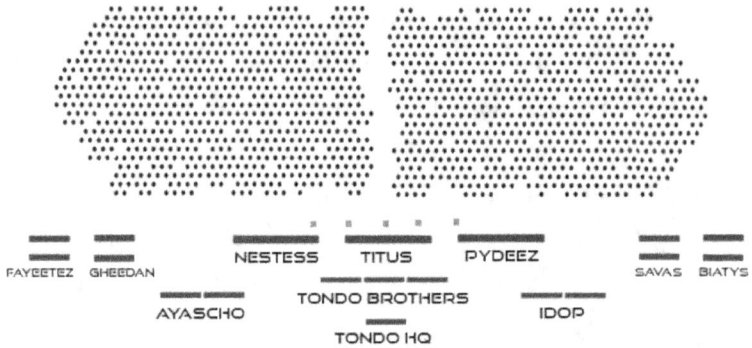

FAYEETEZ GHEEDAN   NESTESS   TITUS   PYDEEZ   SAVAS BIATYS

AYASCHO   TONDO BROTHERS   IDOP

TONDO HQ

"Hornman, sound the Advance to Battle," he calmly ordered the young man standing next to him. The hornman was fearfully gawking at the vast numbers of the massing enemy host. Tondo touched the young man's shoulder, and the hornman refocused. He raised his horn to his lips and blew, but only a pathetic squeak came out. "Spit, boy, and try again!" Tondo ordered. The young man spit, placed his lips on the horn's mouthpiece, and blew. The command blasted from the horn's bell and reverberated across the field. Commands were shouted up and down the line, and then the entire army, archer towers and all, moved forward at a slow and deliberate pace, the foot soldiers beating their metrenas against their shields with every step they took. An archer tower's massive wooden wheel ran over the three sacks of grain left behind by the two wicked kings, grinding the unsolicited offering into the soil.

The Teg-ar-mos Brigade's line of seven-thousand two-hundred-eighty-seven combatants stretched for more than a mile. The center was held by six troops of heavily armored foot soldiers and five archer towers, all under the command of Sutro Megato Titus. To his right were seven troops of heavily armored foot soldiers under the command of Sutro Megato

Pydeez. On Titus's left were seven more troops of heavily armored foot soldiers under the command of Sutro Megato Nestess. On the far right and left flanks of the Teg-ar-mos Brigade, Tondo had positioned his samaran soldiers; ten troops on each flank, arrayed in two main lines, one in front of the other and separated by about one hundred feet. Neva Megatus Ayascho's Headquarters troop and the accompanying troop of Ayascho Brothers were placed between and to the rear of the samaran soldiers and the foot soldiers. Neva Megatus Idop's Headquarters troop and the Idop Brothers troop were similarly placed on the right side. Directly in front of Tondo and between him and the front line of foot soldiers were three Tondo Brothers troops. He positioned himself and his Headquarters command behind them.

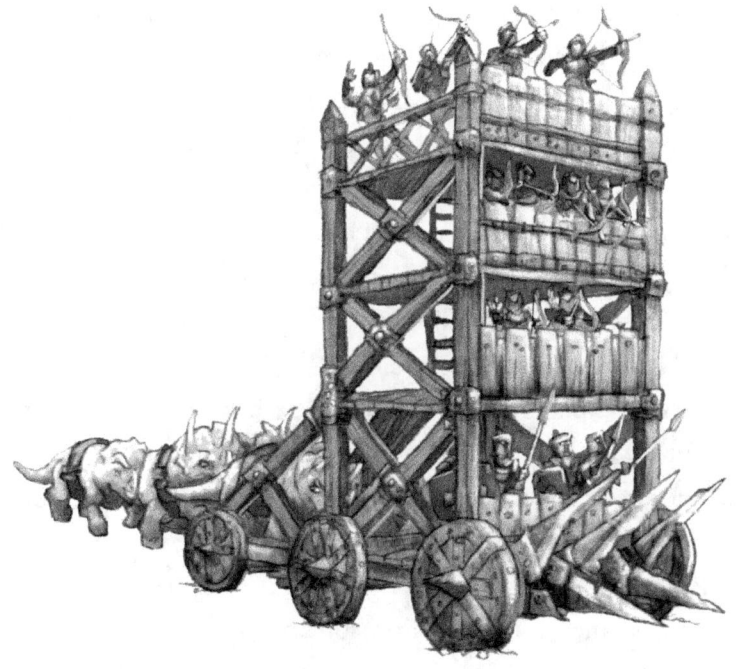

The foot soldiers and towers, pushed by armored thrice, moved forward at a slow and steady pace. The towers had limited maneuverability provided by the application of brakes attached to the giant wooden wheels. The samaran troops advanced at a much faster pace, trotting towards the enemy's flanks. A gap naturally opened between Tondo's foot soldier's line and the samaran troopers, but this gap was covered by Ayascho's Headquarters and Ayascho Brothers troops on the left and Idop's Headquarters and Idop's Brothers troops on the right.

From his perch on the raster's howdah high above the ground, Tondo could see that the combined army of the two allied cities was huge. He was grateful his men at ground level could not see the depth of its full numbers. The forces of each city were clearly divided by a wide gap of nearly one hundred yards. When it became clear that Tondo's samaran troops were heading toward the flanks, the royal banners of the enemy kings' contingents moved toward the threatened areas. From his perch atop the raster's howdah, Tondo could also see two more groups of men with banners, and he assumed these represented the two enemy princes' contingents he'd been told to expect. Other than that, Tondo could detect no other organization in the two separate armies before him.

He was expecting an enemy charge into the center of his line, but it wasn't immediately forthcoming. The enemy seemed to be paralyzed by what they saw advancing toward them. After a surprisingly long delay, he noticed a stirring in the center of the enemy horde, and then groups of men began moving toward his line; slowly at first, but as they advanced, they picked up speed, and soon they were at a full run. He could hear them shouting, "Kill the slaves! Kill the dung creepers!" as they charged. Other patches of men began to break away from the central mass and move towards his line in an uncoordinated charge. Enemy warriors on the flanks seemed confused and not sure how to deal with the mounted soldiers about to skirt around them.

When the mob in the center came within range of the archers, the center tower opened up with a volley of arrows that dropped nearly every man in their leading ranks. When the center tower fired, the other four towers fired their arrows, as they had been trained. The center tower fired a second time, and the other towers also fired, following its lead. A third time, the center tower fired, and the other towers followed suit. The three successive volleys stopped the enemy charge in its tracks. After the three initial volleys, the towers began a steady stream of independent fire, which continued to pick off the now terrorized assailants. The enemy's dead fell to the ground and tripped many others who were not hit, while the wounded cried out in agony and terror, seeding fear into the hearts of their unwounded comrades. Those wounded and still able to move tried to scramble away from the threat, but their retreat was thwarted by their own advancing men. Chaos swelled in the enemy line.

The samaran units started their drive around the enemy's flanks, and as they did, they fired their arrows into the unsuspecting enemy, dropping many and freezing the others in place. As the gap widened between Tondo's center and the samaran soldiers, his two senior lieutenants filled the gaps, firing arrows into any enemy group that attempted to advance.

The impetuous King Pen-dow-mon saw the threat to his left flank—Tondo's right—and charged with his guards into the approaching danger. On the enemy's right flank—Tondo's left—the more cautious King Men-dre-dor withdrew his contingent to a safer position, allowing some of his foot soldiers to advance toward the threat. Prince Pen-dow-mon, who was positioned near the center, took his men and headed for the gap separating the two armies. Prince Men-dre-dor seemed to waiver, not sure what to do with his contingent, his lack of experience clearly revealed.

The foot warriors continued their advance, and after a pause to loose their arrows, the archer towers were pushed forward again. It wasn't long before Nestess's men, in the left-center of Tondo's line, made first contact with the enemy mob. At about fifty feet from the enemy line, and by command, they flung their metrenas, impaling hundreds of their enemy. After loosing their deadly missiles, Nestess's first troop of nearly two hundred drew their swords, and with the shout, "Freedom!" they charged into a gaggle of over three hundred enemy and struggled to push them back. The troop took some casualties and was having difficulty holding their cohesiveness. The enemy slammed into their shields and pushed with all their might. Tondo's men jabbed at enemy warriors' abdomens, armpits, or knees with their short swords, their battle sandals digging into the turf as enemy soldiers began slipping and falling due to the blood-slick grass. Tondo watched as the troops' officers and non-officers scurried from place to place, moving men as needed and shouting orders. Nestess's second and third troops slammed into two other groups of the enemy, and they were having much better success. Tondo could see the enemy waiver under their unrelenting advance.

Tondo's desire was for all samaran troopers to use their bows and engage in melee only if they could attack a king or a prince. Biatys, on Tondo's extreme right, saw his opportunity to attack King Pen-do-mon directly and yelled, "Give 'em the metren!" His lead troop charged and slammed their metren lances into the Otterinian king's contingent, cutting down scores of enemy warriors. The mounted troop hit the king's men with all the force they could muster, but the king's guards hung tough, inflicting moderate casualties on Biatys's men. Biatys's other troops seemed to be hung up and unable to move further around the flank. Tondo could only guess that some unseen terrain feature, possibly a bog, must be causing his samaran troopers to stack one behind the other in a heart-pounding traffic jam.

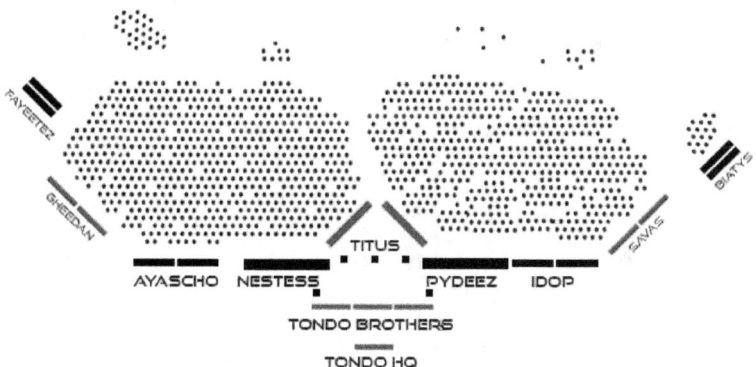

By this time, Fayeetez's lead mounted warriors on the extreme left flank had broken into the enemy's rear and began firing arrows into the surprised enemy's rear ranks. Gheedan's troops began to enfilade King Men-dre-dor's right flank, pouring arrows into his hapless defenders.

On the left-center, a group of enemy soldiers charged into Nestess's seventh troop and were stopped when they hit the shield wall.

"Look zerr, there stands Nestess, like a stonewall!" Tondo's hornman shouted and watched as a look of surprise, followed by a huge smile, covered his commander's face.

The enemy soldiers recoiled at the resistance Nestess's men put up as they hacked and slashed the enemy down. One of the Terratian groups who had engaged his men began to falter under the unrelenting assault of his heavily armored foot soldiers. The discipline and training of his troops clearly showed, and it wasn't long before the enemy mass broke and ran.

Other enemy groups charged into two of the towers, and using metrens and axes as missiles, wounded many of the archers, and sent both towers' lowest level into disarray.

All along the line, enemy conscripts engaged Tondo's well-trained foot warriors. At first, some enemy attacks seemed to make headway while others failed miserably, causing the attackers to become disrupted and confused. An enemy group was able to advance fast enough to engage one of Gheedan's samaran units, inflicting a surprising number of casualties by the ferocity of their charge; however, King Men-dre-dor could not see this gallantry, as he withdrew even further from the onrushing troops under Fayeetez's command.

"What dark power drives these dung creepers?" the king muttered fearfully.

Fayeetez's five troops continued their charge into the enemy's rear, Fayeetez himself at the front of his lead troop as he chased after the fleeing king. His other troopers followed, firing arrows into the backs of the unsuspecting foot soldiers as they charged past their stunned enemy's rear ranks. Gheedan's samaran troop, engaged by the enemy's charge, reacted by drawing their curved sabers—another Tondo design—and began hacking down the hapless attackers. A second samaran troop laid into them and sent the enemy fleeing for their lives after taking horrific losses for their gallantry.

Ayascho sat nervously on his mount. A gaggle of enemy warriors was haltingly advancing toward the gap in Tondo's line. His commander had warned him not to allow the enemy to attack Nestess's flank or break into the army's rear. He had to act; however, the image of a rampaging gorga slithered into his mind's eye, and he shuddered in fear. He clutched the gorga fang hanging around his neck, swallowed hard, and shouted, "Men, we attack! Follow me!"

He led the charge as the Ayascho Headquarters and the Ayascho Brothers troops slammed into the unfortunate cohort of enemy foot soldiers who had wandered too far forward, cutting down many with their long metrens held like lances. The enemy survivors of the charge broke and ran. As the Terratians began fleeing back to their line, Ayascho ordered, "Men, reform, reform!" His command was ignored, and he couldn't stop his men from chasing down the fleeing enemy. His warriors crashed into the enemy's main line and continued their deadly work.

Tondo watched as his line contended with small groups of the foes who had advanced and engaged his men. These enemy soldiers were aggressive and brave, but it soon became apparent they had no staying power. In some cases, their initial contact inflicted a fair number of casualties on Tondo's men; however, his warriors were armored, and the enemy was not, or if they were, their armor was significantly inferior. Tondo's lead ranks were also trained to withdraw after a few minutes of fighting, being replaced by the rank behind them, thereby always presenting the enemy with a fresh force with which to contend. When a rank withdrew, the men reformed at the rear of the brick and kneeled until ordered to stand and prepare to re-engage. They were also given water from the water-boys stationed in the rear.

As the troops advanced, the med-men moved into action and treated Tondo's wounded. They were instructed to carry any severely wounded to the rear aid station where they could be treated by physicians and nurses. Enemy wounded were to be left on the field unattended, not because Tondo didn't want them to be cared for, but primarily because he didn't have the resources to handle the flood of enemy casualties he guessed would be coming.

As the battle continued, the enemy's units began to break faster and faster. Often, when one enemy group broke, it caused a chain reaction, and other groups of enemy soldiers would also flee, although not directly engaged by any of Tondo's warriors. They crashed into the men behind them, throwing them into disarray, as well. Tondo could tell the enemy armies were already beginning to unravel; however, directly to his front, things took a turn for the worse. Several groups of the enemy managed to burst into the lowest level of two of the archer towers, and they were wreaking havoc with his archers and their protectors. Titus, reacting quickly, ordered several of his foot bricks to counterattack in an effort to beat back the enemy assault.

Tondo saw an opportunity to split the allied cities' armies in twain as the gap between them began to widen. He ordered his three Tondo Brothers troops at his front into the breach. He positioned his own Headquarters command where it could take advantage of any opening his Tondo Brothers troops made.

Two of Biatys's troops had now engaged King Pen-dow-mon's contingent; however, his other troops were still stacked up behind the lead units and unable to advance. Nevertheless, many of his men continued firing arrows into the enemy mass, pinning them in place. Savas's samaran troops also loosed their arrows into the front flank of the enemy, cutting them down in swaths.

Suddenly, a mass of enemy warriors overwhelmed the archers in tower four, causing the bowmen to leap from their levels and run for their lives, that is, if they survived the plunge unscathed. Smoke soon began pouring from tower four, and it wasn't long before it became a blazing inferno, causing the enemy victors to also flee for their lives. The sight of the flaming tower strengthened the morale of the enemy soldiers who witnessed it. Titus, whose responsibility it was to protect the towers, quickly formed up one of his reserve bricks and ordered, "To the tower! Follow me!"

The flaming tower inspired a large group of well-motivated enemy warriors to charge Idop's Headquarters troop. "Arm your bows!" he yelled to his men. Hundreds of arrows were quickly nocked. "Loose! Charge!" Idop commanded.

Scores of the enemy were cut down, first by arrows and then by sabers. The survivors of the charge then milled around in a dazed state. Several men from a different enemy group urged their allies to make a charge at Idop's elite Headquarters warriors, but the majority refused to budge, and the attempt failed before it even began.

On Tondo's right flank, King Pen-dow-mon's men continued to resist Biatys's mounted warriors' efforts to advance, but it was obvious, many of the king's men had already fallen, taken down by arrows, and it wouldn't be long before he would have to withdraw or watch his contingent collapse like so many others in his army.

Prince Pen-dow-mon advanced his contingent into the gap between the two allied armies, sensing the trouble that was about to befall the center. Prince Men-dre-dor also saw the threat, and he finally advanced his men toward the gap.

King Men-dre-dor turned his contingent around and readied them to face the onrushing Fayeetez. The mounted commander charged toward the king, and his samaran troopers began firing arrows into the king's contingent. As this was happening in the rear of the Terratian army, King Pen-dow-mon's men on Tondo's far-right flank could no longer withstand the relentless assault by Biatys's warriors, and the king's men broke, sweeping their king along in their headlong flight away from their crazed enemy. This ended the traffic jam and opened the pathway for all of Biatys's troopers to sweep into the enemy's rear.

Titus's counterattack was beginning to relieve the pressure on the archer towers, but they were still in danger. Idop's

Headquarters and the Idop Brothers troops crashed into the main enemy line, killing many enemy soldiers with their metren lances and sabers, sending others fleeing to the rear; however, a lucky throw of a metren by one of the Otterinian warriors pierced the neck of Idop's mount just above its barding, dropping the beast as Idop rolled away. He quickly stood, and a gaggle of enemy foot soldiers charged him. He raised his bow and nocked an arrow, picking off the lead attacker. This did not dissuade or slow the fallen man's comrades as they continued their charge, shouting oaths and profanities. Idop nocked arrow after arrow, and with each release, another Otterinian fell. Surprisingly, the entire charging mass halted and dropped to their knees, pleading for mercy. Idop stood tall, his back straight, an arrow still nocked, as several scores of enemy warriors surrendered to him rather than continue their charge into the maw of death rendered by this terrible foe with his magic weapon.

Pydeez reformed his foot soldier troops and was preparing another push into the enemy's main line. Ayascho's Headquarters and the Ayascho Brothers troops continued to guard the gap between the foot soldiers and the samaran troops attacking on the left flank, Ayascho himself hewing down enemy soldiers with vengeance and power; his men spurred on by his example.

Tondo took his Headquarters troop into the opening in the center of the enemy line, and his men fired their arrows into Prince Pen-dow-mon's contingent from long-range, felling many of the prince's guards and mounts. Fayeetez's personal troop, supported by his second troop, charged into King Men-dre-dor's contingent, throwing his men aside as they headed straight for the king. It was Tondo's order to cut off the heads of the two-headed viper, and Fayeetez was going to follow his commander's order explicitly. His metren pierced several mounted enemies as his armored samaran crashed into the enemy on the right and the left. When his metren broke by the ferocity of his attack, he unsheathed his saber and slashed his way onward, drawing closer to the king as royal guardsmen fell in large numbers. In a flash, Fayeetez was upon the hapless king, who sat on his mount, blinking in disbelief at the horde of crazed men and mounts crashing forward. Fayeetez's saber slashed through the air, and the king's helmet flew free with King Men-dre-dor's head still in it.

Titus had finally swept away the threat to the remaining towers, and the archers quickly reformed and began sending a hail of arrows into the enemy warriors who were not already engaged by any of Tondo's soldiers. Biatys began a race to catch the fleeing King Pen-dow-mon. His men fired volley after volley of arrows into the king's routed guards, dropping both man and mount. Tondo and his Brother troops tore through the breach between the two enemy armies and charged for the enemy princes' banners. When the royals saw the horror of lances bearing down on them, both princes turned and ran, their guards galloping off with them. This further exacerbated the waning morale of their conscripted warriors who witnessed their leaders' display of cowardice.

As word of King Men-dre-dor's death began to spread, the Terratian army started to unravel faster. The rear ranks, witnessing their army's increasingly futile attempts to halt the advancing horde, slowly withdrew, then their slow withdrawal changed into a trot. Finally, they began to flee for their lives at a full run, tossing aside their weapons. Successive waves of dispirited men peeled off the rear of the enemy's ranks and headed for the perceived safety of their camp.

King Pen-dow-mon's proud and impetuous panache had dissipated, and he was now fleeing for his life. "This can't be! The gods won't allow a king to be overcome by worthless slaves," he grouched.

Biatys's men continued firing volley after volley of arrows into the fleeing king's contingent, felling many a man and mount. As the king looked over his shoulder to see how close the enemy was, an arrow struck him in the right eye, and he tumbled from his mount. A handful of his most loyal guardsmen turned their samarans and charged into the advancing enemy in an effort to save their stricken sovereign. Biatys's men tore into them with a vengeance. The lifetime of abuse they had suffered as slaves drove them into a frenzy, and they cut down the king's freeborn guardsmen without mercy. King Pen-dow-mon struggled to his feet and staggered a few steps, holding with both hands the arrow's shaft that protruded from his eye socket. The first of Biatys's men to reach the suffering king put him out of his misery with a metren through the heart.

Prince Pen-dow-mon, unaware of his father's demise, regained his composure. "Men, into the breach!" he yelled. He turned his men around, advancing back into the gap. Tondo's Headquarters and his three Tondo Brothers troops were widening the breach between the two enemy armies, and Titus's men were holding the walls of the breach open.

The enemy soldiers who were still engaged with Tondo's men had lost their will, and they were now exhausted and parched. They began to crumble under the unrelenting press of the more powerful warriors of Tondo's army.

"Your Highness, Your Highness!" a Terratian royal guard called to Prince Men-dre-dor as he galloped up to him at halted his mount. "The king is slain. You now command the army!" he cried.

Prince Men-dre-dor went wild with rage. "Kill the slaves, every one! Kill the outlander savage! No mercy!" he cried, and then he charged his men into one of Fayeetez's troops. The slaves' bloodlust continued to burn, and his guards took a beating at their hands. Nevertheless, with rage in his heart, he and his men fought on, ignoring their losses; however, Fayeetez's men would not relent, and they tore into the prince's guards with the same crazed anger and vengeance Biatys's men had, slaughtering the freeborns with merciless retribution. Prince Men-dre-dor's courage soon failed him, and he turned his mount and ran for his life, but an arrow took down his samaran, pinning the ill-fated prince under its bulk. Fayeetez was the first to reach the luckless prince. He dismounted and approached the disabled and pinned prince on foot, preparing to run the man through with an enemy's metren he had retrieved from the field of battle.

"You're a pathetic sight, Your Royal Highness," Fayeetez spat.

"Spare me! I will grant you your heart's desire. Zanth, women, land; anything you ask is yours," the prince pleaded.

"Oy, how are the mighty fallen. You don't know how much pleasure it gives me to hear your worthless bribes. You are pathetic!" Fayeetez removed his helm, dropping it on the ground, brushing his long, black hair from his face, exposing the slave mark on his forehead. "I am Fayeetez, a worthless slave, but now, I hold your royal freeborn-life in the palm of my dung-slinging hand. Remember me!" Fayeetez's words spewed forth with all the pent-up hatred and guile within his bosom. He raised the metren and slammed its heel onto the prince's head, knocking him unconscious.

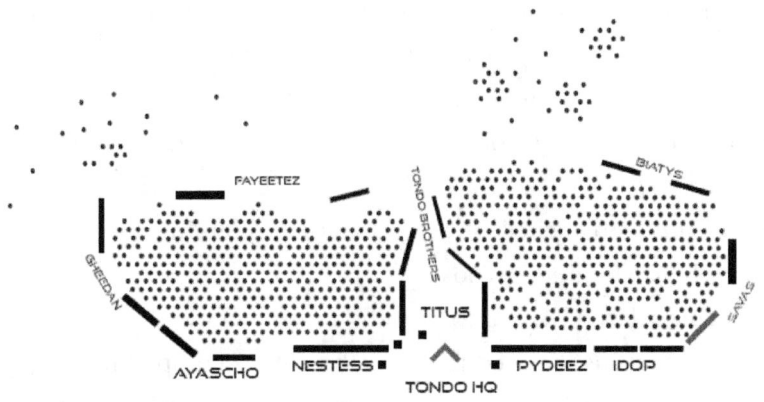

Tondo's Headquarters troop had become engaged with a very stubborn cluster of Terratians, and they stalled his advance. His men finally broke their enemy's morale, and the Territians began to flee. His battle-crazed men chased them down and ran into another enemy group; then they began slaughtering them, as well. Tondo had lost control of his troop and couldn't move them in the direction he desired as they laid into their enemy. Still, two of his Tondo Brothers troops slammed into Prince Pen-dow-mon's contingent, and the Otterinians broke. The prince's mount stumbled, and the prince tumbled to the ground. He stood and faced the onrushing horde.

"I am Prince Pon-dow-mon! You are but slaves!" he shouted. "If you drop your weapons, I will spare your lives!" He was silenced by a metren through the neck.

This was the twig that broke the raster's back, and the combined armies of the united cities dissolved into a mass of fleeing men, all rushing toward their camp, hoping beyond hope that the camp's guards could save them.

Surprisingly, one of Titus's foot troops broke ranks, dropped their shields, and chased after the fleeing men, unmercifully slaying all they overtook. Tondo could see the bloodlust in his men's eyes, and he knew they had gone berserk. He stood atop the raster's howdah glaring in disbelief. *Let them have their vengeance. They've earned it,* his inner voice compelled.

Tondo's disbelief slowly turned to appalling anger. "No, never!" he shouted in godspeak.

He ordered Myron to pull the raster out of formation and charge past his frenzied men. As the raster galloped by, Tondo shouted at his battle-crazed warriors, commanding them to reform. They refused to obey and continued their labor of vengeance for all the ill-treatment they had received as slaves. The raster reached the head of the troop, and Tondo threatened to cut down any man who passed him, but they would not listen or couldn't hear him above the roar of battle as the troop ran pell-mell toward the enemy camp. Tondo feared if his men reached it, his hysterical warriors would massacre every living thing there: men, women, children, and even animals. He could not allow such a shameful finale to mar such a great victory. He stewed in anger for a moment, and as his body began emitting a radiant red glow, a cloud of fire formed in the sky between his out of control men and the enemy camp. A spout of fire descended to the ground, and soon, a flaming whirlwind twisted its way back and forth as if daring anyone to approach. Tondo's men, as well as the fleeing enemy, stopped in their tracks and stared in wonder at the terrible sight before them. Tondo ordered Myron to guide the raster into the midst of his men, and he again commanded them to reform their ranks. This time, they obeyed. The enemy soldiers fell to their knees and begged the lucent commander not to burn them alive.

The whirlwind of fire remained for a while longer, and when Titus arrived to take command of his mutinous troopers, Tondo ordered him to place each man under arrest. The troop was marched back; their heads bowed in shame. The fiery whirlwind soon dissipated, and Tondo gripped the flag pole for support, having been exhausted by his effort.

Ayascho and Idop soon arrived together and sought Tondo's orders now that victory was secured. He told them to guard the enemy troopers and see to the wounded of both sides. He then ordered Fayeetez to reassemble his five samaran troops and follow him into the enemy's camp. The camp guards had lost their will to resist after witnessing the slaughter of their army and Tondo's whirlwind of fire. As his band of warriors entered the camp, the defeated soldiers and camp guards dropped to their knees in surrender and submission, laying their weapons at the feet of his raster and suing for mercy. He could see in their eyes and on their countenances the totality of their defeat. The enemy was spent, and with the loss of their kings, they were fully humbled. Tondo ordered the two kings'

possessions secured by his men, including a substantial cache of funds—more than five hundred thousand bhat from each conquered king's train. There was also a substantial amount of food supplies and other booty. He took control of it all, leaving just enough food to last the defeated host for only a few days. They were now completely at his mercy, and they knew it. He had the loot loaded onto wagons. It was then taken back to his army's camp on the south side of the Wall and placed under guard.

CHAPTER 22

A UNITED KINGDOM

Tondo ordered Myron to lead his raster on a tour of the battlefield. He needed to evaluate the situation and see just how much carnage had been inflicted upon friend and foe. As he began dealing with the myriad of questions his commanders were bringing him at the conclusion of the fighting, King Teg-ar-mos arrived, protected by his contingent and flanked by Master Shergus. "That was the most extraordinary thing I have ever witnessed. Truthfully, I doubted it could be done once I saw the enemy's true numbers, but that seemed to have little bearing on the battle. Your warriors swept them aside like a broom chases dirt. I will present you at a royal dinner tonight so all your peers can honor your magnificent achievement," the elated king proclaimed.

Tondo's expression soured, "My apologies, Your Highness, but there is still much to do. The battlefield is littered with wounded and dying men from both sides, and they must be tended to. The army must be looked after, and the men must be kept under control. I have witnessed some disturbing breaches of discipline, and that must not be allowed to fester and get out of control. There will be plenty of time to celebrate our victory, but tonight is not a good time," Tondo assertively told the king.

The young ruler had grown accustomed to Tondo's brusque ways, especially when he was disturbed, so he accepted the outlander's counsel without objection. "So be it then, but let me thank you here and now, on the field of battle, for your great victory. You have saved the kingdom and the Crown," the king told him as he raised his sword's grip in front of his face in salute.

Tondo bowed in recognition of the honor from his king, then said, "It's a great victory for us all, especially you, Your Highness. Now, you must determine what to do with this victory."

"What do you mean?" the king asked.

"You are now the ruler of all three great cities and their kingdoms. What do you intend to do about that?"

The king's expression changed to surprise. "I don't know. I never believed this could happen. I guess I've got some planning to do."

"Remember, Your Highness, rule with wisdom and humility," Tondo advised. Master Shergus was wearing a proud smile from ear to ear, but he said nothing. The king reined his mount aside and toured the battlefield, accepting the accolades and cheers of his warriors and the obeisance of the many wounded and defeated enemy soldiers scattered across the field of battle.

Tondo spent the remainder of the day tending to his men. All-in-all, they had performed brilliantly. As his men began to calm down from their adrenalin rush, they became more compliant with military protocols, and the command structure regained its full effect.

During his examination of the battlefield, he came across Tretrio, the young messenger who had come to the king's tent while his senior commander was recovering from his wounds. The young man looked up at his commander, saluted, and smiled proudly. Tondo returned his salute and gave him a wink.

As he continued inspecting the battlefield, many of the men began asking about the king's promise to free them, and Tondo answered that it would be forthcoming in due time, to be patient, and tend to their duties as assigned by their commanders. He could see that the men were worried the king might renege on his promise, and that thought had also crossed his mind, although he gave no inkling of his concern. Right now, though, his main burden was to get the wounded treated and the dead buried.

Once Prince Men-dre-dor regained consciousness, Tondo gave an order for him to collect as many of his men as he could and form them into work details for burying the dead. The prince halfheartedly began organizing some of his men, but neither he nor his followers were responding with any urgency, all having fallen into a funk after their dismal showing against the savage beast-man's slave army and their decisive defeat at its hands. Tondo sent both Ayascho and Idop, along with their Headquarters of samaran soldiers, to get Men-dre-dor and his men moving with more resolve, even under the threat of execution, if necessary, should they fail to respond with more vigor. At that moment, Tondo's greatest fear was disease sweeping through the ranks of the victors and defeated alike, and he would do all he could to mitigate that awful threat.

Tondo advised Prince Men-dre-dor he had ordered his physicians and med-men to treat the enemy wounded as soon as his own wounded were cared for. Shortly after the defeated prince passed on Tondo's orders to his men, Megato Ayetoz arrived with members of the King's Contingent and took the prince into custody.

Tondo continued to oversee his army and the defeated enemy, maintaining order on the battlefield. Late that night, he camped on the north side of the Wall with his warriors.

When Assembly was called the following morning, it was determined that eight hundred and three of Tondo's men were casualties; two hundred forty-six killed in action, and the remaining number were wounded; several were expected to die from their wounds. It was difficult to determine the number of enemy losses, but it was no fewer than twenty thousand. At least five thousand Terratians and Otterinians lay dead on the field or buried beneath it. Thousands upon thousands of wounded enemy warriors were lying amongst the unburied dead. Many women from the enemy's camp were walking through the bodies littering the field of battle, searching for a loved one. Mournful lamentations were heard day after day and night after night. The horrific stench of rotting bodies wafted through the air, and swarms of flying creepers and carrion birds descended upon the field of slaughter.

Tondo also received word that the king was dismissing the defenders on the Wall and allowing them to return to their homes. Tondo quickly sent a message to the men from his estate who were guarding the far eastern end of the Wall, ordering them to return to their homes and families. It was undoubtedly the most joyful command he had given in close to two spans. Not one of his men defending the Wall had died or been injured. His thoughts turned once again to the loss of the *Zerio* and its crew, several of whom had manned the defenses before volunteering to serve on the new ship.

For the next several days, Tondo oversaw the cleanup of the battlefield. The dead were buried, the wounded were treated, and all the arms, armor, and other implements of war left on the field and in the enemy's camp were secured. The enemy force was allowed to return to their homes, but not until all the important barons and lords from both defeated cities were taken into custody. Finally, after all was placed in order, Tondo marched his men south, through the massive gates of the Teg-ar-mos Wall, and they returned to their temporary camp.

As Tondo passed through the gates at the head of his men, he was greeted by Lord Riazon. "I said if you were victorious, I would be the first to honor you. I am a man of my word," the lord called. He bowed low as Tondo's raster passed. Tondo returned the lord's bow with a nod and continued on his way to his own camp. He had taken only short naps during the past several days, and he was beyond exhaustion. He retired to his tent, removed his armor, plopped himself onto his cot, draped Taahso's wrap over himself, and immediately fell asleep.

As a brilliant red p′atezas dropped below the western horizon, Megato Ayetoz awakened Tondo with a summons from the king. The army commander sat up, swung his legs over the edge of the cot, and began rubbing the wound on his thigh—it was throbbing and itching. "Yes, megato, what does the king want of me?"

"He has been in counsel with his officials for the past three days, and he wishes you to be there when he issues his decision concerning the status of the two defeated kingdoms," Ayetoz told him.

"Very well, I'll be there shortly."

An irked and tired Tondo took the time to wash the grime off his face, arms, and legs. He also replaced the badly soiled and bloody bandage on his thigh. *You know the king will dishonor himself,* an inner voice harped. *He will not free the slaves. That is your duty, your calling. Your warriors will follow any command you make. It is now your moment, your time to seize power. Claim the throne for yourself!*

He then put on his Munnari armor and armed himself with all of his weapons. He was going to present a powerful presence before the king, even in defiance of the order allowing only one weapon to be carried into the king's presence. His troubling thoughts were echoing in his ears as he prepared himself to act upon his seditious warning.

He quickly limped to the king's tent and was intercepted by Master Shergus. "What's this?" the priest asked as he took stock of all of Tondo's weaponry. "You're not planning to enter into the king's presence so armed, are you?"

"No one's gonna stop me! We will learn if the king nurtures the good seed of honor or the evil seed of dishonor," Tondo growled. He was in a bad mood for being rousted out after only a few short segments of sleep, and he was in no mood to let anyone tell him what he could or couldn't do. In addition to his worrisome warning, he also realized he was under the influence of victor's ego: a sense of supreme self-confidence and overbearing that often fell upon him after a victory. It was a feeling he had known before, especially when he felt he had cheated Death. Nevertheless, he was preparing himself to do battle with king and counselor, if necessary.

He presented himself before the guards in front of the king's tent, glaring at them and silently daring them to stop him from entering. After an awkward few moments, the intimidated guards stepped aside, not wanting to incur the wrath of the powerful megatus, king's champion, and deity's messenger; an outlander surrounded by a faint red aura and backed up by the famed temple sword master gripping the hilt of his sword. He stepped through the entryway, and Shergus followed him, the priest quickly kneeling to the king, who nodded, and then Shergus stood. The gathered men turned and stared at Tondo, each taking the measure of the fully armed and armored outlander, sporting a fierce-looking hairstyle, his red aura slowly fading from view. He could see the king sitting on his elevated throne near the center of the tent. Lord Riazon was the first to approach Tondo and offered him his hand, and they grasped each other's forearm. Many other men followed Riazon's lead, praising him and the army for their great victory. Tondo began to feel some relief, but he noticed Counselor Mordez standing off to the side, observing from a distance, displaying no emotion. Tondo simply eyed him and then turned his attention to the king.

"Welcome, victorious commander of the Munnari War. All hail Tondo!" the king shouted. The gathered men shouted, "Hail! Hail! Hail to the Victor!" Tondo bowed and felt a bit embarrassed as the center of attention, but his stern visage remained. The king then continued, "Now that everyone is here, bring in the defeated prince, barons, and lords."

Ayetoz signaled with his hand, and several men, led by Prince Men-dre-dor, who was sporting a huge bruise in the center of his forehead, were unceremoniously ushered into the tent and placed before the king. In addition to the prince, there were several important barons and lords from the defeated cities; however, they had lost the arrogant stance of royalty or gentry. Defeat was in their eyes, and fear was clearly expressed on their countenances.

"Prince Men-dre-dor, you are the only surviving member of the sovereigns who fought in the battle. Therefore, you will represent both of the defeated cities. You and those with you will now kneel and swear allegiance to me."

The prince hesitated, and Ayetoz gripped the handle of his sheathed sword, enticing the prince to act. The prince stepped forward, and as he did, the defeated barons and lords haltingly followed him. When the prince stopped, so did the others, and the prince hesitated again.

"Oy, do you need additional encouragement? This is what you expected of me, and now it is what I expect of you, my little chetzy. Proceed!" King Teg-ar-mos declared. The prince slowly dropped to his knees, the barons and lords following his lead. "Continue," King Teg-ar-mos urged.

"I, as well as the barons and lords present, and all citizens of Terratia and Otterina, swear fealty to King Teg-ar-mos for now and forever," the prince uttered, and the words trailed off until he was barely able to be heard.

"You will have to speak up. I want everyone present to hear your words. Now, repeat them loud enough for all these witnesses to hear clearly," the young king demanded.

In a loud, strong, but quavering voice this time, the prince repeated his oath, "I, as well as the barons and lords present, and all citizens of Terratia and Otterina, swear fealty to King Teg-ar-mos for now and forever."

"Very good; you may stand." The prince and the others quickly stood. The king continued, "It seems I am in a bit of a dilemma. You see, I promised my slave army I would grant them and their families freedom should they defeat your combined armies. No one really believed it was possible, but here we are. Now, as Counselor Mordez has pointed out, if I free the slaves in my kingdom, that would put us at a disadvantage because the other kingdoms would still have theirs." The king's gaze shifted from Mordez and fell upon Tondo, examining his expression and noticing that his army commander's hand was now resting on the grip of his sheathed sword. Tondo tried to maintain a poker face, not wanting to reveal his concern for the king's next words. The king continued, "I have decided, from this day forth, all three kingdoms will be united into one. No longer will they be referred to as the Kingdom of Teg-ar-mos, the Kingdom of Men-dre-dor, or the Kingdom of

Pen-dow-mon. Now, there is only one kingdom: The United Kingdom of Teg-ar-mos."

A cheer went up from all the victors assembled. The king let them continue their celebration for a long period and then raised his arms to silence them. The defeated men hung their heads in despair as they worried over the future of their lives and their holdings.

"Bring in the markerman," the king ordered. A man with a small wooden box was ushered in. He kneeled before the king, and then he was directed to a place at a table on the left side of the royal tent. He sat, opened the hinged lid of his box, and waited. "Prince Men-dre-dor, I have decided to allow you to become the governor of Terratia and its provinces, under the stipulation that you obey my commands. Can you accept this ruling?"

"Yes, Your Highness, you are most generous," the prince responded, much relieved by the king's generosity and mercy.

"Good. Now, my first decree to you is to have all the slaves under your governance set free," the king ordered.

Relief and joy filled Tondo's countenance, and he quietly uttered, "Praise Batru!" Counselor Mordez's shocked and hateful reaction to the king's demand was clearly visible to all.

Prince Men-dre-dor was stunned. "I can't do that. The gentry would never allow it," the prince cried.

"Ha, this is the choice I present to you, then. Either you free the slaves as I have commanded, or all the commoners, gentry, and royals remaining in the defeated cities will be enslaved themselves, starting with you," the king declared as he pointed to the markerman. The prince swallowed hard and looked to his defeated barons and lords for help. As his eyes scanned their faces, they only lowered their heads. The king stood and ordered, "Set your slaves free or become one yourself!"

The prince shuddered under the threat, glanced toward the markerman, and began to speak, "By the authority granted to me as governor of Terratia, I declare all slaves be freed as of this instant." As the prince watched, the markerman slowly closed the lid of his wooden box.

"Very good," the king said. "Since I have yet to assign a governor for Otterina, I will declare now, before all these witnesses, that all the slaves in that city's jurisdiction be freed, also." He looked over the men before him and continued, "A new day has dawned in the United Kingdom. Slavery is abolished for now and forever."

Tondo almost jumped for joy, but he kept his decorum, although he couldn't hold back the huge smile that filled his face. He noticed Counselor Mordez's look of scorn, but he chose to ignore it.

"Prince Men-dre-dor, you may inform the stewards of the defeated cities and provinces they are allowed to keep their holdings. Megato Ayetoz, you may remove these cavaliers and see that they are treated with the respect due their rank. But remember this, you defeated ones, I will not tolerate any mischief by any of you. You have witnessed the power I wield. Today, I have been generous. Don't make me regret my generosity, for if you do, you will rue that day for the remainder of your lives," the king declared as the conquered men were cleared from the tent.

"Megatus Tondo, step forward," the king ordered.

"Yes, Your Highness?" Tondo asked with a bow.

"Assemble the army in the morning. I will make my proclamation to them personally, and I have some other business to attend to in their presence, as well," the king told him.

"By your command!" Tondo replied with gusto. The king stepped down from his elevated seat and took Tondo by the forearm. The others gathered around them and offered congratulations to both the king and the outlander. Counselor Mordez remained near the tent wall, avoiding the pressing throng surrounding the two heroes and looking more angry and glum than before.

The king's assembly slowly broke up as the gentry withdrew from the tent in twos and threes. Tondo was the last to leave, and he bowed a respectful bow to the king. He returned to his own tent and removed his sword belt. He stood staring at his sheathed Munnari blade, a sword he was about to raise against his king and friend. He recalled his seditious thoughts and felt shame. With anger burning in his spirit because of his frailties and weaknesses, he loudly proclaimed, "I will never again allow myself to be driven by the Tempter's cunning deceit!"

The morning was overcast, and the smell of rain was in the air; however, by the time the army was assembled before the south side of the Wall, the clouds had begun to break, and rays of light poured through the gaps in the clouds. The men had heard rumors throughout the night that the king was about to grant them their freedom, even though Tondo had said nothing about it to anyone. After all of the bricks had formed up, and after an interminable wait of half a segment, the king exited his huge tent, strode to the top of the Wall, taking his position on a foot-high dais above the massive gates overlooking his slave army.

"Warriors of the Teg-ar-mos Brigade," he began, "you are the gallant victors of the Munnari War. Because of your effort and sacrifice, a new kingdom has arisen, comprising all three old kingdoms; The United Kingdom of Teg-ar-mos. Last night, We sent a proclamation to all corners of this new kingdom that states: 'By royal decree, all slaves are to be freed immediately.' Not only have you freed yourselves, your women, and your children, you can also take credit for the freedom granted to all other slaves in this new kingdom."

The men could not contain themselves and began to shout, "Teg-ar-mos! Teg-ar-mos! Teg-ar-mos!" and this went on and on.

Tondo smiled and noticed the joy on Ayascho's face, as well as Idop's far below. Tondo leaned over to the king and whispered in his ear, "This is a great moment in history. Your name will be forever remembered for this decree." The king smiled and allowed the adulation from his army to continue.

The joyous and cheering warriors were not about to let up, so finally, the king raised his arms, and the soldiers slowly quieted. The king began to speak again, "We have some other proclamations that need to be presented at this time before the body of the army."

The king nodded to one of his counselors, and the man stepped forward and shouted in a loud and clear voice, "Neva

Megatus Idop and Neva Megatus Ayascho, present yourselves before the king." The two men scrambled up the stairs and kneeled before the king in front of the elevated dais.

"You may stand," the king quietly uttered. In a loud voice for all to hear, he continued, "Neva Megatus Ayascho, We grant you citizenship in the kingdom." He then placed a hand on each man's shoulder. "Furthermore, We advance Neva Megatus Idop and Neva Megatus Ayascho to the rank of tetzae. Let the scribes record it. Let the heralds proclaim it!" Both men bowed, and Idop couldn't restrain the tear that slowly trickled down his cheek. The king turned the men around, and they faced the army as the king continued, "All hail the victorious commanders!"

The men in the army, as well as the guards on the Wall, began to shout over and over, "Hail! Hail! Hail to the Victors!" Tondo smiled and shouted as loudly as he could until the raucous din slowly quieted.

"Sire Idop and Sire Ayascho, you may return to your commands," the king told them, and the two men quickly scurried down the stairs and returned to their posts in front of the army.

The king nodded to his counselor again. "Megatus Tondo, present yourself before the king!" he shouted for all to hear.

Tondo was taken aback when his name was called. He'd received his reward when the slaves were freed. *What else does the king have in mind for me,* he wondered? He took the few steps necessary to place himself before the king's dais and bowed.

The king returned his bow, placed both of his hands on Tondo's shoulders, and shouted in a loud voice for all to hear, "Megatus Tondo, for gallantry in defense of your king as Our champion, and for your extraordinary efforts in eliminating a threat to the kingdom posed by the combined forces of Terratia and Otterina, We advance you to the rank of tetzus!" The king turned Tondo until he faced the army and then shouted, "All hail Lord Tondo!"

Everyone began to chant, "Tondo! Tondo! Tondo!" The shout continued, and when Tondo raised his arms to silence everyone, they refused to stop. The chant went on, and Tondo soon turned crimson-red with embarrassment. He never liked being the center of attention, and even though he wanted to disappear into the cracks between the stones, he was forced to endure this flattery.

Finally, to his relief, the king raised his arms, and the shout began to trail off. "Lord Tondo," the king said in a quiet voice, "you may dismiss the army."

Tondo saluted the king, performed a crisp About Face, and loudly ordered, "Commanders of the Teg-ar-mos Brigade, march your men to their camps and dismiss them!" His command was repeated down the line, and then the bricks made an About Face and peeled off, one after the other, marching back to their camp.

"I still owe you a dinner of recognition and honor for your achievements. It will have to wait until I return to Anterra. I hope you won't consider it a slight against you," the king said apologetically, no longer using the royal We.

"Please, Your Highness, I can wait. I hope it won't be like the one your father gave me," Tondo told him.

"Ha, I remember how you left during the final match. That was quite the contest. Did I ever tell you, Scar Face slaughtered

Ugly?" Tondo just stared at the king with contempt. "Maybe I can choose a more . . . how shall I say . . . a more genteel manner in which to honor you."

"Thank you, Your Highness, that would be much appreciated," Tondo replied.

The two men remained on the Wall, watching the bricks march off one-by-one. The king and the new lord shared a few comments and enjoyed the moment. When the last brick began its march to camp, Tondo limped down the stairs, mounted his samaran, and followed the army.

CHAPTER 23

A DREADFUL WARNING

When Tondo arrived at the brigade's camp, the men began cheering him again. They were beside themselves with joy. They breathed the exhilarating air of freedom for the first time in their lives, and it was making them giddy. He didn't want to quash their celebration, but he assembled his top commanders and reminded them to maintain order and discipline. He would not allow this happy moment to be turned into a shameful exhibition. The commanders fully understood his concern, so they made sure the word was passed that nothing dishonorable would be tolerated. Any soldier found violating military discipline or King's Law would be dealt with sternly. A few men had to be warned, and those who didn't heed the warnings were taken into custody and allowed to celebrate the remainder of the day in bindings and under the watchful eyes of dour guards angered by their assignment.

Tondo enjoyed the company of his troops all afternoon, moving from one group of celebrants to the next while wearing Taahso's wrap. Later, he retired to his tent, where he wrote a short note to Maaryah, and then he ordered an aide to have an army messenger take it to the estate in the morning. There was much he wanted to tell her, but he wouldn't say it on paper. He had to share his feelings for her in person while gazing into her beautiful golden-amber eyes.

Shortly after he'd finished his note, Ayascho and Idop arrived. He hadn't had the opportunity to congratulate them since the king's morning proclamations. "Sire Ayascho, Sire Idop, please join me." He called his aides and ordered, "Bring food for three, and wine for the two junior gentry," he said with a sly smile, for he was no longer the most junior of the kingdom's elite. "Make sure it's the good food and wine we liberated from the defeated kings," he added. The aides saluted and scampered off. "Let me congratulate you two on your new titles. How does it feel to be special again, Sire Idop, my friend?" Tondo teased.

"Oy, not as special as you, Lord Tondo," Idop countered.

"Now that I'm a sire of this new kingdom, what am I supposed to do?" Ayascho wondered.

"Beats me," Tondo mumbled in godspeak. He continued in world-speak, "I don't know what a lord does, either."

"Aren't you proud? You've achieved the highest rank a non-royal can attain. Also, you're now a Zumar, a kingmaker. Not bad for an outlander-savage-beast-man from the Wilderness," Idop chided.

"Are you suggesting I let the hair on my face grow long again?" Tondo laughed.

"Yes, I am, and maybe you could let it cover your head, too. Why in the names of the Five Shadows did you do that to your hair anyway?" Idop quipped, referring to Tondo's Mohawk.

"I like Tondo's hair this way. I think I might do the same," Ayascho admitted.

The aide returned with a platter of meats and cheeses, and another aide placed two pitchers on Tondo's small camp table, one full of wine and the other full of cool water.

"Ah, look at that, meat! Dig in boys, eat your fill," Tondo told them as he stabbed a couple of slices of meat with his Munnari dagger.

The three ate their fill, sharing war stories while they ate. Ayascho and Idop drained the pitcher of wine and called for another. They soon became quite fuddled. The three laughed and joked with one another, totally unloading all the anxiety and stress that had weighed them down for nearly four spans.

As they continued relaxing and enjoying each other's company, Master Shergus joined them with Pahno at his side. Idop looked up at the master from his seat and asked in a slurred voice, "Oy, great master of the terrible wooden blade of punishment, what brings you here? Do you not approve of how we gained our glorious victory? Do we need a few strokes to set us on the right path?" Ayascho simply smiled at the master and lifted his cup to him in salute, then downed the remainder of the wine still in it.

"What's wrong with these two?" Shergus grumbled.

"It seems the wine has gone to their heads. Please excuse them; we're celebrating our victory," Tondo explained.

"Tutor Pahno has brought word from the Sutro Seer pertaining to you, Ayascho, and the king. Come with me to the king's tent."

"Tutor Pahno?" Tondo wondered. Both priests nodded. "Congratulations on your advancement, tutor." The young priest simply smiled at the compliment and bowed. Master Shergus then turned and exited, Pahno at his heels.

"Come on, Ayascho, duty calls," Coleman said as he slapped him on the knee. Idop raised his cup in salute, downed the remainder of his drink, and tipped over backward in his chair. Apparently, he had passed out. Tondo let him lay there, figuring it served him right for his disrespectful remarks to Master Shergus.

The four men stood outside the king's tent. After a short wait, a king's counselor invited them in. "Ha, Master Shergus, Lord Tondo, Sire Ayascho." The king studied the other priest. "I don't remember you," the king admitted.

"Tutor Pahno," Master Shergus announced. Both priests then kneeled before the king, and Tondo bowed. Ayascho was about to kneel, but Tondo grabbed his arm and had him bow, and when he did, he nearly tipped into the king.

"What's the matter with him?" the king wondered. "Is he ill?"

"Yes, Your Highness, he is. It's called overindulgence," Tondo told the king using the godspeak term.

"Hoy, I hope it isn't serious," the king commiserated as Ayascho swayed to and fro. "Why have you called this meeting?" the king asked, looking to Tondo for an answer.

"Master Shergus informs me, the Sutro Seer has a message for you, Ayascho, and me," Tondo explained.

"Master Shergus, what message do you bring from His Eminence?" the king asked.

"It's a summons, Your Highness. He wishes to speak with the three of you as soon as possible," Shergus told them.

"Did he say what this summons is about?" the king wondered.

"No, Your Highness," was the master's simple reply.

"Of course not. Why should I expect an explanation? Very well then, we will leave first thing in the morning," the king told them.

The others nodded and left the tent, Ayascho's upper arm gripped tightly by Tondo, the new sire's feet hardly touching the ground. After they had exited, Master Shergus pulled Tondo aside and handed him the sealed letter he had written with Maaryah's name scribed upon it. "There's no need for me to keep this any longer," Shergus told him with a grin.

"Thank you, my friend," Tondo responded. When Tondo got back to his tent, he dropped the note into his travel trunk.

Before he left for the city, Tondo placed a hungover Idop in charge of the army and instructed him to deal with the men who had defied orders on the field of battle. He also told him to grant the rest of the men leave, but no more than a third of the army could be gone at a time. It was up to their brick commanders to determine who would be allowed to take leave first and that the leave was to be no more than forty days. Every man would be expected to report back to duty no later than that. Idop asked a few questions while rubbing his pounding head, and then Tondo was gone.

A few days later, King Teg-ar-mos, Ayascho, Tondo, and Master Shergus were standing in front of the doors leading to the Hall of the Guardians. Master Shergus gave the other three instructions. "I will not be going with you. Tondo has done this before, so he will be your guide. When the Guardians ask for your name, respond with King Teg-ar-mos the Unifier; Ayascho of the Wilderness; and Tondo, the Messenger."

"King Teg-ar-mos the Unifier?" the king wondered.

"Yes, you are now the Unifier as proclaimed by the Sutro Seer after consulting with the unnamed god. It signifies a great honor. Now, once you have been given permission to pass, you must advance down the hallway; do not stop nor tarry in any way. As I have explained to Lord Tondo before, a breach by anyone can result in the death of all. You have seen their power, so do not test them. Are my words clear?" The three nodded, but they said nothing. "Then, it is time for you to proceed. I will be waiting here for your return."

Tondo pushed open the ornate and heavy doors, quickly stepping into the hallway; the king and Ayascho following. Shergus then closed the doors behind them.

The Guardian nearest Tondo turned its head, scanned him with a blue laser beam, and spoke in its metallic voice, "Who wishes to pass?"

"Tondo, the Messenger," was his reply.

"You may pass."

The Guardian, on the other side of the hallway, turned and scanned the king. "Who wishes to pass?"

"King Teg-ar-mos, the Unifier," the king responded nervously.

"You may pass."

The first Guardian scanned Ayascho and asked, "Who wishes to pass?"

"Ayascho of the Wilderness," his voice was quavering as he looked up into the huge Guardian's helmed face.

"You may pass."

The three men quickly marched down the hallway, Tondo leading with the king and Ayascho side-by-side, close behind him. Ayascho's eyes were full of wonderment as he gazed upon the huge statue-like Guardians lining the hall. The king was duly awestruck by the powerful temple Guardians' numbers. When he reached the end of the hall, Tondo opened the doors to the Outer Sanctum and stepped in. After the other two had entered, he closed the doors, turned, and looked for the Sutro Seer. He was sitting on his little bench, his eyes closed, and his chin resting on his chest. If his lips hadn't been moving, Tondo would have thought him asleep. After a few moments, the Sutro Seer's eyes opened. He looked over each visitor and then stood.

"Welcome again, Lord Tondo. You have been a very busy man since our last meeting. You have done well for an outlander from a very distant place. Has the infliction of pain on your foes pleased you or sorrowed you?" the Seer asked with concern in his voice.

"It has made me sad, Your Eminence," Tondo told him.

"Do you feel compassion for those you defeated?" the Seer wondered.

Tondo could tell the Seer was worried about how the war had affected him. "I have no animosity to those we defeated. I felt their suffering and spared as many as I could," Tondo said.

The Sutro Seer's face radiated his satisfaction with Tondo's answers. "You are indeed the Messenger." He walked to the king and began to kneel.

"Please, Your Eminence, that will not be necessary," the king told him.

"Oy, thank you, my son. These hard floors are merciless on an old man's knees." He turned to Ayascho and placed his hands on the young man's shoulders. "Ha, the man from the Wilderness. The great unnamed god favors you very much."

"I don't know who the unnamed god is. My god is Batru; he is the one I follow," Ayascho answered.

The Seer looked stunned, and his right hand covered his mouth in surprise. "How do you know that name, child?"

"It is a name I have known all my days. It was taught to me by my taahso when I was a boy. It is also the name the great god has given my people; we are the Batru," Ayascho explained.

"How is this possible? How can you, a wild-man from the Wilderness, know this thing? You must come from a special people; a people close to the heart of the Great One," the Seer said.

"That I cannot say, but my people follow the teachings of Batru. Is the unnamed god Batru? Why wouldn't you call him by his name?" Ayascho asked.

"His name is too sacred to repeat. Only the Sutro Seer is allowed to know his name, and he is never permitted to announce it. This is very unexpected, at least for me. And yet, he has summoned you, and it is my duty to reveal his will unto you," the Seer explained. He turned and faced Tondo and the king. "What you have learned here is not to be repeated," he said in a stern and serious tone. Both men nodded, and the Seer faced Ayascho again. "Let me look into your eyes, young one. Let me examine your soul," the Seer ordered. Ayascho blinked and waited. The Seer moved his face within inches of Ayascho's and stared into his brown eyes, but only for a short moment. "I see you have chosen to nurture the good seeds, just as the Tondo has. The unnamed god desires you to receive his blessing."

Ayascho dropped to his knees, spread his arms wide, and bowed his head. "Great Batru, I am your servant. I will always follow your ways. How may I serve you?"

The Seer placed his hands on Ayascho's head and began to speak as if he were saying a prayer. "My child, I have seen your works, and they are pleasing to me. You are to return to your village without delay. There is a great work for you to perform there. Many of your brothers and sisters suffer at the hands of evil men. You are to save them and then help the Tondo in his continuing struggle. Embrace the seed of hope and reject the seed of discouragement." The Seer removed his hands from Ayascho's head and said, "Please stand, my son." Ayascho immediately obeyed. "You must heed the great god's call, for your sake, for the sake of your people, and for the sake of us all," the Seer warned.

"What does that mean?" the king asked.

"He understands and will obey; that is all that's necessary," the Seer told him. "Your Highness, may I?" the Seer asked as he drew nearer to the king. The young royal looked uncomfortable, so the Seer stopped and waited.

"Is this really necessary?" the king asked.

"Yes, if you are to receive the will of the unnamed god," the Seer explained.

"Very well then, you may proceed," the king responded reluctantly.

The Seer gazed into the king's eyes for a long time, and then he stepped back. "I see a struggle within you; a struggle between what you feel and what you do. You must learn to embrace the good seed of humility and starve the evil seed of pride. This same advice was given to your father, and he chose to set it aside. I hope you are a wiser man than he. Your kingdom will receive the great god's blessings only if it follows righteous principles," the

Seer told him. The king did not respond, and his eyes turned to Tondo. After a few moments, the Seer addressed the king and the new lord. "Now for the two of you: you have much to do. Tondo, you are to accompany Ayascho to his home. Leave as soon as you are able; haste is your ally. When your work there is done, you are to return alone, for you have much to do here, as well. Do you understand?"

"What work, Your Eminence?" Tondo wondered.

"You will understand after your return," the Seer told him. Tondo nodded. "Good. Now, Your Highness, King Teg-ar-mos the Unifier, you must also prepare. There is a new and greater threat rising in the south-lands." Tondo could feel the hairs on the back of his neck stiffen because of the dreadful warning. The Sutro Seer continued speaking to the king, "You must prepare to face its wickedness. It is powerful and merciless, and it desires to crush all beneath its heel. You are to build an army, an army more powerful than the one Tondo built for you. You must take men from all three great cities in your unified kingdom and add them to the army you already have. Tondo is to be your army's commander, and he will prepare the others for their important roles in this struggle. Do you understand?"

"Yes, but who or what is this evil you speak of?" the king asked.

"It is our nemesis, a more sinister threat than what we have just faced. This creature is unmatched by any mortal power from this world," the Seer warned as his eyes turned to Tondo.

"But we have the Messenger. Certainly, we cannot lose," Ayascho stated.

"This evil creature is as powerful as the Messenger, possibly even more so. It will take the combined efforts of many to defeat it, if that is at all possible."

"Why would the great god have me leave at such a crucial time?" Ayascho asked.

"It will become clear as you follow his counsel in faith, child." Ayascho simply nodded. The Seer looked into the eyes of each man, searching to their very core. He inhaled deeply as if bolstering his strength, then he said, "You are the hope of Munnari. Take heed and prepare well." He closed his eyes and uttered a silent prayer. After a long pause, he stepped back and began speaking again, "It is now time for me to resume my meditations. Please excuse me." He returned to his bench. The king was about to ask another question, but Tondo ushered him through the doors before he could voice it.

The king chose to remain in the city, but Tondo and Ayascho hurried back to the army's camp. While on the trail north, they passed a steady stream of army warriors going south, having been granted leave. Among them was Sutro Sestardus Harmon. "Zerr, I am taking my leave and will be returning to the estate to visit my daughter. Is there a message you would like me to deliver for you?"

Tondo thought for a moment, then said, "Yes, Harmon, wait here." He found paper, quill, and an ink pot in his pack and wrote a message to Maaryah; it simply gave her authority to run the estate until he returned. He wanted to say much more; he desired to pour out his heart to her, but he couldn't and wouldn't do it in a note. When he finished the single page, he folded and sealed it, pressing his newly acquired lord's sealing ring into the still-warm wax he'd heated with his tzaah. He then returned and handed Harmon his letter.

"Tell her, I will return as quickly as I can, but it may take more than a span. Also, tell her I would like to continue our conversation; the one we started the night the red moon covered the blue moon. She will understand," he said with a smile. Harmon looked at him in puzzlement, but he did not ask for an explanation. The two grasped forearms in friendship, embraced, and then they were off, heading in opposite directions.

"Victory! Victory!" the messenger shouted as he galloped onto the Tondo Estate manor grounds. It was late afternoon, and everyone was still engaged in their daily labors. A young woman came running out of the barn. The messenger galloped over to her. "Where's lady Maaryah?" the messenger asked.

"She's at the gorn granary, overseeing the loading of wagons being sent to the city. Did you say, 'victory?'" she asked.

"Yes, victory! The war is over!" the messenger shouted with glee and galloped off. He was one of Tondo's regular messengers tasked with relaying communications between his senior commander and Maaryah, so the messenger was familiar with the estate's layout.

Maaryah had just finished supervising the loading of five wagons filled with gorn sacks, the remnants of the last harvest. They were to depart first thing in the morning for Anterra. As she exited the granary, she saw the messenger approaching at full gallop. That was unusual, and, at first, worry gripped her.

"Victory! The war is over!" the messenger shouted as he rode up to her.

"Did you say the war is over?" Maaryah excitedly asked as she hopped up and down on her toes.

The messenger quickly dismounted, "Yes, lady Maaryah, the war is over. Victory! The kingdom is saved!" he exclaimed. He reached into the leather message bag hanging at his side, pulled out a folded paper, and handed it to her. As Maaryah read, her smile grew. It was a note from Tondo informing her the war was indeed over. That was exciting news, but that was not the part of the message she focused on. Tondo wrote that he would return to the estate as soon as possible, and when he did, he wanted to spend some time with her and share his thoughts and feelings. Her heart leapt. *Could he possibly have affection for me? Dare I hope such a thing?* She reread his message, trying to glean more clarity from its few short lines. It was maddeningly vague; however, her hope soared, and she began hopping up and down on her toes again.

When she stopped, she addressed the messenger, "Oeto, you must join me and the others for last-meal and tell us everything you know. I must go now and see that everyone learns of this wonderful news."

Maaryah sent riders across the estate to inform everyone that the war was over, and the king had prevailed. She declared a three-day rest period for all, culminating with a grand celebration on the manor grounds beginning at midday on the third day of rest. When she had finished with this task, she went to her cottage, refreshed herself, and waited for her senior helpers to join her for last-meal as they did every evening. Usually, her assistants gave reports on their assignments and received their duties for the next day from Maaryah. This night, Oeto would be making his report on the great battle.

The army messenger was a bit intimidated, being the solitary male at the table. The only solace he had was the fact that all in attendance, save one, carried the mark of a freedman. The only woman without a mark was Wandra, Scholar Pammon's bondmate, who was now acting as the estate's school teacher while her bondmate served on the Wall. Maaryah had insisted the school remain in operation, and children old enough to attend be sent there and not to the fields until the afternoon. Maaryah had learned the importance education played in lifting someone up; she, herself, being the prime example.

Maaryah allowed Oeto time to enjoy his meal before she asked him to make his report. The army messenger shared his perspective of the battle while posted near Megatus Tondo's command raster, awaiting orders from his commander. It took half a segment or so for him to explain what he had witnessed.

"Fifty thousand enemy? How many men did Sire Tondo command?" Maaryah asked.

"A few more than seven thousand, lady Maaryah," he told her.

"That can't be right," Wandra said with surprise.

"I heard Megatus Tondo and Neva Megatus Idop talking after the battle, and those are the numbers they said," Oeto explained. The women exclaimed their shock and wonder and carried on many side conversations until Maaryah stood and got the attendees' attention.

"Please, Oeto, continue," she encouraged. She took her seat again.

"We knew we couldn't lose because the great god blessed us. Just before the battle was to begin, the blue moon covered the p´atezas, and all our blue weapons glowed. We knew we had the unnamed god's support."

"We saw a black disk growing over the p´atezas, but the darkness quickly fled. I wonder why?" Maaryah was puzzled. She didn't understand that the shadow's track of the eclipse's totality did not cross the estate. "What else can you tell us?"

"That's all I can tell you about the battle. A few days later, the king assembled the army and gave everyone their freedom. And I don't mean just everyone in the army; I mean everyone in all the kingdoms. Slavery is ended, everywhere," he said with emphasis.

"Everyone? Everywhere? Are you sure?" Maaryah asked in wonder.

"Yes, lady Maaryah, everyone. I heard it from the king's own mouth. The whole army did. The king told us that our victory not only freed ourselves, but we freed every slave in the new United Kingdom of Teg-ar-mos," he explained as his expression lifted with pride. The table erupted in another round of exclamations and side conversations. Maaryah's joy was full, and she allowed her guests to carry on until they voluntarily quieted down and waited for the messenger to continue.

"Oeto, is there anything else to report?" Maaryah wondered.

"Ha, lady Maaryah. Neva Megatus Idop and Ayascho were made sires of the kingdom, and the king made Megatus Tondo a lord."

"Tondo is a lord?" Maaryah was smiling broadly.

"Yes, lady Maaryah. For winning the battle and serving as king's champion," Oeto told her.

"King's champion?" Maaryah wondered.

"The kings of Terratia and Otterina challenged King Teg-ar-mos to a contest of champions rather than armies. This was just before the big battle. They tricked King Teg-ar-mos, and Megatus Tondo had to fight two kings' champions at the same time. He won, but he was wounded," Oeto told the guests.

"Tondo was wounded? How badly?" Fear and worry were etched on Maaryah's face.

"He was sliced on the thigh pretty bad. While the army was marching to the Wall, a king's counselor rushed down the formations proclaiming Megatus Tondo had been killed. Everyone was afraid, and some men started weeping. We thought all was lost. Then, Neva Megatus Idop and Ayascho arrived and told us he was alive and only wounded. Then, as we continued our march to the great wall, we saw him standing on top of the command raster. Everyone cheered, and some men even cried. I'm not ashamed to admit I was one of them; they were tears of joy."

"Is Tondo all right?" there was a quaver of anguish in Maaryah's voice.

"I think so, lady Maaryah. He's been limping around camp talking to everyone. One thing did seem odd, though. He was wearing a heavy fur cloak on a warm day. But I don't think that means nothing." Maaryah remembered he wore that same cloak after his hand was injured. She didn't give it a second thought and was relieved to hear Tondo seemed to be recovering.

The women had many questions, and Oeto spent more than a segment answering them as best he could. After that, the women departed and enjoyed three days of rest.

Harmon arrived at the estate a couple of days after the victory celebration, and the first thing he did when he arrived was to search for his daughter. He found her in a gornfield, examining it for planting gorn at the start of the next season. She watched as men and women worked it.

"Papa!" she exclaimed when she saw him. They ran to each other and embraced, and he lifted her off the ground.

"My wonderful daughter, I have missed you so much." He put her down and held her at arm's length. "You look rested; much better than when I last saw you. How have you been?"

"I am fully rested, Papa. When word of Tondo's victory reached here, I gave everyone three days' rest. I nearly slept through all three days. How is Tondo? When will he arrive?" she asked excitedly.

Harmon took a deep breath as a look of concern crossed his face, for he knew the news he was about to relay would devastate his precious girl. "Tondo and Ayascho have been sent into the Wilderness by the Sutro Seer. Megatus Tondo asked me to give you this," he said as he handed her the note. He watched her closely as concern and worry claimed her while she read.

"Oy, Papa, this can't be! Why are the gods treating me so cruelly?" she began to weep openly. Harmon embraced her again and began to stroke her hair, just as he had done when she was a child. She melted into his arms, and he could feel her shake as she sobbed. She then pulled away. "Papa, I must go to him. How long before he leaves?" she asked.

"I don't know, my daughter. He was returning to the brigade after his meeting with the Sutro Seer. He will need to choose men who will go with him into the Wilderness. I guess he'll leave shortly after that is done, and after he gets the carts, thrice, and supplies he'll need. It could take a few more days, maybe a wernt, but no more," Harmon guessed.

"I must leave now, this very instant," she told him.

"Maaryah, it's unlikely you will reach him in time."

"If I must, I will catch up to him in the wasteland," she replied.

Harmon could see there was no stopping his daughter. "Let me get our mounts ready. We'll take four. That way, we can keep two fresh. We can travel faster that way."

"You just got here. I'll go alone," she told him.

"I will not let my daughter make such a long journey to the army's camp by herself, let alone into the wasteland. You get some supplies, and I will ready the mounts."

"But Papa . . . "

"Never mind, daughter, do as you're told," he sternly ordered.

"Yes, Papa." She dashed off, and in less than half a segment, the two were mounted and ambling northward.

Tondo took a few days to plan and record orders for the brigade, then he and Ayascho began selecting twelve men from a plethora of intrepid volunteers who desired to accompany their senior commanders into the Wilderness. It took a few more days to assemble the supplies, carts, and a couple of thrice. Just as all was ready, Hermanez came into camp.

"Boatmaster, it's good to see you. How have you been?" Tondo exclaimed upon seeing the outlander. They grasped forearms and then embraced.

"The king summoned me shortly after I docked, and guess what he did! He made me a citizen and a tetzae for helping to save the kingdom." The other two congratulated him. "Ayascho, the king told me you are returning to your home. You must be excited."

"Yes, I am. But the journey will be long and dangerous," he said.

"I've been examining my charts, and I think there's an easier and faster way to get there. Here, let me show you." Hermanez had his charts, maps, and logs with him. They were his most prized possessions, far more valuable to him than their considerable weight in zanth. He spread a map out on a nearby table, and the three men scrutinized it.

"I understand you still have the map Myron made. Is that true?" Hermanez asked.

"Yes, I do, somewhere in my travel trunk," Tondo replied and went to his tent and rummaged through his personal items. "Ah, here it is." He handed Hermanez the map that was burned into a leather pelt and rolled up like a scroll. Hermanez unrolled the leather and studied it closely.

"Good! Just as I thought. If you look at Myron's map, you can see how the mountains run north and south along this way. If you follow them down to here, you can then compare their location on his map and see how that matches mine. Ayascho's village is right about there, and you can see it looks to be only a few days travel from that cove," he said as he pointed to a place on his map. I can take you to this point in about seven to ten days, and if Myron's map makes any sense, you can walk the remaining distance in, say, another ten to twenty days. That is if you can find a pass through the mountains. What do you think?" Tondo and Ayascho closely examined his map and then Myron's. They looked at each other and smiled.

"This would be much better than two hundred days in the Wilderness and the wasteland," Tondo stated with glee.

And another two hundred for you to return. Also, we won't have to worry about those awful biting varmints or the giant birds," Ayascho added.

"Ha, land-piranha, terror birds, and the return trip; can't forget about all that. If we follow the boatmaster's advice, we could be there in less than a detzamar. We'll do it! We can reduce our team to three others and replace the thrice with three pack samarans. How are we going to get from the ship to land safely when we get there; the terrors?" Tondo wondered as he pointed to the cove on Hermanez's map.

"Let me worry about that. I'll figure out something," Hermanez promised.

"Okay, I'll leave that in your hands. We should leave tomorrow. It will take us about four or five days to reach the dock," Tondo said.

"Let's see," Hermanez mumbled as he examined one of his logs. "Ha! If we arrive at the dock by midday on the fourth day from today, we'll be able to sail that afternoon. If we arrive later than that, we'll have to wait until midmorning of the next for the tide to turn."

"Okay, let's get this show on the road. I've changed my mind. I want to leave right now. Ayascho, secure three pack animals. I will tell the men and choose the three who will go with us," Tondo told them.

"I don't envy you, Tondo. There are going to be some very disappointed faces when you tell them of your decision," Ayascho warned.

"I'll make it up to them somehow," Tondo promised.

Hermanez folded up his documents and placed them in their leather case. Tondo and Ayascho dismissed themselves and headed in opposite directions. By midafternoon, the little caravan left camp.

Maaryah drove her samaran relentlessly. She kept forcing it to gallop, and finally, Harmon grabbed her reins, and they stopped.

"Daughter, I know we must hurry, but we can't abuse the animals this way. We'll kill all four of them. I will take the lead and push them as fast as they can go, but no faster."

"Yes, Father, you are wise. I'm ashamed of myself for treating them so cruelly. Please take the lead," she told him with deference.

They continued on their way, Harmon pushing their samarans as hard as he dared, changing mounts often. When daylight faded, he'd stop and make camp, allowing the beasts to rest and forage for nourishment. Maaryah always pleaded to go on "just a little longer," but Harmon warned of unseen hazards in the dark that might injure their mounts, so she reluctantly complied.

It took Harmon and Maaryah five days to reach the brigade's camp, and he was warmly greeted by his warriors. "Where is Megatus Tondo?" he asked.

"Sutro sestardus, he and his men left for the Wilderness three days ago," a warrior answered.

"Papa, we must catch them," Maaryah told him in desperation.

"Yes, my dear, we'll head north immediately."

"Begging your pardon, sutro sestardus, but Lord Tondo went south, southwest actually. The boatmaster . . . what's his name?" the man asked as he looked to his friends.

"Boatmaster Hermanez," Maaryah clarified.

"Yes, my lady, that's him. Ha, he came into camp a few days ago and met with Megatus Tondo and Neva Megatus Ayascho. And then all their plans changed. They chose three men, packed up some samarans, and headed for his boat," the man told them.

"Oy, Papa, that means they're going by sea. If we hurry, we can catch them," Maaryah cried in desperation.

"Yes, my dear, I'll do what I can. Soldier, fetch us two strong mounts; the ones we have are spent. Quickly now, we don't have time to waste," Harmon ordered. "Also, fetch us a sack of gornbread." The men scurried off, and in less than half a segment, Harmon and Maaryah were on their way again.

Tondo's group reached the bluffs overlooking the floating dock—the one the king had built during the siege. The *Anterra* was drifting serenely offshore. Hermanez shouted and waved. The anchors were pulled aboard, a sail was raised on the ship, and the *Anterra* slowly made her way to the dock. The men and pack animals moved down the dock road and onto the dock itself. The pack samarans balked at stepping onto the planks that extended from the ground to the dock, so the men blindfolded them and urged them forward. Soon, the beasts were secured in the ship's hold. By then, it was nearing midday of the fourth day of their travel from the brigade's camp.

Hermanez sniffed the air, then turned to Tondo. "My lord, I smell a change in the wind. It smells like land."

"Oh, is that significant?" Tondo asked.

"All I can tell you is that it's unusual. Normally we get the Zerio, the southwesterly wind, but we may see a northeasterly picking up. That would be to our advantage," Hermanez told him.

"The great god favors us even with the wind," Ayascho noted.

"When can we depart?" Tondo wondered.

"The tide is about to ebb, so we'll be underway by midafternoon, my lord," Hermanez explained.

"Very well," Tondo told him, "I'm going below to secure my things," he told the ship's master and Ayascho.

"I'll go with you," Ayascho said. The two disappeared below decks, and Hermanez began shouting orders to his boaters as they prepared for departure.

Harmon and Maaryah drove their fresh mounts hard. The samarans were strong and responded well to their urgent rush forward; however, even the strongest samaran must rest, so Harmon reduced their pace to an amble, which was comforting for both animal and rider. When Harmon thought the beasts were rested enough, he picked up the pace. They had left the brigade's camp in the late afternoon, and he knew they wouldn't be able to catch Tondo until the next day if they were to catch him at all.

By late afternoon of the following day, they arrived at the cliffs overlooking the dock. They dismounted, rushed to the edge, and looked down. The dock was empty; it was obvious, the ship had already departed. Maaryah began to sob, tears streaming down her cheeks. She wiped them away with her sleeves, but they kept coming.

Harmon scanned the horizon and saw the *Anterra* in the distance. "Look, child, over there. It's the boat!" he shouted.

She wiped the tears from her eyes and stared into the distance. "We're too late, Papa! He's gone. I may never see him again," and then her tears began flowing once more. She turned and fell into her father's bosom, and he enveloped her in his comforting arms and began stroking her hair.

"He'll return, my daughter. The gods favor him, and he still has much to do. That reminds me. He asked me to give you a message. I almost forgot about it."

She pulled away and looked into her father's face. "What is it, Papa? What did he say?"

"He said, he'll return as quickly as he can. And also tell you, he wants to continue the conversation the two of you began the night the red moon covered the blue moon. He said you would know what he meant."

A broad smile covered her face as she looked out to sea, "I'll be waiting for him."

Tondo and Ayascho stood at the front of the bow, feeling the wind on their faces, mingled with an occasional salty spray. The ship was moving along at quite a clip; the northeastern wind was pushing the *Anterra* along as fast as she had ever moved before. The ship cut through the small sea swells, causing the bow to rise and sink. Tondo turned and looked back toward land—the Anterra Peninsula—slowly slipping away in the distance. He thought he could see some people standing atop the cliffs, high above the dock. They were only tiny dots, so he didn't think anything of it.

His thoughts turned to Maaryah, and he wondered what she was doing at that instant. He recalled a memory of her smile as she sat on a bench before the fire in the guesthouse, sewing or mending one of his shirts. His heart yearned to be with her again, to touch her, to look into her lovely eyes once more. For an instant, he thought of ordering Hermanez to turn the ship southeast and head to his estate so he could be with her, but the Sutro Seer's urging of haste jumped into his mind and chased away the thought.

He turned back and looked toward the horizon and the red glow of the setting p´atezas to his right. Out of the corner of his eye, he caught a glimpse of movement and looked to see a huge dorsal fin pass near the starboard bow. He followed it with his eyes, then turned and looked into Ayascho's face, who had also seen it. They looked at each other as grins of surprise covered their faces, neither saying a word. They turned back and followed the terror's path until its fin sank beneath the swells. Tondo's eyes looked to the horizon again, watching the p´atezas as it sank slowly from sight.

In the golden glow of dusk, a memory crept into his thoughts, a memory of family and friends. Sadness filled his heart as he thought of the suffering his mother and father must be going through, having now lost both of their sons, or so they must believe. He wished there was something he could do to alleviate their pain, but that was impossible.

His thoughts shifted to how exciting his life had become since he arrived on this world. He thought of his newly gained powers and status and the happiness he had brought to so many people, extending from the Batru village to the new United Kingdom of Teg-ar-mos. He smiled because of these accomplishments, and joy filled his soul. *Nurturing the good seeds has its benefits,* he thought. Many referred to him as the Messenger, but the message he carried was simply the love he had in his heart for his fellow man, an innate desire he had nourished from his youth on another world.

His thoughts soon turned to the future. What would they find at Ayascho's village that required this urgent passage? Who or what is this nemesis he must face? Would he ever see Maaryah again?

He closed his eyes and pretended he was home, sitting in his chair, lost in thought as he weaved a basket, a fire burning in the hearth of the guesthouse, Maaryah sitting nearby. *Ah yes,* he noted, *my thoughts always return to her.* He yearned to be there with her again, in his home. Then he fully realized, *Yes, indeed, this world is now my home.*

PRONUNCIATION GUIDE

b´ This low-pitched popping sound is made by pursing the lips together, rolling them inward, and releasing them, creating a low-toned pop.

p´ This high-pitched popping sound is made by pursing the lips together, extending them forward, and releasing them, creating a high-toned pop.

t´ This clicking sound is made by placing the tongue against the palate, and pulling it down, making a sharp, clicking sound.

WORD	PRONUNCIATION
Ab´as	ă b´ăs
Ada	ā´ dä
Adia	ā´ dī ä
Ayetoz	ā´ ē tōz
Agganor	ăg găn ŏr
Andent	ăn´ dĕnt
Anterra	ăn tĕr´ rä
Ardo	är dō
argent	är´ jĕnt
Atura	ä too ră
Ayascho	ī´ ä shō
Bardas	bär´ dăs
bataro	bä´ tăr ō

WORD	PRONUNCIATION
Batru	bă´ troo
Bazi	bā´ zē
Bazio	bā´ zēō
Ben-do-teg	bĕn´ dō tĕg
betzoe	bĕt zō´
bhat	bhăt
Braydo	brā´ dō
Buffo	bŭf fō
Chashutza	chă shoo´ tzä
Chashutzo	chă shoo´ tzō
Dada	dä´ dä
Danner	dăn´ nĕr
Demeos	dē´ mē ōs
defetane	dĕf´ ĕ tān
detzamar	dĕtz´ ä mär
divitz	dīv´ ītz
doez	dō´ ĕz
Dondi	dŏn´ dē
Doros	dō´ rōs
Du	dū
Duba	doo´ bä
Dubo	doo´ bō
Dumaz	doo´ măz
Edder	ĕd´ dĕr
Endet	ĕn dĕt´
Eos	ēōs

WORD	PRONUNCIATION
Ezihod	ē zī´ hŏd
Eos	ē ōs
Fayeetez	fā ēt´ tĕs
Fidus	fī´ dŭs
Fino	fē´ nō
Gangorno	găn´ gōr nō
gartz	gärtz
gee	gē
Gheedan	gē´ dăn
gorga	gōr´ gä
gravetro	gră´ vĕ trō
gravetum	gră´ vĕ tŭm
Grazius	gră´ zē ŭs
Gund	gŭnd
Gute	gūt
ha	hä
habaga	hä´ bä gä
Hani	hă nē´
Harmon	hăr´ mŏn
Haro	hä´ rō
Hermanez	hĕr´ măn ĕz
Hunder	hŭn dĕr
Idop	ī´ dŏp
Ios	ī ōs
Iroesadeen	ī rō´ să dēn
Isse	īs sē´

WORD	PRONUNCIATION
Magheedo	mä gē´ dō
Matti-mas	mä tē´ mäs
meashe	mē´ shĕ
megato	mĕ gä´ tō
megatus	mĕ gä´ tŭs
Maaryah	mär ī´ ä
Men-dre-dor	mĕn´ drĕ dōr
Mordez	mŏr dĕz
munna	mŭn´ nä
Munnari	mŭn´ nä rē
Munnevo	mŭn´ nē vō
Munnoga	mŭn´ nō gä
Myndron	mĭn drŏn
Myron	mī´ rŏn
Namad	nä´ mäd
Namada	nä´ mäd ä
Nestess	nĕs´ tĕs
Nestor	nĕs´ tōr
Nevesant	nĕv ĕ sănt´
Nita	nē tä´
Nu	nū
Numo	nūmō
Oetan	ō´ tăn
Oeto	ō tō
Ootyiah	oo tī´ ä
p´atezas	p´ātĕ´ zäs

WORD	PRONUNCIATION
p´oez	p´ōĕz
Pahno	päh´ nō
Pammon	păm´ mŏn
Pannera	păn´ nĕr rä
Pemmet	pĕm mĕt
Pen-dow-mon	pĕn´ dŏw mŏn
Pendor	pĕn´ dōr
Perdiz	pĕr dĭz´
Pershon	pĕr´ shŏn
Ponti	pŏn tē´
Pontus	pŏn´ tŭs
Ponti	pŏn tē´
Pontus	pŏn´ tŭs
purrant	pĕr´ rănt
Pydeez	pī´ dēz
Rao	rā´ ō
raster	răs´ tĕr
regum	rĕ´ gŭm
Remmo	rĕm´ mō
rezus	rē´ zŭs
Riazon	rī´ ä zŏn
samaran	săm´ ä răn
Sassin	să´ sĭn
Savas	să´ văs
schazu	schä´ zoo
seshtane	sĕsh´ tān

WORD	PRONUNCIATION
sestardi	sĕs tär´ dē
Sevootyiah	sĕv oo tē´ ä
Shadi	shă dē´
Shergus	shĕr gŭs´
Seemo	sē´ mō
Soidentee	soy dĕn´ tē
Stasenar	stă´ sĕn ăr
sutro	soo trō´
taah	tä
taahso	tä´ sō
Tangundo	tä´ sō
Tanzi	tăn´ zē
Teema	tē´ mä
Teg-ar-mos	tĕg´ är mŭs
Teness	tĕn´ ĕs
Tenny	tĕn ē´
T´erio	t´ ĕ rē ō
tetzae	tĕt´ zā
tetzus	tĕt´ zŭs
Tiro	tĭ´ rō
Titus	tī´ tŭs
Tondo	tŏn´ dō
todo	tō dō´
Tono	t´ ō nō
T´orbin	t´ ŏr bĭn
Tretrio	trĕ´ trē ō

WORD	PRONUNCIATION
Tuffen	tŭf fễn
Tumtuo	tŭm´ too ō
tuntro	tŭn´ trō
Turvy	tŭr´ vě
tzaah	tzä
Tzani	tză´ nē
Tzeecha	tzē´ chä
Tzeechoe	tzē´ chō
tzonoe	tzō´ nō
Tzorbin	tzŏr´ bĭn
Uragah	ŭr ä´ gä
Varios	văr ē´ ŏs
Verdeto	vĕr dē´ tō
Vihi	vē´ hē
Wandra	wän drä´
We	wē
wernt	wĕrnt
Yos	yōs
zanth	zănth
Zerio	zě´ rē ō
Zet	zĕt
Zethus	zĕth´ ŭs
zin	zĭn
Zossemo	zŏ sē´ mō
Zosse	zŏs´ sĕ
Zue	zoo

PREVIOUSLY INTRODUCED CHARACTERS

NAME	ROLE
Atura	Atura is assigned to Coleman by the Batru village chief. He is to become her provider, and she is charged with teaching him world-speak, the native tongue.
Ayascho	Ayascho takes an instant dislike for Coleman. During a hunt, their hunt team is attacked by the most fearsome beast in the jungle, a gorga. Coleman notices Ayascho's act of cowardice. Coleman chooses not to expose Ayascho's shame. Ayascho feels he is in Coleman's debt and won't rest until he can reclaim his honor. During their long journey to Anterra, Ayascho and Coleman become friends and allies.
Bardas	Bardas is a guard in Titus's detachment.
Braydo	King Teg-ar-mos's massive bodyguard.
Chashutza	Chashutza is the wife of Chashutzo.
Chashutzo	Chashutzo is the leader of Coleman's hunt team, who was severely injured during a gorga attack.

NAME	ROLE
Coleman	Coleman, an Earthling, who becomes known as Tondo, meaning the visitor, arrives on a distant planet due to a mishap while making an experimental transit from the Earth to the Moon. Coleman nourishes the good seeds and chooses to use his increasing power and influence on his new world to benefit others. He prepares the forces of Good for their great struggle against Evil.
Danner	He is an ex-slave freed by Tondo and the younger brother of Edder. He leaves the estate but later returns and becomes a paid laborer.
Doros	He is the Tondo Estate manor house manservant.
Duba	Duba is Dubo's wife.
Dubo	Dubo, a hunter, is gored and killed by a tuntro. Village tradition requires his family to be banished. Coleman argues for ending this wicked tradition.
Dumaz	Mama and Papa Dumaz are ancient slaves on the Oetan estate. They prepare Maaryah's slave herd's daily food, flatcakes.
Edder	He is an ex-slave freed by Tondo and the older brother of Danner. He leaves the estate and doesn't return.
Eos	He is the Tondo Estate manor house errand boy.
Gheedan	Gheedan is a sharp-eyed guard in Titus's detachment.
Haro	He is an ex-slave freed by Tondo and helper of the estate's blacksmith, Pendor.

NAME	ROLE
Hermanez	He is a black man from an island in the middle of the ocean. He assists Master T´erio in building the first successful ship design in the known world.
Idop	He is the former commander of the Teg-ar-mos kingdom Pannera, the city guards. He becomes a king's counselor and a good friend to Tondo.
Maaryah	Maaryah is a young woman who begins her life as a slave. Through Coleman's intervention, she is freed and is able to reach her full potential. At first, she fears the outlander, but the kindness and respect he offers her changes her fear into love.
Myron	Myron is a merchant from Anterra, the Ancient City. Coleman learns he is more than 600 years old.
Namad	Namad is the tracker in Coleman's hunt team and Nita's father.
Namada	Namada is Namad's wife and Nita's mother.
Nevesant	Nevesant is a young orphaned delinquent who first notices the strange looking Ta-ngundo. He comes to revere the outsider.
Nita	Nita is Namad's daughter. In a moment of weakness, she steals Tzeecha's necklace. Village law demands that she be banished, a sure death sentence. Coleman argues for a more reasonable punishment. Ayascho is attracted to Nita.
Ootyiah	Ootyiah is Oetan's daughter, and she is considered to be the most beautiful young woman in the kingdom.

NAME	ROLE
Otean	Oetan had been granted stewardship by the king of the Oetan Estate. He is the master of all estate slaves, including Maaryah. He was killed by brigands.
Pahno	He is a temple priest of the attendant rank. He serves Master Shergus and Master Varios while they are training Coleman, Idop, and Ayascho.
Pammon	He is the Tondo Estate scholar and schoolteacher.
Pendor	He is the Tondo Estate blacksmith.
Ponti	Ponti is a dim-witted slave on the Oetan Estate.
Pontus	Pontus is a guard in Titus's detachment.
Rao	Rao is a guard in Titus's detachment.
Seemo	He is a young man who is the Tondo Estate samaran handler.
Shergus	Shergus, a master priest serving the Temple of the Unnamed God, is the greatest swordsman in the kingdom. He is sent by the Sutro Seer to train Coleman, Idop, and Ayascho.
Soidentee	He is a senior commander of warriors of the Ben-do-teg Kingdom. After the king is killed by Tangendo, he changes loyalties to his new and brutal tyrant.
Shadi	Shadi is the scent-man in Coleman's hunt team.
Sutro Seer	The senior religious leader and follower of the Great Unnamed God.

NAME	ROLE
taahso	Taahso is the shaman of the Batru village that befriends Coleman. He possesses magical powers that intrigue Coleman and leads him to discover similar powers within himself.
Tangundo	Another off-worlder, whose name is unpronounceable, arrives on the planet shortly before Coleman does. This off-worlder initially is named Tangundo, meaning outsider. Because he has a hairy face, the local populace considers him a beast-man, and they force him into the perpetual mist where an unspeakable horror lives. He survives that encounter and befriends the young orphan boy Nevesant. He begins to nourish the evil seeds within himself.
Teg-ar-mos	King Teg-ar-mos is the ruler of the kingdom where the Ancient City and the Temple of the Unnamed God are located. He is petitioned by the temple's Sutro Seer to send a detachment of city guards into the Wilderness to fetch the unusual outlander, Coleman. After the outlander resuscitates the prince, the king grants Coleman stewardship of a huge estate.
Teness	Teness is a guard in Titus's detachment.
T´erio	He is a priest of the master rank, and he is considered the best carpenter in the kingdom. With Hermanez's assistance and following Tondo's design, they build the first successful ship in the known world.

NAME	ROLE
Titus	Sestardi Titus is a non-officer who leads a detachment of Anterra city guards to fetch the unusual outlander Myron the merchant discovered in the Wilderness.
Tzeecha	Tzeecha is the wife of Tzeechoe.
Tzeechoe	\Tzeechoe becomes Coleman's village mentor and close friend, teaching him the skills he must know in order to survive in the Wilderness.
Varios	Varios, a master priest serving the Temple of the Unnamed God, is the greatest scholar in the kingdom. He is sent by the Sutro Seer to train Coleman, Idop, and Ayascho.
Wandra	She is the bondmate of Pammon, the Tondo Estate scholar and teacher.
Zoseemo	Zoseemo is a young slave owned by Myron, the merchant. He is the first slave Coleman meets. Coleman is shocked to learn that the youthful-looking slave is more than seventy spans old.

DEFINITIONS/TERMS

Anterran Calendar and Daily Time

A typical span is four-hundred days. Every third span is a leap-span, which is four-hundred and one days.

Detzamar

Also referred to as detz, a period of 40 days. There are four wernts in a detzamar, and there are ten detzamars in a span. Detzamars have the following names:

1.	Ant	6.	Du-Ant
2.	Zue	7.	Du-Zue
3.	Dzaah	8.	Du-Dzaah
4.	Tuz	9.	Du-Tuz
5.	Mot	10.	Du-Mot

Wernt

A wernt is a period of ten days. Days have the following names:

1.	Nu	6.	Du-Nu
2.	Tu	7.	Du-Tu
3.	We	8.	Du-We
4.	Gute	9.	Du-Gute
5.	Zet	10.	Du-Zet

Anterran daily time

An Anterran day is twenty-two segments, equivalent to twenty-two hours. A segment is ten intervals long, equivalent to sixty minutes. An interval is equivalent to six minutes.

Anterran measures of distance

march ≈ 15-20 miles
margher ≈ 1 mile
rad ≈ 100 yards
radett ≈ 100 feet
radi ≈ 1 foot
radneva ≈ 2 inches

DEFINITIONS/TERMS

Anterran Military Ranks

United Kingdom Military Ranks

OFFICER RANKS
Wreaths and Bars

REZUS: Military rank inside a split wreath

TETZUZ: Military rank with a zanth horizontal bar above and below

TEXAE: Military rank with a zanth horizontal bar below

KING: (Commander-in-Chief): a crown symbol surrounded by a wreath

PRINCE: One large eight-pointed zanth star surrounded by a wreath

DUKE: Three-pointed zanth star surrounded by a wreath

AMEER: Royal Adjutant of the Army and the commander of all military forces; a zanth circle with crossed swords surrounded by a wreath

SUTRUM MEGATUS: An Army commander of around 20,000+ warriors; four zanth diamonds

SUTRO MEGATUS: A division commander of around 10,000-20,000 warriors; three zanth diamonds

MEGATUS: A brigade commander of around 5,000-10,000 warriors; two zanth diamonds

NEVA MEGATUS: A sub-brigade commander of around 1,500-2,000 warriors; one zanth diamond

SUTRO MEGATO: A wing commander of around 1,000-1,500 warriors; three vertical zanth bars

MEGATO: A troop commander of around 200-300 warriors; two vertical zanth bars

NEVA MEGATO: A brick commander of around 50 warriors; one vertical zanth bar

KING

PRINCE

DUKE

AMEER

NEVA
MEGATUS   MEGATUS

SUTRO
MEGATUS

SUTRUM
MEGATUS

NEVA
MEGATO

MEGATO

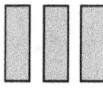

SUTRO
MEGATO

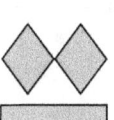

MEGATUS
TETZAE

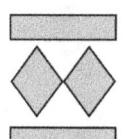

MEGATUS
TETZUS

MEGATUS
REZUS

DEFINITIONS/TERMS

Non-Officer Ranks

SUTRUM SESTARDUS: a senior non-officer above brigade level division or army; three blue stripes plus three blue chevrons and a blue star under the chevrons

SUTRO SESTARDUS: a brigade's senior non-officer; three blue stripes plus three blue chevrons

SESTARDUS: a sub-brigade's senior non-officer; three blue stripes plus two blue chevrons

NEVA SESTARDUS: a wing's senior non-officer; three blue stripes plus one blue chevron

SUTRO SESTARDI: a troop's senior non-officer; three blue stripes

SESTARDI: a brick's senior non-officer; two blue stripes

NEVA SESTARDI: a rank's non-officer; one blue strip

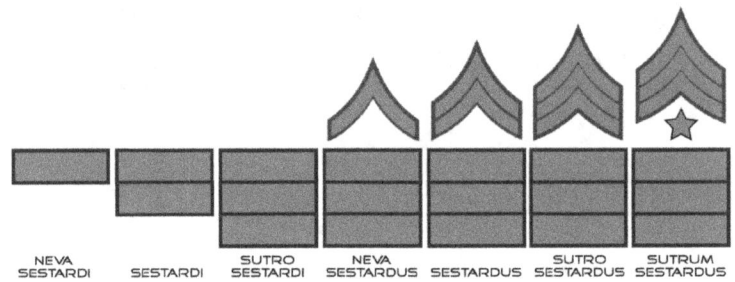

NEVA SESTARDI   SESTARDI   SUTRO SESTARDI   NEVA SESTARDUS   SESTARDUS   SUTRO SESTARDUS   SUTRUM SESTARDUS

DEFINITIONS/TERMS

Arjent

The standard monetary unit of Anterran commoners and the lower-classes, cast from eez (copper). One-hundred arjents equal one bhat.

Batru

The native villager's god; also, the name used by the villagers to refer to their tribe

Bhat

The standard monetary unit of the Anterran gentry, cast from zin (silver).

Creeper

An insect; also, slang for a pest.

Cross-over

To pass away; to die

Detzamar

A 40-day period; refer to Anterran calendar and daily time

Divitz

Cotton

Eez

Copper

Gant

A diluted wine-like drink

Gizz

The world-speak rendering of kiss

Godstone

The world-speak rendering of loadstone.

DEFINITIONS/TERMS

Gorn
The world-speak rendering of corn.

Gravetro
A metal similar to low-grade iron

Gravetum
A metal similar to iron, having the color of brass

Gristening
The world-speak rending of christening; a ceremony in which a new ship or boat is named and launched.

Groundshake
An earthquake

Gumpass
The world-speak rendering of compass

Ha
World-speak for yes; also, an exclamation similar to okay, oh, or well

Hoy
A world-speak exclamation of surprise or despair

Meashe
Food; meal

Megato
A junior Pannera officer

Megatus
A senior Pannera officer

Munnoga-touched
A person who has become insane or is deluded

DEFINITIONS/TERMS
Oy
A world-speak exclamation of surprise similar to oh or ah
P'atezas
The planet's source of light and life; equivalent to the Earth's sun
Panerra
The Anterra city guards
P'oez
Honored slayer of prey
Priest Ranks
Sutrum Seer Myndron Sutro Seer Sutro Adept (aka 'master') Adept Tutor Attendant Neophyte
Purrant
This is a person of authority appointed by a king to oversee local affairs.
Regum
A monetary unit primarily used by the Anterran gentry, cast from zanth (gold). One-hundred bhat equals one regum
Rockman
A slinger
Taah
See tzaah
Seshtane
This is a non-officer rank in the Ben-do-teg kingdom.

DEFINITIONS/TERMS

Span

This is the duration of the planet's orbit around its star, which takes 400.33 days. One day is added to every third span at the end of the detzamar of Ant.

Sutro

Greater; senior, superior

Tza

The inner-power; see tzaah

Tzaah

The inner-power, also known as taah

Vestang

This is a world-speak profanity and disparaging remark. It means snake-legs, something non-existent and/or useless.

Weak-ground

Quicksand

Wernt

A period of ten days; refer to Anterran Calendar and Daily Time

Wur-gor

The world-speak rendering of worker

Zanth

Gold

Zerio

The southwesterly wind

Zerr

The world-speak rending of sir

Zin

Silver

The Coleman Travel Map

Caver's Mountain

Batru's Eye Crater

Magheedo Mountains

Wasteland

Magheedo Plain

The Wilderness

Otterina

Terratia

Antērra
The Ancient City

Coleman's Batru Village

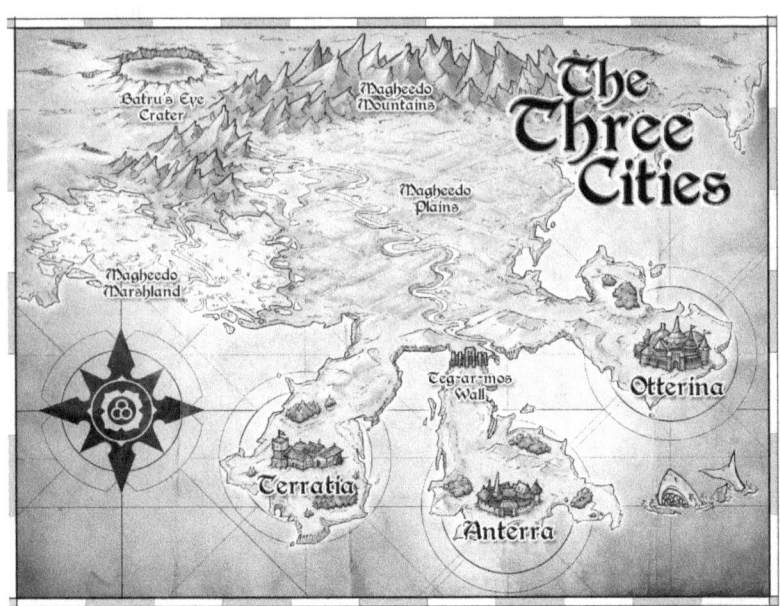

The Three Cities

Batru's Eye Crater

Magheedo Mountains

Magheedo Plains

Magheedo Marshland

Tegzarmos Wall

Otterina

Terratia

Anterra

The Tondo Estate

Penno Estate

Tondo Estate

ML BELLANTE